Nothing Left to Burn

A Story of Alzheimer's Disease

By

Dr. Karen Hutchins Pirnot

BEARHEAD PUBLISHING
- BhP -
Brandenburg, Kentucky

Nothing Left to Burn

A Story of Alzheimer's Disease

BEARHEADPUBLISHING
- BhP -
Brandenburg, Kentucky
www.bearheadpublishing.com

Nothing Left to Burn
A Story of Alzheimer's Disease
by Dr. Karen Hutchins Pirnot

Cover Concept by Dr. Karen Hutchins Pirnot
Cover Image by Dreamstime Stock Photography
Cover Design by Bearhead Publishing

First Printing - February 2015

ISBN: 978-1-937508-36-4
1 2 3 4 5 6 7 8 9

Reviewed By Anne Boling for Readers' Favorite

Nothing Left To Burn: A Story of Alzheimer's by Dr. Karen Pirnot is the story of a loved one slowly fading away. Charlie was a brilliant man; he had practiced counseling psychology and taught doctoral students at the University in Iowa. After moving to Florida, he began teaching there. He enjoyed teaching and cared about his students. He knew his lectures and relished giving them. Then the disease that was slowly changing him progressed to the point that there was no longer any way to deny the effects. Karen is a clinical psychologist and recognized the symptoms early. She found herself watching him and becoming his caregiver. Charlie and Karen clearly love each other but their relationship has changed out of necessity. Charlie resigned from his teaching position, and reluctantly and bitterly he gave up his driver's license. Karen shows amazing patience in her dealings with Charlie. Whether that comes from her experience as a psychologist or from her personality I'm not sure, but the love shines through as she always seems to know just the right things to say and the right way to react to Charlie.

Nothing Left To Burn is a poignant story. Dr. Karen Pirnot has written many books and I've loved them all, but I believe this is her greatest one. She began this book as a way to work through the stress of dealing with her husband's Alzheimer's, but it has become a way of inspiring others and informing them of how to deal with the dreaded disease. She states early in the book that no one can tell a caregiver the correct way to deal with the loved one, but I think that by sharing her and Charlie's story she is demonstrating the correct method. There is so much in this book that I would like to touch on, but this is merely a review. The author's style is conversational. I felt as if she and I were good friends having a cup of tea as she shared Charlie's latest antic. The reader will find some humor in Nothing Left To Burn; they will also find sadness and, at times, triumph. I wish Dr. Pirnot blessings and the strength to continue with her care-giving and I hope she will continue writing.

Comments by Readers

"I believe this book is a must-read for all those involved in the care of loved ones affected with Alzheimer's and dementia-related disorders……..It is a heartwarming description of the challenges Dr. Karen faces providing loving care and advocating for her ill spouse with love, respect and honor, cherishing her marital vows."

**

"It gave a depth of insight into honest feelings/emotions as a caregiver. Your perseverance in your love and care for (Charlie) and planning ahead to meet both (Charlie's) needs and yours is remarkable."

**

"Charlie's determination to keep trying and your patience and compassion SO stood out."

**

"The book is almost shocking at times so, if you're a private person, don't read it. This book will be many things to many people, but above all, it is a beautiful love story."

**

"You have a way of drawing the reader into your life and dealing with what you are going through.

**

"Hard to read…….but, I couldn't put it down. My father is going through this and I am his caregiver. After reading this, I might be able to save myself.

**

"Without the personal information, it wouldn't have seemed real to me. I fell in love with Charlie for asking to have his story told. The emotions were raw, sometimes, brutal, but what else would you expect from real people?"

Foreword

Whenever an author writes a novel "based upon a true story," it always leaves the reader wondering about which portions are true or not. I will save readers that stress by stating ahead of time: Yes, my own husband does have Alzheimer's disease and yes, I am his caregiver. He was a career professional in the field of psychology and a brilliant man by any standard. The flashbacks contained in the book are a real history of our love story and my enduring admiration for him.

Even as I wrote this book I wrestled with the question of whether I would ever want to have it published, given how personal the topic had become. One day while sorting through my research documents, I came across two mementos dating from the early days of my husband's battle with Alzheimer's. In one, he had just left his forty year career as a professor and we were discussing what he would now do with his life. Having not before acknowledged his diagnosis, my husband surprised me by declaring that we should write a book about Alzheimer's disease and that I should study him and document its effect. When I replied cautiously that such a book might best be written at the end of the disease process he scowled and responded: *"True learning comes from the verbal and behavioral testimony of the living, not from the adulterated memories of those who remember a life once lived."* For me, the statement was so profound and, perhaps, prophetic that I grabbed an envelope and on its back wrote down my husband's statement verbatim.

The second memento was written by my husband himself just a few months later. This book was an open project in our lives, and one day I found him in my office reading the chapter I had just written in which he coined the term, "Nothing left to burn." I watched him calmly finish reading, retire to his own office for awhile, and upon returning he presented me with a handwritten declaration stating, with poignant formality, that he was aware that the book I was writing was about him and me as his caretaker, and that he wished for the book to be published for whatever scientific merit it might have for readers. At the time, I thought it was so much like *my* Charlie, always the professor. And now, years later with the disease so advanced, it reminds me without doubt that he wants his story to be told.

The character of "Charlie" is a composite, including the personalities and individual struggles of many Alzheimer's patients I have treated or met during my geriatric work as a Clinical Psychologist. Out of respect for *my* Charlie, behaviors are generalized so as to leave my husband, and all those like him, with the dignity to which they are entitled. The stories that follow portray my own feelings as they occurred during the transition from one stage of the disease to another, and attempt to give a more comprehensive and essential view to readers of the overall caregiver experience.

Chapter One

A Moment of Reckoning

There are a few rare moments in life when you understand truth in a fraction of a second. You distinguish fact from fiction and truth from conjecture. This was one of those times. And, it was a time that would emotionally rip me from stem to stern.

*****

It was such a perfect night. Charlie and I had dinner together, our favorite dish of butterfly shrimp with baked potatoes and cabbage slaw. We were both up to the task of the enormous platters before us. Charlie pulled off two, brown paper towels from the spindle to his right and he placed one of the napkins under my fork. As he did so, his fingers lightly touched the knuckles on my right hand, like a butterfly landing on an exotic flower. His touch still made me quiver. The visceral reaction provided the knowledge that we were, indeed, one of the more fortunate couples going into the golden years.

Small fish jumped from the creek in front of us. It was a beautiful night, one of those magic events you know you will remember on your deathbed. The sun was setting and reflecting on the water, creating a moment of stunning natural beauty.

The shrimp were perfectly butterflied and then dipped in a very light seasoning. They were plump and succulent. As usual, I gave two of my shrimp to Charlie and he finished both halves of his baked potato. I had only one of the potato halves. It was my weak attempt at compensation for having gone off hormone replacement and then having to settle for nothing to speak of in the way of hormones which had regulated my metabolism for the past seventy years. Charlie still had a few pockets of testosterone floating around in his rotund mid-section and was never one to worry about a few extra carbs. We sat next to the window on hard benches and placed our hands on a rough wooden table while we watched the fish flip up out of the water, attempting to avoid becoming dinner themselves.

The night was a bit steamy for April, even in the Gulf coast of Florida, but we weren't the least bit concerned about sitting outside in the fresh air. We were both septuagenarians and we had recently been declared by our family physician to be in "good shape for the shape you're in." That was his way of telling us that we appeared to be free of the usual health concerns which had begun to plague many of our friends. We felt smug and happy that we had both been blessed with kind and sturdy genes and we held hands as we told one another that we would grow old together because surely, the best was yet to come. I looked into Charlie's face, weathered with the years. His usual mischievous pale blue eyes appeared sad and sunken and this caused me to startle inside, although I did not give away my feelings outwardly. We were getting old and I didn't want it to be true for either of us.

Charlie signed the check and we cruised down Tamiami Trail, looking for anything of interest before turning off on the beach road. After parking the car, we took out aluminum chairs from the trunk. We deliberately avoided taking the low, beach chairs as Charlie and I had experienced considerable difficulty extricating our rears from the canvas seat which rested on the pure white sand of Siesta Key Beach only four days earlier. The surface was so soft that we had a bit of difficulty walking on the fluffy sand but we gradually made our way to the edge of the water. We sat watching the sea gulls and terns fight over sea offerings. One of the birds would catch something small and the others would tackle them, hoping for even the slightest scrap which would prevent the need to exercise their own predatory skills. No one bothered the pelicans as they went about the business of diving, retrieving and placing the fish appropriately in their gullets for the final trip to oblivion.

It was our practice to hold hands from the moment the sun began to sink until it dropped into the ocean. Oh yes, we knew for sure that is where the sun rested at night for it gave off a brilliant glow over the Gulf waters when it dashed into the sea, leaving shadows and beams of light for the night to rearrange as it would. If there were clouds like tonight, the show would be spectacular, with backlighting which produced variations of a watercolor art exhibit. It was as if God had taken the sun, splashed it into the ocean and said to the audiences of the world, "Here's the raw material; now, make your own art!"

Charlie said he had a busy week ahead. He considered himself semi-retired and his days off work gave him time to fish the Gulf and spend time teaching the five grandchildren the finer arts of appreciating and conserving nature. He told me that "what's his name" at the office was pressing him for more hours on the job and what did I think of that idea. I frowned and said that it was Charlie's decision but, lately, it seemed that the more hours he put in at work, the more anxious he seemed to be. He looked at me as if I were from another galaxy and the subject was dropped.

When the sunset disappeared, leaving only a faint pastel backlighting, we carefully engaged our arthritic knees, braced and stood up. We folded the chairs and shuffled back to the car, kicking up white coral sand as we went. Charlie asked if we should stop for ice cream. I wanted it about as much as I wanted a tooth extraction without Novocain but I consented. Charlie loved a lot of things but grandchildren and ice cream were right there at the top of the list. The drive into the village took less than five minutes and we were shortly in line at Big Olaf's as we marveled at all the newest flavors. As usual, Charlie got a medium cup of cappuccino chocolate crunch and I got a small dish of chocolate. We reminisced about our years in Sarasota and how wonderful they had been for us and we thanked our lucky stars that the first Florida grandchild had forced our relocation from the Midwest where I had spent the first fifty years of my life.

We took our usual route home, commenting on the road repairs, the neighbor's yards and other things that old, married couples find in common. We approached the intersection where we would make a left turn to curve around into our subdivision and Charlie went past it. He slowed the car and brought it to a halt right in the middle of the road. He turned to me with a look of confusion on his face. "Where's our house?" he asked in a state of near panic.

It was the end that commenced the beginning. It was contrary to every form of logic I had ever learned, but that's the way it was. I knew the truth and in no way was I prepared to accept it as fact.

Chapter Two

The Early Years

Charlie's question and the sense of near panic on his face totally caught me off guard. At first I wondered if Charlie might be experiencing a TIA (transient ischemic attack) in which a small clot lodges in an artery, causing mental confusion or physical incapacity of some sort. Generally, such incidents clear rapidly with little or no resulting effects. I put my hand beneath Charlie's bearded chin and said, "Charlie, you just missed the turn, that's all. We need to back up and then turn left." But deep down, way past terror and denial, I think I already knew; Charlie had Alzheimer's disease.

Charlie still looked confused but he did as I instructed. He made the turn and began to drive in the direction of our house. As he approached the next turn, I softly said, "You need to make a right turn now, Charlie."

Charlie shot me a look that could kill as he said, "I know that! Do you think I'm senile or something?" It was a question best left unanswered.

There was little conversation that evening. Charlie seemed to be deep in a private world of thought. I spent the rest of the evening with the dread of trying to deny something I knew to be true.

We were both mental health professionals. Charlie practiced counseling psychology before our move to Florida. He also taught doctoral students at the psychology department at a large university in Iowa. I practiced clinical psychology in our practice in Iowa for many years and when we moved to Florida, I opened up a small private practice where I assessed and treated both adults and children. Not wanting to undergo the licensing procedure in Florida, Charlie elected to teach full time in Florida.

After retirement age, Charlie dropped to part time teaching and he loved it! He knew his lectures backwards and forwards and he rarely had to prepare to teach. He loved directing dissertations and working with the students in general. He had always been an assertive advocate for students, sometimes at the risk of alienating colleagues. But, for the most part, Charlie was gifted with words and could generally use a bit of semi-truths to convince others of the correctness of his actions.

I loved my professional work and many said I seemed to have a gift for digging in and getting to the heart of the matter. I loved researching years and years back into a patient's history to try to solve a difficult diagnostic problem. Toward the end of my practice years, I assessed many patients with suspected dementia. It was always a difficult procedure, both for the patient and his or her family. As the assessor and the bearer of negative information, it was also difficult for me as well.

When we married, Charlie had no knowledge of the fact that Alzheimer's disease was prominent in his family. Sometimes, relatives were discussed as being *peculiar* or *forgetful* but Alzheimer's was not really a known entity until more recent years. When Charlie's mother began to show signs of dementia, I asked Charlie about the signs I was seeing. His response was that the symptoms were probably indicative of medication effects but even then, I suspected a process of dementia. From the evaluations I had conducted with my own patients, I was pretty sure the symptoms were consistent with those of Alzheimer's disease. Furthermore, I thought the signs and symptoms were evident even in his mother during our first few meetings. Eventually, Charlie's mother was placed in long term care where she ended up not recognizing her only son. But even then, there were a lot of family reassurances that *the big A* was not the real culprit.

Charlie had always been a lot like his mother, both physically and cognitively. They shared some personality traits as well. Naturally, I hoped the mother's disease would bypass Charlie. He had no biological children so I knew he would not pass on the genetic predisposition toward dementia.

Charlie was a wonderful stepfather to my three children and a fantastic "Poppy" to our grandchildren. He taught them all to fish and he would take the whole family on boat cruises that always included fishing and a lunch break at one of the waterfront restaurants on the Gulf Coast where we lived.

After the evening when Charlie got lost on the way home, I began to take notice of actions or statements that appeared the least bit peculiar. It wasn't as if I were trying to *find* mental errors; rather I was more careful not to dismiss errors which did occur. There is sometimes a thin line between the early stages of Alzheimer's and the normal forgetting that occurs with us all as we age. But now, I just couldn't deny or dismiss what I had actually witnessed over the past couple of years.

Most physicians and psychologists now understand that by the time the first symptoms of Alzheimer's are visible, the disease has already been active for at least five years. Some say the figure should be ten years or even more. That would put Charlie right on track with the process of his mother's illness. Unless the onset is abrupt and serious, most people do not detect the early, subtle signs of the disease. The affected person pretty much goes about his or her activities with only minor, temporary glitches in carrying through with activities of daily living. If someone is naturally gregarious and verbally glib like Charlie, it is easier to talk your way out of problems and into a state of normalcy. The aberrant statement or behavior is simply laughed away from consciousness.

Charlie began to refer to his occasional forgetting as "brain farts," or "senior moments." He was always good natured about the mental glitches. After a brief joke, he would seemingly be back to his own brilliant self. I, on the other hand, began to build a scenario which left me suspicious and afraid. A suspicion without confirmation is one of the most resistant emotional events to try to resolve. Most of us need resolution so that we can tackle a problem head-on and go on. But Alzheimer's doesn't work that way. One moment, you are nearly consumed with the thought of what *could be.* In the next moment, that possibility is only a fleeting thought as your loved one reverts to *normal* behaviors and you block out what *could be.*

We went to Las Vegas where I was to receive a book award. We had a wonderful time meeting the award staff and we attended a very entertaining stage show called *Menopause The Musical.* Charlie prided himself on his past Navy navigation skills. My Navy navigator never got lost. It's one of the reasons he was always in he "pilot's seat" when we took trips together But while walking back to our hotel after the stage performance, my flawless Navy navigator got lost. He went deeper and deeper into a part of Las Vegas that was foreign to us both. I asked him several times to turn around and backtrack. He refused. Finally, in desperation and fear of getting into a dangerous scenario in unknown territory, I told my husband that I was going to walk back to the turn we usually took and he could continue on to the hotel if he wished. It was a ploy on my part. I knew my old Navy man would not leave a damsel in distress. He scoffed and then returned with me to a corner I recognized and we made it safely back to the hotel. Before going to bed, Charlie commented. "I don't know why you got so bent out of shape. I was only trying to take a shortcut." I then knew he was capable of attempting to cover his own mental errors and he had probably done it much more frequently and for much longer than I even dared to consider.

When the fall term commenced at the university, Charlie seemed a bit anxious. We discussed whether it might be time for him to fully retire and live his dream fishing on the Florida Gulf Coast. I even urged that course of action. Charlie became angry and he accused me of being jealous that he still had a job and I did not. By then, I had retired from my practice and I had begun to write books. Charlie had oftentimes commented on how content I appeared using my creative skills in another setting, so his abrupt comment took me off guard. When that happened, I generally felt it best simply not to reply.

When Charlie returned from each of his three days of teaching, it was our practice to sit out on the lanai with a glass of iced tea. I would talk about my day and he would relate interactions with students and other faculty members. That fall, Charlie told me things were a bit boring at the university. That was a shocking statement as Charlie had loved his work. He always had stories to tell and would tell me about how successful his students had been after graduation. He always spoke like a proud mentor and I, in turn, would derive such satisfaction from his involvement in his students.

Charlie was no longer providing me any relevant information about his work days that fall. Instead, he would smoothly redirect and then ask me to relate my day's experiences. I began to suspect that his short term memory might be failing and that he simply did not recall what he had done during most of the day. It was one thing to forget something momentarily; it was quite another to forget sequences of normal, daily functioning. And yet, Charlie remained upbeat and witty when in the company of others. When I questioned him about his teaching, he would always remark that he could repeat his lectures in his dreams and that I shouldn't worry about his abilities. "If anything, I'm better than ever!" he would declare with a grin and a swift kiss on my cheek.

It was at about the same time that I began to notice lapses in Charlie's driving. His attention appeared to wax and wane and he increasingly made driving errors such as swerving to another lane or hitting a curb. I suggested a vision test. Charlie went for an exam and he was fitted with new corrective eyeglasses. The driving errors continued.

In the past, Charlie would pick up my son at the Tampa airport after finishing work but after the most recent trip, my son told me in confidence he would no longer ride with Charlie. I asked Charlie directly how comfortable he was driving the interstate and he said, "I'm the best driver on the road." I understood then that one of the signs of dementia is the tendency to exaggerate one's abilities. But, in all fairness, that symptom is not exclusive to the category of dementia.

I discussed the driving issue with my son and daughter. We all agreed that Charlie had appeared to lapse in his driving skills. But, as my son pointed out, "Mom, he's never been the best of drivers." We decided on an approach of caution. Charlie would no longer drive the grandchildren.

At his yearly examination that year, Charlie's PSA (prostate stimulating antigen) test was elevated. That is sometimes indicative of prostate cancer. Charlie agreed to a biopsy which revealed a very slow-growing type of cancer. It is the type that older men usually "die with rather than die from." We and the treating physician all agreed on a *watchful waiting* approach. It seemed as if much of my life was now placed on hold as I watched and waited. I noticed during the exam that our family doctor did not show concern about Charlie's cognitive processing and I cautioned myself not to exaggerate what might be the normal aging process. After all, I didn't want my husband looking for examples of my own geriatric status!

As the spring school term drew to a close, I breathed a sigh of relief. I had planned to try to convince Charlie to retire while he could still be remembered for his contributions to the academic community. Throughout June and July, I would bring up the retirement issue on occasion and Charlie's response would inevitably be, "Sure, we'll see." I felt my husband was being elusive and evasive, not wanting to even consider that he may no longer be in a position to teach. When August arrived, I told him it was time to seriously consider his resignation. He grinned, saying, "I've just signed my contract for another year!" Then, he added, "Let's go out and celebrate!"

I was shocked beyond description! Surely, others must be seeing what I was seeing! On the other hand, Charlie was such a socially engaging individual that just maybe, others also chalked up Charlie's mental omissions to those occasional "senior moments." I simply could not convince my husband that his mind was anything other than its usual efficient self. Professional ethics prevented me from diagnosing my own husband and no professional had yet rendered a diagnosis. He was teaching in a program with other mental health professionals and no one else was complaining about Charlie's performance. I mentally lashed myself for seeing things that probably did not exist. I hadn't practiced clinically now for several years. Maybe I was losing my diagnostic acuity.

The next week, we had five the grandchildren for an overnight while my daughter and son-in-law went on a date night. It was our tradition that we would do a bit of school shopping to lessen the time burden on the parents. I was to take the three older children out while Charlie and the two youngest children all hung out together. The two little ones detested shopping and simply asked their older sisters to pick out things they might need. It seemed the perfect set-up. The children staying home with Poppy would all watch ball games on television and then, they would have an outdoor adventure in the back yard.

I took off with the three oldest granddaughters, declaring that we would have to be back in time to prepare dinner. As I opened the back door to go to the garage, I called out, "Charlie, be sure to watch the children." He blew me a kiss and told me not to worry. "I've got it covered," he said. He was especially happy that the grandchildren were there with him that day.

In the past, Charlie had always been a reliable caregiver. He would have given up his life attempting to protect a grandchild from injury. There had been nothing which would have alerted me that I should think otherwise and indeed, Charlie did watch the children.

I returned home with the three older granddaughters after a two and a half hour shopping trip. I could hear the two younger children in the back yard. Charlie was in his lounge chair and he smiled and asked about our shopping adventure. The girls began to tell Poppy about their shopping trip while I checked on the children in the back yard. They were full of stories and I told them we'd all relate our adventures after I got dinner started.

When I got back in the house, I commented to Charlie that it seemed almost as warm in the house as it was outside. I told him the back French doors were open and I asked how long they had been open. Charlie gave me a blank look. I went back out and asked the younger children about the doors. The youngest one said, "Oh, Grandma, Poppy doesn't care if we leave them open. It's easier to go in and out. We had to check with him every five minutes to let him know what we were doing."

When I then asked Charlie about the doors being open, he said, "You asked me to watch the children; you didn't ask me to watch the doors." I almost startled at that primitively concrete explanation from someone whose abstract abilities were so highly polished. I was used to such sophisticated conceptualizations from Charlie and his statement jolted me and sent up multiple red flags. But, there was dinner to fix and children to bathe, so the response went unanswered. I would have to process it later.

Apparently, the doors had been left open all afternoon, causing a strain on the air conditioner. It had overworked and frozen up. That night, we each slept in separate rooms directly under a fan. The stress on the condenser had been so great that it necessitated a new air conditioner. And, that was to be another story.

Chapter Three

A Mild Escalation

Charlie insisted on handling the issue of acquiring the new air conditioner. Our HVAC system was well over fifteen years old and, with the overstress caused by the open patio doors it was time for a replacement. Charlie talked back and forth with the salesman and when it came time to sign the contracts to do the work, I insisted on being present.

We sat around the kitchen table and the salesman explained that Charlie had picked out a top-of-the line Trane system with a plastic air handling unit that would never rust. I was floored at the expense of the unit which appeared twice as big as that required by our small retirement home. I politely asked the salesman to explain other options that would be suitable for our home. Much to my amazement, Charlie did not react and he did not appear offended that I had asked for other options. We finally settled on a mid-value unit that would probably serve our house for as long as we lived. Even then, I settled for a more expensive unit than I thought necessary.

When the salesman left our home, Charlie went to his computer and began to play a game of solitaire. He had been doing that more lately. When I called him in for dinner, he was somewhat sullen. Finally, he said, "You made me look like a fool." I explained that sometimes, sales persons will start out with the best they have even though other options might do just as well. I asked if Charlie

11

had asked about other handling units and he paused, thought and then said he hadn't thought to do that. Red flag: Charlie always asked about other options available.

On the day the new unit was to be installed, Charlie said he'd supervise. I left the house and came home to find a new air handling unit that was so large I could no longer use two of the storage cabinets underneath it in the garage! But, Charlie seemed happy to have supervised the event and said he'd had a "great chat" with the installer. I was happy we were paying a flat fee rather than a per-hour service that day! My Charlie could charm the fur off a fox.

Charlie began to lock me out of the house. I might be doing yard work in the back or maybe, I would be reading on the back lanai. Charlie would come out to tell me he was running an errand. He would carefully close the French doors and then, unbeknownst to me, he would turn the bolt, locking the door. After waiting an hour and a half for Charlie to return, I asked about his locking me out of the house. He had no explanation. I hid a key outside. Despite reminders to leave the door open for me when Charlie left, it happened several times again.

That fall, Charlie had several episodes which appeared related to the prostate cancer. He would have intense cramping. He missed a day of teaching. But then, the spasm would break and he would be fine for a couple of months. I asked again about his maybe resigning at the winter break. He again became angry and accused me of making up things which put him in a bad light. He appeared increasingly more agitated but he denied his own obvious discomfort.

My daughter commented that Charlie did not appear to be his usual congenial self. Generally at a family gathering, he would take the conversational lead. Lately, he had primarily listened to the conversation. I noticed one day that he was no longer making meals on the outdoor grill. When I told him I missed his wonderful grilled dinners, he said he had "lost interest in that kind of thing."

The agitation grew until one day, Charlie acknowledged that

he had forgotten something while teaching at the university that day. We discussed a mid-year resignation and Charlie would have no part of it. "The students depend on me and I refuse to let them down," he replied. I began to wonder if Charlie might not be the one letting down the students.

Late that fall, both Charlie and I were due for our yearly physical exams. I went in the week after Charlie's appointment. When I had asked him about his exam, he had declared, "I'm in great shape except I need to exercise more." It was difficult to believe that our otherwise insightful family internist had not noticed any cognitive changes in my husband.

I went for my own annual exam to the following week. The physician immediately said he had seen a real difference in Charlie in the six months since he had last been seen and that he'd wanted to verify some of what he was seeing with me. I told him I had seen changes as well. We discussed various possibilities and he asked if there was dementia in the family. I told him of Charlie's family history and he related that Charlie had neglected to mention the prominence of Alzheimer's disease. The doctor said that a definitive diagnosis was nearly impossible at Charlie's age until symptoms progressed. I knew from my own profession that was the case.

We had a wonderful Christmas celebration but Charlie was virtually unable to help me plan and organize as usual. I dreaded his going back to teach the following term and yet, we had no diagnosis of Alzheimer's to prevent just such an occurrence. Indeed, our physician had told me that if dementia was present, it would be best for Charlie to work as long as possible. Research was definitive that it helped to stave off the worsening of symptoms. I thought surely, someone would call from Charlie's office and tell me the axe had fallen. My days had a feeling of foreboding about them.

It was over the spring break in March that the call came. A concerned colleague of Charlie's told me that she was concerned about him and wondered if he was physically okay. She related that Charlie appeared to be missing elements of staff conversations lately and that he seemed preoccupied. He rarely volunteered information in faculty meetings and he sometimes appeared unable to tract conversations. She said she was worried he would be let go. I told the colleague truthfully that I also had concerns about Charlie and that one way or another, I had to convince him that this would be his last term of teaching. The task ahead would be one of the most difficult of my life.

I fixed Charlie's dinner that night. I told him a colleague had expressed concerns about his health. He told me the prostate problems were bothersome but that they were not an issue to his teaching. I told him I was worried about his ability to process new information. He told me he would never resign and that, "They'll have to tell me to get out."

I told Charlie that may be about to happen if he did not tender his resignation. He told me my exaggerations were the only problems he had and that his teaching abilities were "just as sound as they've always been." I told him I feared he would be forced out rather than be allowed to resign with dignity. He had taught for forty years and was now in danger of being forced to leave his position.

After some consideration, Charlie finally came to me and he acknowledged that he was having some problems. "I'm forgetting student's names," he said somewhat blandly. That was another thing I had noticed as of late; his emotions were becoming blunted. For a highly expressive man, that was a critical change.

That night, I typed his letter of resignation. He signed it and promised to deliver it to the department head the following Monday. On Sunday night, I left Charlie a note on his home office desk reminding him to turn in the letter of resignation. I waited all day Monday with nerves on edge, hoping he would not change his mind.

Charlie's car pulled into the driveway at 5:30 that evening. I was out front reading, not remembering a word I had read. Charlie got out of the car, came to where I was sitting and said, "That went really well!" I breathed deeply for the first time that day. He told of how he had handed in his letter of resignation the first thing in the morning. His resignation was announced at the faculty meeting in the afternoon. I asked Charlie how he felt and he said it was probably good timing because he was forgetting more and he didn't want to end up hurting the students. I told him I was proud of him and that the children were also relieved that he would now formally go into retirement. I couldn't help but ponder how easily Charlie's resignation had been accepted. Perhaps, the university was relieved as well.

Chapter Four

Chicken Little Arrives

Charlie's prostate problems seemed to intensify and he was started on medications that seemed to bring some relief. His mental status seemed to alter significantly and we were unsure as to what might be medication effects and what might be signs and symptoms of escalating cognitive problems. Charlie finished out the teaching term and had a wonderful retirement party. But, he didn't go fishing as expected.

Since our move to Florida, Charlie had talked about how he would fish every day following retirement. I waited and he didn't fish. In fact, Charlie did little except run errands. He seemed to be forgetting how to cook and I gradually took over more and more of the chores around the house. His memory deteriorated rapidly to the point that we both agreed he would go to the doctor. He refused to allow me to accompany him.

Charlie returned from his medical appointment and I asked what he had told the doctor about his memory problems. He panicked and yelled out, "I forgot to tell him about my memory problems!" Charlie got back in his car, drove back to the doctor's office and demanded to see the doctor. "I forgot to tell him about my memory problems," he told the nurse.

Our doctor kindly accommodated Charlie. My husband was immediately prescribed a trial on Namenda, one of the newer drugs prescribed for Alzheimer's disease. The medication had an almost positive overnight effect in that the anxiety and agitation ceased. But the memory difficulties did not abate.

It seemed that Charlie had difficulty initiating activity. But, if the activity was suggested and encouraged, he would usually go ahead. He would generally enjoy himself. I mentioned that I missed his home-cooked meals and he stared at me as if he had forgotten that he was the family cook. We gave my daughter the outdoor grill. Her husband was a splendid grill master and their grill had just literally blown up on them that very week.

Traditionally, Charlie had always managed the bills. One day, I discovered our checking account had been electronically hacked. About ten thousand dollars had been stolen from two accounts! I immediately went to the bank and Charlie accompanied me. The bank personnel tried to explain that hacking accounts via stealing information on checks was becoming a new and well-established scam. Charlie just did not seem to understand the concept. I had continually asked him to do on-line checks and he said he didn't trust computers. The bank assistant explained to Charlie how on-line bill paying was actually more secure than writing out checks and sticking them in the mail. I worked with the bank, turning in fraud claims.

When we got home, I asked Charlie if it might be time for me to take over the checking and billing duties. He seemed frightened. He was afraid of trying new computer technology. He went to his desk, pulled out the two checking account folders and handed them to me. I established on-line bill pay and we've had no further problems. That was the beginning of my taking over one activity after another.

The children, the grandchildren, the doctor and I were all increasingly concerned about Charlie's escalating memory difficulties. The doctor suggested a brain MRI. Charlie was perfectly willing to undergo the procedure. He kept denying he had his mother's disease but I think he was also frightened about what was happening to him.

The doctor explained that the results of the MRI showed moderate diffuse brain atrophy. We three discussed that it might be time for Charlie to give up driving. Charlie became agitated and he refused to consider the possibility. The doctor gave me a brochure in which an independent medical facility would test persons suspected of being physically or cognitively impaired. My task then became how to present the testing to Charlie in such a manner that he could retain a modem of dignity.

Charlie became agitated and had escalating memory deficits. The medication Aricept was added to the Namenda. Again, he had an initially positive response. It was almost as if the medications were buying us all time to prepare for what was yet to come.

Chapter Five

An Unkind Transition

It was again time for my yearly physical. Our physician commented that I looked tired and my blood pressure was elevated. I acknowledged that Charlie's problems were a source of stress for me. I told him I was not sleeping well and I knew I needed to begin to take over more caregiving duties. I told him I needed to get an appropriate Power of Attorney and we both discussed how, unless a patient voluntarily signed permission for a POA, it was a difficult legal process. The doctor asked if maybe a cognitive evaluation might be something that Charlie could relate to as an academic. I said it was worth a try.

I talked with Charlie about my assuming more responsibility in the house and he admitted that he was relieved I was primarily managing most of the running of the household. I suggested that a cognitive evaluation might help us both understand what areas of his brain might be affected so that we could make plans. "What kind of plans?" he asked. I teared up as he asked, "Are you thinking of putting me in a home?"

I began to shake and then, I took several deep breaths. I went to his chair and sat on the footstool in front of him. I took his hands in mine. I told him that we could no longer deny that he had the dreaded family disease and that his symptoms would only worsen. I asked him if he understood and he nodded his head. "I understand," he replied blandly.

Nothing Left to Burn - A Story of Alzheimer's Disease

I told Charlie that it would never be my intention to place him in nursing home care unless I absolutely could not handle him. I told him there were various services we could look into and that the children would be there for him as well. I told him I loved him dearly and that his problems were my problems and we would handle them as a couple.

I got up and hugged him. He received the hug and yet, he seemed unable to return the hug. I understood we had now gone even more deeply into the disease.

We agreed that Charlie would schedule a cognitive assessment with a specialist in neuropsychology. When I returned home from running an errand one day, Charlie announced he had an appointment! I was pleased that he had actually scheduled the evaluation. Unbeknown to me, Charlie had actually gone to the psychologist's office and had asked to see her. The psychologist interrupted her schedule, thinking that someone from the University where Charlie had worked was concerned about an intern she had working for her. She felt it highly invasive that Charlie would show up unannounced and was later to conclude that his behavior was undoubtedly symptomatic of cognitive impairment.

Charlie was actually feeling upbeat on the day of the evaluation. I filled out some forms and then, left the office as the testing continued for three hours. Charlie called when I was finished and I picked him up. We made an appointment for a feedback session for about ten days from that date. On the way home I asked Charlie to describe the tests he had been administered. He could not remember anything about the testing but he thought he had "nailed it."

Charlie continued to run errands in his car. I always felt relief when his car pulled into the driveway. Oftentimes, he would deposit items and then tell me he had to go back because he had forgotten something. When I would ask him about the list I had made for him, he would reply, "I forgot to look at the list."

I knew we were in for a tough time ahead. When you forget about the list of items to help you remember what to get, you're sinking deeper in the mental mud of Alzheimer's

When we returned for the follow-up visit to the office of the neuropsychologist, the doctor asked Charlie how he thought he had done. "Great!" he answered with a grin. The doctor looked toward me with sympathy in her face. I immediately understood and I bit my lower lip to control my own terror at what I was about to hear. I could see the results in her eyes.

Premorbid cognitive functioning (functioning prior to the onset of disease or injury) for Charlie was estimated to be in the Very Superior Range of intellectual abilities. Although verbal testing demonstrated that he could still "talk the talk," the testing revealed Charlie could no longer "walk the walk." Although some of his testing was in the Average range of abilities, other skills were in the Below Average to Deficient range. Overall, this was a substantial and heartbreaking decrement in mental abilities.

The examiner expressed concerns about Charlie's ability to drive and he got highly defensive. She handed me the same brochure our doctor had given to me just weeks ago.

Charlie became paranoid. He started to follow me around the house as if he did not trust me. He asked where I was going and with whom I would be. In reality, my activities now consisted of going to the gym three times weekly so that I could be strong enough to help Charlie. His gross motor abilities were declining as well. He shuffled his feet as he walked and he had difficulty rising from chairs. Although it was a dream of mine to get away for a day, I did not feel comfortable leaving Charlie for extended period of time.

One evening, Charlie fell asleep watching me. He was in his chair and apparently, in a deep sleep. I saw movement and looked over at him. He appeared to be grabbing for something on the small table next to his chair. All of a sudden, he grabbed an invisible object and he aimed his hand at me as if he were holding a gun. He clicked the invisible trigger twice and then put down the invisible gun.

The following day, I told Charlie about the incident. Being

an old Navy veteran, he had always kept guns in the house. Even though the guns were locked away, I told Charlie I was scared that he might do something that he would be unable to live with. He agreed to get rid of the guns. A neighbor who knew of Charlie's diagnosis kindly came and took away all the guns and ammunition.

That night, I slept for eight hours and awakened refreshed the following morning. Finally, I had inadvertently identified at least one of my own fears of the past few months! Sometimes fears are so realistic and terrifying that we just cannot bear to bring them to the conscious mind in order to acknowledge them. When the threat was finally gone, the image could then surface and I could acknowledge my own fears.

Chapter Six

Losing the Parts of the Self

My children and I were on the verge of doing an "intervention" when Charlie finally agreed to take the driving test. He was frequently losing his sense of direction and he was scaring me with his errors in driving judgment.

When Charlie finally agreed to make an appointment, I could hear him talking on the phone and he appeared to be attempting to influence the examiner. He talked about having been a navigator in the Navy and how he had been driving for nearly sixty years. He related that he simply wanted assurances that he was still a safe driver.

When he hung up the phone, I asked who he had called for the appointment. He said he had called a local driving school. I told Charlie that he was referred to a specific program at one of the local hospitals. That test would consider overall cognitive abilities as well as a test on a simulator and an actual behind-the-wheel driving test I insisted that nothing short of such an evaluation would give the family any realistic idea of his real driving potential. He reluctantly agreed to cancel the appointment with the agency and to contact the one to which he was referred. I could see Charlie was very angry with me now that I was in a position to challenge his overall abilities. He expressed anger with the neuropsychologist who had diagnosed cognitive deficits. He had always been able to convince others of his way of thinking and that was no longer an option for him.

Charlie did follow through. He called the driving assessment agency and scheduled an appointment. He told me he did not want me to go and give them any information whatsoever. The appointment secretary explained to Charlie that I must drive him to the evaluation and that he was to bring his driver's license and identification with him. He was also to bring a list of medications he was taking. He defiantly asked me for a ride and knowing he would forget about the medications, I made a list to give to the agency. I set the paper on kitchen table where we always left notes for one another.

On the day of the evaluation, Charlie "forgot" to pick up the list of medication I had placed on the table for him. I picked it up, placed it in my purse and then gave it to the secretary when we checked in. I gave Charlie his cell phone, turned it on and asked him to call me when he was finished. I told him we would go out to eat dinner afterwards if he wished. I left and went home and began to write to keep my mind off Charlie's testing procedures.

The testing consisted of cognitive testing, a simulator and on-road testing. If all went well, the testing would last for three hours. Charlie called after two hours and happily announced, "I'm ready!" I knew what was going to happen. Nevertheless, my heart began to race and I found myself breathing heavily to prepare for what I was going to hear.

I arrived at the testing center in ten minutes and was immediately escorted in. When asked how he thought he did, Charlie replied with an aire of confidence that he thought he had done very well.

The examiner said Charlie had made several errors, some of them critical. She said Charlie had talked nonstop through the driving experience, apparently attempting to influence her with his ability to do two things at once. She told him he was a "highly social" man and that that particular trait was not always a positive, particularly if cognitive problems are in evidence. She explained the errors he had made and Charlie immediately got defensive. The examiner said it was time for Charlie to turn in his driving license. He escalated the verbal anger and the examiner began to pull back. I knew I must take over.

I took Charlie's hand and I told him that it took a lot of courage for him to have voluntarily undergone the examination. I told him the children, the grandchildren and I were all proud that he took the responsible approach and that that we would now be in a position to help him get where he needed to go. He calmed a bit and the examiner relaxed. She explained again the great risks to Charlie and others should he continue to drive.

I told Charlie it would be awful if something happened to him. I also asked him to think about having to live with the realization of having hurt someone else. I knew he would think about the grandchildren.

Finally, Charlie asked, "When should I turn in my license?"

The examiner said that it would be best to do it immediately so that there would be no urge to drive. Charlie looked defeated and unable to express his own pain and I began to cry for him. Then, I immediately took his hand, pulled him up from the chair and led him out to my car.

I drove to the driver's license office and explained that my husband needed to surrender his license to drive. We sat down while the attendant looked up information on the computer. She asked Charlie if he was voluntarily surrendering his license and he said, "Yes." I was so proud of him! I squeezed his hand in love and support.

Charlie took his license from his wallet and handed it to the attendant. She cut up the license and explained that should Charlie ever wish to drive again, he would need to undergo an examination. He smiled and said he had just had an examination and apparently didn't do too well. He smiled at the attendant and said, "It was news to me!" I asked him how he felt but he was unable to come up with any feelings about the current experience. I knew I personally felt relieved that Charlie could no longer hurt himself or others with his vehicle. But I also cried for the part of Charlie that had just disappeared. He had lost his identity as a full-time college professor. Now he had lost his identify as a driver. Charlie had driven for sixty years and was now totally dependent upon others to go where he wished to go.

We went out to dinner and Charlie was very quiet. After about forty-five minutes, he said, "So I guess when I get better, I'll have to take the test again?" And I knew, we had sunk even lower in the quicksand of Alzheimer's.

Prior to the driving evaluation, I had arranged with a neighbor who sold used cars that should Charlie fail the evaluation, the neighbor would pick up Charlie's car. The morning after the evaluation, I texted the neighbor about Charlie's testing results. The neighbor texted back saying he would pick up the car early the next day. That morning, I told Charlie we needed to clean out the car and take out all his personal possessions. He took out a few things and I then searched the car for documents and personal items. I went back into the car three times, discovering Charlie's possessions that he had obviously overlooked. His car resembled the disarray of his old university office. We decided to wash the inside and outside of the car so the neighbor wouldn't have to do so much work before selling the car. I asked Charlie to clean certain parts but he was not able to follow directions. I told him, "First you do this, and then you do that." He would start and then, forget the directions. Finally, I gave him a task which only had one step. His coordination was such that he was agonizingly slow, with poor end results. When he left saying he was just too tired, I finished cleaning the car. It took over four hours. I called Charlie out and he was so pleased that the car looked so good. "We did a great job, didn't we" he asked.

When I awakened the following morning and went to look out the front window, Charlie's car was gone. It was sold within a week and I put the proceeds of the sale of the car into a transportation fund for Charlie.

The somewhat sudden loss of Charlie's driving privileges sent me into hours and hours of research into services available in our community. I got the bus schedule and would encourage Charlie to take the bus for short distances as the bus stop was only a block and a half away. I arranged an application for the special bus that took persons with disabilities. That involved having our doctor certify that Charlie had a cognitive handicap that necessitated alternative transportation. Lastly, I got in touch with a not-for-profit private transportation service that could take Charlie to places where he could fish for the day and do other things that were not available to him with the regular bus services.

I decided I needed the advice of an elder attorney as a means of planning ahead for Charlie's needs. One was recommended by my estate attorney and I got an appointment within a couple of weeks. It was a very helpful consultation. His recommendations were ones which I would initiate in the coming months.

One of the recommendations was that I get an immediate Durable Power of Attorney for Charlie so that I could act in his behalf for all financial, real estate, business and health transactions and decisions. Unless Charlie would sign it voluntarily, I would have to go through a lengthy procedure to have him declared incompetent to manage his affairs. As Charlie was a mental health professional himself, that would have been a cruel blow and I wanted to avoid that at all costs. I elected to simply present the facts. I explained to Charlie that as I was already acting in his behalf, we needed a formal document saying he was giving his permission for me to do that legally. We talked for quite some time and finally, he said he thought it was probably necessary. He was no longer responding to emails and he had forgotten most of his passwords on the various accounts he used to handle.

I called the attorney and asked that the document be drawn up. I was fearful that Charlie would have a change of heart on the day of the signing. Before we went to the attorney's office, I again explained to Charlie what the document meant. I told him he would be giving me authorization to make calls for him and sign documents for him. He said, "That's a good idea." I asked him to repeat several of the sections of permissions to assure me that on that particular day, he did, indeed, comprehend what he would be signing.

When we got to the attorney's office and were escorted into the conference room, witnesses were presented and the attorney came in to greet us. I explained to Charlie in their presence what he would be signing and he said it was okay with him. When the attorney asked him directly about the document, Charlie responded, "She does all this for me anyone. I just don't remember most of it. I have a lot of memory problems." He then added, "But I do understand that I am giving her my permission – and I do." The attorney smiled and nodded his head. The documents were signed and witnessed.

That night, I thanked the powers that be that Charlie had a lucid day and was able to give me informed permission to act for him. It was a precious gift of love and trust that I treasure to this day.

Chapter Seven

Meltdowns

All the lights were on in the house even though it was bright daylight outside. I would go into the kitchen to turn off lights and then notice the cabinet doors and drawers were open. Each and every time that happened, I would ask Charlie to go turn off the lights and close the open doors so as to try to remind him. I felt that as long as he continued to do routine things, his mind just might cooperate. Charlie would always comply but soon, the lights would be on again and the doors open. That is how I knew that the routines he had so taken for granted for over seventy years were no longer a component of his knowledge.

In a twenty minute time frame, Charlie might ask me the same thing three or four times. Each time, I would try to factually answer his concerns with as much patience as possible but I found myself growing a bit irritated. Charlie began to prepare for the following day's bathroom activities by laying out everything he would use. At first, I thought it a clever compensation and said nothing. But then, the items were laid out on the bathroom counter at three in the afternoon! Then, he began to turn down the bed for sleep at about the same time and I would simply go in and make up the bed again. My patience was being used up by trivial things that I had never before had to face as routine events. As a psychologist, I tried to reason what Charlie must be thinking with the type of brain atrophy apparent in his testing. For the most part, I was proud of myself for staying the course in the early stages of the disease.

But then, the meltdowns began. The meltdowns were mine, not Charlie's. I began to raise my voice in frustration. I immediately felt guilty and went to Charlie and apologized. One time when I did not react quickly enough with an apology, he looked at me like a two year old child and said, "Don't yell at me." I felt like a heel and silently chastised myself for being so thoughtless. Charlie's simple statement had a profound effect on me. It made me pay attention to my own maladaptive behavior and I vowed to try harder.

As Charlie's behaviors deteriorated, I knew better than to react, but I was now the wife, not the clinical psychologist. At times, I just wanted to scream. But, I knew that would upset Charlie and he was forever present. Each and every repetition of questions would build to a climax and I would then vent my frustrations and feel immediately guilty. I got so I'd go in the other room so that Charlie wouldn't see how angry I had become at things he simply could not control. Even when I told myself this was not Charlie irritating me, it was still *someone* and that was enough for the frustration to begin to externalize.

I went for long walks but had already developed knee problems which made the walks less relaxing. The walks had always had the effect of getting me in touch with nature, something that I could count on to relax me and help me to a more positive mood. I continued to go to the gym but oftentimes, Charlie's appointments would interfere with that schedule. After having received a power bill for fifteen dollars more than expected, I began to follow Charlie around and turn out the lights. It felt as if I were following around a toddler, picking up the toys in order to have some semblance of order in my own home. I didn't feel disappointed that I had capitulated to Charlie's omissions. At least, I could help to control the power bill.

Of course, it was Charlie's home too but more and more, it felt as if he was a visitor in the house we had built together. He couldn't start the gas mower so I got an electric mower. Then, he couldn't figure out how to avoid the cord during mowing so that became my job. I asked him to pull some weeds while I mowed. He pulled up the flowers I had planted the previous month. When asked to edge the sidewalk and driveway, he brought the edger to the driveway and then looked at it. "I don't know what to do with it," he said. And my heart cried while I mowed, edged and pulled the weeds on a hot, Saturday afternoon. The sweat pouring out of my body felt cathartic. I went into the house sweaty and exhausted and I told Charlie I loved him. He smiled but he no longer automatically reached out to caress me. That also had stopped some time back.

I now had to help Charlie change his tee shirts. He simply could not get them over his head. It was as if his coordination was affected such that he could not reach back. I purchased several patterned button down shirts for him and he seemed to like the change. I always got shirts with blue coloring so that his beautiful blue eyes would be highlighted. The bright shirts also complemented the wonderful smile he continued to display for almost everyone, including me.

Every morning, Charlie would take a shower and spend a great deal of time in the bathroom. I decided it might be best for me to use the other bathroom, the one we had always reserved for guests. It saved being frustrated at not being able to meet my own hygiene needs and it gave Charlie the opportunity to fully take care of his own hygiene. Even though he would shower faithfully, he began to neglect washing his hair. I would have to remind him every other day or the grease would build up and I could detect an odor.

Oftentimes, I would need to remind Charlie to change his clothes. He would put on clean underwear but would wear the same outer clothing day after day unless reminded to change his shirt and pants. He didn't seem to notice stains and soil. He had always been a sharp dresser and this was just another loss to absorb while I began to monitor what he wore out of the house.

Sometimes I marveled at the fact that as a child, I played the adult. My mother had died when I was a toddler and I became highly adept at anticipating the needs and moods of grownups so that I could stay in one family or another. Now, those skills were again put to use. This time, I was functioning with an adult mind and having to respond to childlike moods, thoughts and behaviors.

Chapter Eight

A New Language

As in all cases of Alzheimer's, word-finding became problematic. Being highly verbal, Charlie was usually able to compensate and make his thoughts known, at least in the mild to moderate stages of the disease. He would look at the television guide and tell me he was studying the "menu." The remote control became the "clicking thing," and his computer games of solitaire became the "card show." One day, I watched him on the computer. I was concerned he might be trying to access something I needed such as our bank accounts or other financial information. I thought I had changed passwords for all of the important accounts, but Charlie seemed to be very creative in finding information I had neglected to secure.

I asked Charlie what he was doing. He appeared to be surfing the net. He responded, "I'm putting things into the computer." I watched him for a while and indeed, he was going onto various sites that appeared to interest him. I asked my husband just what he was putting into the machine and he said, "I'm telling it what to do."

When Charlie began to lose common words for food, I labeled everything in the pantry, hoping the written connection might help him in finding whatever he sought. During the transition from the mild to moderate stages, Charlie retained a remarkable amount of ability to name most common things. I attributed that to his outstanding verbal skills in general and I was pleased he was still able to make common associations. It greatly assisted me in understanding his needs.

Nothing Left to Burn - A Story of Alzheimer's Disease

During the transition from the mild to moderate stages, Charlie's short term memory was virtually nonexistent. I used clues to ascertain about how far back his memory was lost. For example, one day, I took him to our favorite brunch place after he had successfully vacuumed all the carpets in the house. More and more, food items were becoming effective reinforcers for tasks accomplished. On the way to the restaurant, Charlie asked if the restaurant had breakfast or if we could just have lunch. That initially startled me as we had been going to the brunch place for over 25 years now. We loved the restaurant precisely because it served both breakfast and lunch. So, I ascertained from Charlie's comment that he was now bouncing back and forth, with an unreliable memory that now reached back about 25 years.

Once seated at the restaurant, I gave Charlie a menu. He began to look at it and he then asked, "Do they serve breakfast here?" I assured him they did and he said he would have something that I felt would irritate the recent dental work he'd just had done the day before. He looked at me with an expression that suggested I was the nutty one and he commented, "That was years ago, you know. I think you're getting a faulty memory, love!" I smiled at Charlie and replied that at our ages, we could expect some lapses.

I then suggested to Charlie that he might want to order something soft. I could immediately tell he was having trouble with that concept as it related to food. I asked him if he wanted breakfast or lunch and he said he wanted breakfast. I told him that was a great choice as there were so many soft things such as eggs, pancakes, oatmeal and such. The suggestions seemed to help. When the waitress arrived with our drinks, Charlie immediately said, "I'll have something soft, please." The waitress looked at me and I smiled. She then asked Charlie what he wanted to order and, pointing at me, he said, "Ask her first." I knew he had already forgotten my suggestions. I ordered and Charlie grinned and said, "I'll have the exact same thing! She took my idea!"

Little by little, the teenage granddaughters were called "toddlers" and the cupboards became "holding things." With a couple of questions, it was not generally difficult to rename the objects correctly in my mind. I thought much of Charlie's object renaming to be rather creative. At times, the television was the "show box" and at other times, it was back to being the TV. Most of the time, shoes were called shoes but at times, they were called "foot coverings." All tools became "machines" while all pots and pans became "cooking things". I noticed that much of the renaming of common household items resembled the object naming of a preschooler and it helped me that I was once a parent and could look into Charlie's creativity and extrapolate a new meaning for a common word.

Chapter Nine

The Day the Bus Changed Routes

Charlie decided one day that he would explore changing buses to get to places further away. He decided to go to Sarasota Square Mall to walk around and then have lunch. We discussed where he would get off to transfer and I wrote down the bus numbers for him and handed the note to Charlie. Before Charlie left, I asked about his cell phone. He took it out of his pants pocket and said, "I even charged it this morning!" Charlie stuck the note and the cell phone in his pocket and went out to catch bus number fifteen a block and a half away from our house.

As I had an appointment that day, Charlie was going to take the bus to Sarasota Square Mall to spend most of the day. When he was finished with his activities there, he would call me to pick him up. I finished my chores around mid-afternoon and then, went home. Charlie was not yet home but that set off no alarms with me as we had both agreed on a late afternoon pick-up time. I took the rare alone time as an opportunity to go out to the front patio and get in some recreational reading. It was pure heaven! I turned on the water fountain and laid back. I had nearly fallen asleep when Charlie called at 4:15 PM.

I picked up Charlie at the mall and immediately I told him I was proud that he had made the longer trip by himself. I asked him how the transfer had gone. He grinned from ear to ear and replied that he had not had to transfer buses at all. I asked how that was possible and he replied that the bus had simply made a right turn and taken him to the other mall. From there, he was able to get a bus to Sarasota Square Mall.

This confused me. I knew the bus did not turn in that direction and I again asked the question of Charlie. His reply was the same. "I don't know why but the bus turned right there today and it took me to Southgate Mall. I ate lunch and then got on the bus and it took me to Sarasota Square Mall." I asked Charlie if he had transferred to bus number seventeen and he said, "I think so. It took me to the right place anyway." I had to drop the conversation for the time being. We were getting nowhere. It was evident Charlie had already forgotten the morning ride.

For several days, I tried to think about how Charlie might have gotten to the right mall the wrong way. Finally, I had the light bulb effect in my brain and I asked, "Charlie, did you stop at the Publix grocery store to get a paper on the way to the mall the other day? He said, "I think maybe I did but you'd better check that out." I then asked if maybe, he had walked across the street to catch the bus to Southgate Mall. He said, "That could be." Then, I related how he could have gotten to the wrong mall, asked someone for the bus to Sarasota Square Mall and finally ended up there. He replied, "That could be exactly the way it happened!"

It dawned on me that because Charlie took the bus nearly every day and always got off at Publix, he had also acted out that routine on the day in question. After getting the paper, he normally went to a nearby restaurant around the corner and got tea and a pastry before catching the bus home. The pastry shop is on a north -to-south street while Publix is on an east-to-west street. Since he hadn't gone for a treat on the day he was to go to the mall, he went directly across the street from Publix and caught the bus to the wrong mall. Had he gone to the pastry shop, he would have crossed the street going north and south and he would have caught the bus back home. When I explained the mistake to Charlie, he said, "Lucky I didn't get my treat today or I would have come back home! I would have missed my big adventure at the mall!"

Nothing Left to Burn - A Story of Alzheimer's Disease

This was another important message for me. Even though I had given directions to Charlie, we had not discussed his need to stop for a newspaper. Therefore, he went with the known and got off where he normally got off the bus. As usual, he went across the street to catch his ride back. Only this time, it took him to another mall. He recognized his mistake and asked how to get to the right place for his pick-up. Although Charlie did a good job of asking how to get where he wanted to go, the incident scared me enough that I remembered to ask Charlie about all his needs whenever he went out using the bus again. I asked him what he would do if he found himself in the wrong place and he said he would take out his cell phone and call me. That was a source of comfort. He still understood how to ask for help and who to call.

When Charlie mentioned that he had eaten at the wrong mall, I asked him why he then went on to Sarasota Square Mall instead of coming back home. "I didn't have my treat yet," he replied simply. Well, of course. I should have anticipated that one!

I wondered what other adventures lay ahead of us. After all, Charlie was only in the *mild* stage of the disease.

Chapter Ten

Charlie's New Talents

Charlie had always been a bit of a klutz with things like tools but lately, he was picking up some new talents. We had the new gas lawn mower into the shop four times in six weeks when Charlie tried to pull the cord to start the machine. I have no idea what he did but he had somehow pulled the cord from its casing. That's when we got the electric mower. The repair costs were ruining my budget!

One of his major chores was to make up the bed after I had washed and dried the sheets. Being a former Navy man, he had always had a great talent for getting the sheets on nice and tight. Charlie told me Navy men could always "bounce a coin on the top sheet." He had shown me several times early in our marriage just to make his point. One day, he came to me and said, "You should come in here and look at this." I went in with a feeling of caution. One of the corners of the fitted sheet had torn badly.

Charlie looked at me with fear in his face and he said, "It musta happened in the washing machine. It musta torn it apart." I knew that was not the case as I had taken the sheet set from the dryer, folded it and given it to Charlie. But, he obviously feared punishment and that look went straight to my heart.

"You're probably right, Charlie," I said. It's a powerful machine and those sheets are getting old. He smiled and asked if he should leave the torn sheet on the bed. I smiled back and went to the linen closet, got a new fitted sheet and put it on the bed after having removed the torn sheet.

Nothing Left to Burn - A Story of Alzheimer's Disease

When someone tries their best and still screws up a task, there is no gain in pointing out the obvious. It was only a sheet.

I was outside power washing the front patio area. Charlie came out and wanted to help just as I was finishing and winding up the cord on the power washer. I said I was tired and could really use some help moving things back into place. Charlie carefully moved back two chairs and then he began to hurry. He carried a small rattan table over to the patio, lifting it slightly over the wrought iron gate with pointed spindles. He ripped the rattan. I saw the incident but said nothing as Charlie then went to get a plastic statue in the form of a child. While bringing it into the patio area, he dropped it and one of the arms of the child broke off. I said nothing as Charlie tried to put the arm back in place. The child statue ended up with its right arm resting on its head. My back had been turned away from Charlie and I guess he reasoned that I had not seen what he had done.

Afterwards, we both sat in the chairs to rest. I stared at the statue and Charlie followed my eyes. "He musta had an accident," he said. I replied, "I guess so, Charlie." Charlie got that scared look on his face and he asked, "Is somebody in trouble?" This was a complete departure from the confidence my husband had displayed before the onset of his illness. I took my husband's hand and I said, "Charlie, the important thing is that people are willing to help other people. We can always replace things that get broken but a helper, well, a helper is something pretty special. Thank you for helping, Charlie." I later put a spare ceramic tile on the table with the torn rattan and it works fine to this day. I glued the arm back on the child statue. The arm is just a bit off, but neither Charlie nor I notice it.

Charlie developed a talent for breaking the things he touched. That's how I learned of his coordination problems. I studied him and sure enough, one day, I saw a slight tremor in both hands. Of course, Charlie wasn't going to be bringing me my good china or a plate of hot food. But, for as long as he could possibly manage it, I vowed that Charlie was going to be my helper.- for the good of us both. I think it was even written in my wedding vows.

Chapter Eleven

There's a Place for Us

When Charlie and I married as middle-aged adults, we danced to the Barbara Streisand song "There's a Place for Us." We were madly in love and oblivious to everyone on the dance floor. Like most couples in a fog, we figured we'd be the way we were on that special day for the rest of our lives.

Every so often after Charlie's diagnosis of dementia, I would put on the CD which contained the Streisand song and Charlie and I would dance. One night I put on the song and I asked Charlie to dance with me. "Why?" he asked and my heart fell to my shoes.

"It's our song, Charlie," I replied with teary eyes.

"Do we own it?" He asked.

"Yes," I answered, "we own it."

Charlie rose from his chair and awkwardly held me as he shuffled his feet around the wooden floors of the great room in our house. It would be our last dance; it was just too painful for me. Charlie was shuffling a lot now. No matter where I was in the hours, I always knew where Charlie was.

More and more, I was losing Charlie emotionally as well as cognitively. Charlie had always been a *touchy-feely* kind of guy. Even when engaging in an interpersonal conversation, his hand might be on the shoulder of a student, faculty member or friend. His natural affection was one of the qualities that attracted me to Charlie. Giving affection was much more awkward for me. Having lost a parent when just a toddler, I had learned to do without hugs and kisses as routine reinforcement. When I had my own children, I got used to giving and receiving affection and I loved it! Charlie's touches had seemed special from the very first touch. I grew to love them and even to crave his ongoing attention.

One of Charlie's most famous talents was his outstanding backrub. I was generally the one to do the physical chores around the house while Charlie was far more adept at running errands. If he had to drive to stores five or six times a day, he never complained. I tried to teach him some of the routine house maintenance chores but generally, he would bypass a critical step and I would end up bailing him out. He always felt badly that he was not gifted in coordination but he was so appreciative of my talents that I could almost always count on a wonderful, healing backrub at the end of the day.

His new emotional blandness was so subtle that it took me a while to catch on. He still smiled but his facial features lacked definition during emotional discussions. He stopped reaching over to touch me. The routine hugs ceased. After a while, he no longer initiated sexual interactions and he seemed confused by my advances. At that time, I believe I also distanced myself from close contact, probably to protect myself from what I could not have. I had been accomplished at self-protection as a child and now, it came naturally to me.

I still tried to hug Charlie whenever he left the house. I would put my arms around him and hold him for a few seconds. He had always returned the hug - and then some! Generally, a good-bye kiss on the lips would follow. But now, when I would hug Charlie, my arms were the only arms doing the hugging. When I would release him, he would smile and say, "That's nice." I would kiss him on the cheek because a direct kiss on the lips just seemed too intimate for me when Charlie did not understand the significance. After the cheek kiss, Charlie would leave the house.

Charlie would still allow me to take his hand when we went out together. Oftentimes, it was my reassurance that he was still with me. He struggled to get out of my car and would lag far behind me if I didn't go to him and take his hand. My hand in his seemed to reassure Charlie that we were still a couple and that he was in safe hands.

If Charlie couldn't see or hear me when we were in the house, he would seek me out. He would stand and look at me and I'd say something like, "I'm still here, Charlie. I'll be sure to let you know if I leave the house." It's one of the frustrating things that Alzheimer's patients do. They probably need ongoing reassurances that the person they most trust is still there for them. When cognitive reasoning begins to fail, perceptive senses become the form of knowing.

Chapter Twelve

Fishing for All Sorts of Things

As much as Charlie loved to fish, he seemed to have forgotten that he could go fishing any time he wanted now that he was retired. Even though he had no car, I would drive him places and he also had the transportation I had already arranged. I wrote Charlie notes with pictures of fish on them as a reminder. Sometimes he would look at the note and say, "You draw well." At other times, he would not even look at the note. Inevitably, I would need to remind Charlie to call for a fishing trip and then, stand by as he made the arrangements.

Sometimes, I asked Charlie to pack up the car and we would go out to Turtle Beach in the late afternoon. Charlie would cast out his line and walk the beach as I sat in a chair and read. He would always keep me in sight. He glanced to where I was sitting and he smiled, in seeming satisfaction that I was still there. Or, perhaps, he was just happy to be at the beach. The late afternoons at the beach were precious to us both. Charlie usually threw back any fish he caught. I would try to read but would inevitably end up simply gazing at the tide as it ebbed and flowed. Sometimes, I would get into a synchronized rhythm with the tide so that I would relax my body and my mind would be momentarily freed of its own constraints of duty and obligation. The rhythm of the tide would stimulate visual images of times spent with Charlie, times when we were carefree and we thought we had the world by the tail. Those were times when Alzheimer's was a word that belonged in the verbal repertoire of others less fortunate than we.

These were the days when Charlie's behaviors and abilities would vacillate between the mild and the moderate stages of the disease. One day, he might be capable of doing a certain chore and the next day, he would have no clue as to how to do the same task. Sometimes, the behaviors would change from one hour to the next in the same day. Most of the time, Charlie would vehemently deny he was as cognitively impaired as he was. On occasion, he would seem to realize the extent of his own decompensation. At those times, I saw fear in his eyes and my heart would bleed for his awareness.

I had been keeping a sort of unorganized diary so that I could record and understand the backward progression of the disease. Also, I wanted to chart my own reactions to ascertain when I overreacted to things and when I displayed a reaction of true concern regarding Charlie's safety. I had always had a somewhat perfectionistic view of what my own abilities should be and at times, I caught myself unnecessarily projecting those expectations onto others. Charlie had never been one to expect a perfect performance from himself and now, I understood that I must attempt to pattern my own expectations after those Charlie had always held.

I noticed that Charlie's expectations for himself were primarily centered on food. While other tasks began to become far too complicated for my husband, he was continually able to find some means to feed himself. When he could no longer remember how to operate the stovetop and oven safely, he used the microwave. On occasion, he would ask about setting the timer on the microwave but for the most part, he retained that ability well into the moderate stage of the disease. For foods Charlie routinely reheated, I put a laminated heating chart on the counter by the microwave.

Although he could no longer cook for the two of us, he was capable of getting a simple meal for himself. That allowed me freedom to leave the house without fear that he would be malnourished or that he would be put in harm's way by attempting to feed himself. I stocked the refrigerator with protein drinks, hard-boiled eggs, cut up carrots and celery and various containers of leftover foods such as cold, cooked chicken and casseroles which Charlie could heat up in the microwave. I always printed out directions as to how long to cook the leftovers in order to heat them and I taped the directions to the top of the container.

One day when I woke up feeling the need to have a day alone, I decided to power wash the driveway and walkways of my son's house. I had just given him a ride to the airport the day before for a trip abroad. On the way, he had mentioned that he needed to borrow my power washer to do the work soon. I thought I could surprise him and also get some time for myself. I told Charlie what I was going to do and he asked to be dropped off at the grocery store for his usual routine of getting the paper, walking over for a pastry and tea and taking the bus home. I asked him if he remembered he needed to do his three chores that day and he said he would do them as soon as he got home. "I promise," he pledged as he got out of the car at the grocery store parking lot.

For the past month, Charlie and I had decided he would do three chores a week so that we would both contribute to the running of the house. He was to sweep the floors, dust, and then vacuum the three area rugs. These were all one-step procedures and Charlie had demonstrated his ability to complete each task. We discussed what his lunch would be and there was nothing to prepare. He would take out the prepared turkey sandwich and the small container of fruit for his lunch. He asked on the way to the store if he could have chips as well, so we added them to the luncheon menu. I felt confident I could have a day of alone time without Charlie risking any kind of catastrophe to himself or to the house. And, of course, he could always call me on my cell phone if he ran into difficulties.

I spent five hours doing the power washing and my son's place looked decidedly better. I was soaking wet, dirty and exhausted, but it was one of those good types of physical tiredness – when you feel you have really accomplished something meaningful.

I returned home to find Charlie at his desk, eating a muffin. I asked him to unload the power washer from my car and to put it in the shed while I scrambled into the shower. When I showered and dressed, I realized my back was very sore from standing on the concrete so long. I told Charlie I was going to stretch out on the sofa. I asked if he had done his three chores and he turned away from me. "Oh, Charlie, I was so hoping you'd try to help out while I was gone," I said. He saw my disappointment and went to his office in an obvious retreat. He would always go into an avoidance mode now rather than endure any kind of confrontation.

After a while, he came to the sofa and asked if we could go out to dinner. For some reason, his request just infuriated me and I told him I was exhausted and since he hadn't been thoughtful enough to do his chores, there was no way on earth we were going out to eat! I thought he was going to cry. At that moment, I hated myself for my failure to put Charlie's needs first. In retrospect, it was just one of those moments when the frustration of what I could no longer have combined with the fatigue of the day became the predominant feeling and I acted it out.

I immediately apologized for my outburst. I rose and said that I was disappointed that the work had not been done but that there was plenty at home for us to eat. Charlie immediately went back to his office. I now understood that the man who had counseled so many people to handle their emotions could no longer handle mine. Furthermore, Charlie actually appeared afraid of my anger when previously, he was an expert at soothing over my stronger emotions.

That night in bed, I finally pulled together what was bothering me. Charlie was such a giving person and now, I was doing all the giving and he was doing all the getting. I wasn't sure what to do about that but I vowed to fight for Charlie's love and attention for as long as he was capable of reciprocating in any manner. In my earlier adult years, I had done the bulk of the giving and that was my choice. But, when meeting Charlie, I finally realized how good it felt to be taken care of sometimes. I vowed I would fight for that for as long as possible.

The following morning, I reminded Charlie that he would need to do his three chores before we went to get groceries. He asked if we could go to brunch if he did his chores and I told him we could do that. I engaged myself doing business work on the computer while Charlie completed his three chores. We then went on our weekly grocery outing and took the groceries home and put them away. I asked Charlie to choose where he wanted to go to brunch and he said, "We should go to that place we both like." I knew what restaurant that was and we took off in my car for a place by the water.

The restaurant was crowded and when we were finally seated, I knew it would be a while before we were served. I ordered and then, Charlie said, "I'll have the exact same thing she told you." While we were waiting for our food, I decided to try to talk with Charlie about my unmet needs. I explained that sometimes when someone is sick, the other person has to do all the work and that the giving person doesn't mind a bit. But then, the person doing all the work begins to feel that maybe they are not appreciated. Charlie's eyes brightened a bit and I thought he was tracking me. "Am I the sick person?" he asked.

My heart began to thump and I told Charlie that his mind was sick and that was why he had so many problems remembering. He surprised me by saying, "So you must be the one doing all the work!"

I responded that yes, indeed, I sometimes felt overwhelmed and that sometimes a simple "thank you" would be enough to keep me going. "I can do that," Charlie responded. We both decided that each day, Charlie would try to do one simple thing to let me know he appreciated having me take care of everything for us both. When we got home from our brunch and a short drive, Charlie wrote a note and put it on his desk. I went in to dust the desk as Charlie always left muffin crumbs and I didn't want to attract ants. On the top of his desk, I saw his note. It said: "Every day, do something nice for Karen." It melted my heart! It was such a tiny thing but it gave me sustenance for the next round.

That night, Charlie said he was going to make a frozen pizza for us for dinner while I relaxed on the sofa and watched a baseball game. My back was still a bit tight from the power-washing job the day before. As I lay on the sofa, it occurred to me that making the pizza was Charlie's *nice* thing for the day. It brought a smile to my face.

Charlie got out the pizza box from the freezer and I told him he needed to add some vegetable toppings. I told him to preheat the oven and he said he didn't know how to turn it on. I got off the sofa, went to the kitchen and turned on the oven to 400 degrees and went back to the sofa. Charlie asked what to put on the pizza and I told him we had mushrooms and spinach but that he should defrost the spinach. He asked how to do that so I got off the sofa, went to the kitchen and put the frozen spinach in the microwave and defrosted it. I returned to the sofa. I gave Charlie running accounts of the at-bats for the Tampa Bay Rays as he was a big fan. He called out that he couldn't open the small can of mushrooms. I went to the kitchen and opened the can of mushrooms, drained them and went back to the sofa. Charlie called out, "I'm putting the spinach and mush-rooms on the pizza," and I told him he was doing a great job. I also said I was so happy that he was making the dinner for us that night.

The oven was then preheated to the correct temperature and it beeped. Charlie startled and said, "Uh, oh," and I told him it was time to put in the pizza. I asked him if he had used all the spinach and mushrooms and he said, "There's a little bit left." I got off the sofa and went to the kitchen to take a look. There was a spoonful of spinach and about ten mushroom pieces on the pizza. I put on the rest of the vegetables and opened the oven, telling Charlie to put in the pizza. He did so and I then set the timer and went back to the sofa. Charlie followed me and sat in his lounge chair.

The timer went off indicating it was time to take out the

pizza. Charlie said, "Uh, oh," and I told him it was time to take out the pizza. We both went to the kitchen as I suspected my job was not yet quite done. Charlie opened the oven door and was about to reach for the hot pizza pan when I said, "Charlie, NO!" I handed him two hot pads and he took out the pizza. I handed him the knife as he said he wanted to cut it. He did a credible job, cutting the pizza into fourths. He then put two pieces on my plate and two pieces on his plate. He beamed at me and said, "See, I told you I could do it!"

I said, "You sure did, Charlie. Thank you so much. I love you for doing this." He glowed with happiness and a sense of achievement.

We took our plates into the family room and I sat on the sofa. Charlie looked so very pleased with himself. I sat there wondering how my job had probably just increased with all the things Charlie would do for me each day. As it turned out, that was to be the last of my *nice* days. Charlie forgot to look at his own note and I eventually put it in the scrapbook so I'd be sure to remember the day he voluntarily did something nice for me.

Chapter Thirteen

Cleaning the Computer

One of Charlie's friends called him to ask why he hadn't returned his email. Charlie told the man he'd been just too busy lately and he said he preferred to talk on the phone anyway. The conversation lasted about twenty minutes and when Charlie hung up the phone, I asked about his emailing habits. I reminded him that he needed to keep in touch with people so that he'd know what was going on. I was concerned that Charlie seemed to be pulling further and further away from us all. When I again asked about his emails, he finally said, "I don't know how to do it."

I told Charlie we needed to check his emails but he had forgotten his password. I went into the computer and had the password changed to one I now knew. I logged onto his computer and saw there were six hundred and thirty-seven email messages in his box!

Charlie then confessed that he really hadn't done emailing for about a year "or so." I told him we needed to clean out his emails and he said he didn't know how to do it. I asked if I could delete the ads and simply print out anything from a friend. We could then email the friend and tell them that Charlie preferred not to email and instead, he requested that any friends simply call him with news. I spent some time cleaning out and sorting and finally, we were down to the last message. Charlie sat patiently in the extra chair in his office while I did this. When I told him we were down to the last message, he said, "I just don't know how you do that!"

Emailing had been required in his work and it hadn't been that long ago that he had routinely performed that task.

Every week after that, I checked Charlie's emails and printed out any messages that seemed important. Soon, the only messages he got were ads and spam. I debated whether or not to keep the computer but Charlie still used it to play solitaire and I didn't want to deprive him of that pleasure.

As a child, I used to say the Lord's Prayer nightly. I always asked to keep safe those I loved. It gave me a certain peace of mind to think I was being watched after as well. I was beginning to think I needed some extra help so I now added the 23rd Psalm to my nightly offerings. And still, the issues with Charlie escalated. I knew I couldn't ask for a reversal but surely, God had enough power to stop the insidious disease from worsening for a while. When it kept getting worse, I asked for the strength to handle the day-to-day issues. Some days, it seemed my prayers were heard and on other days, God seemed to have turned a deaf ear to my prayers.

There were days when I almost felt desperate to handle everything coming my way and there were days when I reveled in the feeling of having things under control. No matter how much education or counseling or support you have, the emotions just keep on flip-flopping. I used a lot of self-talk and some removal of myself from stressful situations. I talked to my friends and I researched ideas on the computer. The thing is, it just keeps coming on, no matter how good and practiced your coping skills.

Chapter Fourteen

A Short Respite

My fifty-fifth class reunion was fast approaching and I had to make a decision. Finally, I got on the computer and looked up the prices of a round-trip airplane ticket. On impulse, I got a ticket. I called my daughter and son and explained where I was going and they immediately assured me they'd step in and make sure Charlie was taken care of.

I would be gone four days total. Two of the days would predominantly be travel days and the other two days would be spent with my high school friends. I also agreed to do a benefit book-signing fundraiser for the local historical museum. I worked hard to schedule activities and transportation for Charlie for the four days I would be gone. He would have various activities, some of which were routine and others which would be new and hopefully, stimulating for him.

When the day of my departure came, I had notes all over the house for Charlie. The Scat Plus bus (special needs bus) came to pick up Charlie just before I was to leave for the airport. I asked Charlie to show me his cell phone and then, I kissed him good-bye and he was off on his adventure!

I checked all my notes and was satisfied I had covered any anticipated potential crises. I left my car parked in the garage but took both sets of car keys with me. I took off the knobs from the stove so that Charlie wouldn't be tempted to use the stovetop. I texted my daughter and son that I was on my way!

Nothing Left to Burn - A Story of Alzheimer's Disease

The travel turned out to be a real hassle with cancelled and delayed flights. I finally arrived at my destination in a rented car at 10:30 in the evening, totally exhausted but assured by texting with my daughter that Charlie was at home and ready for bed. The next two days with my friends were truly a respite, even though there were ongoing activities.

On the morning of my departure for home, it was raining hard and I had to have the rental car turned in at the airport by noon. It was over a three hour drive so I immediately set off in a driving rain on roads that were somewhat foreign to me. The driving concentration left me a bit weary but I successfully turned in the car at the airport and then got myself a fruit smoothie and sat down to read. My flight would not take off for another hour.

At about the time I was to board, there was an announcement that the plane I was to take had mechanical trouble and they were "checking it out." Supposedly this was a ten to fifteen minute process. Two and a half hours later, we boarded. Two and a half hours was the layover I was to have at the Atlanta airport before I connected to return to Florida. I began to get an uncomfortable tightness in my stomach. I texted my daughter telling her there was a fairly high probability I'd have to spend the night in the Atlanta airport as my scheduled flight was the last to leave that night.

Before the flight landed in Atlanta, the young woman next to me looked up my boarding gate for me. I sighed when she told me we were landing two concourses away. When I deplaned, I heard the announcement for the final boarding of my flight. I literally flew through the concourse, down the escalator, into the train and up the escalator to the concourse in which my plane was boarding. I sprinted to the end where I saw the attendant closing the door. I literally screamed out, "Please, please let me on that plane! My husband has Alzheimer's disease and if I don't get on this plane, he'll be alone tonight!" The woman probably thought I was crazed! She looked at me, looked at the door and then, opened it! I thanked the powers that be that they had not yet detached the walkway from the plane.

My heart was literally pounding in my chest and my bad leg felt as if it had detached altogether from my body. But I was on the plane headed back to Charlie. For me, it was a victory, one of the occasional ones you get when you are the caregiver of an Alzheimer's patient.

After landing in Sarasota, I got my luggage and then headed to the long-term parking area to retrieve my car. The warm, moist Florida air seemed to hug me with all things secure and known. I paid for the long-term parking and headed out toward home. I turned on the radio and turned up the volume as I tried to loosen the muscles in my tight body.

I hoped Charlie had already gone to bed. It was nearly midnight and I just wanted to crash in bed after checking on him. But, when I entered the house, Charlie was sitting on his lounge chair. His two hands were tapping his knees in anxiety. He looked scared until he heard the door. He got up, looked at me and smiled so broadly I though his lips might burst with joy! I went to him, gave him a hug and said, "It's time to go to bed now, Charlie." He turned around and headed for the bedroom. Within three minutes, he was sound asleep, safe in the knowledge his caregiver was home.

During my absence, Charlie lost his cell phone and the $100 in cash I had given to him. I was proud he had done so well and relieved that nothing worse had happened.

Chapter Fifteen

The Downward Slope of Degradation

I now had to monitor everything. I would find ice cream in the refrigerator instead of the freezer. Charlie put the butter tub in the oven. Dirty rags from the garage would turn up with the clean laundry in the drawers. The toilet Charlie used would not be flushed. Charlie would beg me to go see the grandchildren several times a day. I explained limitations and boundaries, all to no avail. I knew the bundles or tangles in the brain were now getting more pronounced.

In Alzheimer's disease, neurons are the major cells destroyed. Neurons carry messages from one part of the brain to another, transmitting memory as they go. The electrical charges which carry the messages from cell to cell are disrupted and cell death occurs. The brain literally shrinks (atrophies) and the shrinkage is generally the worst in the brain area called the hippocampus. This is the area in which new memories are formed. Gradually, fluid in the brain spaces becomes larger and the synapses (potential cell connections) no longer carry messages. I could almost visualize this happening in Charlie's brain. At times, it helped to visualize this shrinkage as it reminded me I must have fewer and fewer expectations of Charlie's performance. It was almost as if Charlie was giving me a map of his brain via his current behaviors.

I understood that, at this stage of the disease, Charlie's brain now had considerable plaque. Plaque is formed when protein clusters build up between the nerve cells. The dead and dying cell strands then form tangles or bundles which further inhibit communication from one nerve cell to another. Science has not yet identified the exact cause of cell death in Alzheimer's disease but it is currently believed that these tangles are a major contributor to the decline of brain functioning.

In the normal brain, the brain transmits messages in orderly strands of information, much like a train moving down a railroad track. In the Alzheimer's brain, the transport strands become tangled. Because of the tangles, nutrients cannot move through the strands and they cause the tangled strands to die. The brain tangles fall apart and they are eventually absorbed by the brain.

As a scientist, the knowledge that Charlie's brain now had an unseen Alzheimer's look was knowledge that tended to depress me. The visual image was just another sign of foreboding. As a spouse and caregiver, that knowledge both angered me and created searing emotional pain which had to be assuaged so that the caregiver role could emerge in a productive manner.

We all understand that when brain cells are used, they tend to strengthen and increase connections. If brain cells are not connected, they are of little use. This is why it is critical that infants and young children receive ongoing brain stimulation. Since we're born with all the brain cells we will ever have, the only way to go is down. Once the Alzheimer's process starts, the domino effect is initiated and the only treatment available consists of stalling tactics.

Having ongoing access to the phone at his desk, Charlie would continually make unnecessary calls to service providers. He would call to see if his vision or eye insurance was still valid. Of course, he never had the insurance information in front of him so he always struggled to try to communicate to a particular representative what it was he wanted.

Since I was now in charge of our household business, there was no reason for Charlie to be calling. But, as that was a task he had traditionally assumed in our marriage, there were times when the brain would be triggered to recall that particular task and he would then go about assuming the responsibility without any current information that would facilitate the communication. I must say that the representatives were, without question, patient and kind with Charlie. I think that his stage of dementia was now pretty much apparent to all and they were no doubt trained for situations such as that experienced by Charlie. On occasion, Charlie would call out to me and I would take over the conversation, apologizing for the inconvenience and thanking the representative for his or her time. It is all just a part of the caregiver role and is pretty much generalized to the problems of all patients with dementia.

On one particular day, Charlie had called a health service provider and apparently they asked for his Social Security number. I happened to be in the kitchen and Charlie yelled out to me, "What's a Social Security number?" I was appalled that this distant memory had been lost but I went into the den and asked why the provider needed it. She explained that Charlie was cancelling a life insurance policy he'd had for nearly fifty years and he was ordering something else. I asked Charlie to go outside and check for the mail while I explained to the woman I had just paid the policy and we wanted no changes. I now dreaded receiving phone calls when I was not immediately ready to take the call. I had arranged for most business calls to come through my cell phone but apparently, I had left holes and gaps in my arrangements.

I oftentimes wondered if the Alzheimer's brain was nearly a reverse of the child's developing brain function. Being a professional in child developmental issues, it intrigued me to think that Charlie might simply be going backward in his ability to process the world. But, of course, it isn't as simple as that.

Swiss psychologist Jean Piaget formulated a developmental stage theory which allowed for the maturation of the brain function as it formed greater connections. At first, the child learns about his or her immediate environment via movement and sensation. Children younger than two years can begin to form ideas about how their movement affects things around them. When an object disappears from sight however, it is as if the object no longer exists. At times, I saw this in Charlie, although it was not related to a sensorimotor experience. Rather it was related to the cells which no longer gave memory about an object. If a backwards brain process was in effect, this sense of an object existing should have been one of the last things to go. In fact, it was one of the first, simply because the immediate memory goes first. In the Alzheimer's brain, even if you see a new object with a mature brain, the object no longer exists moments later.

Piaget's later developmental stages consisted of children learning appropriate associations and beginning to formulate the ability to do abstract thinking. Although many of my friends insisted that Alzheimer's seemed to be a process of becoming cognitively childlike, for me, it seemed much more a result of the initial deterioration of short term memory functioning. If you don't remember the correct wording of a conversation, you simply cannot intelligently respond. You begin to withdraw from social interactions due to the uncertainty of what is occurring. As the disease progresses, you lose more and more memory, giving you fewer and fewer available responses to the world in which you exist.

For Charlie, it seemed as if his moral development remained long after his cognitive skills had declined. For that, I will remain forever grateful. That allowed for social interactions into the moderate to moderately severe stages of the disease. American Psychologist Lawrence Kohlberg theorized that children also go through moral developmental stages in which they gradually learn to consider the perspectives of others as well as the world at large. Kohlberg's stage four called Maintaining the Social Order seems to hold fairly fast with most Alzheimer's patients until they reach the more severe stage of the disease. For Charlie and for most at his level of functioning, he seemed able to maintain a sense of social order. Again, that would be consistent with the memory functioning going backwards in time. Most young school children are taught rules and regulations such that they can act socially with respect toward others and consideration of the rules of social order.

When deterioration begins in the part of the brain that inhibits self-focused and hedonistic activities, the caregiver understands that the Alzheimer's patient must be protected not only from others but from him/herself as well. The first time I got a hint that that particular stage was forthcoming, I added the Beatitudes to my nightly prayers. In addition to the nine blessings from the Sermon on the Mount, I would always add two more, one facetious and one in honor of the caregivers: Blessed are those with Alzheimer's disease for they shall create chaos. Blessed are the caregivers for they are the more creative of the Earth.

Chapter Sixteen

The Appliance Terminator

Every so often, Charlie had a banner day. This was one of those days. He managed to disable the dishwasher, the washing machine and the outside fountain all in one day! His creativity never ceases to amaze me. The neurotransmitters that are functioning yet must be misfiring in rapid succession!

Charlie is not supposed to touch or try to operate any appliances now except for the microwave. But he tries to *help* me from time to time. Today was one of those days. When the dishwasher finished the dry cycle, I opened it to allow the hot air to escape so the dishes could cool and I could put them away. There was a thick layer of suds and water in the bottom of the dishwasher. At first, I thought the drain might be plugged with waste and I dreaded calling for a repair. But then, I thought to ask Charlie a question.

I had long since given up asking Charlie to use words to describe actions I considered questionable. So, I asked, "Charlie, can you show me the soap you put in the dishwasher before you started it?"

Charlie went to the sink cabinet and pulled out the liquid soap we used to wash items in the sink. He handed it to me with a big grin on his face. I instantly understood that he had used the wrong soap for the machine and I thanked him for his help but asked that he allow me to choose the soap "next time." I knew he wouldn't remember that but it seemed to be a courtesy that I might want under the circumstances.

Nothing Left to Burn - A Story of Alzheimer's Disease

I unloaded the dishwasher and placed all the dishes in the sink. I then scooped out all the suds and then, the water. Fortunately, there wasn't much water in the bottom. Easing down on my bad knee, I cleaned out the bottom of the dishwasher with cold water, hoping to get out most of the soap residue. I then ran a short cycle, hoping not too many suds would appear. When the cycle ended, I opened the dishwasher and marveled that I had lucked out! There were no suds and the water had all drained. I put the dishes back into the dishwasher, put in the correct soap for the machine and started the appliance.

"What does F5 mean?" Charlie yelled from the laundry room.

I entered the room and looked at the washing machine. Indeed there was a signal from the machine that it was in distress. I looked in the manual to see what horrible thing had happened to my relatively new, high-tech machine. I opened the machine and sure enough, the *high suds* warning the machine had issued was correct. I asked Charlie what soap he had used to put into the machine and he showed me an old bottle of laundry detergent that did not have the HE (high efficiency) symbol on it. How he managed to locate the obsolete bottle was beyond me but I immediately understood what I needed to do. I looked into the machine and saw one pair of dark underwear. Charlie had apparently had an accident and had remembered that the underwear needed to be washed. He put in the one pair of underwear and proceeded to *help* me by running the machine.

I sent Charlie to do a chore outside while I scooped out the suds, thinking my hands were getting truly cleansed today. I then switched the setting from warm water to cold water and ran a short cycle. Following the completion of the cycle, I was again rewarded with a clean and fully-functional machine. I rewashed the underwear in the deep sink, feeling way ahead of the game in appliance repair. A second before the end of my self-satisfied smile, Charlie said, "Uh, oh!"

Charlie was standing at the front door pointing out at the

fountain. There was foam literally spewing from the base of the fountain which was overflowing and running into the flower beds nearby. Charlie looked scared so I immediately assured him it was not a huge problem, even though it was. I told him we could remedy the situation as soon as I understood what had happened.

The chore I had sent Charlie to do while I fixed the washing machine was a simple one. I had just emptied and cleaned the fountain and it looked beautiful! I normally added a couple tablespoons of bleach to discourage bugs and mildew after filling the fountain base with water. As I was already in the laundry room, I knew that Charlie could not take the HE bleach we used for the laundry. He had to use the regular bleach stored in the shed. I even thought to give him a scoop, telling him how much to put into the fountain.

Again, I asked Charlie to show me what he had used in the fountain. Instead of going to the shed as anticipated, Charlie went to the garage and brought me a bottle of HE bleach. Again, I had no idea how it had been placed in the garage. More Charlie creativity, I reasoned. He sometimes helped me to put away grocery items after we had made our weekly trip to the grocery store. I asked Charlie to bring me the bucket and I emptied the fountain, being careful to direct the bleach water onto the driveway rather than the flower beds.

When we got close to the bottom, I asked Charlie to help me topple the fountain so as to fully empty it. I then rinsed it out and refilled it. I went to the shed and got the regular bleach and handed Charlie the scoop and measured out the right amount of bleach for the fountain. Charlie poured in the solution and I then turned on the fountain. Charlie clapped his hands as the mechanism worked flaw-lessly.

I went into the house to get us an iced tea and told Charlie we would sit outside and listen to the fountain while the towels were washing in the washing machine. Charlie stared at the fountain. When I came outside, he said he thought we should have a decoration on the wall above the fountain and I agreed it was a good idea.

He suggested we go out and shop for something and then have lunch out. Charlie was always looking for a meal out but on that day, I would deny him. We had to watch out budget.

I remembered that we had two metal decorations on the back fence that might look good above the fountain. I suggested Charlie go out back and pick the one he would like to see above the fountain. I sat back and relaxed on the lounge chair. Within five minutes, Charlie was back with the metal butterfly. I told him it was the perfect choice.

Charlie wanted to put up the butterfly immediately but I knew it would involve drilling into the concrete wall. I asked him to sit and admire the garden with me and we would then do the task together. Charlie talked about a garden we had planted twenty years ago when we lived in Iowa.

After finishing the iced tea, I took Charlie into the garage and got out the drill and put in the cement drill bit. I asked Charlie to get the tap con screws and he asked what they were. I showed him the special concrete screws and then got out an extension cord and we went to the front to install our metal butterfly.

I managed to drill successfully through the concrete and put in the screw to hang our butterfly. When it was properly installed, we both stood back and Charlie had a big grin for me.

"It's just perfect," I said to him as I placed my hand on his shoulder and gave him an affectionate squeeze. He did not back away as he generally did with physical contact.

I gathered almost all the work tools and asked Charlie to bring the extension cord into the garage. He asked, "What's an extension cord?"

It was at that instant I understood Charlie was entering another phase where common words were now sometimes unavailable to him.

In case you're wondering about the flowers, I did have to replace them. The annuals apparently do not thrive on bleach water.

Chapter Seventeen

Deceptions

Little by little I was learning how to protect myself and Charlie financially. He would try to buy stamps on our weekly outings to the grocery store and I would assure him we already had several books of stamps at home. I instructed Charlie to bring the letters he wished to mail and place them on my desk. That way, I could screen the letters to see that they were not soliciting money or trying to run a scam on Charlie. By now, he could not distinguish a legitimate solicitation from one that was fraudulent.

For the most part, Charlie's letters were torn up and placed in the recycling bin. There was no reason he should have any letters to mail as by now, I was doing all bill-paying online. But, there was still healthcare correspondence in his name as well as letters from his old colleges. Even those had to be screened as Charlie would try to write checks to send donations with money we didn't have. Whenever something would come in his name, he would diligently open and study the correspondence. I would watch as he studied the letters and then, as he carefully placed the letter in another envelope. I then went into his office and offered to stamp the letter for him. I would open the letter and screen for solicitations and then discard the letter as required.

As time went on, he would ask me, "Can you read this for me? It's a very confusing letter." In that manner, I came to screen nearly all correspondence that came to our house. It seemed as though when Charlie asked me to read something, he had a bit more control and dignity than when I automatically sorted through the mail and simply handed him flyers that we would recycle. Sometimes, we sat together at the kitchen table and opened the mail together.

More and more, Charlie wanted to be out of the house. Usually, he would come into my office in mid-afternoon and ask, "How about if I take you out tonight?" That would be my clue to respond that I would fix dinner for us both and then, we'd take a ride.

"Can we have a treat too?" Charlie would ask with a grin. Generally, it would be a given that we would stop for a yogurt or a tea and pastry. That seemed to be enough for Charlie to relax for a while longer.

After dinner, we would get in my car and I'd ask where Charlie wanted to go. He would frown for a few seconds and then smile and say, "Why don't you choose tonight?" It would be the same answer each night because Charlie could no longer conceptualize the plan of the city and the sites he wished to visit.

I would take off to a known destination. Generally, it would be a place where we could either cross over water or end up by the water. Charlie's Navy years would always be something he would value and being by the sea tended to settle and relax him.

At the end of our ride, I would stop at a quaint place in the village of one of the keys or else at a well-known place on the mainland. After ordering our yogurt or tea and pastry, Charlie would busy himself devouring his treat. He would always remain silent unless I brought up a topic of conversation. By now, the remembering had to be at least twenty years or so back in time. Charlie would devour his treat and leave me sitting there slowing enjoying what I had ordered. He would tidy up the table and rise to take his dishes or trash to be disposed of as I sat and watched his movements. He shuffled and sometimes, stumbled. I internally visualized that it would soon be time for a walker.

When finished with his task, Charlie would return to the table and stand, hoping I would finish quickly. He was always in a hurry to go somewhere and always in a hurry to leave. If I asked Charlie to sit while I finished, he would comply and then tap his knees in anxiety until I rose. Then, he would smile and say, "Time to go home."

Sometimes, Charlie would verbally woo me with possibilities of walking the beach or walking St. Armand's Circle where there were quaint shops available to browse. It was his way of manipulating me to get out of the house. But, as soon as we would get to the Village on Siesta Key or the Circle near Longboat Key, he would immediately ask for a treat and we would skip the time together. Charlie never forgot to eat, but that was about all he remembered those days.

Chapter Eighteen

A Rainbow Day

Sometimes, relief comes when you least expect it. Several months before, I had taken Charlie to the VA medical facility close to our house. Even though I knew he was low on the priority list for treatment, I had hoped to get him enrolled in the adult day care group at the Senior Friendship Center. Charlie's attendance at that group would give me a few hours of respite for three days a week. The cost of the day treatment was way more than we could afford and our only hope of getting the treatment for Charlie was that it be VA approved.

It was a Saturday night when the phone rang. Unfortunately, Charlie was standing right next to the kitchen phone and he picked it up. I immediately tensed, just waiting for a solicitation that Charlie would probably support. Instead, he said, "This is Charlie."

I then heard Charlie telling the caller he did not understand and finally, I asked him to hand me the receiver. I introduced myself and the caller said, "Thank goodness. I was getting nowhere with your husband."

The woman introduced herself by name and then told me she was with Bay Pines VA Medical Center in Clearwater, Florida. She said Charlie had just been approved for the group at the senior center and that someone from the center would probably call me on Monday. I was so excited I probably forgot most of what else she related to me that night. I do remember saying, "I do so hope he's right for the group." The caller then replied that she thought, based upon her brief conversation with Charlie, he would be a perfect addition to the group. Sometimes, I forgot how Charlie's current condition must impact others. His abnormal presentation was becoming common-place to me.

When I hung up the phone, I explained to Charlie that he had just been accepted into the group at the friendship center. He asked, "Will there be veterans there?" I gave him a hug and told him he would meet many veterans and he would be able to talk over old times with them. He was elated!

On Monday, I got a call from the director at the Senior Friendship Center. She assured me she had just spoken to the VA representative and that, indeed, Charlie was approved for the group. She related that their agreement with the VA allowed that the fees would be paid but that we would have a small copay. She would email me forms to take to our doctor regarding Charlie's current medical needs. When the forms were faxed back to her, she would do a phone intake with me to get other relevant information regarding Charlie's current functioning.

I waited for the email and then downloaded it and printed it out. I filled out what I could and took the forms to the doctor's office requesting they be filled out and faxed back to the Senior Center. For the first time in months, I went to sleep at a normal time that night. Furthermore, I slept through the night.

Lately, I had caught myself tensing up in my stomach and my back. Whenever Charlie would solicit information, I did well in relating to him what he wished to know. But after several such questions over a period of time, I felt myself tense and I knew the tension was probably taking a physical toll on my own health. I would either need to get some in-home companionship or I would need to find affordable services outside in the community. I could also see that Charlie was craving social attention. And now, the VA group would provide us both the relief we needed. I would now have some of my days back; I would have hours at a time when nor-malcy would be the rule rather than the exception. I would have long periods of the day when I could attend to my own needs and dare to envision what I wanted to do with the rest of my life.

Chapter Nineteen

A New Beatitude

Several of the neighbors had noticed changes in Charlie and they asked me about his condition. I was forthright with them. There was no reason to withhold information and I reasoned that I might need their assistance from time to time.

On occasion, one neighbor would mow our lawn for us. Perhaps, he had noticed my exhausted look as of late. The nurse next door came to volunteer her assistance again should Charlie have medical problems such as choking. I knew I could contact my neighbor who was a member of the highway patrol should Charlie become belligerent.

One day, I got Charlie to read a book. Charlie was not interested in engaging in activities but I knew he had once been an avid reader. He had not read for several years now. So, I started him off on a book I had just finished. It dealt with a former military Special Forces man who had become a private detective. I thought the military aspect might hold Charlie's interest. As it happened, that was the beginning of an intense reading program.

While I worked in my office, Charlie would sit in his lounge chair and read. Every few minutes, I would rise. There was a two-fold purpose to that action. My right leg was badly in need of a knee replacement. If I sat too long, it would buckle when I rose. So, I would take the opportunity to exercise it and go to where Charlie was reading. I would immediately ask him to tell me what he had read. He always stopped his reading and related something in the chapter to me. He actually did a pretty good job.

I then noticed that if I asked him to tell me the story when he had already put down the book, he would be unable to relate the story. Sometimes, he had a blank look to his face and at other times, he would make up a story from several books he had read, some of them from decades before. It didn't bother me. It was an experiment of sorts. As a psychologist, I thought there might be a possibility that Charlie was stimulating his brain neurons for at least the time he was reading. That was more than he had done before initiating the reading program. He also seemed a bit more settled while he was reading. Even though he was apparently unable to encode the information into short term memory, he was at least giving those brain neurons a temporary work out!

One afternoon, I was sitting outside reading a book when a neighbor stopped her car and came to where I was sitting. I offered her a drink which she refused but she did accept a seat near where I was seated. She said, "I don't know if you know it or not but my husband gave Charlie a ride home yesterday. When my husband told me what he had done, I wondered if it was alright for him to have picked up Charlie, so I thought I'd check with you."

I told her Charlie occasionally hitch-hiked when he got tired of waiting for the bus to come. I was still driving Charlie for his morning routine of getting the paper and then going for a tea and pastry before taking the bus home. I explained that I had instructed Charlie to call if he felt he was waiting too long for a ride home but that he did not always do that.

The neighbor explained that her husband had seen Charlie near the bus stop with his thumb out. He had pulled in the driveway of the retail establishment close by and then gone to where Charlie was standing. He explained to Charlie that he was a neighbor and he then asked if Charlie needed a ride home. Charlie accepted. I assured the neighbor that it was okay to help Charlie out. And I gave her my gratitude for her husband's compassion.

Charlie then saw or heard me talking with the neighbor outside and he came to the door. He did not seem to recognize the neighbor so I introduced him and told Charlie where the neighbor lived. Charlie then smiled and said, "Oh, yes, your brother was kind enough to take me home today!"

The neighbor looked at me as if to say, *So, this is how your days go, right?"*

That night when I went to bed, I added a new Beatitude in my prayers: *Blessed are the neighbors for they shall safely return my husband to me.*

Chapter Twenty

The Very Long One Hour Trip

Things at our house weren't going particularly well but I was determined to see it through and find simple pleasures for us both. For months, Charlie had begged me to go on a trip with him. We had diligently saved before our retirement. We had always traveled well together before and had planned several future trips abroad. That was now impossible. Even with protection, Charlie's problems with incontinence seemed to restrict distance and time. And, I couldn't imagine us getting separated in an environment that was unfamiliar to us.

I was to receive a book award in Miami, Florida. At first, I thought I would drive but I then thought better of trying to anticipate Charlie's needs on a five to six hour car trip. I got airline tickets out of Tampa and thought the one hour plane flight was something both Charlie and I could manage. I paid extra for aisle seats for us, feeling confident Charlie could get to the bathroom quickly should the need arise. Also, I was sure I could monitor Charlie's reactions while sitting directly across from him.

Charlie ruminated about what to take the day before the anticipated journey. I made out a list of clothing and necessities for him and he began to pack his bag. For the awards ceremony, he was to take a blue blazer, a white shirt, grey slacks and a tie I had picked out for him. He agreed to wear protective underwear on the plane.

It was not long before I noticed Charlie was substituting

items on the list and attempting to sneak things past my attempts to monitor his packing. He was packing all sorts of treats for himself, some of which just might melt during the plane flight and damage the clothing.

I removed unnecessary items when Charlie went to the bathroom and he never realized they was gone. I explained that we could get food at the airport if we were hungry and that packing treats would take up room essential for the clothing we needed to take. Charlie sulked and then removed the remaining treats and put them all into a plastic bag which he would carry on the plane. The treats bag seemed to act much like a security blanket did for a young child so I let it go.

The blue blazer turned out to be an ongoing problem until we left the house the following morning. Charlie took the blazer and placed it over the back of a kitchen chair. I asked about its placement and Charlie said he would wear it on the plane. I explained that both of us would pack the clothes we would wear to the awards ceremony as we did not want to risk getting them dirty before we would wear them. Charlie simply would not accept that explanation. I put the jacket back on a hanger and told Charlie I would pack his jacket, slacks, shirt and tie the following morning just before we left the house. Twenty minutes later, the jacket was visible on the back of the kitchen chair.

I explained to Charlie that he could take another jacket on the plane if he needed one but that his dress jacket had to be packed in order that it remain clean. Lately, Charlie's eating habits had declined and he nearly always had food stains on his shirts and pants. He never seemed to notice the need to wash his clothing. He would wear the same clothes for days if I didn't take them and put them into the laundry basket. I took the jacket back to the bedroom and again hung it on a hanger and hung it over the closet door. Charlie's pants, white shirt and tie were folded on the top of the dresser and he seemed unconcerned about those items.

When I again saw the blue blazer hung over the kitchen

chair, I left it there overnight. The following morning while Charlie showered, I took the blue blazer from the kitchen chair and replaced it with Charlie's tan jacket. I packed the blazer, the white shirt, the grey pants and the tie Charlie was to wear to the awards banquet. I zipped up Charlie's suitcase and wheeled it to the kitchen door leading to the garage. I placed the plastic bag containing Charlie's treats on the table next to his jacket. I went to pack my own bag.

When Charlie came in to have breakfast, he looked at the jacket and his bag of treats. He sat down to eat breakfast, seemingly pleased that he was about ready to go on his trip. I smiled with the satisfaction of a caregiver having solved another problem. Charlie had apparently wanted to take a jacket on the plane. Since I had mentioned taking the blue blazer, it was fixated in his mind that the blue blazer was a jacket he was to take. When I substituted the tan leisure jacket, he associated the travel clothes with that jacket instead and the problem was solved! With Alzheimer's, it's a hit-and-miss proposition. You just need to take an educated guess as to how the mind is functioning.

My son picked us up right on time and drove us to the Tampa airport. Since I had already downloaded our boarding passes, we simply needed to go through security and find our gate. I had already gone through Charlie's bag to assure myself there would be nothing in the bag to attract the attention of security personnel. I should have known better.

When we got to the scanning belt, Charlie had to be told to empty his pockets and place the contents of his pockets in the bowl so everything could be scanned. He didn't *beep* while walking through the scanner and I congratulated myself for convincing him to leave behind his heavy metal Navy belt buckle so it wouldn't cause problems with the scanner as had been the case during past plane travels. I was putting my shoes back on when a guard approached Charlie and asked why he was attempting to bring a knife on board. I immediately went to Charlie's side and looked into the dish. Sure enough, he had managed to slip his pocket knife into his pants pockets when I wasn't looking! I pulled the guard aside, explained my profession and my husband's diagnosis. Security confiscated the knife but said they would return it to us if I filled out some forms. I told the guard to consider the knife a gift to the TSA.

Charlie used the bathroom three times in the forty-five minutes we waited to board our flight to Miami. I think he didn't want to do anything to embarrass either of us and he was overcompensating. I was so grateful to him for his thoughtfulness. I smiled at him as I led him to the boarding gate. Then, they called our group to board. The one hour flight was without complications. At one point, Charlie began to tap his legs with the palms of his hands. Lately, that had been a signal of distress of some sort. It frequently occurred when Charlie was in an unfamiliar situation. I suggested he look into his snack bag. That did the trick! I reasoned that if you were using your hands to eat, you couldn't use them to tap your knees.

Lately, I had been reinforcing Charlie with snack items in order to encourage positive behavior. Although I tried to make the snacks healthy ones, he would generally sneak in some items laden with sugar. He immediately pulled out a candy bar and I was surprised. I had no idea we had anything like that in the house for him to have packed. Charlie seemed as happy as a three year old with a chocolate Easter bunny so I elected to simply let him enjoy what had so obviously snuck by me despite my careful planning.

When we landed in Miami, I got down Charlie's bag. It was very heavy and he was not able to balance it in order to place it in the aisle. I lifted the handle and told him to go ahead of me. I lifted my bag down from the overhead compartment, smug with the satisfaction that my months at the gym had resulted in at least some upper body strength. We walked into the terminal and Charlie immediately said, "Uh, oh!" I could tell he was confused but I couldn't fault him for that. There were thousands of people and many possible ways to go in order to get to the ground transportation area where we would catch the shuttle to the hotel.

I studied the area for a moment and then said, "This way, Charlie."

"How do you know where to go?" He asked.

I pointed to signs above our heads and replied, "Look" Charlie. The signs tell us exactly which walkway to take."

"Did they do that for us?' he asked.

"Yup," I said with a smile. I took Charlie's hand while wheeling my bag in the other and we made our way through the maze to the ground floor.

As soon as we got outside, Charlie said, "I have to pee."

I immediately did an about-face and lead Charlie back inside to the restrooms which were thankfully right by the exit door.

We went back outside and I asked an attendant where to stand to catch the shuttles to the hotels. He pointed to the middle island and Charlie and I made our way there.

I told Charlie the name of the shuttle we were to board. He watched the oncoming traffic like a hawk! Finally, he pointed and with a great deal of excitement, he shouted, "There it is! I found it, didn't I?"

After boarding the shuttle, Charlie pulled out his wallet and handed me a dollar bill. I asked what it was for and Charlie told me we should tip the driver. I smiled and thanked him for the dollar. Before we arrived at the hotel, I dug into my purse and pulled out a larger bill. At the hotel, I gave the driver my bill as well as the dollar Charlie had contributed.

Our room was one with two double beds. I did not know how our two nights would go as we had not slept in the same bedroom for about a year or so now. I was aware of the fact that Charlie was up at night as I would oftentimes see the light under the master bedroom door in the wee hours of the morning. I immediately unpacked Charlie's bag and hung up the clothing he would wear to the awards ceremony. Charlie said he was hungry so we went down to the dining room and had an early dinner.

That evening, there was a *meet and greet* event in which authors receiving awards would be able to meet one another and talk about their books. Then, there was a marketing presentation which would go well into the evening. Fortunately, we could pull away at any time without anyone thinking anything about it.

We took a couple of our books down to the lobby area where a hundred or so authors had already congregated. I talked with a few authors while Charlie mostly listened in. I met several fascinating people who had come from many different countries and continents. I gave the CEO of the review and awards company a big hug of appreciation and then hugged the president who told me to go to the meeting room before all the seats were taken.

We made our way to the meeting room and took seats on the aisle. I again planned for a quick exit should the need arise. By the time the first of six speakers was halfway through his presentation, Charlie was already tapping the palms of his hands on his knees. I whispered to him that we would go when the speaker had finished and he said, "Good. He's not making much sense."

During the applause for the speaker, Charlie and I made our exit and went back to the room. I showered and then, Charlie and I went through brochures and decided that we would call a cab in the morning and spend time at a waterfront mall where we could dine, watch entertainment and watch cruise ships come into Miami. The awards ceremony the following day would not start until five o'clock and that would give us time to explore the area safely, with all the conveniences Charlie would need right at hand. I climbed into bed with Charlie and we snuggled while watching television. When he dozed off, I went to my bed and snuggled in for what I hoped might be a good night's sleep. We were only a couple of miles from the airport and the planes took off and landed during the night. The guests came and went, always allowing their doors to slam shut.

I was beginning to slip away when Charlie got up and started to pace the room. He was in and out of the bathroom for a couple of hours before returning to bed. He immediately fell into a deep sleep while I remained awake for the balance of the night.

The next morning, Charlie was up and into the shower bright and early. I put a pillow over my head and tried to catch some sleep but my efforts were in vain. Once I'm awake, I simply cannot relax my mind. I turned on my cellphone and there was a message from the company CEO who was also a friend. She asked if Charlie and I might join her for brunch so that we could catch up on our personal news. I told Charlie that we'd have to scrap our plans for going to the waterfront mall. It wasn't a problem as he hadn't remembered them anyway. He opened the blinds, momentarily blinding me and then said, "Good that we don't have plans; it's raining anyway and we didn't bring any umbrellas!"

We decided to walk to a convenience store three blocks from the hotel. Charlie wanted to stock up on things for the room. He had pointed out to me that we had a refrigerator in the room, "And we don't have anything in it!"

We took off walking while it drizzled a bit. When the rain came, we ran into the parking area of a Checkers. Charlie got a drink for me. He felt it was payment in kind for the fast food place letting us use their canopy to get in out of the rain. When the rain all but stopped, we made our way to the convenience store and picked up some bottles of water and some snacks. By the time we got back to the hotel, we were pretty well soaked but the exercise had been good for us both. I blew my hair dry and changed into dry clothes. I mentioned to Charlie that he should change his pants as they were wet from the rain. He said he didn't have another pair. I told Charlie I had packed another pair for him. He told me he didn't like that color of pants and he had taken them out of his bag when I wasn't looking! I handed him the pair he had worn on the airplane and he refused to put them on. "They're airplane pants," he explained. It shocked me that someone with a doctorate degree would revert to the use of such basic, concrete thinking. Charlie went to brunch with the CEO wearing wet pants and we all did just fine.

After lunch, we decided to just watch college football games and *chill out* in the afternoon. It turned out to be a good decision. Charlie had several of the snacks we'd purchased in the morning and he was very content. I felt the relaxation was probably the best thing for us both.

Nothing Left to Burn - A Story of Alzheimer's Disease

We spent time dressing for the awards ceremony. When I came out of the bathroom, Charlie was dressed in his grey slacks, white shirt, blue blazer and tie. There wasn't a spot on the clothes and Charlie momentarily took my breath away! He was so handsome and he had obviously worked very hard to dress himself properly. I knew his efforts were for me and I told him he looked just wonderful. He told me, "Well you look so beautiful that I wanted to look like I belonged with you." My heart melted. Every so often now, some of the Charlie I married leaked out from the tangled masses in his brain. These glimpses were becoming fewer and fewer as I craved them more and more.

We made our way to the banquet room. I lead Charlie to a section of seats at the side of the stage and I again chose aisle seats. We talked a bit with the authors in front and to the side of us and then, the ceremony began. After the greetings from company executives, the authors were asked to line up and come to the stage to receive their award medallions. The CEO who was barely five feet tall presented the medals. We all had to bow down a bit as she placed the medallions over our heads. The last person to receive a book award was the actor/producer Eric LaSalle. I believe he played a physician in the television show ER and he has also starred in movies. He is a large African-American man and when preparing to receive his award, he knelt in front of the CEO, bringing a burst of laughter from the audience. Even kneeling, the recipient was still taller than the diminutive CEO!

It was then time to eat and socialize. A generous array of finger foods was offered and we all roamed, ate and learned a little bit about one another. Charlie and I finally took comfortable chairs while we finished our food. A reporter came over and asked if she could interview me about one of the books I had written. I had no objection so she took a chair next to me while Charlie remained in the chair on the other side. After five minutes, Charlie got up and stood between the reporter and me and said he was going to get some water. I nodded and the interview continued. Charlie returned and again interrupted the interview, handing me a cup of water. He wanted to talk. I motioned for him to sit as the interview proceeded. Charlie got up and announced he was going to the bathroom and I nodded. The reporter asked if I was currently working on a new book. I answered that I was writing a book about someone with Alzheimer's and she asked if it was perhaps, an immediate family member. I smiled and verified that was, indeed, the case. Charlie was now pretty transparent in his deficits.

After the interview, I lost Charlie for a while and asked people if they had seen him. Finally, I spotted him by a group of people with looks of puzzlement on their faces. I inched up to the group as Charlie was saying, "I'm sure we know one another. Now where have you been recently that we could have met" I whispered in Charlie's ear that it was time to go as the group looked at me with concern. We went to sit down and Charlie immediately began his tapping routine. Normally, I would have stayed another two hours but I knew our night was at its end.

The following morning, we packed our bags and I went down to the lobby to sign out as Charlie hit the bathroom one last time. I talked with friends until Charlie came. The shuttle arrived and we all headed to the airport for the return trip. Charlie and I got our boarding passes and then went to a restaurant to have a generous breakfast. I thought if Charlie was satisfied in his stomach, other successes might follow. After eating, we headed to security. I knew Charlie no longer had his knife so we should get through cleanly this time. I did, but Charlie did not.

This time, the beeping was so loud that everyone in the area turned to look. I was dumfounded! I went to the area in my stocking feet as Charlie told the screener he could not have his belt. Somehow, Charlie had managed to sneak in his metal Navy belt. The guard asked Charlie to remove the belt and Charlie refused. I again intervened with the guard. Finally, Charlie agreed to detach the metal buckle and place it in the dish to be scanned while leaving on the fabric belt itself. We collected our belongings and headed to our gate to board the plane.

Once home, Charlie visibly relaxed while I unpacked. He came into the bedroom and asked if he had done a good job on the trip. I told him he had. I was exhausted as Charlie had again wandered the previous night. He came to me, placed his hand on my shoulder and said, "Well, it was only an hour trip you know."

The trip from Miami to Sarasota only takes an hour. From my perspective, it was the longest hour trip I had ever taken!!

Chapter Twenty-One

Nothing Left to Burn

My days were now totally centered on and around Charlie's needs. I was grateful that he was able to attend the day care group. At first, he resisted but ever-so-gradually, he seemed able to fit in and to see some benefit from the group. When he returned home from his group, I would try to be outside waiting for him. We would sit out front and talk about his day. Sometimes, he remembered what he had for lunch. Some days, he remembered that he had talked with someone or at least, he thought he had. On one day, he might recall a memory exercise and on another, a trivia game. Charlie would never forget the day when Ace came to visit the group. Ace was a former guide dog who came to visit the Senior Center. He was always the star of the day. Charlie would bring treats to try to lure Ace to his side. Ace was non-demanding and he required no recall and no planning. He was simply there to love. It was as if Ace could provide something I could not and he made Charlie happy. I vacillated between being happy for Charlie and jealous that I could no longer offer that kind of simple joy to my husband.

While Charlie attended group, I would go to the gym. It served three purposes for me. First, I got out all my frustrations by vigorously exercising. Secondly, it allowed me a chance to social-ize. People there knew about Charlie's problems and they would always show caring and concern for us both. The third benefit of regular gym attendance was that I was maintaining the body strength I required to assist Charlie. I always left the gym feeling invigorated, as if I had some sense of control to my life.

Sometimes, I would treat myself to a Subway sandwich while I ran necessary errands. I always had a book with me and sometimes, I would sit outside and pretend I was in a small European café with Charlie. It helped me to recall the wonderful years we had experienced together. I recalled conversations, visual and aromatic sensations and the closeness Charlie and I had taken for granted back then. But, there is a time for everything and that was then and this is now. My remembering helped me to put my current caregiving roll into perspective. I had been blessed with wonderful years with Charlie and now, my role of caregiver would be undertaken with just as much commitment and energy. It was not a focus on martyrdom or anger from current burdens; rather it was a realization that Charlie would not have done less for me had the tables been turned. I could have my memories while I was alone and I would have my caregiving duties when with Charlie.

I almost always had an errand to run while Charlie was at group. I always took him to the grocery store with me but on group days, I took care of everything else at my own pace. Charlie shuffled and was extremely slow now in both gross and fine motor movements. As I still maintained a fast gait in my mid-seventies, it would be a frustrating and lengthy outing whenever Charlie accompanied me. I could do almost anything when alone. And then, in the mid-afternoon, I could go outside and sit in the sunshine and read books or just rest. Just closing my eyes and listening to the birds or to nearby children's voices would settle my mind. The aroma of blooming flowers would settle my soul for what was yet to come in the day.

Once in a while, there was a glimpse of the old Charlie but for the most part, I was living with a man I did not know. At first, I was grateful for these occasional glimpses of the old Charlie, even though they were simply teasers and I knew I would shortly be disappointed that he could not stay with me. But now, there was only brief evidence of the man I had married. I steeled myself against feeling that kind of love. Losing it again and again and again was just too big of an emotional price to pay. If I stayed more in the caregiver role I was able to keep my love for the *real* Charlie better intact. It was a way of preserving my heart.

And then one day, Charlie broke my heart in such a way that I thought it would never mend.

It was a simple day. We went to a ceramics shop and I painted a small, ceramic Christmas tree while Charlie watched. He seemed awed that I could do something so lovely. Then, we went to lunch in a Scottish pub and talked about Christmas preparations. Charlie seemed distant but lucid. He spent the afternoon reading while I attended to business matters on the Internet. Charlie again wanted to go out to eat but I told him we would have leftovers. I asked if he would like to finish the pasta Alfredo from the previous night's meal. He went into the kitchen and looked in the refrigerator and then, he said that would taste good. Charlie said he could heat up the pasta so that I could finish my emailing.

As usual, Charlie asked me what to do to heat the dinner. I told him to take out the pasta, the container of peas and the Alfredo sauce. Then, he should dump the pasta into a glass container and add the peas and then the sauce. I told him to stir the contents and to place it in the microwave for two minutes. There was no sound for a minute. Then, I heard the refrigerator door close. I figured Charlie had gotten out all the contents but then, I saw him go to the family room and sit in his chair. I asked if he had changed his mind about the foods. He said he still wanted the pasta.

I went in to where Charlie was seated and looked at him. He looked tired and defeated. I was sure Charlie had not retained the simple three-step instruction I had given him in order to heat the pasta dish. I chastised myself for not giving the directions one at a time. I said nothing. Then, I thought to ask Charlie if he'd like to have me heat the pasta while he relaxed. He nodded that he wanted that. I prepared the pasta and added vegetables and served Charlie.

Nothing Left to Burn - A Story of Alzheimer's Disease

He didn't want to sit at the table. Instead, he watched television as he ate. On several occasions he experienced a gag reflex and I encouraged him to eat slowly, chew well and take frequent sips of water.

I could see a sun-downing effect as we ate our meal and I thought Charlie might soon be asleep. When we finished our meal, I cleaned up the dishes and went to sit in a chair beside my Charlie. He looked very sad and I wondered if he was having a moment of rare insight into his disease. I asked him if he could share what was on his mind. He shook his head and I took that gesture as a sign that he was not able to formulate any coherent thoughts. Instead, he surprised me by asking, "Tell me what's in your mind." Then, he added, "Please."

"Oh Charlie," I began. "It's just that it's so difficult to watch you struggle so. Sometimes, I have these urges to just light a fire in your brain and burn out all those bad cells that make you forget things."

Charlie stared at me with a look of defeat on his face and tears in his eyes. Then, he said, "There's nothing left to burn."

My heart broke and this time, I believe it shattered. I wondered if I could even find the pieces to attempt to reassemble them. I was unsure that I wanted to.

Chapter Twenty-Two

Boundaries, Intrusions, Ruminations

The toilet was now frequently unflushed with contents greeting me as I entered the bathroom. Intrusions in my private time became the norm. Charlie developed compulsive checking routines that involved the doors, the pantry and the refrigerator. At night, he would go to each and every exterior door, open it, slam it shut and then open and slam it again. He then toyed with the locks for several minutes. He would do this several times a night. When I had tucked Charlie in the room for the night, I would go around and secure each door. Charlie would inevitably leave at least one of the doors unlocked. The door to the garage eventually became unseated and had to be reinstalled due to Charlie's obsessive behaviors. He ruminated about whether he should take a jacket whenever we left the house. I reminded him that we always carried spare jackets in my car in case it got cooler at night. Then, Charlie would ruminate about whether I had a jacket.

My husband was now becoming emotionally and cognitively younger than the youngest grandchild who was eight years old. When I changed clothes, he would come into the room and *sneak a peek.* Unless I locked the bathroom door, he might just barge on in. I began to lock the bathroom door. On occasion, Charlie would get up from his chair and come to me and start to pinch my breasts. I finally interpreted that as Charlie's need for some type of personal intimacy. I would smile at him, tell him he had a good idea and lead him to the bedroom and we would simply lie down and *spoon* for a few minutes. When Charlie then said, "This is boring," we would get up and I would resume my activities while Charlie watched television.

Generally, Charlie failed to close the bathroom door when he went in to take care of his own needs. When the grandchildren came to visit, he would entertain them by taking out his dentures. He would make potty jokes with the youngest child. He would talk about my younger son who had died several years before. He had forgotten about my son's death and it was painful to have to remind Charlie daily that I had lost a child. In Charlie's world, dead people were now alive and living persons were sometimes dead. It was a daily bombardment and, were it not for his attendance in the friendship group, I honestly think I would have become physically and emotionally bereft of any normal feelings.

On grocery day, Charlie would always stock up on blueberry muffins and chocolate chip cookies. After a few days, he would come to me and ask, "What happened to my cookies? Where did my muffins go?" I would explain that had eaten them but he simply would not accept that answer. Instead, he would accuse me of eating his treats. If I denied having taken the treats, Charlie would ask, "Then, where did they go? He seemed totally unaware of his own actions these days. Of course, most would conclude that Charlie had simply forgotten but there was more to it than that. He seemed to have lost a lot of cause-and-effect connections in his brain.

One day, I asked Charlie to scoop the leaves out of the fountain in front and to turn on the fountain so as to keep the water fresh and circulating. Charlie went outside and came back in about three minutes later. He told me he couldn't clean the fountain so I asked, "Why Charlie?"

"I can't find the net."

"Well, look around, Charlie. You always keep the nets in the garage. If you put them there, just go get them and then, scoop out the leaves."

A half hour of searching failed to turn up the nets. So I asked Charlie to just scoop the leaves out with his hands.

"I can't."

"Why not, Charlie."

"I have on a shirt with sleeves that are long. I'll get them wet," he responded.

"Charlie, you can roll up the sleeves and then scoop out the leaves," I suggested.

"I can't."

"Why not, Charlie"

"Because I have on a clean shirt."

"You could change your shirt, Charlie. If you get it wet or dirty, you can just change your shirt."

"I can't."

"Why, Charlie?"

"I like this one and I have it on now."

This is how it would go if I requested a simple task. It would oftentimes consume an hour and on some days, it was an hour I did not have to spare. On that day, I decided to do the task myself. Charlie could not find the nets to scoop out the leaves so I scooped them out by hand while Charlie continued to look for the nets. I got out all the leaves and filled the fountain to a few inches from the top. I was going to put in a couple tablespoons of bleach to keep the water clean but could not find the special bottle that we always kept in a cabinet in the garage. I set about trying to find the bottle of bleach so that I could complete the task. After forty-five minutes of searching, I was finally able to locate the bottle in among Charlie's fishing supplies. I never have figured out the thinking in that one but the five minute chore took us one hour and ten minutes!

I wanted to try to keep Charlie engaged in daily functions for as long as possible but on some days, that just plain wore me out. And then, there were the hours that were consumed with instructions, modeling and helping to carry through with a task. The alternative was of course, to do the task myself. But then, Charlie would have no opportunity to try to remain stimulated by daily activities.

Nothing Left to Burn - A Story of Alzheimer's Disease

As I write this chapter, I have had three phone calls that I have had to attend to, none of my own doing. Charlie still browses the Internet but now, he has little idea as to what he is finding. Almost daily, I get calls about things he has ordered. Most are free samples but many are upgrades to the computer or items for which we have no need. Just yesterday, I sent back two magazines and something that said "Invoice Enclosed." I marked the items "Not Ordered, Return to Sender" and put them back in the mailbox. If you don't stay on top of things like that, you can get into a financial mess.

My life was now much more ordered than I had wanted it to be in retirement. While I was still working, I had envisioned sleeping in and going to bed whenever I felt like it. But if you have a husband who gets up and wanders at night, you need to attend to activities in which he might generate the potential for personal harm or harm to the house in which we both live. A brief check will always insure me that Charlie is safely in bed watching television or else in the bathroom trying to attend to his own needs. I am grateful that Charlie does still attend to his personal needs, no matter how long it takes.

I am now starting to give myself brief respites. I might go to a book store, browse and then, have a cup of tea. I might go to a store to window shop, even though we no longer need frivolous things for the house. Yesterday, I went to a ceramics shop where I could paint figurines. I decided to do something for my daughter's new house. I spent nearly five hours in the shop, watching people come and go. I made friends with three babies who thought I was interesting. I had brought a bottle of water and a power bar for lunch and I simply stayed and took my time. I got back home fifteen minutes before Charlie arrived home from his group at the Senior Friendship Center. I was able to stay the course the rest of the night, simply because I had cleared my head and relaxed my body with something nonessential to our daily lives.

Charlie just came into my office, completely soaked. I had asked him to water the plants in the back. I can see the entire back yard from my office and I was able to watch him attempting his watering task. He did manage to get some water on the thirsty plants but somehow, he turned the spray nozzle in such a manner as to soak his shirt, shorts, shoes and socks. He just came in with a huge grin on his face and said, "I watered everything – especially myself!" Those are the moments for which I now live; they are brief moments when Charlie is one with the world.

Chapter Twenty-Three

Christmas Shopping

Our Christmas shopping this year would be decidedly different. I ordered many things online and then, took Charlie out to get stocking stuffers. Even that was confusing to him. I would ask him to go down an aisle and look for a certain item, keeping an eye on him to be sure he didn't wander. Inevitably, he would forget what he was to look for and would return to where I was and ask for clarification. Then, we would go down the aisle together. I'd pick up an item and ask him if he thought this would be suitable for one of the grandchildren or for our son or daughter. He would agree with anything and everything I picked out. He was no longer able to discern one item from another but he was excellent at saying "okay" to the choices I made. Charlie had become every woman's perfect yes man!

Charlie loved Christmas so I made it a point to take him out to look at the lights after dinner. Sometimes, we would focus on the neighborhood. It was okay to take a neighborhood tour several times as Charlie never remembered from one day to the next. We took trip to neighborhoods that were notorious for lavish decorations and we also went to commercial areas that traditionally went out of their way to celebrate the season. He loved the lights, the music and all the festivities associated with the season. For the past few years, the grandchildren have come for an overnight after Thanksgiving. It gave their parents a day to shop free of the gift receivers and it also gave the grandchildren the opportunity to help us decorate the house inside and out.

This year, I told the grandchildren we would need lots of help and they assured me that they would be up to the task. On the day they were to come over, Charlie went on a six hour fishing trip while the grandchildren and I decorated the house. Three of us took the outside duty and three volunteered to put up the tree and decorate the interior of the house. I was totally amazed by how self-directed they were and they all did an outstanding job! We were just finishing up our hot chocolate when Charlie walked in the house with a bag of freshly-caught fish. His eyes were filled with wonder! It was the face of a child who was mesmerized by the beauty of the season.

On days he was home, I tried to find things to occupy Charlie's mind. He would always beg to go out. One day, I might take him with me to pick out a gift for a certain family member. In the past, he would have definite ideas about what we should gift. Now, he seemed pleased to be a vicarious shopper and that was a sadness that consumed me for many days. With Alzheimer's, you lose your loved one in bits and pieces. Others have told me they think it is far better to lose parts of a loved one prior to death so that you get used to the feelings of loss. For me, each loss was simply another twist of the knife.

After shopping, I would sometimes take Charlie for a light meal in a nearby village. We might then go for an ice cream. Then, Charlie would fall asleep in his chair while I attended to unfinished chores. I would oftentimes wake him to tell him it was time to go to bed. He would initially fall asleep and then, he would awaken and stay awake for hours, watching television.

I began to notice that Charlie seemed unusually tired on certain days. I tried to remember if he might have exerted himself physically. There did not seem to be any direct correlation of physical activity and mental fatigue. Sometimes he would complain of physical pain and the areas of complaint were always vague and varied. One day, his eye might bother him. On another day, there was pain in his arm. On another day, his leg or hip would bother him. Oftentimes, he had indigestion and so forth. Initially, I attempted to connect the complaints to activities or to medication effects but that task always proved fruitless. It scared me a bit because I began to think that I might someday ignore a sign of physical pain that could prove significant. For the most part, I relied on the physician's pronouncement that, other than being overweight, Charlie was in pretty good health for a man approaching eighty.

The thing that struck me about this phase of the disease was that despite Charlie's inability to process the immediate environment, he remained highly verbal. It was as if he was producing a class lecture from memory except that he might be talking with a neighbor or someone we would meet at a store. He remained unfailingly social and many people would have no clue as to his cognitive dysfunction while talking with him. I can't tell you the many people who would comment to me later, "What a delightful husband you have!" It always surprised me but it also delighted me that they recognized Charlie's core personality. So often, the Alzheimer's effects got in the way of Charlie's ability to demonstrate his intellect and his personality and even minor successes were becoming more and more important to him. As long as Charlie stayed in the past, he seemed more socially successful. When he had to deal in the present, he generally failed miserably.

I was now catching myself trying to spare Charlie social embarrassment. Before we would go into a room or a restaurant, I would check his fly and make sure it wasn't open. Sometimes, he would unzip his fly in the car and I was never sure why. I would check his clothing before we left home and would oftentimes ask him to change a shirt or a pair of pants. He would always appear surprised if I pointed out a stain. I would remind him to use the restroom. I would remind him to eat slowly. I would remind him to use his napkin. I got accomplished at leaning over and whispering in Charlie's ear and then gently stroking his cheek as if we were simply having a moment of intimacy. With close friends, I didn't have to do that but in a new situation, I never felt it necessary to educate others about Charlie's condition as Charlie's sense of pride was always my paramount concern. I wondered if it was really *my* pride that caused me to do all the checking and anticipating but in the end, I am pretty certain it was because I felt protective of Charlie. I had done similar things when my own children were very young and it wasn't out of a sense of pride for myself; rather it was to spare them potentially difficult social situations.

Chapter Twenty-Four

Do Unto Charlie

You learn a lot about yourself when you're a caregiver for a loved one. I never talked down to Charlie before the onset of Alzheimer's disease and I made a vow that, no matter how childlike he got, I would never talk down to him. Every day I reminded myself of the Golden Rule. I tried never to do anything to, for or with Charlie that I would not want done to myself. I didn't always succeed and for that, I have to live with my own short comings. But in my nightly prayers, I always reminded myself to Do Unto Charlie as I would want Charlie to do for me were the situation reversed. On many days, it was my saving grace.

You can read lots of "dos" and "don'ts" on the internet if you're a caregiver. Some will apply to your particular situation and many will not. After doing your own research, I think you must become your own scientist. It's a trial-and-error kind of disease and you'd best be prepared to make mistakes and to congratulate yourself when you stumble upon a solution that brings a momentary feeling of success. I say momentary because in Alzheimer's disease, the course is not lived year-to-year. It is a moment-to-moment course and the caregiver must be both creative and flexible. If you don't have the patience of the Biblical Job, then use your creative mind to develop a challenge that will bring relief to the situation.

I learned to do simple things for complex situations. If Charlie complained that his eyes hurt and there did not seem to be any basis for the complaint, I would get a sleeping mask and ask him to sit in his lounge chair and sit back. I placed the sleeping mask on his eyes, rubbed his forehead and he would fall asleep. I concluded he might be sleep deprived and as a result, a headache ensued. If he complained of pain in his arm, I would get one of my silk scarves and tie up his arm and ask him to rest. He loved the feel of the silk and it seemed to soothe and relax him. Perhaps, he only wanted attention and no longer knew how to ask for it. The complaints of physical discomfort were the closest Charlie would come to trying to define some need within him. The five minutes it would take to attend to his immediate complaint oftentimes brought me valuable time after Charlie felt soothed. If Charlie's leg hurt, I would wrap a towel around his leg after warming it in the microwave. He loved the feeling of warmth and would frequently sleep while his leg was wrapped. When he tapped his hands against his legs, I took his hand and walked up and down the driveway, talking with him about the blooming flowers or about how large our grapefruits were getting. When back inside, Charlie would then again be distracted with the television. If you attend to symptoms rather than to trying to guess an underlying cause, you may just stumble upon a possible etiology of the complaint. If not, what does it matter? You have consoled someone dependent upon you and you have done it with compassion and respect.

For some persons with Alzheimer's, television is confusing, as are mirrors. The diseased brain simply cannot comprehend duplicates of a person or people on TV that do not live in the house. At this stage, this was not an issue for Charlie. But, when it happens, the caregiver can simply cover the television screen with a towel. The same works for mirror confusion. Once covered, there does not seem to be any awareness that the object of confusion is still in its usual place.

Simple also was my philosophy when taking Charlie on outings. I would ask Charlie to do a simple chore and when he completed the chore, I would smile, thank Charlie and we would get into the car. When shopping for stocking stuffers for Christmas, we would go to Target with a list of things to look for and Charlie and I would go aisle by aisle. I had to remind Charlie several times during our journey down one aisle what we were to look for and even then, he would still ask three or four time what the items were for. Each question brought only a short response from me, something like, "A can of plain nuts, Charlie." I always used his name. I wanted him to remember to respond to something which was long familiar to him.

If Charlie tried to wander to another aisle, I would have him hold onto the cart so that I could keep track of him in a crowded store. I also used to do that with my young children and it was a life-saver at times when the stores were crowded. If Charlie did not get agitated during an outing, I might again treat him to a sandwich or a salad at an inexpensive restaurant. I noticed that if I rewarded Charlie with a trip or a treat *after* he had completed a chore at home, he would be more likely to complete the task next time. This would be true even when Charlie did *not* remember what task he had done. I surmised some type of rudimentary connection remained to the behavioral model of reinforcement for positive behavior. This is a behavior which is generally instilled in very young children.

We no longer had company very often but when we did, Charlie was always given a task so as to feel he was contributing to the interaction. Sometimes, I would whisper to him to ask a question of the guest. It would always be something I knew about the guest's current activities. Charlie would smile with satisfaction that he had stimulated a conversation. Once commenced, the conversation was able to sustain itself without any intervention from Charlie. On occasion, Charlie would ask a question that had already been answered by the guest but our company always knew a bit about Charlie's problems and they were always extremely kind in repeating the information to Charlie. As much as possible, I tried to give Charlie the same courtesies as our guests but with some adaptations. When bringing in drinks, I would always put a lid on Charlie's drink so that if he spilled, it would not disrupt the conversation. I brought in treats that Charlie could easily eat, without much probability he would choke and become the center of attention. I would encourage guests to sit in places so that Charlie was closest to the bathroom. When he got up, it would not disrupt the conversation. With a lower probability of accident comes a higher probability of success.

So, we would go on our outings and I would invite Charlie to lunch. If he didn't act out, that was a wonderful way to reinforce him as he so much loved to go to restaurants. If the restaurant was not crowded, I ask to be seated away from others so that I could talk privately with Charlie. Eating out was oftentimes a great time to talk about expectations as I usually had Charlie's full attention, at least, until his food arrived! I sometimes had to remind Charlie to close his mouth and chew quietly and I didn't want others to hear my prompts. Even to me, it sounded as if I were picking on Charlie!

When we finished our meal, I would take Charlie by the hand and lead him outside to the car. On one particular day, he must have been very pleased with the outing. He said, "I like you. I really, really like you," and he smiled. It melted my heart and I again resolved to be as respectful as I could be while Charlie continued to regress in time and abilities.

On one winter day while eighty-eight percent of the nation was covered in snow, it was eighty-four degrees in Sarasota, Florida. I felt the inside of the house getting warmer and warmer and that puzzled me. Generally, as the temperature rose outside, the interior of the house would be shaded by the giant live oak trees in the front and the back. They would keep the house cool, even without the assistance of the air conditioner.

I went to the thermostat and was astonished that it was turned to the heat setting! I asked Charlie if he had touched the buttons to change the temperature and he nodded that he had. I told him I had set the thermostat to the current temperature so that it would remain stable.

"That's why I changed it," Charlie replied.

"Why did you change the temperature, Charlie," I inquired.

"So it wouldn't be the same all the time," Charlie replied.

"But Charlie, we want the temperature to be stable while we're in the house."

"Nothing is stable," he answered. And he walked away. I never really figured out that one. I wondered if he was talking about himself, but I'd never know.

I put more notes around the house. I put notes on the thermostat, the front door, the back door and the dishwasher. Charlie thought that was a good idea. His pleasure at seeing my notes made me even sadder.

On some days, Charlie slept excessively and on other days, not so much. I guess it all evens out but I can't help but think his erratic patterns took their toll on him physically. One thing is for certain: Charlie slept much more than his caregiver.

When Charlie got home from group one day in the fall, he looked a bit pale. I asked if was feeling alright and he nodded that he was. He went to the bathroom. Five minutes later, he went to the bathroom again. When he came out I again asked if he had a problem. He denied any problems and asked to go out. I had heard about a gingerbread house display at one of the malls and decided Charlie might like that. He would especially like it if we paired our outing with a light dinner.

We got to the mall and after walking fifty feet, Charlie asked me to slow down. I was already walking less than half my normal pace but I slowed down and took his hand. I asked what Charlie wanted to do first and he said, "Let's eat." We each got something light and sat in the food court, watching crowds of people begin their Christmas shopping. Then, we decided to go to the gingerbread house display. We were halfway there when Charlie looked at me, panicky.

"Bathroom?" I asked.

Charlie nodded and we made a beeline for the restroom. I waited about five minutes while Charlie took care of his needs. We then walked to the display and Charlie said he wanted to skip it. He decided we should go into Costco to look around. We had no sooner gotten into the door when Charlie immediately asked an associate to direct him to the restrooms. I waited by the entrance and told Charlie to meet me right there. He was gone for twenty minutes before I began to panic and started toward the restrooms. I saw Charlie come out the hallway and head for an aisle with a look of apprehension on his face. I yelled at him but he didn't hear me. He began to walk away from me. I literally ran toward him, calling his name. He finally turned around and smiled.

"Time to go home, Charlie," I said. He did not argue with me. I believe Charlie had a bad episode with his prostate cancer but he wasn't really able to describe his symptoms in order for me to help him. The following morning, he woke up feeling just fine.

It was approaching Christmas so I told Charlie we would begin to get the Christmas dinner supplies during our weekly trip to the supermarket. I had a list of a couple of dozen items and Charlie had his list of three things. He always took a separate cart. I think it reminded him of when he did all the grocery shopping and felt more independent. Charlie and I met in one of the aisles and I told him I was ordering a precooked turkey and that I might have to wait in a line at the deli counter. I told him to meet me in the usual place by the checkouts in a few minutes. It took ten minutes to order my turkey and when I got to the checkout lines, Charlie was nowhere in sight. I looked up and down every aisle but I could not spot Charlie. I went to the checkout and began to place my items on the conveyor belt as I continued to look for Charlie.

I was now beginning to seriously worry. Charlie was wandering a bit more lately and I feared he might have left the store without me. Since I sometimes dropped him off at the store to get his newspaper, I thought he might have decided to take the bus back home, forgetting I was at the store to transport him. My items were placed in the cart and I began to head for the exit. Then, Charlie appeared with his sack of three items. He smiled and said he was waiting on the bench by the door.

"Charlie, that bench is not visible from the store. I couldn't find you and I got a bit worried," I said as calmly as possible.

"Oh, don't worry," Charlie replied. "I knew I was on the bench."

Chapter Twenty-Five

Slipping into My Own Journey

A lot of caregivers have told me they related to the five stages of grief proposed in the book **On Death and Dying** by Elisabeth Kubler-Ross. The author wrote her book in 1969 and it has been well referenced in thousands of articles, journals and books since that time. The first stage of the grief process is called Denial and it logically deals with the idea that people deny an impending death as a defense mechanism. To my knowledge, I never experienced that stage. As a psychologist, I recognized the initial signs and symptoms of Charlie's dementia. The symptoms were almost immediately undeniable for me. Kubler-Ross's second stage is simply called Anger. I don't know any caregiver who could ever deny their anger concerning the mental and/or physical suffering of someone they loved. I have to admit, I delved into this stage periodically. I always tried to direct the anger toward the disease and not toward Charlie who was the victim of the disease. Anger would surface with renewed vengeance whenever it became apparent that Charlie's brain was further compromised. For me, it was a back and forth process, rather than a stage in which you would experience anger and then resolve and move past it.

The third stage of the Kubler-Ross grief process is called Bargaining. In this stage, the person afflicted with a disease and/or her/his loved ones bargain for some kind of reprieve. I knew as a psychologist that Charlie's disease would only get worse. This stage never factored into my caregiving role. The fourth stage called Depression was one which I battled daily as Charlie got worse. I tried to monitor my own wellbeing but this is sometimes difficult when the problems pile on, one after another. Some caregivers lose weight while others gain. Some experience insomnia while others sleep excessively as an avoidance mechanism. I tried to eat healthy meals as I knew I could not help Charlie if I did not tend to myself. Also, I did not want to become ill and miss out on the lives of my grandchildren. On many occasions, being included in their lives kept me afloat for another day. If I experienced two sleepless nights in a row, I would yield to a sleeping aide. Generally, a pain reliever which combined a sleep aide would be enough to relax my aching body and allow healing sleep to come.

The next day, I would always be grateful that I had yielded as the renewed energy of sleep gave me feedback on the need for occasional assistance. On days I worked out at the gym, I allowed myself to have "Karen days" and after a fleeting period of personal shame, I eased into a routine of pampering myself for the hours Charlie would be in his group. I vividly remember one particular day in December. The stores were filled with holiday decorations and gift ideas. I had just come from the gym and my body felt alive and renewed. It must have shown on my face. It seemed as if every associate in the store took the time to smile at me and wish me well. On days I ignored the need to care for myself and instead, caught up on neglected tasks, I would pay the price in lack of wellbeing. Since my upbringing was that of non-selfish service to others, this was a giant leap for me and one which would become my saving grace as Charlie's condition worsened. I avoided a clinical depression and was much more ready physically, mentally and emotionally to be there for my husband.

The final stage of Acceptance of a terminal condition is one which I never really bought into due to Charlie's diagnosis. I never understood how anyone who loved someone with Alzheimer's could accept the diagnosis. I do believe we can all believe the diagnosis and then accept the fact that everyone who contracts the disease will die. I think if anything, I simply resigned myself to the fact that Charlie would gradually deteriorate until his brain or body could no longer function. For the most part, the grief state of Acceptance is probably one of emotional detachment as the inevitability of death approaches. I know I detached at various times during the stages of Charlie's illness. But my detachment was more one of being better able to help Charlie through his own process of deterioration. I couldn't help him if I was angry at the diagnosis. I couldn't help him if I took his thoughts, actions and emotions personally. I couldn't help him if I was in so much pain as a spouse that I could not think through what to do in one unusual circumstance after another.

I think stages and groups and help aides are great. Some of us require more direction and more planning while others of us are more comfortable being a bit more spontaneous. I don't think general principles apply to every situation in similar groupings of diseases and I believe they must be used with caution such that the caregiver does not compare him or herself according to a model and then, fall short and be in further misery. If you try, that's usually enough. If it isn't, then reach out. Someone will always be there. It doesn't matter if you need five minutes or five hours to regroup. As long as you recognize the need to do so without thinking yourself to be a failure, you meet the caregiver guidelines in my book. I didn't want to be a parent again, but as I repeated so long ago, "For better and for worse." And no, none of us, no matter how talented and how well trained, can fully comprehend how "worse" the worse can be until we are smack dab in the midst of it.

Charlie asked to go to a pharmacy. He needed more guards for his underwear. We were about to get into the car when he had a bowel accident. It took nearly an hour to get Charlie cleaned up and ready to go. When we got to the pharmacy, I asked that he sit in the car while I ran in to get the guards. The store was crowded and I took longer than I had intended. But, Charlie remained in the car. When I returned and started the car engine to leave, Charlie said he needed a newspaper which he could have gotten if he'd gone in with me. I took him back into the store and he got his newspaper. I asked if there was anything else he needed while we were there. He pointed to the candy bars and I told him we had treats at home. We were on our way home when Charlie said, "We forgot the toothpaste."

"Another trip, Charlie," I said.

The thing with Alzheimer's disease is that it just defies all logic.

Chapter Twenty-Six

The Last Christmas Hooray

As the holiday season approached, I always got into the proper spirit and looked forward to hosting the family. This would be my fifty-fifth year as hostess and it would also be my last. I chuckled as I remembered my first Christmas dinner at my duplex at the tender age of nineteen. I had meticulously planned and organized the dinner for my stepmother and two brothers. When I pulled the turkey out of the oven, I underestimated the weight and promptly deposited my beautifully roasted bird on the kitchen floor! I remember my husband laughing at me as he placed the turkey on the platter saying, "Five second rule applies here!"

I had come a long way since that first dinner and I knew this would be a special event for me. I was fully comfortable in passing the tradition on to my daughter. What I had not anticipated was how all of Charlie's well-meaning "help" would be such a draining hindrance to the preparations.

I thought I would be clever and use my time wisely so as not to get overly stressed. I ordered a precooked turkey. I made some cold dishes ahead of time. As anticipated, Charlie asked how he could help. I got out ten sacks filled with stocking stuffers from the closet. I showed him where each sack had been marked with the name of a child or a grandchild. I told him to place all the items in one sack into the matching stocking before proceeding to the next named sack of goodies. I thought it was a foolproof operation. I should have remembered that Charlie was an expert at getting around foolproof plans.

One stocking would not hold all the goodies. One item would not fit in the stocking. I suggested that Charlie empty the stocking and repack it. He did so and then, he told me he had two items left over! I dropped my cooking and went into the great room where the ten stocking hung proudly on the shelf. I told Charlie it was okay to leave the leftover item on the shelf in back of the stocking. He smiled and proceeded to the next stocking.

When Charlie yelled, "Uh, oh!" I hurried back into the great room. The disaster was quite obvious. Charlie had somehow knocked several of the filled stockings off the shelf and the contents were strewn over a fairly large area on the floor, all mixed up together.

"What happened, Charlie?" I asked

"They just fell off."

"All by themselves? They just fell off all by themselves?" I asked with a grin as I began to pick up the items and place them in the respective stockings.

"I think I helped a little," Charlie answered.

I filled the socks, gave Charlie a kiss on his cheek and then Charlie asked, "I did a good job, didn't I?'

"Yup!" I replied as I went in to make the sweet potato casserole.

"I want to do something else" my husband said. He was into the Christmas spirit as well and I didn't want to deny him his own sense of joy.

"We're going to eat outside on the lanai so could you perhaps clean off the table before I put on the table linens Charlie?" I asked.

"What?" he asked. I realized I had provided too much information in my request.

"Please clean the table outside, Charlie."

"Okay," he responded. He came into the kitchen and pulled a kitchen towel from the rack. I immediately surmised he was planning to use the towel to clean the table.

"Oh, let's do it a different way," I suggested. I went to the laundry room and got down the bottle of glass cleaner. I handed the bottle to Charlie and gave him a roll of paper towels. "Just spray the cleaner on the table and wipe it down with the paper towels," I instructed.

Charlie looked at the bottle of cleaner and then at the paper towels. "Okay," he said as he exited to the lanai.

I was proud of myself that I was able to keep Charlie busy while I was doing the Christmas dinner preparations. But, after twenty minutes, I hadn't seen nor heard from Charlie and I became suspicious. I went to the lanai and there was Charlie. He had apparently poured the entire bottle of cleaner onto the four foot by eight foot table and was trying to clean up the liquid with paper towels. He was down to his last paper towel! When I had handed the roll to Charlie, it had been a full roll!

"Wow!" I exclaimed. "That's really a clean table, Charlie! How about you go in and wash your hands and I'll just finish up polishing the table." Charlie smiled and went back into the house. I got out the bucket and sponge and cleaned off the table.

I was just finishing the table when I heard another, "Uh, oh!" preceded by a crash. Charlie had somehow managed to knock off all the stockings but one from the shelf.

I went into the great room and Charlie had a sheepish look on his face. "I was just looking," he said in explanation of the disaster on the floor.

"Okay, don't worry, Charlie. Let's just leave them on the floor for a while. I need to get a couple of things in the oven."

"But, it's all messy," Charlie answered.

"Yeah, it is but I don't think the stockings care right now."

"Can I look at my stocking?" Charlie asked. His was the only one not on the floor.

"Sure," I said. I would later suggest he put everything back in his stocking, knowing when he *officially* opened his stocking with the family gathered around, everything would be new – again.

After a while, Charlie came into the kitchen. I was preparing some muffins that were favorites of the grandchildren while also making some meatballs as a pre-dinner snack in case things weren't ready when everyone arrived. "I want to help some more," Charlie requested.

I thought for a moment and then asked Charlie if he would please blow the leaves off the front walk. "Sure," he answered. He headed out the back door to the garage.

After about ten minutes, Charlie came back into the house. "Something wrong?" I asked, knowing full well that he hadn't gotten the blower going.

"It doesn't fit anymore," Charlie explained.

"What doesn't fit, Charlie?'

"The thing that goes in the machine to make it go on," he answered. "It doesn't fit anymore."

I frowned and then realized that my husband could not figure out how to put the battery into the blower. He had known how to do that just two days ago! I finished filling the muffin tin and placed the muffins to bake in the oven. I went with Charlie back out to the garage. The battery was still in the charger. He had forgotten how to depress the lever to release the battery. I did that and then placed the battery into the blower. Charlie looked amazed and asked, "How did you do that?" Then he patted me on the back and added, "You always were good with machines." Lately, all tools were called machines. I went back into the house and Charlie called to me to go look at the front walkway. He had blown off all the leaves alright. He had blown everything into the fountain! Oh well, that was a task for another day. The walkway looked nice.

Charlie came in to tell me that some of the lights were out on the tree. I went in to look and sure enough, it appeared as though one of the light strings had malfunctioned. I reasoned that it might be the fuse and I told Charlie I would attend to it later. I heard nothing for some time and finally, Charlie came into the kitchen. "I fixed the lights," he said. "But now, more lights are out."

I went to the tree and there were more lights out. I looked at the strand of lights and it was hanging loose. "Charlie, what did you do?" I asked.

"I tried to turn the lights back on," he said. The tree was the prelit kind and Charlie had removed the wires from the branches. I knew I didn't have time to fix the lights as the final preparations were being made. I told Charlie I'd fix the lights later and he wasn't to worry about it.

I asked Charlie to please change his shirt. It was stained from all the glass cleaner he had spilled on it. He couldn't figure out what to wear so I said, "It's Christmas, Charlie, why not wear a red shirt."

I checked my dinner and then went to the garage. I found a spare set of lights and strung them on the tree and then plugged it in again. Everything worked, although the prelit lights were still dangling from the tree. Charlie walked back out of the bedroom and commented on how good I was with machines. He carried a red polo shirt on a hanger and asked, "Is this red?"

My hand went to my chest and then I took a deep breath and said, "Good choice, Charlie. Now, please go put it on." I didn't have time for another loss, even though it was simply a color-naming loss.

Before I knew it, the family had arrived and for the first time in fifty-five years, I was not ready. I took out a prepared shrimp cocktail, got out the meatballs and placed the men in the great room while the girls, my grandson and my daughter all helped set the table, mash the potatoes, arrange the desserts and do last-minute preparations. I was amazed with their efficiency and Charlie seemed content talking with our son and son-in-law while snacking on goodies.

Our son carved the ham with the cloves I had so patiently put on before cooking the ham in a homemade peach sauce. Our son-in-law carved the oven-roasted turkey while I put out all the rest of the holiday dinner. We had our feast and it was nearly flawless. Charlie sat next to me by the grandchildren and he listened to the

111

conversation with obvious pleasure. He was not able to track the conversation long enough to think about a reply. But he was so very happy. He was with his family.

We lingered at our Christmas dinner while the grandchildren got antsy to open gifts. We adults all understood that it was the last Christmas at Grandma's house and no one was particularly eager to end the magic of Christmas dinner outside on a seventy-five degree day in December. We talked of Christmases past and we speculated on new traditions to come. We opened gifts and told more stories. We opened our stockings and yes, everything was new for Charlie. Everyone cleaned up while Charlie and I sat watching all the younger people take charge. I was exhausted and my eyes were filled with tears of acknowledgment that something was at an end. But, my heart was also filled with joy at what Charlie and I had established and nurtured.

Chapter Twenty-Seven

Looking for Light

It seemed that new losses were now day-to-day rather than month-to-month. A light bulb went out in the kitchen. Charlie had changed a bulb in a lamp just a week ago. Today, he could not figure out how to unscrew the bulb. He got a small ladder in order to get a better angle. But, Charlie could not coordinate climbing the ladder. I changed the light bulb when Charlie went to the bathroom. When he came out, he looked at the brightly burning light and said, "Good, that job is finished. Anything else I should do?" Maybe tomorrow, Charlie will know how to change a light bulb, but, probably not.

We arranged for Charlie to go on a fishing charter with a gift certificate he had received for Christmas. We called the special needs bus to pick him up at home and deliver him to the marina. That night, Charlie said he would make his lunch to take with him in the morning. He got out a hardboiled egg. I watch him peel the egg as he struggled to make his hands cooperate with the task. When the egg was peeled, there was nothing left but the yolk. Charlie gave up and went into the bedroom to watch television. I asked if he needed me to make a lunch for him. He looked very sad as he responded, "Don't bother." I closed the door and I soon heard the snoring sounds that assured me he was asleep for the night – or at least, for some of the night.

I made Charlie's lunch and put it in a bag in the refrigerator with his name on it. I got out the insulated bag and placed some dry goods in it. I then wrote Charlie a note which said his lunch was in the refrigerator. I instructed him to take out the sack containing the prepared lunch as well as the two bottles of water and place them in the insulated bag. I further instructed him to put the bag on his shoulder while he waited for the bus.

Charlie arose early the next morning and showered, ate something and then went out to the bus. Previously, he had always arisen before me on fishing days. He was quiet and respectful of my need to sleep in. I heard the front door close and I quietly got out of bed to check on my husband. He did have the insulated bag on his shoulder and was waiting for his ride. I checked the refrigerator and the prepared lunch and the two bottles of water were gone. When the ride came, I went back to bed. I didn't go back to sleep. I just lay in bed watching the sun dance on the ceiling of the bedroom, wondering again if I could stay the course. I reminded myself to put one foot in front of the other and to just keep going.

At nine-thirty that morning, the phone rang and it was Charlie. He was supposed to be somewhere out in the Gulf waters with a fishing rod in his hands. Instead, he asked if I could come and get him. I asked him if he was out fishing and he said, "It was cancelled. There was a note on the door." I was stunned! In the past, the fishing charter had always called if the trip was cancelled. I asked Charlie if he was still at the marina and he said he had gone to breakfast. I asked where he was and he replied that he was somewhere in downtown Sarasota.

Picturing the geography, I was aghast because of the realization Charlie had apparently crossed a busy highway in order to find a restaurant in a dense shopping area instead of simply calling me from the marina. I asked why he had gone to a restaurant and he said, "I was hungry." Well, okay, I guess I set myself up for that one. Then, I asked again if Charlie could tell me the name of the restaurant and he said he wasn't there anymore.

"Where are you, Charlie?"

114

"I'm walking."

"Charlie, I want you to stop walking and then, tell me what you see."

"There's a church right behind me."

"What church?"

"It has one of those big tunnel things on the top."

"You mean the spire, Charlie? It there a big spire on top? Does it sorta look like a really long ice cream cone, Charlie?"

"Yeah, but the cone is upside down."

"Okay, now is there a sign around by the door?"

"Nope."

"There's no sign?"

"Yeah, there is a sign but not by the door."

"Okay, tell me what the sign says, please, Charlie."

"I'm walking right to the front of it."

"Good. What does the sign say, Charlie."

"First Baptist Church. That's what it says. And then, some other stuff."

"Is there an address on the sign, Charlie?"

"Nope. No numbers."

"How about above the church door?"

"I'm walking back."

"Okay, when you get to the front, look up and see if there are any numbers on the door."

"I'm back."

"Okay, do you see any numbers above the door, or to the side of the door?"

"No numbers."

"Okay, do you know what street you are on, Charlie?"

"The busy one, where all the shops are."

"Okay, it's probably Main Street then. Can you tell me what is right across the street, Charlie?"

"Lots of shops."

"Maybe you could walk to the corner and tell me the name of the other street."

"Okay, I'm walking now."

I could hear the effort of Charlie's steps and the shuffling of his feet. I think we used about five minutes of his cell phone minutes but he made it to the corner. "I'm looking now."

I waited and then, Charlie said, 'there's no sign on this corner."

"Is there anyone else nearby, Charlie?"

"No. I guess it's still too early for people to be out."

"Charlie?"

"I'm still here."

"I just Googled the area and I think I know where you are. I want you to go back to the church and stand or sit in front of it. Don't walk. Please don't talk with anyone and just wait. Can you do that?"

"Yeah."

"Charlie, please don't try to hitchhike. I am coming for you. Please promise me you won't stick your thumb out and take a ride."

"I'll put it in my pocket."

"You mean, your thumb? You'll put your thumb in your pocket?"

"Yeah."

"Good plan, Charlie. Now walk to the church while I'm still on the phone."

"I'm walking."

I knew I'd have to buy another phone card for Charlie before he went on his next excursion. Finally, he said, "I'm there."

"Okay. Is there a bench you could sit on?"

"Nope. Just some steps."

"Okay, please sit down on the steps."

I heard some groaning and then Charlie said, "Okay, I'm down."

"Good job, Charlie. Now put your thumbs in your pockets and sit tight until I come to pick you up, okay?"

"Okay. How long will you be?"

"I'm not sure, honey, but don't move from where you are."

"I won't. Can I call if I need to?"

"Of course you can, Charlie. I'm leaving now."

I drove to downtown Sarasota and ran smack dab into a motorcycle convention. Many of the main streets were totally blocked off and others were so congested I couldn't make a left turn. It was almost half an hour since I had talked to Charlie. The phone rang and Charlie asked, "Did you forget where I am?"

I told Charlie I was in a traffic jam and he should sit tight until I arrive.

"My butt hurts," Charlie said.

"Okay, you can get up but don't go anywhere, Charlie."

"A car just stopped and asked if I was lost."

"Please tell them your ride is almost there, Charlie. Tell them thank you."

"Okay. A few seconds later, Charlie said, "They left. They coulda taken me home and then you wouldn't have to."

I'm almost there, Charlie. I can see you now so hang up the phone and go out to the curb. I can't park so you need to get right into the car."

"Okay."

I retrieved Charlie after nearly an hour. He got into the car and said, "It was fun eating somewhere different."

I later found out that the fishing charter had called to tell Charlie the trip had been cancelled. He took the call and then, promptly forgot the message. When Charlie and I got back home, I began to research how to place a tracking system on Charlie's phone. The line between responsibility and respect for Charlie's independence was very thin indeed.

Chapter Twenty-Eight

Playing Double

In the past, Charlie and I would each always drive ourselves to a doctor appointment. But this time, I would drive Charlie and I would also go in for his consultation. I knew full well that Charlie could no longer give reliable information such that his physician could make informed decisions. I had Charlie take out his new insurance cards prior to leaving the house. It took him twelve minutes to locate the cards in his wallet

We signed in and gave the receptionist the new insurance cards and then waited a short time to be called in. There was a new nurse and she quickly ascertained that Charlie was not a reliable reporter of his own status. Yet, she was respectful and she continued to direct questions toward him until he would say he didn't remember. Then, I would respond with the information she required.

Charlie's blood pressure was much lower than when he had been working. As his went down, mine went up. But then, that was predictable. During the consult, our doctor was interested in why Charlie had apparently discontinued some of his medications. "I just decided they weren't right for me," he would say, without any extrapolation on why or when he had taken or discontinued a certain drug. We discussed Charlie's needs and finally settled on a drug regimen that I would monitor. Charlie verbally agreed to my taking over that responsibility but, on the way home, he became angry at having had to yield his last bastion of control. Before leaving the medical

118

facility, I provided the doctor with a copy of my comprehensive Power of Attorney for Charlie and he gave me a copy of the DNR (Do Not Resuscitate) that we had recently signed. From now on, whenever Charlie had an appointment, we were a twofer.

That night, I placed Charlie's medications in a small cup so that he would remember to take them the following morning. The next day, I heard Charlie in the kitchen. He was in the pantry getting more medications and placing them in the cup. I told him we had agreed with the doctor that I would monitor the medications and Charlie said, "You don't do it right." I asked Charlie what I was doing wrong and he told me that I was not putting in all the over the counter medications and that he wasn't going to take the prescribed medications every day. Medications seemed to be some sort of point of control for Charlie and for months and months, he would undermine my attempt to dispense and monitor his medications.

We had also changed health insurance the first of the year and I needed to get Charlie's medications set up through a mail service. That took a bit of doing as I had to converse with the company myself. They insisted on talking with Charlie who had no clue as to how the mail process worked. Finally, I asked if I could email or fax my Power of Attorney for Charlie so that they could have it on hand whenever Charlie's medication needs required a discussion. I now had to do that with each and every agency that we had to deal with, whether it was for healthcare needs or financial arrangements. At times, even with the Power of Attorney in their grasp, the agent on the line would insist I get Charlie on the phone so they could get verbal permission from him to talk with me. Even though Charlie and I were partners and I now had the controlling duties in the relationship, some people still insisted on talking with the "policyholder" or the "man of the house." It was just one of those things I had to decide: do I take a stand on this one or not? Generally, I ended up including Charlie out of respect for Charlie's feelings.

We were also partners in all our outings together. One day, Charlie asked if we could go out. I told him we had several errands.

"And then we can have lunch, right?" he asked. I told him we might do lunch out if our errands ran late.

I asked Charlie to get into the car and as I was locking up the house and Charlie said, "Uh, oh."

"Which *uh-oh* is happening, Charlie?" I asked

"Bathroom," he answered. "I have to pee."

Several minutes later, Charlie came out holding his underwear, slacks and socks. "I need to wash these," he said.

I took the garments and placed them in the deep sink to soak and help Charlie pick out more clothes, complete with guards for his underwear. After over half an hour had elapsed and we were preparing to get into the car, there was another "h-oh," from Charlie and he raced from the garage into the house. He again came out with soiled clothes. I asked if the underwear guard had failed. "Maybe," he answered. "Maybe I didn't put it on right," he added.

So back into the bedroom we went where I picked out another set of underwear and I installed the guard into the underwear. Then, I got another pair of slacks. The socks were okay this time. Another forty-five minutes elapsed before I had soaked the clothes and prepared to leave again.

This time, we didn't make it to the back door before Charlie said, "Oh no!"

I had no doubt what had happened this time. The odor was nauseating. I took Charlie to the bathroom while he stripped. I had him get into the shower which I rinsed the garments in the toilet and then took them to the deep sink. I rinsed out the first garments which had been left soaking and put them into the washing machine and started them washing. I then rinsed the soiled garments and put them into an antibacterial solution to soak. Charlie had showered and I said that maybe we would have to stay home today. He looked like a horribly disappointed three year old and his eyes filled with tears. Yes, I caved.

I insisted that Charlie wear full underwear protection and initially, he was resistant. Finally, he said, "I'm hungry. Can we go out if I wear the underwear you want?" I looked at the clock and sure enough, it was already after noon. I told him we could do that and he immediately donned the underwear and finished dressing. It was now about three hours after we had initially planned to go to run errands. I asked Charlie how he felt and he said, "Great!" I knew from experience that once the accidents had occurred, he was generally okay for the rest of the day. And so, we two errand-runners left the house together. We didn't run any errands that day but we had a good lunch together. I talked while Charlie ate and afterwards, he commented that we were a pretty good team at getting things done. All through lunch, I silently ruminated about how bad it could get before we fused into a single person with dementia.

Chapter Twenty-Nine

Knee Problems

I was in need of surgery for my right knee. I was no longer able to walk my preferred three to five miles and lately, even getting up from a sitting position brought pain and inability to put weight on the knee. I was trying to hold off on surgery until the summer when one or two of my granddaughters would be available to assist me in the recovery process. Charlie was simply not capable of being a caregiver, although he desperately wanted to be available to me.

Working out at the gym continued as a three-times-weekly event and that resulted in continued use of the knee as well as increased upper body strength. But, I could tell that the knee joint was failing by the week and I was silently praying my knee would not give out before the summer. I iced it daily to take down the swelling. Each and every day, I would lie on the sofa after dinner with the ice pack on my right knee and Charlie would look concerned.

"Is your knee hurting you?" he would ask.

"Yes, Charlie, it's the same old problem."

"Then why don't you go get it fixed?"

"I need surgery, Charlie."

"Then go get it."

"I'll need a lot of help afterwards. So, I'll wait until the summer when the girls can come over and help."

"You should do it now. I can help you."

"Charlie, you have to go to group. You won't be home."

"Oh, yeah, I got it. You need somebody to be here and I gotta go to group, right?"

"Right?"

I was always amazed when the same conversation would occur nightly but I knew that for Charlie, it was a new conversation each and every night.

Sometimes, I went to my office after our dinner. There was always work to do. I sat so that I could look directly into the great room where Charlie sat on his recliner. Sometimes, he looked very confused. At such times, he would become agitated. I always went in and inevitably, Charlie would be concerned because, "The show just doesn't make any sense."

I immediately understood that Charlie had turned to a current show and he could not follow the dialogue to make sense of the story. I would change to another channel that featured reruns. Charlie loved to watch reruns of NCIS and lately, he had become interested in the reruns of The Andy Griffith Show. As soon as I got a rerun, Charlie smiled and his anxiety subsided. He would sit for hours if I needed to work. He seemed oblivious to the fact he had watched the same show two days earlier and he was always interested in how the show would turn out in the end. I sat doing my work, wondering when and if the day would come that I would have to cover the television screen because it confused my husband.

And then, the day came that I had a different kind of knee problem. I saw Charlie pick up the phone and sometimes, that signaled problems. I asked who he was going to call and he said, "I'm going to call Seth."

"Seth who?" I asked with growing concern.

"Our son Seth," Charlie replied. "I want to go to a movie and it's one you won't like. Seth always likes to go to these kinds of movies so I'm going to call him."

"Don't!" I yelled as I hung up the receiver and hurried to the bathroom. I knew my outburst startled Charlie and he immediately retreated to his office.

Nothing Left to Burn - A Story of Alzheimer's Disease

I went to the bathroom and fell to my knees as I hugged the toilet and sobbed. Seth had died seven years earlier and I now knew that Charlie had no recollection of the tragedy. I wondered if Charlie's future inquiries would be an ongoing turn of the knife in my heart in the weeks and months to come. I allowed the sobs which gripped my chest like a vise. I couldn't help it; the instant memory of the loss of my son was too unexpected. There had been no time to prepare for my own response. I had to let the pain flow out so that reason could take hold of me. Finally, I struggled to rise and I rinsed off my face with cool water. I went back to Charlie's office and said, "Charlie, Seth can't go to the movies with you anymore."

Charlie looked at me with a confused expression. Then he shrugged and said, "Oh, okay." Charlie was willing to let it go but his lack of pursuit did not result in the easing of my own pain. The tightness was with me throughout the day and into the next. It had brought me to my knees and I had doubts that I could rise again should it reoccur. Charlie's memory failure was so deep now that he had an unexpected means of repeatedly hurting me without the slightest intention of doing so. The losses were accumulating too rapidly and it felt at times as if I were a windshield on the car that navigated the highways daily and repeatedly got hit by gravel. There were so many cracks in the glass that the windshield was in danger of shattering and potentially disabling the vehicle.

Chapter Thirty

Outings and Innings

I was now very selective in the outings of togetherness for Charlie and me. It was a weekend and Charlie wanted items for his own personal hygiene. I was pleased that he still attended to his personal needs and so, I asked him to make a list. He took an hour and a half to write five items: toothpaste, mouthwash, bar soap, tissues and an ointment for a sore in his mouth. We set off for Target to pick up the items and then, we would go to brunch. I allowed one day for brunch and one night for pizza and otherwise, I would fix our meals.

On the way to the store, I talked with Charlie about how we would clean the house the next day. He would dust and then vacuum the area rugs while I pretty much did everything else. Charlie asked if we'd go to lunch afterwards and I reminded him we were going on this day after we ran our errands. He replied, "Then, why do I have to clean the house?"

I immediately understood his correlation between doing something and being reinforced. I replied, "Because, it's the right thing to do, Charlie." Charlie looked at me with confusion and pouted.

We got to the store and I waited several minutes while Charlie struggled to extricate himself from the front seat. If I tried to help him out of the car with my hand, he would generally reply, "I can do it myself." So, I waited and waited and finally, Charlie was upright.

We slowly made out way to the front of the store and I asked Charlie to get out his list. He spent three or four minutes getting it out of his shirt pocket and unfolding the list he had made. We entered the store and Charlie got a cart. It was easier for him to move a bit more quickly when he had the support of the cart.

"They have food here," Charlie commented.

"Yes, they do, Charlie, but we'll go to lunch after we drop our bags back home," I replied.

I guided Charlie and the cart to the two aisles containing the items he wanted. He looked but could not find what he wanted so I asked which item he was trying to find. He pointed to toothpaste and I directed him to the brand he usually bought. We found the box containing toothpaste that also helped to keep gums healthy and Charlie put it in the cart. He then spent two or three minutes looking for the next item. I told Charlie I was going to pick up a couple of items for myself and not to move from the aisle he was in as it contained everything on his list. I was gone three minutes and Charlie was still looking for the second item on the list.

I pointed to the place containing the mouthwash. Charlie picked up an expensive bottle and I pointed to a bottle that seemed to be the same except it was a store brand for two dollars less. I picked up the store brand bottle and read the ingredients to Charlie. "They're exactly the same, Charlie," I said. "Except this brand is two dollars less," I added

"I want the one with green on it," Charlie replied. I tried to convince him that the items were the same and we would save money but Charlie could not grasp the concept. He repeated that he wanted the green bottle. I caved. It wasn't worth an argument in the store. But, that conversation went on with the next three items as well and each time, even though the item Charlie wanted and the store brand were identical, he insisted on the one in the color he wanted.

In all, we were in the store for twenty five minutes finding Charlie's five items. On the way to the car, I talked with him about letting me purchase items on his list the next time. We again talked about how different looking items can actually be the same thing.

When we neared our house, Charlie turned to me and said, "It's wasteful to buy some of those things you buy. You should buy the store brand, you know."

I sneaked a peak at Charlie as I pulled into the garage. I turned off the car engine and placed my hand on Charlie's hand and said, "You know, Charlie. Sometimes you come up with the greatest ideas! Next time, I _will_ buy store brands!"

"Then we can go out to eat, right?" he asked. I gave him a look of doubt and he said, "But we will save money. What else would we do with it?"

I grabbed the bag of Charlie's items, raced into the house, tossed the bag of items on the table, went to my office, opened the back door, went out to the lanai and let out a gigantic growl. I didn't care a bit that the neighbors probably though I was crazy!

After I vented, I went to the kitchen and told Charlie we would put away the items we had purchased after we had our brunch. It was _Season in Florida_ when many tourists were visiting and I wanted to get to the restaurant before the noon crowd arrived. I asked Charlie where he wanted to go and he responded, "The usual place, I guess."

As we had three usual places and Charlie obviously no longer had any idea of the names of the restaurants I said, "Okay, I'll choose then."

"No, that's my job," Charlie replied.

"Okay, then, which one?" I asked.

"The one I like."

"And what will you get at the one you like?" I asked, trying to narrow down the field.

"Maybe pancakes."

"The big ones, Charlie?"

"Yup, the big ones that cover the plate." Well, that knocked out one of the choices. I at least had a general direction now so I backed the car out of the driveway and headed north.

"I think I'll have the mushrooms, Charlie," I said, hoping to trigger a memory in my husband.

"Me too," Charlie replied.

"Well, which do you want then, Charlie, the big pancakes or the mushrooms and eggs?"

"Both," Charlie replied with a big grin. "I'm really hungry after all the work I did."

How could I deny such a simple request? I knew exactly where to go now!

We got to the restaurant and Charlie's grin increased. Lately, his face was showing excitement he couldn't express verbally. But pleasure was about the only emotion readily available to Charlie. His previous intense range of emotions was now a thing of the past. While Charlie struggled to get out of the car, I said, "Here, Charlie, take my hand. We need to get in there and get our names in. It looks as if it's already getting crowded. Charlie allowed the hand up this time.

Inside, the crowd was gathering and I was about to put our names on the waiting list when I glanced toward the large, raised table to the right of the waiting area. There were only two people sitting at what was known as the *community table,* so I asked if we could be seated there. We were accommodated and I helped Charlie onto the raised seats. He immediately looked at the menu and I reminded him of what he had said he wanted to eat earlier in the day. He smiled and agreed that he still wanted those items. When the waitress came, I was ready with both of our orders. As I ordered each item, Charlie nodded his head in agreement of the choices he had earlier verbalized to me.

The other couple was seated one seat away from Charlie and both the man and woman were on the same side. Charlie elected to sit across from me. It was a habit we had established early on in our relationship. I loved to look at his sea-blue eyes and he loved staring in my garnet-colored eyes.

Since it was already crowded, it took a while for the waitress to bring us our drinks. She set my iced tea in front of me and then, she set a coffee cup in front of Charlie and poured in his decaf coffee. She also gave Charlie a glass of ice water as requested. She left to attend to others. Charlie asked, "Is this all we're going to have?"

The woman seated next to Charlie turned her head and raised her head as if to question him. I smiled and she turned away. Charlie asked, "What will we talk about? You said we should talk." And the woman stared at him again. I was so used to Charlie's childlike conversation that I guess I sometimes forgot how it must impact others.

"Well, we could talk about the things we just got, Charlie. We could talk about how you need to put them away when we get home."

"Okay, what did we get?" Charlie asked. That produced another stare. I could see it out of my peripheral vision and I just ignored it. Charlie seemed oblivious.

I began to talk about how we were going to purchase store brands to save some money. "What's a store brand?" Charlie asked.

Charlie and I talked about store brands until our entrees arrived. Then, Charlie didn't talk at all as he dug into his order, an order large enough for two.

I couldn't help but overhear the couple to Charlie's right. They were a couple about the same age as us. I listened to the ease of the conversation and I saw how the man would sometimes reach over and lovingly touch his wife. I listened to the laughter and the shared memories and the plans they made. I began to get jealous, so jealous that my body began to shake. It was just a tremor, as if I were cold, and yet, it unsettled me to my core. I told myself, "Just breathe, Karen. Just breathe; it's all you have to do right now." It was such a simple thing. It was self-talk at its most basic level and, I guess it worked. The tremors subsided.

I left half of my meal on the table and Charlie reached over and began to eat from my plate. He did leave a piece of toast on my plate and then, he allowed the waitress to clear the table. I reminded

Charlie quietly to use the restroom and he got up and headed that way. The lady turned and smiled at me. Then she asked, "Alzheimer's?"

I nodded and she said, "Bless you."

I had to get up as tears were forming in my eyes. Those two little words of understanding from a stranger just buckled me. I smiled a quick *thank you* as I was unable to speak. I went to the front and paid the check and then waited until Charlie came out of the bathroom five minutes later. We walked to the car and I helped him in. We drove home. Charlie was satiated and I felt barren and bereft of any feelings whatsoever. "You got a stuffy nose again?" Charlie asked. He had apparently noticed my occasional sniffles as I attempted to ward off a full-blown breakdown.

"Something like that, Charlie," I replied as I pulled into the garage.

Charlie went immediately to the television and turned it on. He pressed the wrong buttons and finally, I came to his rescue and got the television working. He came across a rerun of the Tampa Bay Rays baseball game. I remembered it well as it was one of their better games last season. Charlie mentioned I should come and watch and I told him it was a rerun from last season. "That's nuts," Charlie said. "I'm seeing it today so it must be on today." I decided to leave that one alone. Charlie watched all nine innings, without the slightest knowledge of having seen it just a few months ago.

We aren't meant to raise children in our seventies. That is the time of special trips, of memories of children and grandchildren, of holding hands and writing creative works and not worrying so much about what others think of you. It is not the time to raise children.

Chapter Thirty-One

Equalizers

Three of the grandchildren were coming today, along with the family dog Franny. My grandson was attending a birthday party and one of the granddaughters was spending the day with a friend while her parents hosted an open house. The family would move into their new house in two months and my son-in-law, who is a realtor, was hosting the open house. I had extra groceries and had baked some treats in preparation for the arrival of the children.

The minute the grandchildren arrived, they went to the pantry and the refrigerator. They always arrived hungry, even if they had just eaten! Today was no exception. I think it may have to do with different foods being available. Charlie immediately joined the children in the kitchen. Even though he had just finished his lunch about twenty minutes earlier, he went about preparing things, mimicking the actions of the children. The U-shaped kitchen was becoming crowded and chaotic. Finally, I chased Charlie out of the kitchen and he went around to the eating bar. He stood and continued to watch the children preparing their various foods. Then, he went back into the kitchen. Food was gradually becoming Charlie's prime way of relating to people. The more he tried to *help*, the more frustrated the granddaughters became. They were not used to his boundary problems and obviously, he was trying to help while actually making a nuisance of himself. I suggested he try to read his current book while the granddaughters ate and then, we could do something outside. Charlie retreated for a while, got engrossed in his book and seemingly forgot that the grandchildren were visiting.

The youngest granddaughter and I went out to play catch with the baseball while the older two got out another outside game and busied themselves. Apparently, Charlie heard us and he came outside. He didn't join in on the games as he would have done in the past. The youngest granddaughter invited him to play catch and he declined. The two older ones then asked if Charlie wanted to play badminton with them. He said, "I'll just be the looker." The older girls turned so as not to show their amusement and embarrass Charlie. At nearly seventy-eight years of age, Charlie was still a handsome man but I fully understood that no one would really classify him as a head turner,

For a while, Charlie appeared content to simply sit on a chair and watch us play. But then, he suddenly got out of the chair and went to the neighbor's house. Their garage door was open and I saw my neighbor's son was there with his family. It appeared as though the young man was loading up his family to take off in the car. I called to Charlie to come back home but he didn't hear me.

Charlie was apparently talking with the neighbor's son about our grandchildren. He was telling the man the children's ages and I heard the oldest granddaughter yell out, "No, Poppy, I'm seventeen now." That was an ongoing thing with Charlie. Each time he saw the grandchildren, he'd ask them what grade they were in and/or how old they were now. Each and every time, they answered him patiently. I threw the baseball to my youngest granddaughter and overthrew it. When she returned the ball to me, she said, "Poppy's losing track of us, isn't he, Grandma?" I told her she was very observant and I reinforced her for sticking with her Poppy, despite the fact that he couldn't do things with her that he had previously done with ease.

In a couple of minutes, Charlie came back to our house and I asked him what had prompted him to go to the neighbor's house.

"There was a baby crying and I thought I would help," Charlie replied. I also had heard the baby cry but had not even given any thought to trying to interfere with the situation while the grandmother, mother and father of the children were there.

"What would you have done to stop the baby from crying?" I asked Charlie.

"Maybe a treat?" he replied.

"But, the parents of the children were there, Charlie," I stated, hoping he would get the connection that the children were being properly care for.

"Oh," Charlie said and then, he nodded. "Well, I would have brought treats for them too."

It was a fun afternoon with the grandchildren but I couldn't help but think about how active Charlie and I had previously been whenever grandchildren were at our house. They had loved their fishing outings with their grandfather and they were now all avid fisherpersons. But, Charlie could no longer drive them to fish and when he was fishing, he seemed to lose track of their needs now. Charlie was withdrawing from social contact when it involved immediate information processing. It was not because his love for the children had diminished; rather his ability to interact was compromised. While we played games in the kitchen, one of the grandchildren would go to the room where Charlie was watching television and they would simply keep him company for a while. Then, they would return to where the action was and another child would sit with Charlie for a while. This was all spontaneous action on the part of the grandchildren. They seemed to have a keen sense of their time with Charlie being limited and my love and respect for them grew intensely with every act of kindness.

Later that evening when the grandchildren were again with their parents, Charlie turned to a television show which sounded new to me. He asked me to come in and see what had happened to the stars of the show. The show was Hot in Cleveland, with Betty White as the ageing lady of the house. Charlie said the characters were all wrong. I asked in what way they were wrong.

"The tall lady got thin," he said.

I couldn't figure that one out so I asked, "What else, Charlie?"

Well, the one that flirts just doesn't look like herself."

I was still drawing a blank. So I asked Charlie if there were any other differences.

"She got taller," Charlie said. "The one from Minnesota got taller."

Finally, the light bulb lit up in my mind and I asked, "Charlie, do you think this is the *Golden Girls?*

He nodded and finally, I understood his confusion. "Charlie," I asked, "did you want to see the Golden Girls?"

He smiled and said he did. I looked in the guide and found the reruns and turned to that channel. Charlie was happy as a clam! "Finally, they look just right!" he declared.

This was a different kind of confusion. I realized that Charlie somehow recognized Betty White but he was back twenty to thirty years and was confusing that show with a current show. I realized I must now take into consideration that what Charlie sees might be distorted. If not distorted, his mind was juxtaposing the past to the present and that could be problematic if I did not become instantly aware of such processing. I vowed that I would look for clues so that I could be aware earlier regarding the nature of his confusion. If I could lessen the confusion, I would lessen the anxiety.

I was becoming a chess player. In his brave attempts to function in an ever confusing world, Charlie would move around pawns of thought, feeling and sensation and it was up to me to try to attempt to disallow him to capture my Queen, the queen being my stamina and my sanity. If I could anticipate moves, I would not be quite so immediately disorganized when other crises arose.

There is an awful lot to this caregiver role. No one can ever tell you what to consider until it happens. And, quite frankly, Charlie's transitions were oftentimes so subtle and so abrupt that anticipation was nearly impossible. My job was not so much trying to stay ahead of the disease. It was more a challenge of trying to figure out what the disease was doing to him via nonverbal clues and peculiar phrasing in conversations. Sometimes, I tried to visualize Charlie's current brain, with random sparks of yesterday, confused thoughts about today and virtually no thoughts of tomorrow. And then I had to stop my own thinking. It only produced anger and a sense of injustice. Even a jellyfish deserves better instincts than Charlie struggles with day after day after day.

Chapter Thirty-Two

Assessing Myself

At times, I thought I was doing a good job in the caregiver role. I was still being careful to take care of myself, despite erratic sleep patterns and ongoing unexpected crises. I still used Charlie's group time to run errands and I knew that, in this phase of the disease, I really needed to do things more relaxing for myself. It just seemed that there were oftentimes way too many hours in the day.

It was Sunday and on Sundays, I asked Charlie to tell me anything he wanted to do the following week on the days when he wasn't in group.

"I want to get a haircut," he said.

"Okay, on what day do you want to do that, Charlie?"

"Tuesday."

"Okay, Tuesday would be a good day. Shall I call Scat Plus for a ride?"

"Can't you take me?"

"Charlie, you usually want to go early and I need to have time in the mornings to get prepared for the day."

"You can prepare if I'm gone."

"Yes, Charlie, that's the idea. So shall I call for your ride to the barber for Tuesday?"

"No, I want to do it."

"Okay, but remember you must write a note and call tomorrow."

"I'll remember."

"Okay, I'll write the note and put it on your desk."

"Okay. Can we go out tonight?"

"Where?"

"To eat."

"Charlie, we just went out yesterday."

"When?'

"We went out yesterday. We had brunch together."

"We did?"

"Yes, sweetheart, we went out to lunch together and we had a wonderful time."

"Charlie smiled and said, "Oh, good!"

I wrote the note for Charlie and put it on his desk. The following day when he returned home from group, I asked if he had called for his ride before he left for group. I knew he had not but sometimes, it was a bit less threatening if I followed up on things in the present tense."

"Oh no, thanks for the reminder," Charlie said.

"I'm going outside to read, Charlie. When you make the call, please come right out and tell me."

"Okay."

I went outside to the lanai to read before I began the dinner preparations. Charlie did not appear. When I went back inside, I asked Charlie if he had called for his ride.

"Yes," he said. "I called for the ride." I didn't follow up on that and I have only myself to blame.

The following morning, Charlie showered and had breakfast while I showered. I came into the kitchen fresh from a night of five hours of sleep and felt fairly refreshed.

"Can you drive me to the barber?" Charlie asked.

"Charlie, you told me you called for a ride."

"I did."

"Then, why do you need a ride from me?"

"They were busy. I called and they were busy."

"And you just hung up then? You hung up and didn't call back. Is that it?" I asked.

"I guess."

"Okay. I know the haircut is important, Charlie. I'm going to have a protein drink and then, I'll take you to the barber."

I was getting my purse and keys to take Charlie to the barber when he ran to the bathroom. It would be nearly two hours later before we got Charlie cleaned up and into the shower (again) and dressed in clean clothes. I took him to the barber and asked when I should pick him up.

"I don't want you to pick me up."

"How will you get home, Charlie?"

"The bus stops right there – see?" Charlie asked as he pointed to the bus stop right in front of the barber shop.

"But, Charlie, that bus won't bring you home from here."

"I'm going to Publix and then to Panera," he stated. "The bus goes right there."

"And then, how will you get home?" I asked.

"I'll hitch a ride so you won't have to come for me."

"No, Charlie, that's not okay with me. If you need to go to Publix and Panera, that's okay but you must call me from Panera."

"Okay. I wish you wouldn't treat me like I was three years old."

"I'm sorry, Charlie. I know you're a grown man but sometimes, I worry a lot about your memory."

"That's why I have the phone." That one took me a minute to process. I guess Charlie felt that as long as he had the phone, he could call me and I would be his memory.

We decided Charlie could have his time with the barber and then go on his errands. He again promised he would call from Panera after he'd had his treat and read the paper. I immediately high-tailed it back home, changed my clothes and went about mixing the fungicide needed to spray my ailing grapefruit tree. I had to get it sprayed before it started to blossom. I had the large ladder up and was spraying the top leaves on top and underneath. Needless to say, the solution was showering down on me. Had I not had on goggles, a mask, gloves and long sleeves, the solution would have saturated me. As it was, my allergies were kicking in and I was beginning to itch. I thought I would finish in ten minutes and then hop in the shower. Charlie was probably just about to finish with his haircut so I had plenty of time.

My cell phone rang. I had put it in my pants pocket so it would be handy for calls while I sprayed. I clicked on and greeted the caller.

"Hi, it's me," Charlie said.

"Yes, Charlie?"

"Can you come get me?"

"Where are you?"

"At the barber."

I thought you were walking to the bus stop to go to Publix and Panera, Charlie."

"My feet hurt." After Charlie's accident that morning, I had told him to put on different shoes as his were wet from the cleaning process. Apparently, the new shoes were bothering him enough that he felt he could not walk. At a time like that, it was useless to argue. It was best to simply retrieve my husband and bring him to a place of safety.

"I'll be there in less than ten minutes, Charlie." I tore off the mask, goggles and gloves and put the fungicide solution in the garage. I was already itching and in serious need of a shower. I retrieved my license and car keys and sped off to Charlie's location. He was waiting in front of the barber shop. I unlocked the door and Charlie struggled to seat himself. I reminded him to buckle his seatbelt.

"Thanks for the ride," Charlie said with his childlike grin. Then, he looked at me again and added, "You don't look so hot."

"I don't feel so hot either, Charlie. I've been spraying fungicide on the grapefruit tree and it's making me itch. I need to finish the job and hop in the shower."

"Well, I could have done that, you know."

I smiled at my husband, barreled on home, finished the spraying and then, hopped in the shower.

That night while Charlie watched television, I tried to read but could not focus. I asked myself if I was up to the task of trying to help Charlie through the intense episodes yet to come. The disease would progressively get worse. I wondered whether I should even be the one to do it. I wondered whether the prostate cancer could progress and take my husband away before he no longer knew me. Then, I hated myself for even thinking such a thing. I gave myself a negative assessment. And then, I reminded myself that I would breathe and breathe and breathe and just take each minute as it came until it was time for someone else to take over.

Chapter Thirty-Three

The Uncontrolled Executive

It was way too apparent now that Charlie's executive functioning was grossly impaired. Executive functions are brain-controlled activities that originate in the frontal lobes of the brain. The lobes are right behind the forehead and they are critical to thinking and planning. They are essential to the smooth daily operations we all take for granted. Our major decision-making, consideration of consequences and working memory are all essential to being able to plan and organize one's day.

In dementia, the frontal lobes are oftentimes the first to experience impairment, but damage is frequently subtle and difficult to spot. When the dementia is of the progressive type as that seen in Alzheimer's disease, the caregiver must take for granted the fact that not only will abilities *not* improve, they will diminish until only basic, instinctual activity is evidenced. For most people, the frontal lobes continue to become more complex and well-developed from adolescence through adulthood. In Alzheimer's patients, it is abruptly halted in development and then, gradually, the lobes begin to atrophy. So basically, there is a working physical body with nobody in charge to make logical and positive decisions. There is no one in charge of the body to organize and plan the day. There is no one to say that a function should be started, stopped or continued. There is no one in charge to adjust when a new situation occurs.

Nothing Left to Burn - A Story of Alzheimer's Disease

Charlie's executive functioning had always been a cut above the norm, except for his ability to attend to multiple events at the same time. Because of his well-developed executive system, he fooled a lot of people for a very long time. But now, he was able to fool no one. Even on days when the lobes worked their hardest, they would wax and wane and at peak, they remained grossly impaired. Charlie could no longer initiate activity without prompting unless it related to something he had done in his childhood. Examples of this would be bathing, dressing, eating and turning on a television set. He could no longer hold pieces of information in his mind in order to plan a day. He had problems honoring limits, particularly as it related to others' personal spaces. Emotions were sometimes disconnected or absent. There was a paucity of ability to think about consequences such that I had to think ahead constantly in order to keep Charlie from potential harm.

Taking control of executive functioning is probably one of the most emotionally-laden duties of the caregiver. This is particularly true if the major caregiver is a spouse or an adult child. It is agony attempting to explain to a grown man or woman why they cannot do something or go somewhere unsupervised or unaccompanied. Days have to be planned and organized at a time when life should be a time of boundaries stretching and time being meaningless. It is a time when the caregiver must structure the day and prioritize tasks so as to conserve energy and motivation. If you can't develop a good sense of humor or you don't have the ability to think on the spot, caregiving an Alzheimer's patient might best be left to those who can better go with the flow. It's not a character deficit. It's simply a fact.

I had always considered myself to be a highly reliable person who would do what I said I would do. Furthermore, I would do it well and I would do it without griping. It's what I was taught as a child and since it had always worked in times of stress and trauma, I failed to let go of it until Charlie's condition forced me to take a serious look at my own personality. At times, I liked what I saw and at other times, not so much. My standards were way too high for someone without an executive in charge. I had always told others I was not the type of person to be a decent caregiver to those with diminished capacities. But, in the end, I was wrong about myself.

The big things were easy to handle; my own organizational skills worked their best in situations that demanded a clear head and quick action. But, the small things…that was another matter. Simple things that go wrong have always bothered me primarily because they are so preventable. Simple things are the building blocks to more complex tasks and if Charlie couldn't or wouldn't do the simple things, the complex tasks always took way too long to complete and I would get irritated. Structure is very important as dementia progresses. It's important for the one with dementia to understand when and how things will happen so that anxiety and frustration are reduced. So, each and every day, Charlie and I started out with me providing a very light and simple summary of the first expectation of the day. There was also a written schedule posted on the refrigerator. Lately, whenever I would give a request to Charlie, I would prepare it with a reinforcer.

I might say, "Charlie, remember this is the time to pick up your clothes."

"What should I do with them?" Charlie would ask – yes, each and every time.

"Put them in the clothes hamper. When you put the clothes in the hamper, come out to the kitchen."

Assuming Charlie performed the task, I might reinforce him with a glass of iced tea outside and a bit of conversation. It didn't matter whether I was attentive five minutes or five hours. For Charlie, time didn't have a lot of meaning anymore.

If everything went well, I would remain relaxed and ready for whatever needed to be done next. But, oftentimes, Charlie would divert his attention. Sometimes, he would wander outside to pick up sticks or just look around. He might go to the bathroom and spend fifteen or twenty minutes. He might go back to his desk and look through papers again. Then, I would have to give him the same instruction again. This time, I might be a bit less patient. If Charlie was again diverted, the third instruction would be a bit terse.

If Charlie asked me the same question again and again, I would also lose patience. Even if I wrote down the answer for him, he would often ask again and again. He seemed to need to receive the answer from *me* rather than from a visual prompt. There was a strong element of perseveration in Charlie's thinking. Perseveration is the irritating notion of doing something again and again. It's as if the mind gets stuck. But then, the executive was not available to stop the activity.

I wondered if his visual skills were deceiving him but an eye examination verified Charlie's eyesight had not changed. I began to suspect that visual images might be distorted at times. Charlie would oftentimes claim his eye glasses "didn't work."

We might be sitting in the family room together, Charlie watching television and me reading. Charlie would endlessly study the program guide and sometimes he would say, "The programs are all wrong here."

"Charlie, are you on the right page?" I would ask. "Remember, its Thursday today."

"Well, the programs aren't right on Thursday then."

"How are they wrong?"

"You can't even see them."

"Charlie, I don't understand."

"You sure don't!"

"I mean I don't understand the problem, Charlie. How are they wrong? It's eight o'clock now. Look at Channel 11. The show *Monk* is supposed to be on. Is it listed there?"

"You can't see anything."

"Oh, Charlie, is the page blurred or something?"

"Yes, that's what's the matter. My glasses don't work anymore."

"Charlie, we went to the optometrist last week. You have new glasses and you told me you could see better than before."

"Then, they changed them. They don't work now."

"Would you like me to check the channel for you?"

"No." I wait for over a minute while Charlie changes the channels with the remote control and then Charlie says, "You change it. The buttons on the menu are all wrong too."

I turn the channel to the program Charlie wants and go back to my reading. I am trying to figure out what could be bothering Charlie but I chalk it up to some sort of visual distortion. Sometimes, medications will do that and at other times, it could be simply the faulty processing of the brain. The executive in Charlie's brain had jumped ship and now, the mates were in charge with no training in actually guiding the ship.

We decided to go to Sebring to meet friends from the East coast who had rented a condo there for a couple of months. They were a wonderful and understanding couple who had known us for over twenty-five years. As luck would have it, Charlie had an accident the morning we were to travel to Sebring. Fortunately, it wasn't a granddaddy accident and we were able to take off on time. I had Charlie bring two extra pair of full protection underwear as well as an extra set of clothes. I had written the directions in large, bold lettering so that I could read the words easily as I drove.

We stopped once for a bathroom break and I was feeling a bit too haughty about the progress we were making. I thought I had planned for each and every possible negative incidence, fool that I was. Charlie picked up the directions sheet and he said, "I'll be the navigator, just like when I was in the Navy." I knew there was a turn coming up just outside a small town so I asked Charlie to read the direction to me. He read the turn we had just taken so I asked that he read me the next one. He did so, telling me to turn left at such-and-such a state highway.

We came to the intersection and Charlie said, "This is it. Turn left." The direction seemed a bit off to me but I also knew it was a jog in the road so I turned as Charlie directed. He was in seventh heaven being the navigator!

As luck would have it, we had turned the wrong way and we were now coming into Sebring way north of where we wanted to be. Charlie kept nagging me to "turn there" and to "turn there," obviously trying to make a correction. Finally, I stopped at a gas station and asked where to catch the highway we needed. We weren't too far away and we were able to make our way to the restaurant to meet our friends, being only five minutes late. As we were getting out of the car, Charlie said, "You sure aren't very good at directions."

I wanted to punch him but I just needed to relax so I breathed deeply and prepared to meet friends who would relax me and validate my day-to-day efforts with Charlie. We stayed at the restaurant for two hours and Charlie said precious few words the entire time. He had forgotten the couple had visited us in Sarasota the previous month and I think they were a bit taken aback at how much he had slipped since then

On the way home, Charlie immediately picked up the instructions and I immediately tightened my grip on the steering wheel. I saw a Dairy Queen to my right and pulled in there. I ordered two chocolate cones and handed one to Charlie as I took the directions and folded them up. I was pretty sure I knew where we had missed the turn. The distraction satisfied Charlie as his hands were busy – as was his mouth!

We stopped a couple of times for bathroom breaks for Charlie. When he got back into the car after the first stop, I began to hear a series of three beeps. They seemed to happen about every three to four minutes. Charlie didn't hear the sound. I checked my instrument panel and nothing was amiss. I asked Charlie if he heard the beeps and he said he did not. I asked if he had brought anything with him that might have such a sound and he denied bringing anything. As we progressed, I began to worry that the car might be malfunctioning in some way. There were no lights on the instrument panel that would suggest such a malfunction. And yet, the beeps continued and I remained a bit on edge. I thought I'd stop by the car dealership in a couple of days to have the beep checked out.

I saw where we had missed the turn and noted it on my directions in case we traveled again to Sebring. We pulled in the driveway and into the garage. Charlie went into the house, went into the bathroom and then, went to the family room and turned on the television. I again heard the beeps.

I went to Charlie and said, "Charlie, the beeps are coming from you! What do you have that would be beeping?"

Charlie stood up and I searched his pockets. When I pulled out his cell phone, I finally understood the mystery of the beeps.

"Charlie, you need to charge your cell phone."

"Why?"

"It's beeping. It needs to be charged because it is beeping. By the way, Charlie, why did you take the phone when you know I have my phone?"

"I always take it when I go out. Usually, I don't turn it on."

I prepared a light dinner for us both and had to laugh at my own anxiety at the beeping mystery phone. After dinner, I checked my emails and then went to get the ice pack to ice my bum knee. I lay on the sofa icing the knee and watching the program Charlie had on. I commented to Charlie that we would be taking another trip next week to meet friends.

"Oh, that's nice," he said. "But I wish we could meet Susan and Jeff," he added. "It's been way too long since we saw them!"

They were the couple we had just met that afternoon. The executive was not just gone; it was dead and buried.

Chapter Thirty-Four

Medication Madness

Shortly after our trip, Charlie and I just had another go-around about medications and I didn't handle it well. It came up too suddenly and it caught me off guard. I heard him in the pantry and it sounded as if he had pill bottles. I had a sack of old medications way in the back of the top shelf and I feared he might be into them. I chastised myself for not disposing of them after the last visit to the doctor when several had been discontinued. I went into the kitchen and asked Charlie what he was doing.

"I'm getting rid of all those medications that give me the runs."

"Charlie, you needn't bother yourself with medications now. Remember you promised the doctor you'd let me handle them for you," I said as calmly as I could.

"You aren't giving me the right ones. You're giving me the ones that make me worse."

I gasped, thinking that Charlie had some rudimentary awareness that he was failing.

"Charlie," I replied, "you take the medications so that you don't get worse, but some things just can't be helped."

I went to where Charlie was and took the medication bottles out of his hands. I was shocked to see they were the meds I had supposedly hidden away so that he wouldn't get at them. I told Charlie he was not to worry about the meds and I began to walk away.

"You're trying to make me worse," he said. I looked at Charlie and he was glaring at me. He went back to the pantry and got out old bottles of vitamin supplements and started putting those pills in the cup in which I would set out his prescribed medications nightly. I said, "Charlie, why don't we prepare lunch now. We have some turkey dogs and we also have sliced turkey for sandwiches.

The attempted distraction didn't work. Charlie ignored me and continued to put over-the-counter pills in his pill cup. I tried again to distract him.

"Don't you dare try to tell me what to take! The stuff you give me give me the runs."

"Charlie, please come sit down," I suggested. Charlie ignored me.

"Charlie, you have the runs because of the problems you have. Prostate cancer can sometimes do that to you. And, your brain is not doing what it's supposed to do either, Charlie. Sometimes it tells your body to do things you don't particularly like."

"Listen here," Charlie yelled. "The medication I take is supposed to get rid of the prostate cancer. And if you're telling me it's my memory problems, you're crazy. You're just trying to make it worse."

Charlie was paranoid and I recognized it as such. And yet, he was not yielding. I fought off tears at Charlie's accusations and then I asked Charlie to come into my office with me. I had him sit in a chair while I pulled out his medical file. I picked out the list of medications he had been taking and showed him where the doctor had prescribed a generic for a medication he took for his prostate. "Look, Charlie, the generic is written in the doctor's handwriting. It's the same medication you were taking for your prostate. The name is different because it's a generic."

For ten minutes, Charlie studied the paper. He then reviewed each and every medication and he handed back the paper. I asked him if he now remembered the doctor telling him that he wanted me to put the medications out for him. Charlie accused the doctor of "making a mountain out of a molehill" but he finally said he remembered "something like that taking place."

I went outside to water the orchids in order to try to let go of some strong emotions. Pretty soon, Charlie came out and asked if I wanted to go get some chocolate cake. I was unsure as to where that thought originated but I told him our son was coming over shortly and we needed to be home. Charlie went to his office and began to reread the Sunday paper we had just purchased earlier at the convenience store. I then wondered if he had read something in the paper that triggered his reaction. Shortly, Charlie came back into my office and asked if I wanted a candy bar. I surmised that Charlie might be trying to tell me he was sorry he had upset me. But then, Charlie really hadn't realized any of my moods lately, so that might not have been it. Still, it smacked a bit of a child trying to make restitution to a parent for being naughty.

Trust had always been something that was unequivocal between Charlie and me. It was one of the straws that wouldn't break the back of the camel. And now, I had to worry about increased paranoia and what that might do to my ability to act in Charlie's behalf.

My son came over and we had a good discussion about his life and mine. We both agreed that despite setbacks, we had made steady progress in the directions we had set for ourselves. We sat out on the lanai with the sun on our shoulders. It was mutually rewarding and I went back inside the house determined to try to give Charlie some pleasure on that day.

I suggested we take a ride to the home my daughter and son-in-law were building. We hadn't seen it for about a month now and my daughter said the floor tiles and kitchen cabinets were now installed. I drove the car through some scenic areas and then, we found the new home. We explored the downstairs and had just gotten upstairs when we heard voices below. Three sets of feet came pounding up the stairs and three sets of arms reached out saying, "Grandma!" My daughter had brought the five grandchildren to inspect their new house and the children's presence had given me an unexpected surprise! We stayed a half hour at the house while the children inspected the woods behind their house. At one point, they rushed into the house saying there was a young deer outside in the forest. We all went out to look and sure enough, that young doe was just as interested in us as we were in her. She stared at the children for a long time before retreating back into the woods. Just seeing the grandchildren had lifted my spirits and I felt refreshed and ready to take on whatever came my way.

I decided to try to prolong Charlie's outing so I took him to the Dairy Queen where we each got a chocolate cone. I deliberately drove the long way home so that Charlie would remember having had a good day with me. He had seemingly all but forgotten the outburst in the morning and I would not mention it. After dinner, he again retreated to the television set and I elected to do a bit of writing in my office. Charlie was interested in the Olympic events in Sochi so I got the correct channel for him and he was as contented as a recently fed and diapered newborn infant.

Later, when I went into the family room to join Charlie, he smiled at me. I was never sure anymore what he was seeing or thinking. I asked, "Is something on your mind, Charlie?"

"Some people would have put me in a home by now, wouldn't they?" he asked.

I got up and went to Charlie and hugged him. "That's a long way off for both of us," I said.

In the end, we had managed the day and for the most part, that was now our mantra – just try to manage the day.

Chapter Thirty-Five

Finding Charlie

It was becoming more and more difficult to find Charlie. The man to whom I had been attracted nearly three decades earlier was slipping away and in his place, a demanding stranger was living with me. In order to remember *my* Charlie, I would try to find a certain look in his eyes or a phrase that suggested the man of long ago. The best times for that seemed to be when Charlie was watching television. He would occasionally utter a phrase that would remind me of the man with the mischievous smile.

I was in graduate school when I first met Charlie and the meeting was brief and not at all monumental. I was a forty-seven year old woman in the Doctoral program at the University of Iowa when Charlie came into my classroom. There were only six of us accepted to the program and we were told we would work closely with nearly all the professors in the program. Each of the professors in the program was to come to our room for an introduction so that we would know them when we met in the hall or in a scheduled class. Charlie was in a suit and tie and right away, his sparkling blue eyes suggested a lot more than the exterior was willing to divulge. He cracked a few jokes and left. For nearly three years, I had no contact and no interaction with him.

During my last year in graduate school, I was writing my dissertation and preparing to go out on internship. I decided to sign up for a class in forensic psychology as I thought it might come in handy in my intended profession as a Clinical Psychologist. Charlie would be my professor. On the first day of class, I was immediately put off by Charlie's behavior as well as his style of lecturing which seemed to be a series of one story after another. I noticed the younger students seemed enthralled by Charlie. Perhaps, they expected that if he kept on talking, their assignments would be less-ened, a burden we all wished for daily.

Charlie was a chain smoker and in those days, there was no policy stating a professor could not light up in the classroom. Char-lie entertained us with story upon story and I will admit that his firsthand knowledge of his subject was superb. He talked about his cases and how a psychologist could be critical to the preparation of a difficult court case. But, for me, there did not appear to be sub-stantial preparations in the lectures and I sometimes wondered if I was getting my money's worth for the course.

At the end of the semester, we were all asked to give evalua-tions of the professor's course. I debated about what to write and then, I told Charlie exactly what I thought about the course. I doubted that I would ever hear back from Professor Charlie about the feedback I had given. I hoped the feedback would not enter into the consideration of my course grade. But, even though we were not required to sign our evaluations, I felt it only respectful to do so. Two days later, I got a request from Charlie to go to his office.

I knocked on Charlie's door and he asked me to come in. When I went to close the door, he asked that I leave it open. That was also a customary practice. When you had an opposite-gendered student in the room, the door generally remained open.

"I wanted to talk with you about your evaluation," Charlie said as I sat on the chair in front of his desk.

I began to shake and I clutched at my own hands to steady myself. On the evaluation, I had told Charlie that I sometimes felt disrespected by his behavior in class (e.g. his smoking and his ongo-ing stories) and I thought that he was entertaining but that he obvi-ously had a brilliant mind. I did not feel he was well-prepared to give the students what he actually had in his mind. I had written that he did not seem prepared for the classes and that I was unsure that I was getting my money's worth in his class.

Charlie told me he had never received such an honest evaluation and I wondered if he was simply easing up on me before he went for the kill. But then, he continued by explaining that he was, indeed, feeling a bit burned out and that he did not use course materials well. Instead, he was choosing to pass the class time relating old stories which were comfortable and known. Charlie then shocked me by asking if I would consider working with him on a current forensic case. In the field of psychology, forensic work involved working with attorneys on case development, jury selection and witness preparation. Charlie explained to me that he was a bit stuck trying to "humanize" the prosecutor in the case and that I might be able to offer insight that would move the preparations along.

I told Charlie I'd have to think about his request and also, check with my advisor. Charlie said he had previously included students in forensic cases and that the students had always thought of the forensic experience as a sort of short internship. I asked a few more question and left the office somewhat intrigued. For one thing, I had never thought about forensic work in my field. For another, I was impressed that someone with Charlie's credentials would not only consider a student's negative evaluation as a positive thing, he had obviously valued the person inputting the feedback.

As it turned out, my work with Charlie on forensic issues was an instrumental part of my training as a Clinical Psychologist. Charlie would teach me that if a psychologist takes the stand as an expert witness and is not prepared to answer for his or her *expert* opinions, then that psychologist deserves to be taken apart by an attorney who *has* done his/her homework. The same would be true of the attorney who asks a question of a witness without knowing the answer ahead of time.

Every so often, I saw that kind of reasoning in Charlie's current thinking. He would look at me with a question mark on his face, as if he were considering whether or not I had the credentials to make a certain decision or suggestion. At first, the looks spooked me out as I thought it was distrust on Charlie's part. But now, I reasoned that he was simply asking me to back up my facts as an expert witness. When I looked at Charlie's requests in that way, I found myself taking on a more positive feeling in my responses where previously, I had felt insulted. Where previously, I had looked at the exterior (Charlie's verbalizations and his expressions) for explanations, I now began to look within myself for important clues. Oftentimes, when the exterior betrays you or makes you feel estranged from your own grounding, you simply need to look within for a different kind of centering.

That insight was something that would carry me through the truly difficult days. I would think back to my own learning and then, realize that the lessons in learning were always the same. But the lessons were learned in different situations involving different persons. For me, the difficult life lessons were almost always lessons of loss. And, although the lessons were similar, I now realized I was progressing through a highly structured program that required increasingly more integration of the heart and the mind.

My first loss lesson was a devastating and severe lesson for one so young. I was but a toddler when my mother died and from that point on, I believe I began to favor the cognitive resolution over the emotional one. I understood that I would survive the loss with the support of loved ones in my extended family, but I remember it as an ongoing series of losses which carried me through my childhood. In young adulthood, a series of miscarriages flipped me back to the emotional center I had managed to avoid as a child. It was a private pain and it oftentimes excluded others. But, I learned that emotional pain would not break me. In middle age, the loss of my first husband from lung disease forced me into a more balanced thinking about loss. Despite his own self-destructive smoking behaviors, he was my first love and the father of my children. I loved him to the day of his death. Even though I felt his emotional loss keenly, the logical consequences of behaviors began to help me integrate the loss as something somewhat expected in life. If any-thing, it tended to remediate the feeling of abandonment and cau-tiousness that had permeated my childhood years. I guess I could say that I had probably earned a Bachelor's degree in accepting losses at that stage.

And then, my younger son died and my childhood fears flooded in and nearly wiped out both my cognitive and emotional reserves. For some time, I felt life had little meaning. Even though I loved my children, my husband and my grandchildren with all my heart and soul, I feared I had to quit loving so deeply in order to pro-tect myself from emotional implosion. But, strangely enough, that did not occur. For a while, I did have to know where everyone I loved was at the end of the day, but, fortunately, that need was short-lived. In the end, I guess I came out of the experience with a Mas-ter's Degree in losses.

There are so many ways to lose love. The abrupt severance of the mother-child bond was one which, as a child was not truly com-prehensible. So, as a child, I simply began to interpret the world in a way which would result in the protection, guidance and security I had lost with the death of my mother. When I as a mother, I then felt the loss of my own child, the depth of the loss was such that I actu-ally gained a renewed sense of how deeply pain can penetrate and begin to bend and break old truths.

And then Charlie came, with his ability to both frustrate me and bring me to a level of love I had never anticipated. A soul mate type of love is much different from that of a mother-child relation-ship. It is one which both draws you in and spits you out. And then, it draws you in yet again so that you reach a higher understanding. It is close to an unconditional acceptance of whatever form of love is available at any given time. It is a weathering kind of love in which you either grow from your willing participation or you revert to immature behaviors which result in either building a safe cocoon or lashing out at the world in anger for what has not been bestowed. I

156

knew as soon as I confirmed Charlie's diagnosis of Alzheimer's that I was now in the Ph.D. program for Lessons on Loss.

And so, every day I would look for the Charlie that had taken me into the Golden Years of life. That Charlie might occasionally and briefly be found in a spoken word or a glance. He might be recognizable in a predictable move or the way he approached a friend or a neighbor. Even in the moderate stages of the disease, Charlie was still bullshitting his way through life in a charming way. The old Charlie was just getting harder to spot now. But it was there, if only I took the time to look hard enough. It would have been way too easy to miss Charlie had I not recognized he was still there but that I must look inward to find him.

Chapter Thirty-Six

The Nebulous Napkins

"I can't get my drawers open," Charlie declared one day.

I grinned, trying to think of which drawers Charlie was complaining about. He wasn't in the bathroom so he didn't require assistance with his protective underwear. From where I was sitting in my office it sounded as if Charlie was in his office when making the remark. I went in there, expecting he had a jam in one of the drawers in his desk. Sure enough, he was tugging at two drawers, trying to get into them. His efforts were to no avail so I decided I'd better give some assistance before he yanked off the drawer pulls. I asked Charlie to rise from his chair so that I could sit and get a good look at the jammed drawers. I tugged and sure enough, they would not open. I finally pulled out a section of three drawers from the unit that sat underneath a counter. I decided to approach the problem from the back of the cabinet. I got a long knife and tried pushing down what appeared to be a mountain of soft material. With that effort, I was able to ease open one of the drawers.

I gasped when I saw dozens of napkins that had apparently jammed the drawers when Charlie went to open them. I asked if there might be napkins in the other drawers as well and Charlie answered, "Maybe."

I used the same technique to ease open the second drawer and there were even more napkins than in the first drawer. I took them all out, counting them as I went. There were fifty-two napkins in the two drawers, along with everything Charlie normally stored in there. Actually napkins might be stretching the concept just a tad. Charlie always tore off a square sheet of paper towel to use as a napkin. He would oftentimes eat breakfast or lunch at his desk as he played on the Internet. Sometimes, I asked him what he was looking at on the computer screen and Charlie would answer, "Whatever they put up for me." Charlie would click on a picture and then study whatever came up. Apparently he thought the news articles were written especially for his interest!

I was curious about the purpose of Charlie's peculiar napkin collection. So, fool that I was, I asked, "Charlie, why are all these napkins in your drawers?"

"Because I put them there."

"But, Charlie, they are used napkins and you should throw them in the trash when you are finished with them."

"I'm not finished with them."

"Sweetheart, when you finish the meal, you are finished with the napkin."

"Nuh-uh," Charlie explained. "They are still clean. I try to keep them clean so I can use them again. It's wasteful to throw them away."

"Charlie, if you save them to use again, why do you keep getting new ones instead of using the napkins you have saved?"

"I forgot."

"You forgot about the napkins or you forgot why you are saving them?" I asked.

"Maybe both," Charlie responds.

I thought for a moment and then I suggested, "Charlie, Maybe I should just go to your desk and get napkins whenever we need them."

Charlie frowned at me and said, "No you shouldn't do that. Those are the napkins I'm saving for next time I need them."

I do not know why Charlie has been hoarding napkins. I wonder if it has something to do with his safety needs. I wonder if it has something to do with his more frequent bladder and bowel problems. I wonder if Charlie just likes to look at napkins. He folds them very carefully, first in half and then into quarters. He seems to derive enjoyment from the act of folding. Maybe it brings some sort of organization to a brilliant mind infiltrated with chaos. At best, Charlie has given me a clear glimpse into the workings of his mind. At worst, even though I am trained to assess and understand Alzheimer's disease, I have no clue about what many of the symptoms mean.

**

We had a very busy week in mid-February. I decided to make a large batch of vegetable soup which would tide us over for three meals. We were attending baseball and softball games for three of the grandchildren. The games would be held around the times we generally ate our evening meal. A quick soup warm-up would be just the thing. The bonus would be that everything in the soup was not only nutritious, it was soft so that Charlie would not experience any choking problems.

I made the gigantic batch of soup just before Charlie returned from group on a Monday. He really loved the soup and he remarked that there was enough to last nearly all week. He rose from the table and said he would clean up the dishes for me. There were only two soup bowls, two spoons and the pot of soup which I had left cooling on the stove prior to placing the leftovers in a large container. I rose and thanked Charlie for his kindness. I went to my office and began to answer emails. Suddenly, I heard what appeared to be liquid pouring into the sink. The faucet was not on so I knew Charlie was not rinsing the soup dishes. I ran into the kitchen in time to stop Charlie from pouring the entire remaining pot of soup into the sink!

"Charlie, I wanted to save the soup for other meals," I said as I took the large soup pot from Charlie's hands.

Charlie pointed to the small container he had gotten out and said, "The soup won't all fit in the container. You can't just leave it

160

on the stove, you know," he added with a smug aire of authority. I immediately realized that Charlie had not thought of the obvious solutions. He had not thought to either put the leftover soup into a larger container or else, get two containers to fill.

Charlie's thinking was now squarely in the stage of the pre-school child. Abstract thinking and cause and effect were now nowhere in the conceptualization mix. Now, I had to monitor every offer to help with even the simplest things.

Chapter Thirty-Seven

Undermining the Caregiver

By the third year following the lost house incident, I considered myself a caregiver as opposed to the earlier stages of Charlie's disease, I had thought of myself in terms of *helping* my husband with things he could no longer do. By necessity, I was now in a more authoritarian position but I tried to guard against taking a parenting approach. Whenever possible, I shared responsibilities. If my son, daughter or grandchildren were there to take charge of Charlie, I willingly yielded. Three days a week, the Senior Center would be Charlie's caregivers for about six hours. I considered those hours my *sanity time*. For the rest of the time, I was Charlie's sole caregiver. Most of the time, we were getting into a comfortable routine that would allow us both to see our world as somewhat predictable. This required that I learn how to spot potential problems as well as anticipate potential solutions to those problems. Even with my doctorate degree in psychology and my years of working in geriatric services, I still had a lot to learn. I think any professional caregiver will also tell you the same thing. Due to the idiosyncratic nature of Alzheimer's, no one approach works for everyone. In a group of Alzheimer's patients at a long-term care facility, it might be possible to divide dementia patients into groups depending upon shared needs. But as far as the individual caregiver is concerned, educated guesses were still a primary source of caregiving.

I was beginning to notice a decided difference in outings with

Charlie. Without going into detail, almost all my friends had some notion that Charlie had dementia and that the dark circles around my eyes were a result of sleepless nights and ongoing stress. For the most part, they were very understanding and they tried very hard to support the caregiver. On occasion, friends or members of Charlie's family would also try to support Charlie but it would oftentimes end up undermining the caregiver.

When we were out with friends, it was not at all unusual for Charlie to remain silent. Some might try to bring Charlie into the conversation by commenting on something in the present that had recently occurred. Charlie would always smile and oftentimes comment, "Yes, Karen took me there," or "Oh, Karen does that for me now." That would be followed by the friend reinforcing Charlie for the trust he had in me and for relinquishing duties which were best accomplished by others. In other words, they were reinforcing his willingness to trust the caregiver

On occasion, an old friend would be with us and I encouraged the friend ahead of time to recall past memories as that would be Charlie's strength in conversation. When talking about current events, he would basically remain mute and continue to eat. On occasion, there were those who would make comments on Charlie's physical well-being and their comments would generally refer to Charlie's exterior presentation. Many people had no notion of the various physical ailments which threatened his functionality at any given time.

But, when people then began to tell Charlie something to the effect that he was just the same as he'd always been and that he shouldn't let others try to convince him otherwise, I'd tighten up and hope the conversation would not proceed. Even though they were well-meaning and probably hoped to boost Charlie's moral, it oftentimes had the effect of undermining the caregiver. For example, one day, we'd just returned from a lunch with a friend who was visiting. She had taken the approach that *there's really nothing the matter with Charlie.* She talked on and on about how Charlie could do about anything he'd always done and that he shouldn't rely so much on me. I'm sure the intentions were to give Charlie a sense of efficacy but it had the opposite effect.

Not long after we got home, Charlie remarked that since there was nothing wrong with him he was going to begin to take back the things he'd been letting me do. He declared he was going to apply for a job the following Monday and also, that he was finished with his group. He went out to get the mail and instead of giving it to me to sort, he went through the mail and took everything except the flyers. He asked for the checkbook back and he made out a check. I had been doing online banking for months due to the hacking fiasco that had occurred when Charlie managed our monetary funds. Then, Charlie went to the recycling bins and threw out the rest of the mail.

When Charlie went into the bathroom, I checked the recycling bins and I took out the electricity bill (which had been torn in half) and also the quarterly bill for my own life insurance policy. When Charlie returned from the bathroom, I told him I'd mail the bill he'd made out the check for in the morning when he went to group. He asked me, "What bill?" I went to my office with the bill and stuck it underneath the computer so that I could make out an electronic check the following day.

But, that was not the end of the problem. Charlie then said he wanted to go and take the driving test again because there was no reason he could not drive. He used his friend's observations that he was the same old Charlie as *proof* that I had been making up his mental limitations and his need for assistance. He got out all the prescription bottles and forbade me to "interfere" anymore. He called several people he'd found in his phone book and made several calls. None of them were home. He told me he was going to call the University where he'd taught and see if he could get his old job back. He instructed me to call the Senior Center and cancel his participation in the group he attended three times weekly.

During this time, I said very little. I had hoped the passage of time would simply allow the short term memory deficits to go to work. It would be nearly three hours before I saw the effects of that luncheon conversation wearing off and I surmised that Charlie's ability to keep even trace memories of the luncheon was a factor of how badly he wanted to be *normal* again. In the meantime, I silently cursed the well-meaning friend who wanted to buoy Charlie's spirits at my expense!

I knew Charlie had finally forgotten the experience when he asked, "Can we go out tonight?"

I asked where he would like to go and he answered, "Where I like to go." As that generally meant I should remember his favorite places, I agreed to go out, thinking he might then get accustomed to seeing me in the caregiving role when I took the wheel of the car. We ran some errands that night and then had a bite to eat at a new restaurant. It was a burger place and generally, Charlie and I do not eat red meat due to elevated cholesterol. But this place had chicken, turkey and veggie burgers so we decided to give them a try. It had just been highly recommended by a relative we both trusted. It was well worth the stop and by the time we'd finished eating, Charlie and I were again one with his disease. We were who we were and the disease was only a small part of our consideration. I relaxed and simply enjoyed what was available to us.

We decided to drive to the beach to watch the sunset. We got there as the colors emerged. There was a natural art show right before our eyes! Yellows played in and out of the light cloud cover while the oranges and reds danced among the clouds like ballerinas winding daintily through a thick forest they had known forever. It was almost as if the show was orchestrated and I found myself setting the show to music in my head.

We were standing about six feet from the water, watching the ebbing and flowing of the surf. Charlie looked at me smiling and he put his arm around me. I told him his arms felt good.

We stood for several minutes and then Charlie shocked me by saying, "I'm not okay, am I?"

I wouldn't lie to him but neither would I cause him grief.

"No, neither of us is really okay anymore, Charlie. We're getting older now. But it really helps when we trust one another, doesn't it?" I turned to Charlie and he allowed me to hug him. I stayed in the hug while he patted my back as if he were attempting to console me.

"What are you thinking?" I asked, wondering if this was one of those rare break-through moments. I longed for him to say something really profound.

"The surf is really loud, isn't it?" he replied.

I hadn't gotten what I'd really craved but I had gotten what was offered. And I knew instinctively that the caregiver trust was back. For Charlie and me, that was a very good day's work.

Chapter Thirty-Eight

Learning Along the Way

I was beginning to categorize my caregiving duties so as to better conceptualize them. The categories fell into groups I would name, Activities of Daily Living (ADL's), Interpersonal Activities, Emotional and Behavioral Needs and Safety Concerns. Of course, each category had subcategories and those needs would change depending on the pace of the progression of the disease.

Activities of Daily Living: For me, these were the most boring and non-rewarding caregiver duties. For others, they might bring a sense of regularity to the day and that in and of itself could be reinforcing. For Charlie, dressing, grooming and bathing and problems with incontinence would be considered ADL's. Rather than laying out all grooming aides in the mid afternoon as Charlie had been doing, everything was now put out on the bathroom counter at night just before Charlie went to bed. The visual stimulus would be a reminder to brush his teeth, comb his hair and such. Every other day, I'd put a note on the glass shower day reminding Charlie to shampoo his hair. An oily odor would always be an indicator that the task had not been completed.

Charlie would put out the clothes he was to wear the next day. Oftentimes, he would put out the same slacks for the next day, oblivious to stains and wrinkles. When he was busy with another chore, I simply tossed the soiled clothes in the laundry basket and replaced them with others that were clean and that I knew were favorites of Charlie's. He had certain clothing that he felt comfortable in and I would not try to alter that need by putting out clothing with which he was unfamiliar. In order to reduce confusion over clothing, Charlie and I had gone through his wardrobe and donated things he did not routinely wear. That way, when he chose a garment, it was likely that his choice was a perfectly acceptable one. Sometimes, Charlie's selection would seem to get *stuck* in his mind. He would wear a particular blue shirt with a Navy emblem for days and days. I purchased two other shirts of the same color and ordered Navy emblems to sew on so that Charlie could make the choice he wanted and he would still be in clean clothes.

Charlie had always worn boat shoes for casual wear and we kept those polished. He wore them so thin in the soles that they squeaked when he walked across the floors of the house. I bought him socks with gripper circles on the soles so that he could walk quietly around the house and not risk falling on the well-shined floors. Charlie could not reach down to put on his slip-on shoes so I got a shoe horn with an extended handle and he did just fine. On occasion, I would need to assist him in putting on a knit undershirt or a tee shirt. He had a favorite jacket with a button-down front and he was soon unable to button the buttons. I removed the buttons and sewed in a zipper and the problem was solved.

We didn't know the etiology of the incontinence so we decided to simply protect Charlie at all times. I brought home several different full protection underwear and Charlie experimented until he felt comfortable with one particular pair that felt very similar to his underwear. From that point on, there was no great concern about occasional bladder accidents other than to be sure we had a spare pair with us if we went outside the house. Whenever we were out, I would always remind Charlie to use the bathroom before we left where we were visiting. Charlie got so used to the reminders that one day when we went out to eat, he leaned over and asked me if it wasn't about time for me to suggest he use the bathroom!

Most of the time, neither of us drank caffeinated beverages

because of the stimulating qualities of the drink. I figured that should I want a drink with caffeine, I could do it at a time I was alone. That way, Charlie didn't feel deprived. At night, we restricted liquids to water only and even that was forbidden within three hours of bedtime. For Charlie's benefit, I used the logic that if we did not drink fluids, we would not have to get up to use the bathroom and disturb our sleep. Naturally, there was a protective cover for Charlie's mattress should an accident occur in bed. When Charlie had his occasional bouts of diarrhea, I would steel myself for the task ahead and assist Charlie in cleaning up. I was careful never to make comments that would be shaming to him. I tried to reassure him that this was all part of the problems in ageing and that we would both help one another.

Emotional and Behavioral Needs: Many of those afflicted with Alzheimer's disease or other dementias can get aggressive with their caregivers. This was never the case with Charlie and I was grateful that aggression was not one of his common symptoms. Sometimes, medication is necessary to help with aggressive behaviors.

Oftentimes, if the caregiver can understand the underlying triggers for the aggression, it can be short-lived. I personally do not believe aggression toward a caregiver (or anyone else) should be ignored in the hopes it will subside. It teaches negative behaviors and that is reinforcing to the aggressor. Speaking softly but firmly and acknowledging the anger may assist in remediating the behavior while you try to help problem-solve what initiated the action. At times talking a brief walk with the aggressor can help to soothe anger or frustration. Sometimes, music helps to reduce the tension. At other times, a simple distraction can make the aggressor stop and redirect his or her behavior.

Agitation was a problem for Charlie from time to time. He would pace, going from room to room. Sometimes, he would tap his hands on his knees or his thighs. Sometimes, with the tapping, I would pick up his hands and play a game. I remembered the simple hand tapping of "Peas Porridge Hot" from the nursery rhyme and Charlie would always like the action and the participation with me. Generally, the agitation would subside by the time the game was played out. I would always ask Charlie if he was getting "cabin fever" because he oftentimes wanted to go places. If I didn't have time for a short trip, I'd take him outside and we'd walk around the house while I pointed out the flowers that were currently blooming.

One thing I caught onto early in the disease was that Charlie did monitor *my* expressions. If I displayed worry or anger, his agitation might increase. So, I was expectedly parsimonious in my worry look from that time on. Charlie seemed to find joy in my laugh and so, I tried to display it more frequently. Perhaps, it was reassuring for him as he so oftentimes saw me as a serious person.

Hallucinations and paranoia can seriously affect both emotions and behavior. With Charlie, it was frequently associated with a medication that either was new or else, it had run its course of effectiveness. There were a couple of times when medication was not the culprit and I then understood that the brain dysfunction Charlie was experiencing was causing misfiring in the brain. I immediately made sure that there were no objects readily available so that Charlie could injure himself – or me. I also tried to get Charlie to watch nonviolent television programs thinking the violent programs might provoke feelings of anger and paranoia. On the occasions that hallucinations and delusions did occur, I did not attempt to convince Charlie that what he was seeing or hearing was not real. Rather, I would take his hands in mine and direct his eyes toward me and start to tell him a story from the past. It would be a pleasant story, usually of a time we shared and cherished during a vacation many years ago. Most of the time, this redirection seemed effective in helping the brain to readjust.

With Charlie, the paranoia seemed to be the most difficult for me. I guess that when you are a caregiver, it is sometimes seen as a personal assault when the one you love begins to accuse you of unjustly acting against his or her interests. I had to learn that the attacks had nothing to do with me and everything to do with the insidious disease which inhabited Charlie's brain. I could afford to hate the Alzheimer's disease but I could never afford to hate a husband who depended upon me in such a childlike manner.

For me, the personality changes in my husband were even more heartbreaking than the behavioral changes. Had Charlie been a quiet and reserved individual prior to the onset of his disease, it might have been a bit easier to assimilate his presentation as the disease progressed. But, Charlie was just the opposite. He was an outspoken and socially gregarious man who craved social interaction and attention. It was the first actual change that my daughter noticed. "He's just not the same, Mom," she said.

When previously, Charlie might have gotten angry about a perceived injustice, he was now bland. Generally, he had an opinion on pretty much everything but as the disease progressed, he could not retain information long enough to formulate an opinion. If he did venture to pass judgment on something, it was an unemotional statement. If he did attempt to comment on something, his views would be increasingly distorted. Sometimes, Charlie had a "potty mouth" when previously, he could be almost prudish about the same topics.

One of my attractions to Charlie had been his vibrant personality. I was basically a shy individual who had been trained to speak out. When in a crowd of people, I would oftentimes remain silent, preferring to simply take in the conversations of others. But now, as Charlie's personality disintegrated before my eyes, I frequently had to take the lead in conversations with others. Generally I would find a way to bring Charlie into the conversation by asking him to relate details of a vacation twenty years or so earlier. He had been a superb travel guide then and now, even with his impairment, he could still relate details I had long ago forgotten.

One of Charlie's more recent annoying habits was that of dismissing people abruptly. It might be a neighbor or our son-in-law or a friend or relative. Charlie would listen to the conversation for only so long and he would then dismiss the person by saying something to the effect that we had things to do or surely, they must have things to do. At such times, I would often ask Charlie to get something for me from the kitchen or elsewhere while I talked with the person or people involved. Sometimes, Charlie would come back to the gathering and we would then end the get-together in a friendlier manner. At other times, Charlie would simply disappear and I would explain about Charlie's level of tolerance for stimulation.

I tried to schedule social activities in the daytime as Charlie would sometimes have trouble with sun downing effects. This is when the affected person experiences anxiety, agitation, irritability and/or confusion around twilight time. I didn't want Charlie to become overly stimulated so that he would not fall asleep and have a restful slumber. So, for the most part, we avoided nighttime activities. Sun-downing effects were not so prominent at this stage, however, and I could readily attend to Charlie's needs.

Safety Needs: When Charlie had his first hallucination about a gun some time ago, I had immediately removed the guns from the house. Now, I tried to find places to put kitchen knives so that Charlie would not have ready access to them. Because of his hoarding and rummaging behaviors, I needed to assure myself that Charlie would not come across things that could put him in harm's way. I went through all the drawers and cupboards in the house and hid things that were potentially problematic. I disposed of other things such as duplicates of can openers and other cutting and opening devices. Charlie had always had a short, well-trimmed beard and he still wanted to shave himself. Rather than risk cutting by using a razor, I got him an electric trim device that had a protective guard next to the cutting blade.

If I saw Charlie rummaging in drawers, rather than challenge him, I would always ask if I could help him look for the desired object. He was not always able to verbally name the object he needed but he could describe it to me. I would then tell him to look in a certain drawer. I did this even though I could have gotten it for him as it seemed more respectful for him to locate what he had put so much energy into. While Charlie then retrieved the desired object, I would bring a sense of order to the drawer he had demolished!

Charlie and I agreed that his desk would be only for his things. That way, he had six special places he could rummage to his heart's content! I would occasionally go through the drawers when he was attending group. I did this to assure Charlie's safety. Besides the 52 napkins I once found, he would occasionally place silverware, keys, and other objects he had taken from other drawers. He never seemed aware that I had taken some items back to their preferred locations. I always went through trash cans when Charlie was away. It oftentimes saved me from a reduced credit score because of lost bills and notices!

I had already planned with my son and daughter to secure the house if and when Charlie began to wander. My son planned to put in a dead-bolted keypad entry and exit system when I decided we needed them. My daughter suggested an identification bracelet. I asked Charlie if we could get matching bracelets and he frowned, saying, "Do you think I'm going to get lost?" I decided to wait awhile on that but I did order one that I stashed away in my desk drawer. Our neighbors were all aware of Charlie's illness and they all offered to be on the lookout in case he wandered. I had recent photos of him in my desk drawer as well as on my cell phone so that potential helpers would be able to identify him in an emergency.

I had gotten Charlie a pay-as-you-go cellular phone and I got email messages whenever service days were about to expire. I knew it was a matter of time before Charlie would no longer be able to call but while he could, it was a task which brought him a sense of security. You can have a tracking device put on a cell phone for people with dementia. The only problem is that the phone has to be powered on in order to track. Charlie rarely had his phone on. In my mind, you simply do whatever makes you feel more secure about your loved one. The only caution I would offer is to try to anticipate how the affected person will feel about any perceived loss of respect and/or independence.

Interpersonal Activities: When going on outings with Charlie, I generally tried to go before sunset and to places with which he was familiar. I preferred more frequent outings of shorter duration so as to lessen the potential for anxiety and other problems in controlling the body, physically and cognitively.

Generally, Charlie and I were with people who had familiarity with his disorder. If on occasion, we were thrust into a situation in which the person or group were unaware of Charlie's brave fight to remain solidly in life, I would carry specifically annotated business cards. Should Charlie do something that would raise eyebrows, I would simply say, "Here, please do let me give you my business card. I'm an author and there might be a few of my books that would be of interest you." I would hand the card over. There would be a brief note on the back about Charlie's Alzheimer's condition and as the person read, I would simply keep talking about one of my books. Generally, the unwary person was immediately able to grasp the situation. The business card always worked and Charlie was never aware that a person or a group had awareness of his social faux pas.

When going to restaurants, we would generally go during non-peak hours. I would ask for a booth as not only would I have Charlie's attention seated directly across from him, the padded booths helped to absorb sounds such that remarks would not be overheard by others. If we had to wait, Charlie would become anxious and go to the hostess several times asking if our names had come up on the list. I also tended to choose restaurants in which the service was fairly quick as Charlie would get frustrated waiting for his food.

Fortunately, in the area in which we live, there are many retired people as well as several facilities catering to those elderly citizens with dementia. Most of the wait staff in highly frequented restaurants are highly understanding of having to alter menu items. I always help Charlie choose a menu item in such a way that he believes he is ordering his own food. If he appears anxious on a particular outing, I might ask if I can simply order for both of us. If the food is delayed, I oftentimes ask Charlie if he'd like to use the restroom so that we can have refills on our drinks and "not worry." It seems to make sense to him and it occupies the time necessary to the preparation of the food.

I've mentioned that even with the preparations I make prior to even considering traveling with Charlie, not everything can be anticipated. For most of us caregivers, it is not too much trouble to travel with our charge early in the process of the disease. When it gets to the point that the preparations do not result in a journey that is in any way rewarding or is, indeed, just too frustrating, it is time to discontinue traveling with your loved one. If Charlie mentions travel, I frequently turn on the travel channels and we take a visual journey together. At other times, I might get out the photo albums I made after returning from our vacations years ago. Just reviewing the cities, the countries and the experiences seems to make Charlie forget we're not actually there. The bottom line is, if you need to travel and take your loved one with you, be prepared to return early and just deal with it!

When Charlie and I are with others, he may use a round-about way to explain a concept or to identify an object. For example, Charlie might say, "We should have brought a reflection thing in the dark." I might say something like, "Yes, Charlie, you're right. We probably should have brought a flashlight with us."

When in a group of people, I try to get eye contact with Charlie so that our communications have a better chance of being understood. Sometimes, I touch his forearm to get his attention and redirect it to my face. It's a small gesture which signals in a tactile way that he is to attend to me. If Charlie says something inappropriate, I will try to redirect the conversation and ignore what he has said. I oftentimes smile at the individual to whom an inappropriate comment was made to let them know I appreciate their understanding. When with a group, I will oftentimes hold Charlie's hand so that he will not wander away and treat others to his unique ways of misunderstanding and interpreting his world.

Nothing Left to Burn - A Story of Alzheimer's Disease

I've heard caregivers talk to dementia patients with a "baby" voice and it irritates me to no end. It serves no purpose in my mind other than to emphasize to the patient and to others that they are in the presence of someone with diminished capacity. In fact, I don't even like adults talking with children in a condescending voice, whether it be by word selection or by tone of voice. Even those with advanced dementia are generally capable of one and two word instructions. With Charlie, redirection was almost always an effective means of bringing social behaviors under control. For example:

"We talked enough," Charlie might blurt out suddenly. "I want an ice cream now."

I would take his hand and say, "That's a great idea, Charlie. (Validation rather than criticism) "We'll do that on the way home." (Reinforcing the need but delaying) "Now, Susan wants to know about that opera place we saw in Verona when we visited Italy." (Redirecting) Charlie would totally forget his gustatory needs and give an intelligent travelogue about the sites in Verona, Italy."

I would be careful to always stop and get Charlie what he had requested, even if he no longer remembered. After all, it was generally such a small request and some part of him had really wanted that ice cream.

If Charlie started telling "potty stories," I would intervene immediately with something like, "Whoops, Charlie, I've misplaced the napkin for my drink. There's one on the table there (point). Would you please get it for me?" Since thoughts stay in the head of the Alzheimer's patient for such a short time, by the time Charlie walked two steps to get the napkin, he would have forgotten the inappropriate joke he was about to tell.

I never took Charlie to a business meeting but I would oftentimes take him to a social event in which I had a greater opportunity to intervene should he run into trouble. If you force your loved one into a situation you know from experience will be difficult to handle, you have set both yourself and your loved one up for disappointment.

When we got together with family for holiday events, I never really worried about Charlie. It was a given that Family would accommodate and understand. Charlie and I would discuss before leaving the house that there were certain expectations such as "talking nicely" and saying "please" and "thank you" to people who helped us. Otherwise, it was somewhat up to family to adapt to Charlie. If Charlie became anxious, I might suggest one of the grandchildren get out a photo album or tell "Poppy" about the latest baseball game. Charlie would almost always let us know when the stimulation was enough. He would either begin to clear up the clutter around him or he would stand up and say, "Time to go home now!"

During one gathering, one of my granddaughters came to me and said, "Grandma, Poppy asked me four times what grade I'm in."

"Did you tell him?" I inquired.

"Every single time," the child replied.

"Then, that's four times more that I love you to the moon and back," I responded. That simple validation always had the effect that the grandchildren felt reinforced for having the compassion to continue to interact with their Poppy.

If family members asked if they could help, I never took the martyr approach and declined the opportunity for assistance. My son-in-law might take Charlie to a movie. My son might invite us to brunch and take the initiative in talking with Charlie while I *spaced off* a bit and rested my mind. My daughter might make up a card just for Poppy to let him know how loved he was. There would be messages from each of the grandchildren. I would put it on Charlie's desk as an ongoing reminder. In the end, it was those small acts of kindness and compassion that helped me to hang in there year after year after year.

If the children or grandchildren would ask about Charlie, I always answered truthfully. When you try to hide the truth, you not only make the situation even more complicated, you deprive those willing to help of a learning opportunity as well as the opportunity to show their loved ones how much they are appreciated. Never did the grandchildren appear embarrassed about their Poppy. He was simply a wonderful man who had an insidious disease and he was coping the best he could.

Chapter Thirty-Nine

Handling Intimacy

When I first realized Charlie had begun the horrid process of losing himself, I think I pulled away emotionally. It was an almost immediate response. It was instinctual – a sort of leaving him before he was allowed to leave me kind of thing. But, that was short-lived as I began to understand that he would leave in bits and pieces and that much of my husband would continue to be mine as long as I fought for him.

When Charlie began to display prominent dependence upon me, I had to acknowledge and handle the feelings of resentment that flooded me at times. I thought I had enough on my plate without taking on all the responsibilities of Charlie's life as well. And, it's difficult for most adults to consider a sexual relationship with someone who appears childlike. For most of us, it initially appears as if we might be in an incestuous relationship! I did some visual imaging and I used my professional knowledge of neurology to reconfigure my expectations of Charlie. I researched the things I did not know or could not remember from my training. There is a wealth of information on the Internet these days. You have to pick and choose which articles best fit your needs.

Sexual intimacy was always a natural and intense part of our relationship and that would continue for some time. But then, Charlie's prostate cancer made intercourse difficult and frustrating for him and we conceptualized other ways to maintain a physical relationship. Having both taught Human Sexuality in college, we were fortunately on the same page. As the years progressed, touching and cuddling became more commonplace while other forms of sexual intimacy were put aside.

As physical intimacy waned, our shared history became an important component of couple's intimacy. We reviewed scrapbooks which held our history of vacations and our professions. Charlie never tired of reviewing a travelogue or a recounting of a day I remembered. Instead of making future shared memories of us as a couple, I began to conceptualize myself as a caregiver who would protect Charlie's functionality as well as attempt to keep him safe. Holding hands and touching became more sensual for me. At times, I would welcome the touch and at other times, I would almost cringe with the realization that the simple touch was all there was. But, I vowed that whatever form of intimacy was available to us, it would not cease until the day one of us succumbed to death.

Hypersexuality (an excessive interest in sex) sometimes affects Alzheimer's patients and that can be problematic if the caregiver is not willing to assist the loved one in easing the sexual tension. Interest does not always mean the person wants sex; rather it may be a manifestation of tension that surfaces as sexual interest. That was never a problem with Charlie as we seemed to ease into a less sexual relationship over the years. But, Charlie did manifest resistance to being touched at times. At first, it would hurt my feelings and then, I realized that the changes in his brain probably made him hypersensitive to touch and he had no control over those sensations.

Some patients with Alzheimer's disease actually forget their loved ones. Others want to establish sexual relationships with new people and this is one of the most difficult thing for the spouse/caregiver to handle. Reassurances of continued love and support are about the only thing that helps to keep a connection in such circumstances. But even then, it is a slow death for the spouse being rejected.

For the most part, I'd have to say that Charlie and I maintained a sense of connection for all of the years he battled with the disease. It was displayed in different ways and at different times as the disease progressed. But, the connection was always there. Intimate means personal, familiar, and it does not necessarily need to be a thing of the past in Alzheimer's disease. That is not the case for all couples under the same circumstances and you must not play the blame game if your loved one no longer understands that you are there to share a life together.

Chapter Forty

These Are a Few of
My Unfavorite Things

It is Sunday and Charlie is eager to go to our weekly brunch. It is still tourist season and I know every place will be crowded. But the outing is important to Charlie so I keep our routine. I think if we go a bit earlier than usual, we might beat the noon rush. So, we head out and go to Charlie's favorite restaurant. It is very crowded but they are taking orders as people wait so that when we get seated, our orders will immediately be turned in to the chefs. While we wait, Charlie reads the Sunday paper and I answer some emails on my smart phone.

We eat at the community table Charlie likes. He can always try to talk with other customers. There is a man from Wisconsin sitting alone and he talks to us about how much they like Sarasota. Soon, our food is delivered and Charlie begins to devour his lunch. I caution him to go slower as I am afraid he will choke. Later I tell him to use the bathroom.

After finishing our brunch, we decide to take a ride to the home our daughter and son-in-law are building. Charlie likes the drive. We pass a grocery store on the way to the new home and I ask Charlie if he needs anything. He says he is fine. We had just grocery-shopped the day before. The house is coming along well. It now has all the floors tiled and the kitchen cabinets, counter tops and appliances are all in. The pool has been caged and the lawn has been graded. Charlie and I are so happy for the children.

I haven't been sleeping well again and I'm pretty sure it's allergies keeping me awake. Days ago, I had asked Charlie if he would sweep the leaves every day as they tended to make my allergies flare up. Every day he forgets. When we get home, Charlie immediately goes into the bathroom. He may be in there for some time, so I go outside to sweep the leaves that have fallen from the live oak tree. In the early spring, the leaves all fall off as the new leaves appear so that the tree is never bare. When the new leaves appear, they are accompanied by pollen. I decide to rake some of the leaves and bag them for the waste management truck which will come in the morning. When I am finished, Charlie comes out.

"I need a Sunday paper," Charlie says. This means he wants me to drive him.

"Charlie, you read the paper at the restaurant."

"Yeah, but I didn't *get* a paper," he argues.

This is true. However, Charlie has read the paper and it seems a waste to purchase it just so that Charlie can have a physical paper to throw away. But, he simply won't let it go. I guess these notions just get stuck in his head. It's not worth the argument so I take Charlie to a gas station a mile away and he goes in to purchase a paper.

When we get home, I watch my husband as he sorts out the ads and puts them aside. He then takes each section of the paper, unfolds it and looks at the front page. Then, having barely read a word of it, he stacks the entire paper and takes it out to the recycling bin in the garage. He is apparently satisfied that he has *gotten* the paper.

Later that day, Charlie wants a treat. He says he wants a cup of flan. I am in the kitchen so I pull the flan from the refrigerator, get a spoon from the drawer and take it to Charlie who is already watching television. He takes a bite, looks at the spoon and says, "You brought me the wrong spoon."

"Charlie, it's a spoon," I say trying not to become irritated. "What's wrong with it?"

"It's one of those that don't match." Well, Charlie is right. I have bought four extra stainless steel spoons because we use up our set of eight rapidly.

"Charlie, it still scoops up the flan just fine.'

"But, it doesn't match," Charlie looks at me and adds, "So the flan doesn't taste the same."

It's useless to even attempt to understand the logic. I go to the kitchen drawer, pull out one of the eight matching spoons and take it to Charlie. He's happy as I go back to the kitchen, rinse off the offending spoon and place it in the dishwasher. *Remember that one, Karen* I tell myself. If I can remember Charlie's quirks, I can save myself aggravation. But then, I am angry because I have to remember so many things that aggravate Charlie. I am tense today and easily irritated. And I fully understand, there is so much more to come. I rationalize that as soon as the live oak has its new leaves, I will feel better and I will be more patient. That's probably a lie but at least it works for that particular day.

It is now four-thirty in the afternoon. Charlie has closed the front door and he begins to close all the blinds. I immediately feel trapped in my own home. I go back and open the front door so that the sun can shine in from the glass storm door. I ask Charlie to please leave the blinds alone. He has started his sundowning process a bit early. He goes into the bedroom to begin to lay out his clothes for the morning. As he is taking the pillows off the bed, I remind him that it is early to start preparations for the next day. He says "Okay" and I know it is meaningless as Charlie will repeat the routine the next day, and the next. Even with notes all around the house, he still does his routines. Soon, he will lay all his personal items all over the bathroom counter. I can only hope we don't have unexpected company.

I love having the house open and sunny. I love to be in tune with nature. It has always been a relaxing force for me. Now, Charlie's disease attempts to shut me off from almost everything that is soothing and assuring. While some battles I choose to avoid, I am taking a stand on Charlie's compulsive behaviors and I will not yield. Every afternoon, I undo what Charlie has done. Sometimes, he simply repeats the routine but at other times, he doesn't seem to notice. It is these small, annoying and never-ending things that are among my least favorite things in the caregiving role. I'm not sure why but the compulsive behaviors seem to give me the feeling that the house is no longer my own. It accommodates only to Charlie's personal needs.

A few days ago, a friend I hadn't seen for a few months thought I looked worn out and that I had aged considerable. I know she was right and still, it hurt me to have my own observations verified. She was very supportive but I knew that despite her love and support, my problems with Charlie would not go away.

A few days later, I break down. I want Charlie to see how his routines are frustrating and unnecessary. I haven't slept for two nights now. I am tired and the pollens outside are getting stronger. Charlie has not swept up the leaves as he promised he dutifully promised and the pollen is rampant. When I leave the house today, I deliberately leave out all of my things on the bathroom counter. It's a spiteful thing to do and, at that moment, I really don't care. I don't put away the breakfast dishes. I just leave everything out on the counters like Charlie does. I close the blinds like Charlie does – in the middle of the day. The house looks closed up and simply horrible. Then, I simply go out, do my work out and run errands, feeling tired and unappreciated.

Charlie arrives home from group and he does notice things are different. He begins to laugh which is *totally* the wrong thing to do when I'm having a meltdown. He has no clue as to what my big-time, childish hints are meant to convey and he continues to laugh. I try to explain that his compulsions sometimes get me so annoyed that I have to let him know the effects they have on me.

"They don't bother me," Charlie replies.

"I know, Charlie," I reply with tears in my eyes. "But for me, a sense of order is really important."

"Then, why did you make such a mess?" he asks.

As it is now later that same day, I am beginning to regain myself so I ignore Charlie's answer and I begin to pick up the things in the kitchen and open the blinds. Just letting in some light helps a little bit. I walk into the bathroom, intending to put away my personal things on the counter. Then, in a moment of spite, I simply leave it there. My thinking is that if Charlie sees my things there tonight, he might just understand how annoying it is for me when I have to contend with his laying-out rituals time and time again. But later, I go in and put away my things. I know Charlie will not remember my message and instead, he will be upset that he has no room for his personal items on the counter. His being upset tonight is not worth my trying to make a statement.

I know I am being childish acting out like this. But, at times, it seems as if my very sanity depends upon my being able to look around my house, inside and outside, so that I might assure myself that there is beauty and organization to life. It's important that I own up to these things. My melt-downs are proof of my frustrations, proof of my sense of an unjust rule and proof of my humanity.

Chapter Forty-One

A Prayed-For Hiatus

Charlie has suddenly started to help around the house and I am shocked! It is allergy season here and every morning, he sweeps the leaves in front. On Saturday, he cleans the bathroom as best he can. I will get what he has missed when he is at group. This has gone on for about two weeks. I try to think about what Charlie has been eating or doing that might account for his sudden willingness to help out. As I am writing this, Charlie comes into my office. Fortunately, the computer screen is not visible to him. He asks if we can go out to brunch and I immediately suspect why he has been willing to help. I remind him of our agreement to eat out once a week and he fades before my eyes. I have to do something immediately.

"Charlie, are you helping out to show me you care about the house?'

"Yeah," he says. "And I can see you are busy so I'm helping you."

I am astounded! I haven't had Charlie display this kind of awareness for months! I know I have to reinforce it but I wonder how I can do it without breaking my own rules.

"Charlie, let's not waste our time together eating out. I'll make a brunch here and then, we'll drive to Venice, walk the streets and look in the windows for interesting things"

"Then can we go get a gelato at that Italian store?" Charlie asks, his blue eyes twinkling in anticipation.

"I was hoping you'd say that!" I answered. I saved my document and went to make brunch.

We drove to Venice after cleaning up the lunch dishes and Charlie barely said a word. He appeared deep in thought but he was not able to convey those thoughts to me. I asked him several times to share his thoughts but he just looked frustrated and remained silent. We walked the main street in Venice and we went into a couple of shops. In one store, Charlie asked me to "Go away and don't come back for a while."

I wandered to another aisle but was not about to leave Charlie alone. Finally, I spotted him in the check-out counter and I waited until he finished with his purchase. It looked to me as if he had maybe purchased a card. We went to get our gelato and then, we drove back to Sarasota. By then, Charlie was nearly mute.

After dinner that night, I sat with Charlie while he watched his two game shows. I fed him clues so that he could participate. When the shows were ended, Charlie got up and went into his office. He came back to the great room and handed me a card saying, "I got this for you."

On the outside of the envelope was written "Karen." The greeting immediately saddened me as Charlie had always used my nickname of "Sam" when presenting something personal. That nickname had had its birth on our wedding night. After a hectic day, Charlie had rented a house on the beach at the tip of Long Island in New York. After dinner, we showered and then lay on the bed, both heated with expectation. Strangely, I was very nervous and I said, "Charlie, I have the strangest feeling I've been here before." It was a reference to my first marriage and I immediately knew it was a stupid thing to say. But, Charlie was unaffected. He took my chin in his right hand and tipped my head to plant a gentle, reassuring kiss. While doing so, he said, "Then, play it again, Sam." And the nickname stuck with me for twenty-five years, until the day Charlie forgot it.

I opened the envelope Charlie had presented and took out the card. It was of those artistic Blue Mountain Arts cards that had special verses. The front of the card said, "If my heart could speak to you, you would know how much you mean to me." I was touched and somewhat astounded. It seemed to be some kind of recognition on Charlie's part that he had deep feelings even though the words were no longer there to verbalize those feelings.

Inside the card, Charlie had put a paragraph sign on the writing at the side of the card. He had handwritten, "My feelings exactly."

The card read, "Sometimes, I forget that you can't see into my heart or know what I'm feeling when I think of you.

This is for the times when I don't tell you how wonderful you are or how much I love you and appreciate your presence in my life.

This reminder from my heart expresses all my special thoughts and feelings for you – because sometimes I forget to tell you how very much you mean to me."

The card is signed at the bottom, "Your Charlie, 'til the end of time!"

I couldn't speak. It was as if time had granted a small window into Charlie's brain and he took advantage of that window and gave me something for which I had been longing.

Charlie asked me if I liked the card and, holding back tears, I told him it was the very best present he could ever have given to me. He literally glowed with a sense of pride. I hugged him. Then, I went outside to try to compose myself.

I wondered for quite some time if my recent meltdown had somehow upset Charlie to the degree that he accessed a part of himself I thought had been lost to the ages. I had no explanation for his voluntary participation in simple chores and his spontaneous display of his feelings. I wondered if I had somehow stumbled upon a miraculous treatment for Alzheimer's disease, some sort of emotional shock treatment. But then, as suddenly as it had appeared, the window to Charlie's soul disappeared. It was a teasing window which both delighted and tortured me. It would be the last of his giving for a very long time. But, Charlie's card remains in my desk drawer where each and every day, I take it out, read the verses and remember who Charlie and I were together.

Chapter Forty-Two

Strange Noises in the Night

Charlie nearly always goes to sleep now very early in the evening. Lately, he's been producing some strange noises. His breathing is not always regular. There may be a few seconds in between intakes of air and his stomach will rise and fall rather than his lungs. I watch him as he seemingly struggles to recapture a rhythmic breathing pattern. At times, he has a rattle to the intake of breath, much like someone with a respiratory infection. At those times, I go to him and check him for a fever but he has none. Oftentimes, Alzheimer's patients will succumb to infections and/or pneumonia and I want to catch an infection before it become troubling to Charlie's body. Charlie's blood pressure has gone way down and that is also a frequent occurrence in people with dementia. It is almost as if the entire body is slowing down to accommodate for the lack of brain cells able to convey vital body functioning messages.

There are so very many things that could go wrong at this time. I've talked with my adult children about providing a safe environment for Charlie while still allowing him some sense of dignity. It's a thin line and I oftentimes question myself. When Charlie rummages in the medications, I ask what he is getting. Since he finds everything I hide, I have no assurance that he will not someday take a medication in the wrong dosage. I have a lockbox and I am considering putting the drugs in there. Charlie would be devastated if he didn't see his pill bottles on their usual place in the pantry. I have left vitamins and supplements there so that he can touch them when he needs to do so. It seems to have a calming effect on him just to look at the pill bottles. So, I again hide the prescribed medications and I leave the supplements in the pantry. Sometimes, Charlie picks them up and touches them. At other times, he will open the bottle, carefully take out one pill and put it in the plastic cup beside the supplement bottles. I know then that he has a trace memory of having done that for himself for the past fifty years. I can always hear him scrutinizing his pill bottles. When he is finished, I go in and check to see that he has added only one pill. If so, I leave the small cup for him to take in the morning. If he has accidentally added more than one pill, I take out the additional supplement and place it back in the bottle. In the evening, I add Charlie's prescribed medications to the small cup and he will take it in the morning.

Charlie has always gotten up before me in the mornings. Lately, he will sleep in on days he does not go to his group. Usually, when I enter his room, he is in the shower. Sometimes, he has been in the bathroom for an hour or so and I simply keep myself busy with computer work until he finishes and dresses. Several times lately, Charlie has still been in bed when I enter the room. I always stand still while my heart pounds. I go to him and feel for a pulse. His pulse will be very slow and I immediately go to check his pill cup. It is still there, with all the pills not yet consumed. I relax and stroke Charlie's arm and he awakens and smiles at me. I tell him I will shower first and he should just stay in bed and awaken gradually. I go to the bathroom and shut the door, locking it. Lately, Charlie has been bursting into the bathroom and playing peek-a-boo when I am undressed. I think I understand the childlike need and I make it a point to lay naked with him in bed after such episodes. I want him to understand limits and boundaries for as long as possible.

While in the shower, I silently go through what I would have done had Charlie not had a pulse. It is shocking to me that I would be thinking these things and I wonder if I am such a bad person that I want Charlie to go silently in the night. Then again, I don't want that. It is only my stress talking.

We continue to attend the activities of the grandchildren. When at a baseball or softball game, Charlie eats nonstop. My daughter and I look at one another and she gives me a *what does it really matter* look. I agree. I watch Charlie get up from his chair. During the hour and a half the game is in progress, he gets up five times. He comes back with a hot dog and he demolishes that. He rises and goes to get French fries and he eats ravenously. He gets up to use the restroom. He comes back with a Reese's Peanut Butter Cup and eats that. He rises and says he will use the restroom again, forgetting he used it ten minutes earlier. He comes back empty-handed and sits for about three minutes. He rises and goes again to the concession stand. They now know him by name and he thinks they are his friends. He comes back with a package of chips. He asks about the game and I give him a recap he will not remember.

Later that night while Charlie is watching television and I am working in my office on the computer, he says, "Hey, when are the kids playing ball?"

"Charlie, we went to two ballgames today. We went to the softball tournament in the morning. Just a while ago, we went to the baseball game. Clay got a double play at second base and Celia got out two guys at home plate."

"She did?"

"Yes, Charlie, she did."

"I'm so proud of her. Not many girls can play catcher in that league."

"Right, Charlie."

"What did Clay do? Did he play today?"

"Yes, Charlie. Clay was the starting pitcher and he did well. Later, he played shortstop and he made a double play."

"That's good for somebody that's only six, right?"

"Sweetheart, Clay is eight, going on nine now."

"When did that happen?"

"While you were eating, I guess," I said, tongue-in-cheek.

"Oh," Charlie said, not really comprehending my droll attempt at humor.

Nothing Left to Burn - A Story of Alzheimer's Disease

There are still days that are relatively calm and others that are a series of one surprise after another. The latter are becoming more frequent as Charlie finds ways to reveal the depth of his compromised brain. Those are the days that I lay awake at night and wonder if I will find Charlie sleeping the final sleep the next morning.

Charlie wanted to go to the mall the other day and I told him I would take him in an hour. He said he couldn't wait and he would take the bus. I got up from my work and asked him to wait but he was already out the door, headed to the bus stop just down the street. I chased after him but with my bad knee, Charlie was now faster than me. That in itself was disconcerting! Charlie got to the bus stop just as the bus pulled up and he got in. I felt reassured that he would be delivered safely. Lately, I fear having him cross the streets alone. The bus would take him to the mall entrance. Charlie was to call me when he was ready to come home and I'd pick him up at the mall. After two hours, there was no call. I tried calling his cell phone but he had not turned it on. I tried calling several more times without success. Finally, I got in the car and drove to the mall, knowing full well that the chances of my finding him were not all that great. I searched to no avail and then had the mall office page Charlie. No one came. I went home and there was Charlie. I asked him if he had taken the bus home and he said, "I didn't have to. I met a man at the mall. He's a Vet too and he brought me all the way home."

"Charlie, that could have been a dangerous decision, you know" I said trying to remain calm.

"I think he knew I wouldn't hurt him," Charlie replied with a look of concern on his face.

"Charlie," I said, with growing concern. I had raised my voice.

"You should really work on keeping your emotions in check," Charlie said. That stopped me dead in my cognitive tracks. I looked at Charlie who was looking quite self-satisfied.

Then, I started to laugh and I said, "Yeah, I guess you're right, Charlie." He walked away feeling very superior that day!

That night was a sleepless night for me. I had visions of Charlie trusting the wrong person. I played versions in my mind of how I might restrict Charlie from such ventures on his own. Then, I weighed his need for dignity and a sense of independence. In the end, everyone who really loved and cared for Charlie was in agreement; there were many ways to succumb to death. Charlie had always said he'd go out fighting. He wanted to be a warrior to the end. We all knew that and we all respected his right to choose.

Chapter Forty-Three

Spinning off the Merry-Go-Round

I have been checking out all the information on the National Alzheimer's Association website to see if I've missed any important information that might have recently appeared. I do that regularly as they are a wonderful resource for information and support for the caregivers. I am checking out the latest research about the disease when Charlie comes into my office.

"I need different underwear," Charlie says.

"Charlie, I just bought a huge package of the kind you like. There's no blue underwear in the package, Charlie. You said you don't like the blue underwear, only the grey."

"Okay, I only like the grey then," Charlie replied.

"Then what's the question?" I ask.

"It doesn't fit right."

"Charlie, we've tried out several brands of underwear and this is the only kind that you *DO* like," I respond in mild frustration. I try to pin him down. "What bothers you about the underwear, Charlie?"

"It gets wet. It doesn't work."

"Charlie, if you have an accident, your underwear will get wet. That is the time that you take it off and put on another pair of underwear."

"I don't have accidents. I'm not a little boy."

"Yes, of course, honey, but sometimes urges just creep up on us and we can't help it. Just change your wet underwear, Charlie."

"But then, that one won't work either."

It's a circular argument based upon a faulty premise and I cannot argue it. Probably, when the underwear gets wet, it feels different and Charlie is thinking it doesn't fit. I think for a while and then I say, "Charlie, I think what you're telling me is that we got exactly the right kind of underwear." This tactic is called *reframing*.

Charlie looks confused so I continue. "See, that underwear is supposed to collect moisture from your body that you don't need. If your underwear is getting wet, then it is doing a wonderful job. It is doing just what it's supposed to do. But, when the underwear does its job, then you have to take it off and get a pair that is dry."

"So it can take more moisture from my body?" Charlie asks.

"Yes, exactly, Charlie!" I am pleased that he has tracked my reasoning. There is a bit of the scientist in him yet!

"So, I don't have to get new underwear?" Charlie asks, needing additional assurance.

"That's right, Charlie. You got exactly the right kind of underwear and it's doing a good job."

Charlie studies my face for a few seconds. I have no idea what he's looking for but pretty soon, he turns to leave my office and he says, "Sorry, I gotta go pee!"

Charlie leaves and I shake my head. Averting disaster is what it's all about these days. I think about Charlie's underwear and I wonder why babies have diapers named Loves or Pampers or Huggies, all names that seem to imply a natural process of love and acceptance. Why not make adult diapers with names that convey automatic acceptance of what is happening in the body? I spend about five minutes wandering in my mind, trying to come up with acceptable labels for adult diapers. Even though I always refer to them as underwear to Charlie, I know they are diapers. I think about a brand I would name Tender for Men. It would have a fake fly opening painted on the front of the underwear. But no, that would confuse an Alzheimer's patient and probably, he would dig through the padding trying to open it. So, what about something named

Alluring? It would be for women and it would have paper lace on the leg openings. But, that might scratch and annoy women with needs for paper underwear. Then, my mind wanders to the commercials about adult protective underwear. There is one in which a burly man announces that you can "Guard your manhood" by wearing their product. It makes me ponder whether one's manhood lies in the urethra. Probably not, I reason. I think about starting a company called "Geriatric Glamour" but decide against it as I then switch my thinking to what I will prepare for dinner.

Most of our days are like this now. We have outings. We eat nutritious meals. We get on the merry-go-round and we go up and down on the horses. On some days, we wind to an end and we get off the amusement ride. On other days, the ride just never stops and we wait for an opportunity and then, we just spin off and hope that we'll not land in harm's way.

Chapter Forty-Four

Long-Distance Friends

A long-distance friend sent me flowers today. I emailed her my gratitude but I wonder if I really conveyed how much her support really means to me. Another long-distance friend sent a loving email and of course, I replied. My sister is a long-distance friend who takes my words and assesses them for need and for over seventy years, she has been my constant. My long-distance friends need to know that on some days, their words of love and support are really all that keep me from breaking. The words are what motivate me to clean up Charlie's messes and to tell him fifty times that today is Thursday. Many are the days that the words of a friend touch my heart and bring me to tears, all in a good way. Words are a means of stress relief, the same as lifting weights or running. Sometimes, words simply assure me I have the strength to get up and do it again. Sometimes, the words assure me that in an insane situation, I have remained sane. At other times, a word or two simply assures me I am loved, whether I have done my duties with grace or with frustration and anger. My friends are the wind beneath my wings.

As I think back over the months and years my friends have stayed with me in times of stress, I am amazed by their loyalty. They live in at least six different states, thousands of miles from where I live and yet, I feel I can go to them at will. One lives in Canada and another in Australia. Many have known me for nearly seventy years now. Some know more about me than I know about myself. I might send a perfectly innocuous email about my day and my long-distance friends read my moods and my needs. They answer back in just the right way. Sometimes, when I am unable to put into words what I have faced that day, I might send a chapter of my manuscript and they will immediately attend to its actual as well as its implied content. Even though they are long-distance friends, they are not superficial friends. They are friends of the heart.

Each and every one of my friends has faced heartache in her life, some more than others. One lost a job she loved. Another lost a son. Others have faced bitter rejection from family and friends. One friend's husband took his life and yet, she persevered and raised her children. Another was widowed and still another was betrayed by a husband. We World War II babies were raised with the understanding that self-sufficiency is not only a desirable trait; it is a must. But, we also learned the value of love and support for those who might have it *worse* than we. Of course the *worse* past was always situational. We sturdy long-distance friends seemed to grow with the understanding that life owes you nothing and that fairness is a circumstance to be wished for and not taken for granted.

My long-distance friends take some of the burden from my family and my immediate friends here in Sarasota, Florida. I think to the times that my days were so flooded with grief that there were not enough people immediately available to lift the burden from me. But, with each and every email, the tension would ease; my heartbeat would revert to a more normal pace; my fears would subside just enough so that competence could overcome the fears of inadequacy. And I would go on.

And so, thank you, my long-distance friends.

Chapter Forty-Five

Uncertainties

Charlie had a choking episode while at his group. He was eating meatballs and rice and he probably gulped down the dish without chewing properly. He is always so eager to eat that he takes way too much in his mouth, chews rapidly to soften the food, and then he swallows food that is not properly chewed. As a result, he has choking episodes from time to time. The first time it happened, Charlie was scared and he insisted on going to the emergency room of a nearby hospital. It cost hundreds of dollars while we sat and waited for the episode to pass. I talked with the nurse and we both agreed this was something that we could handle at home.

The Senior Center tried to call me several times but my phone was not ringing. When Charlie got home, he told me about the episode. He related how the nurse had stayed with him until the spasms stopped and he then went back to join the group. He spoke without anxiety and in a bland tone of voice. After telling me about the choking incident, he said, "I really had a good day."

After Charlie related the story, I looked at my phone log and I was shocked to see I had over a dozen missed calls. I then realized that my phone setting must have been on the *silence* mode. When I checked, sure enough, it was on the silence setting. My granddaughter changed it back for me. Several days ago, I had let a child play games with it while I went about helping with chores and inadvertently, the setting had been changed.

Nothing Left to Burn - A Story of Alzheimer's Disease

Two days later, one of the nurses from the Senior Friendship Center called me to tell me in more detail about the incident. She said she had twice used the Heimlich on Charlie. I responded that I had once used it with Charlie as well and that I also tried just rubbing Charlie's back and that seemed to relax him. The nurse said she thought it was spasms and I said the doctor and I were unsure as to whether it was related to Charlie's diagnosis of Barrett's Esophagus (a pre-cancerous condition of the esophagus) or to the malfunctioning of the frontal lobe due to Alzheimer's. The nurse also commented that Charlie did not really seem anxious about the choking episode. I related that in the past year, his emotions have become remarkably bland. I commented that prior to the onset of the Alzheimer's symptoms, Charlie had been emotionally quite demonstrative. The nurse reminded me that I needed to be continually available by phone and I thanked her for helping Charlie in his time of need.

I hung up the phone realizing that I now had to be available 24/7, even when Charlie was in the care of someone else. For a moment, I felt like a prisoner but then, the feeling passed and I was simply grateful that Charlie had gotten through another choking episode.

The next day was a busy day as Charlie and I were going to look for a new sectional to replace the two sofas we had used for the past twenty years. We finally found one that suited Charlie just fine. It had a comfortable power recliner built in as well as a cup holder for his beverages. Lately, there had been some spilling events as Charlie reached for his glass on the side table next to his easy chair.

"Now, I don't have to reach so far and there's a special place for my glass!" Charlie said proudly as I paid for the sectional with my credit card.

The sectional would not be delivered for five days. Since my daughter was holding a garage sale prior to their move, I decided to take Charlie's lounge chair as well as my own to the sale. They sold immediately and that left me with the problem of attempting to acclimate Charlie temporarily to the two remaining sofas which he rarely used. I tried moving the coffee table over so that he could lean back on the sofa and put his legs out as he had done on his old reclining lounge chair. He told me that arrangement didn't work for him. I tried moving in a wing-backed chair from the bedroom and placing an ottoman in front of it. Charlie said that didn't work either.

For the next four nights, I continually tried to make Charlie feel comfortable while he watched his nightly television programs. Nothing seemed to work and I finally realized it was the *change in what was known* that was the problem rather than the chairs themselves. I gave him my sympathy and told him we just had to *rough it* and he finally fell asleep on one of the sofas.

We were about to head to the grandchildren's baseball game when I noticed that Charlie's shirt had spots of food on it and his pants were very dirty. I asked him to change and he said he'd change "tomorrow." There was just not time to argue with him at that moment so he went to the game in dirty clothes. As it turned out, he got food all over his dirty clothes at the ballgame anyway. Again, it was a lesson to me that some things are just not important enough to argue about. Here's Charlie's reasoning on the subject:

"See, those players have on dirty clothes too," Charlie said, looking somewhat defiant.

"But, Charlie, that kid just slid into home plate. Of course his pants are dirty now."

"They probably were dirty before."

"Why is that, Charlie?"

"It's probably not the first time he slid into base, you know."

Later that day, we were to meet my daughter's family at a nice restaurant to celebrate my grandson's ninth birthday. I asked Charlie to change his clothes for dinner. I modeled by changing the clothes I had worn to the ballgame.

"I'll change tomorrow," Charlie said.

"Charlie, this is a nice restaurant and anyway, we both agreed that we'd try to look nice for Clay's birthday party."

"Will Clay change his clothes too?" Charlie asked.

Nothing Left to Burn - A Story of Alzheimer's Disease

I thought of the baseball uniform Clay had on earlier in the day and I responded, "Of course he will, Charlie."

"Okay, then I will too," Charlie said. He willingly went to the closet and pulled out a nice pair of slacks and a clean shirt. He came out of the bedroom grinning and I told him he looked wonderful. I quickly ran to the bedroom to retrieve Charlie's dirty clothes and I buried them in the laundry basket so he would not wear them the next day.

The following morning was our usual grocery-shopping day. I reminded Charlie that we would not go to brunch because we had just been out the previous night. He tried to argue that the birthday outing "didn't count" but I held my ground. We took off for the grocery store.

As usual, I took a cart for the items I would need for us for the coming week. Charlie took another cart and got his newspaper, chocolate milk and other necessities for the week. We were to meet at the checkout.

When we got to the checkout, Charlie immediately put his items in my basket and took the other cart to the store entrance. I began to put the items on the conveyor belt and was frustrated with what I saw. Charlie had again gotten himself a basketful of treats. There were several people lined up behind me and I didn't want to make a scene by attempting to put back items. So, everything went on our grocery bill.

I had not anticipated the bill would be large as I still had several frozen items as well as foods in the pantry that would be used for our weekly meals. The grocery bill was only $76.57 but Charlie's treats alone totaled $44.26! I showed him how much we had spent on the treats when we arrived home. He smiled and said, "I guess I get a lot of good things this week, don't I!"

I just looked at Charlie until he said, "You look confused."

I said, "I don't think I'm confused, Sweetheart. I'm maybe a bit frustrated is all."

"Same thing," Charlie replied as he eagerly opened a package of blueberry muffins.

I was still uncertain when to take a stand and when to let things go. I was gradually learning to let things go simply to maintain my own sanity. Eating was such a pleasure for Charlie. And, I had to admit: he was SO good at it!

Chapter Forty-Six

Relevant Beatitudes

Blessed is the Senior Friendship Center for they can provide joy to Charlie that I cannot. Charlie still attends his group three times weekly and he is content to eat cookies, sing songs and wait for the visiting dog Ace to come. He loves to sing and lately, the leader has been asking him to read funny stories to the group. He really likes the attention he gets there and I am so happy he can still feel a sense of personal worth.

My ability to provide joy to Charlie is by now, mostly in the form of taking him to visit the grandchildren so he can vicariously participate in their lives. Last night, we went to another baseball game. We figured it to be a runaway as the team we were to play was unbeaten.

At one time during the first inning, my daughter said, "Mom?" I turned and she was sitting with a young man.

"This is Kevin," my daughter said. I shook hands and said I had heard about the young man. He was renting the house next door with two male housemates. All three men were in spring training with the Baltimore Orioles at the Sarasota complex. They were all pitchers.

The game was intriguing as our team was hanging tough. Our granddaughter was the team catcher and she was allowing no one to escape home via passed balls. Our grandson got on base twice and both times, he stole home. Then, he went in to pitch and, with the bases loaded, struck out the side for a win for our team!

After the game, my daughter told me the Orioles pitcher had texted his agent saying there was a little stud (meaning my grandson) on the mound and that the agent should keep the kid in mind for future business! Charlie had to laugh about that one and it was a joy to see him experiencing such a good time. But, perhaps even more importantly, I caught myself laughing out loud and it took me a moment to recognize the sensation of really feeling good all over!

I knew I had to work on myself. As a child, the world had seemed magical and exciting. Of course, it was also sad after the early death of my mother. But, during past adversity, I had always chosen to allow the pleasant to override the sadness of life. Lately, I caught myself allowing my mind to dwell on sadness for periods of time. Perhaps, that is somewhat normal in the aging process and it was even more pronounced with what Charlie and I were going through.

Lately, a feeling of chronic tiredness would set in unannounced. On those days, I would take myself away from the house and go to where people were doing normal, everyday activities. One time, it might be to a public park and at another time, maybe the mall. I loved going to the ballpark to watch softball and baseball. Not only was the game entertaining, the families there cheering on their athletes always reminded me of days spent with my own children in their younger years. Generally, I would come home refreshed and with a better sense of the fact that Charlie's story was just part of the grand scheme of things.

~~~

It was moving week for my daughter and her family. I went to the house to prepare for a garage sale and because Charlie was not in group, I took him with me. I designated tasks and sometimes he would do a simple task but at other times, he would just stare at me with a blank look on his face. He was forgetting so many things now and it just broke my heart. I asked him to pin tags onto the clothing hanging up and I watched while he attempted the task. His hands would shake and he stuck himself with pins several times. I teared up and directed him to another task. There was very little he could do anymore without supervision and assistance.

During the actual garage sale, I took Charlie to the mall and picked him up after the sale had ended. I didn't even tell him about the fact that I would be helping at the sale and he seemed to have forgotten all about it.

When I went over to help pack up the house in preparation for the move, Charlie again asked if the family was moving. Every day, I would tell him about the move, hoping he would remember that we would soon have to go to another house to visit the grandchildren. Again, Charlie wanted to help with the preparations. My daughter finally had him pack up the pantry. Charlie spent more time looking at the food than he did packing up the dry goods, but he did seem content. Afterwards, he told me it was "very hard work." He stood watching me and two of the granddaughters pack and he appeared amazed that we were able to get things so easily organized for the move.

On the day of the move, my daughter and son-in-law had to go sign their closing papers. Charlie and I went over to their home while the movers were taking out boxes and furniture to the moving van. The family dog was getting a bit hyperactive with all the commotion so I put her in her cage. She sleeps in the cage at night and she routinely goes into the cage in the daytime to sleep. After I put the dog into her resting place, she immediately started to bark and pace. I put a chair next to the cage and asked Charlie to sit there and talk with the dog. Immediately, the dog calmed down and Charlie had an important job to do. The dog seemed to sense Charlie's vulnerability. It was as if she and Charlie had some unwritten form of kinship.

It was a very long moving day and Charlie began to decompensate as the hours went by. He paced and he tapped his hands and he asked the same questions over and over again. Finally, I stopped trying to help inside and took Charlie outside and told him we would go home. Charlie looked at the moving van and asked, "Are they moving?"

Blessed are those with Alzheimer's disease for they shall eventually forget everything that makes them anxious.

Chapter Forty-Seven

Sensory Distortions

As my daughter was going to take our old sofa and loveseat set to the new house, Charlie and I went to several furniture stores and finally, Charlie found a sectional that seemed to suit his needs. Two of the sections reclined and the sectional also provided good support for him to rise out of the chair. I went to pay for the sectional and arrange for the delivery. The salesman asked "Alzheimer's?" and it took me by surprise. Most people did not pay attention to Charlie when we were out together. Or perhaps, they were just polite and didn't want to ask. I wondered what behaviors of Charlie's the salesman had identified as Alzheimer's symptoms.

The salesman saw the surprise on my face as I nodded that he was correct. He told me his mother suffered from the disease and that he had picked up the classic symptoms of blandness in Charlie's speech. He also said Charlie's word selection seemed a bit "off" at times. It really took me back that a stranger could now recognize the dementia in my husband, simply by his speech. Charlie's persuasive verbal intelligence was now definitely a thing of the past.

On the day the sectional was delivered, I stood back and looked at the setting in order to see how to accessorize and make the room inviting. The sectional was a dark leather color and the two large pictures on the wall did nothing to make the room look bright and warm. Just as I was thinking what to do about the pictures, Charlie came into the room.

"I don't want those pictures in the bedroom," Charlie announced referring to the two paintings we'd had on our bedroom wall for the past twenty years.

"Why is that, Charlie? You told me you loved those pictures."

"Well, maybe I did but they've changed," Charlie said.

"How have they changed?" I asked.

"They look all weird now. I don't like them."

I thought and thought and then realized that Charlie's visual distortions probably made the pictures look odd. The pictures were treasured renditions of ballet dancers. The artist had also studied medicine. The dancers' bodies featured beautiful muscles and veining in the arms and the legs of the dancers. For Charlie, the nearly translucent skin of the dancers now seemed distorted. As the disease progresses, this is a common occurrence in Alzheimer's. As noted earlier, caregivers sometimes have to cover a television screen or a mirror because the images create confusion for the patient. We had purchased the paintings at an art gallery shortly after our marriage. At the time, we had thought of the dancers as performing the dance of love that Charlie and I had felt for one another. Now, they had become a source of anxiety and confusion. It was just another loss, albeit a cruel one.

I immediately took down the pictures of the dancers and placed them in a closet. I took the pictures from the great room and hung them in Charlie's bedroom. His face instantly brightened. One of the paintings had a circle and another had a square. Both were decorated in metals and subtle earth tone paint colors. "These are better," Charlie said. "They didn't get all weird like the others," he added.

We went picture shopping together. I wanted to assure myself that whatever we had in the room with the television set was something that would relax Charlie rather than cause him anxiety. We finally settled on two pieces of art that would complement the room. Charlie was very appreciative and he said, "You decorate really good." Even though I was now getting used to the simplicity of Charlie's speech compared to the verbal sophistication I had learned to love in the college professor, it still took me by surprise at times.

~~~

"Charlie, why is the drain strainer out of the drain in the laundry room?

"I took it out to pour something down the drain."

"But, Charlie, the drain stopper is supposed to be in there to catch things so they *won't* go down the drain."

"But that wouldn't work. You should know that."

"Why wouldn't it work, Charlie?"

"Because the things to go down the drain are too big to go through the stopper thing."

"That's the point, Charlie. We don't want bigger things to go down the drain. So, we put in the drain stopper and then, we don't clog up the drain."

"But then, the stopper gets all clogged. You should know that."

"Charlie, that's what a drain stopper is for. It picks up the larger objects and then they don't get caught in the drain and clog up the drain."

"That's stupid! All you do is clog up the drain stopper instead."

I couldn't argue it with Charlie. The logic simply wasn't there anymore. It's another thing I have to monitor now. But it did explain why I was having to pour drain cleaner down the four sink drains in our house so often – not to mention the two visits by the plumber!

~~~

It took less than a week for Charlie to break the recliner in our new sectional. Charlie loved the sectional and he loved to play with the motorized control that made his recliner go up and down. I cautioned him each time he used it to be sure he got the sectional all the way up and locked before trying to rise from his seat. I was sitting right there when he destroyed the mechanism.

We were both watching a Florida college baseball game. After a busy day of errands, I was attempting to rest my body before preparing our evening meal. Charlie began to press the button which allowed his seat to rise.

"Going somewhere?" I asked.

"I need to pee," Charlie answered. He began to struggle to rise and I could see his chair was not in the fully upright position.

"Charlie, you need to press the button more. Your chair isn't fully upright, honey."

"I gotta pee!"

"Okay, Charlie. Let me help you then." I could see the sense of urgency in his face and I wanted to try to help spare him another change of underwear.

"NO!" He yelled, "I can do it myself!"

I could see Charlie struggling to get up. He was bracing his legs against the bottom of the recliner which was not yet fully upright. I put my own recliner upright and rose to help him. As I got to my feet, I heard a "*twang....bing*" as if something had snapped or been stressed. I ran to help Charlie get upright and he raced to the bathroom.

While Charlie was in the bathroom, I attempted to push the button to put the recliner into an upright position. It went a bit further but then, stayed in that position, a bit short of fully upright. I attempted to put the seat up and down several times but it would not snap into position. The first thing on Monday, I would call the furniture company and ask for assistance.

~~~

"I want to go to the beach," Charlie said one morning.

"Sweetheart, we can go to the beach but we need to wait

until more tourists are gone. It's going to be very crowded if we go now. But, we'll go soon and we'll pack a lunch and make it a day."

"No, I want to walk into the village for lunch."

"Honey, I don't think either of us is up to that right now."

"Maybe you're not, but I can certainly walk in. Maybe you'd better exercise more and get yourself in shape."

"I'm trying, Charlie but we're both going toward eighty now and you know I've got that bum knee."

"You should get it fixed then. I want to go to the beach and walk into the village."

"Okay, Charlie, I understand. Oh, I need to go to pick up a couple new pillows for our sectional. Want to go?"

"Mine doesn't work. They gave you a bad one."

"You mean your sectional recliner, Charlie? I know it doesn't work. I'll call tomorrow and get someone to take a look at it. Now, do you want to go with me to look for pillows?"

"I guess."

"Okay, go hop into the car and I'll be out shortly." Charlie always took a long time to get in the car so I usually sent him out ahead. By the time I had finished doing a small task, he was usually seated and I would remind him to buckle his seat belt.

On the way to look at pillows, Charlie remembered a couple of things he needed. I told him we'd just go to Target and pick up his items and look for pillows at the same time. When we got to the Target parking lot, I asked Charlie to get out. Most of the time, he will stay in the car seat until reminded to get out. I watched him trying to extricate himself from the front seat.

Some time ago, I had pushed the front passenger seat pretty far back, making it easier for Charlie to get into and out of my car. But lately, even getting in with ample foot room was becoming very difficult. Charlie kicked at the door several times before being able to place his feet on the parking lot pavement. The door was severely scuffed and I winced at the time I had taken just two days ago trying to remove all the scuff marks on that door.

When Charlie was finally out of the car, I locked the door and said, "Let's go, Charlie." He was agonizingly slow and I could see there was no way he could walk the beach anymore. I would have to find a clever way to convince him that a picnic lunch was a much better adventure. I finally settled on simply telling Charlie we'd have a picnic lunch on the beach and I'd then drive into the village and we'd get an ice cream for dessert. If I could remember my own plans amidst all the other distractions, they just might work!

~~~

It looks as if Charlie can no longer make up his bed. He used to make beds for us both but now, I make up my own bed. And now, I'll need to make up Charlie's bed. I washed and dried his sheets and handed them to him. He went in to attempt to make his bed. I sat working on the computer and could see him from my office. He struggled to put the top sheet on the mattress instead of the bottom sheet. Then, he went to put on the other fitted sheet and of course, it didn't work. Charlie sat on the chair in his room and stared at the sheets.

I went into the bedroom and showed Charlie how to correctly put the sheets on the bed. He smiled and said he would remember. I know we have passed another milestone and now, I shall add but another small chore to my list.

Chapter Forty-Eight

A Reality Check

I really thought I was taking care of myself but a reality check proved otherwise. Last night, I made the mistake of looking in the photo album. I was trying to locate a picture of one of the grandchildren. I found the picture without much frustration and right next to the grandchild's glowing face was a picture of me taken about a year ago. I was astounded at how I had aged in a year!

Later that night, I looked in the mirror as I washed my face, applied moisturizer and brushed my teeth. My entire face was lined where a year ago, only the area around my mouth had lines. It was a shock and a wake-up call. I had always told my own patients that stress was one of the greatest enemies of the aging process. And now, I was the perfect example. I was not proud to stand out in that way.

The following morning, the lawn care man my neighbor used for her lawn agreed to blow off the accumulated leaves and pollen from our roof. He did an outstanding job and it motivated me to rake the leaves, mow the grass and apply new grass seed to the bare spots on the lawn. I had been raking for about an hour and a half when Charlie appeared. He'd gone out with a friend and had been dropped off at the curb. He said, "Oh, you decided to rake the lawn."

Foolishly, I said nothing and watched as Charlie walked into the house. I should have asked for his help but I didn't, thinking he was still fully capable of noticing that his wife was *busting her butt* trying to make the lawn look nice. I also wanted the pollen off the lawn as it was preventing me from sitting outside in the front while I read in the afternoons. Even as a child, I had multiple allergies and the pollens seemed to be prolific this spring.

I vigorously raked away and on occasion, witnessed Charlie looking out the window of his office. I got angrier and angrier as I felt how unjust it was for me to be doing the bulk of the hard labor in and around the house. I worked myself into a wonderful fit of anger and could actually hear my own heart beating. As I tossed in another handful of leaves and pollen into the plastic yard waste bag, it finally dawned on me what I was doing. I had help available. It really didn't matter whether Charlie simply couldn't conceptualize that I needed help or whether he was simply trying to avoid work.

I went inside the house and said, "Charlie, I need help outside here."

"Shall we call somebody?" he asked.

"I was thinking you might be able to help me, sweetheart."

"I'm having a snack."

"Yes, I see that Charlie but I need help outside and you are the only other person who lives in this house. I'd appreciate your helping me."

"I don't like to rake. It hurts."

"Okay, Charlie, I understand that it makes your back hurt. So, how about if I do the raking and you toss the piles into the yard waste container?"

"You shouldn't do the raking."

"Why not, Charlie?"

"'Cause of your allergies."

"I'm glad to know you thought about that. So, if I rake and you pick up the piles, the wind won't blow the pollen into my nose."

"You might be right."

"But, I can't do it anyway," Charlie replied.

"Why not, Charlie?"

"I have my going out clothes on."

"Okay, I see that. I am going to get us glasses of ice water while you change your clothes."

"No."

'No, what, Charlie?"

"No, I don't want ice in my water." (It always helps to check out a response that may appear contrary or negative before you make an inappropriate conclusion!)

Charlie went into the bedroom and came out with work clothes on while I got the drinks prepared, complete with caps on the top in case they got knocked over.

We went outside and I pointed to a pile of leaves that I had not yet put into the yard waste container. I took the rake and showed Charlie how to pick up the leaves and deposit them in the container. He had done it dozens of times in past years but I no longer took for granted his routine abilities. I watched while he got up a load of leaves and then, I went to get another rake.

It took us some time but we finally got up all the dead leaves and pollen. "The grass is greener now!" Charlie remarked. I had to admit that with all the dead debris off the lawn, it looked one hundred percent better!

"I'll mow the lawn now," Charlie said, forgetting that he'd already had multiple causalities with the lawn mower and that chore was now on my *to do* list.

"How about I do the lawn while you get out the blower and clean off the lanai and the driveway?" I asked. Substituting a chore generally resulted in a husband who was pleased to be able to do anything at all. Charlie headed for the garage.

I was just finishing up mowing the small front section of the lawn when Charlie came out with the blower and said, "They made the starter thing so you can't get it out now."

I frowned and thought back to not so long ago when Charlie had experienced difficulty getting the battery out of the charger. We went together to the garage. I feigned having a difficult time getting the battery out and then pushed down on the button that released the battery from the charger base. "You're right, Charlie," I said while quickly putting the battery into the blower.

For fifteen minutes, Charlie blew debris from the concrete

surfaces. I noticed that he was going over some areas several times even though it had already been blown clean. I smiled in recognition of how at about four or five years of age, our grandson had done the same thing when he tried to help me with yard work. I managed to scatter the grass seed and clean the mower while Charlie worked and then, we went into the house to prepare dinner.

Remembering the image in the bathroom mirror the previous night and being acutely aware of the tightness in my back and the heaviness of my eyelids, I told Charlie we would order out for pizza for dinner. I wrote down what to order and Charlie placed the pizza order by phone.

That evening, I lay on the sofa thinking about all the unnecessary stress I had caused myself in the past few months. Tending to someone as a caregiver is stress enough without causing additional problems to myself. I vowed that night that I would try to reach out to whoever was available when feeling worn out. I simply had to change my lifelong habit of trying to be independent, even when it worked against my own natural needs. The reality check in the mirror had shown me that if I could not give myself a break from traditional expectations for performance, there was no reason to expect anyone else would do so either. Charlie needed to know that as long as he was capable, there were expectations both as a spouse and as a homeowner. There was no need to over-think what Charlie might be thinking or experiencing. I simply needed to state my case while respecting his current abilities.

Chapter Forty-Nine

Ballpark Conversation

We were sitting at a baseball game on a Saturday morning. The team was doing well and Charlie and I were both relaxing. Then, he reached into the breast pocket of his shirt, pulled out two cards and said, "I want you to order more of these."

I looked closely at the cards. They were business cards from when he used to do legal consultations such as case analysis and witness preparation. Charlie had not done that kind of work for over fifteen years now.

"Charlie, you don't do that kind of work anymore," I said as I pointed to our granddaughter who was now at bat.

"Well, I want to do it again so I need more cards," Charlie replied.

I took a deep breath and tried to think of some kind of distraction. "We'll go to brunch today instead of tomorrow. Remember, I'm going shopping with the girls tomorrow. So, we'll go today," I said with emphasis.

"Will you order the cards today?" Charlie asked.

Again, I paused. We were in a crowd of parents and I did not want to have any kind of confrontation with my husband. "I think we have a lot of them at home," I said, as I again pointed to the home plate area as I heard the umpire yell, "3 and 2: full count!"

I heard the bat crack and knew our granddaughter had hit another ball to the outfield, driving in a run. I was certain it would distract Charlie. But, I was wrong. He persisted.

"I took all the cards we had at home."

I frowned and asked, "What did you do with them, Charlie?"

"I've been passing them out. How else will I get business if I don't pass them out?"

Well, I have to tell you I was suspicious of anyone who would even accept a card from my husband, but I was also curious. "Who are you giving the cards to, Charlie?" I asked.

"Everybody."

Oh-oh, I thought to myself. Then I asked, "Who's everybody, Charlie?"

"The people in the group."

Okay, I thought silently. "And who else, Charlie?"

"The people on the bus."

Not so okay, I thought. "Anybody else?"

"Yeah, the people at the restaurant I like," Charlie answered.

I had to think about that one. "Charlie, did you go somewhere after I dropped you off for a haircut?"

"Yeah, I went to the restaurant I like."

"Charlie, you promised me you'd get right on the bus. You promised me you'd take the bus home and if you didn't want to wait, you were going to call me. Do you remember that?"

"Yeah. I did all that. I went to the restaurant on the way and then, I took the bus home."

"Charlie, you didn't have time to eat and then take the bus home."

"Oh. I guess someone gave me a ride then."

Well, at least he had forgotten about the business cards. It was a good Little League game but I found my mind wandering. How long should I wait before I further restricted Charlie? He had so few privileges already.

I watched my grandson get up to bat and smack a grounder into the right outfield. Then, as usual, he stole the other three bases and scored a run. I had to smile at the little imp. He was every team's nightmare if he got on base. But then, reality came to smack me in the face – again.

"So, are you going to order the cards for me?" Charlie asked.

I smiled at Charlie and said, "Sure, Charlie. Now, why don't you think about what you're going to have for our brunch right now?"

"Are we going out?" my husband asked with a grin.

There was no more mention of the business cards.

Chapter Fifty

Dancing to the Music

It seems as if I've been dancing to the music nearly all my life. Both of my parents were musicians, my mother being a concert pianist and my father a vocalist. In times of stress, songs have taken on increased meaning for me. Sometimes they help me to externalize a particular period of pain and at other times, they seem to enhance the joy I feel about every day, common experiences.

Lately, certain songs have teased out pain and disappointment. Last week, I turned up the volume on the radio when I heard Bonnie Tyler singing "Total Eclipse of the Heart" (lyrics by Jim Steinman, 1983, from the album Faster Than the Speed of Night). Ms. Tyler is a Welsh vocalist who is blessed with a haunting voice that seems to capture some of the sense of helplessness portrayed by the lyrics.

In particular, a certain strain caught my ear and my heart:
"Every now and then, I get a little bit angry
And I know I've got to get out and cry.
Every now and then
I get a little bit terrified
But then I see the look in your eyes.
Every now and then
I fall apart
Turn around, bright eyes
Every now and then

I fall apart.'

By the time we get to the verse:

"I don't know what to do and I'm always in the dark;

We're living in a powder keg and giving off sparks,"

I begin to release the uncertainties of my abilities to care for my husband. I begin to mourn for the loss of who we were.

At first, there's a trickle down my left cheek and then my right eye releases the tensions of my mind and the pain of my soul. Soon, I am sobbing and it feels good; it feels so very, very good. Bonnie continues to sing:

"Once upon a time there was light in my life

But now there's only love in the dark

Nothing I can say

A total eclipse of the heart."

I go to the lanai and I am alone with nature. The birds sing to me and the wind takes the pain I am releasing and finally, I hear nothing but the birds. I begin to smell the flowers and I begin to think about children, and faith and birthday parties, I am now grounded. I have taken back the soft parts of me vital to my caregiving duties. And, it's just in time. For fifteen minutes, I have allowed myself to listen to the music and it has a healing effect. Charlie has returned from his group. He comes in the front door and runs to the bathroom saying, "I gotta go pee."

Chapter Fifty-One

Hints and Hypotheses

I think I'm beginning to figure out a few things that distinguish Alzheimer's disease from other dementias. Basically, it's the quality of thinking, or lack of it. As I look back through my own notes about the progression of the disease in Charlie, I notice the value of the conversations I entered. Ever-so-gradually, Charlie's ability to conceptualize has gone from that of a highly intelligent man to that of a preschool child.

My younger brother suffered dementia as a result of an automobile-related accident. As with Charlie, my brother's short term memory was also taken. But there was no gradual deterioration in his ability to formulate responses based upon conversation. My brother was able to conceptualize until his death. He was simply not able to remember his own conceptualizations.

With Charlie, the conceptualizations are simply not there. One might argue that the Alzheimer's patient is simply unable to get a *clear channel* through the brain in order to access the concepts. But, I would argue that the concepts are not there to try to encode into the brain at all.

Oftentimes, when I catch Charlie looking at the television screen with a confused look, I'll ask him what he is thinking. He is never able to tell me. In fact, he seems confused that I have even noted the confused expression on his face. Sometimes, he seems to react after the fact to something he sees. He might have a brief interaction with a grandchild and afterwards, I might catch a smile on his face. When I ask him about the apparent feeling of pleasure, Charlie is not able to define the basis of his own emotions.

Although Charlie's ability to greet people remains appropriate, his ability to engage in a current conversation is now nearly non-existent. He can no longer engage in creative thought or bring new ideas to the surface in order to verbalize them. There is no ability to initiate ideas and there is no insight about what Charlie might be experiencing in the environment. One would think that the opposite of coming up with one's own ideas would be to repeat the ideas of others. But even that ability is nonexistent unless the information was encoded in Charlie's youth. It's almost as if Charlie has forgotten how to think about the things he knows from experience.

If you cannot remember what you really know, you cannot check out new knowledge and compare it to what you have already learned. You cannot organize and analyze the information. Therefore, new experiences become virtually worthless. It makes the curse of forgetting a blessing. You don't know what you are missing because you do not remember what you have experienced. One of the cruelest aspects of Alzheimer's disease is that most victims never even realize they have the disease or that they have changed in any way. When others notice or make comments, it only further serves to confuse and frustrate them.

Some might equate this state of being to that of the newborn infant. And yet, we know from scientific study and personal observation that the infant mind is akin to an absorbent sponge and that personal meaning is formed via associations. An infant will naturally discover the world while the Alzheimer's victim is content to stay within a world which is barely knowable.

At a recent gathering in the new home of my daughter and her family, the adults were all asked to hide plastic Easter eggs after the brunch that my daughter had prepared. The five grandchildren would then hunt for the eggs. Each child was to look for a different colored egg so that the egg count would be evenly distributed among the five children. Out of courtesy, my daughter asked Charlie to hide a basket of blue eggs. He struggled up from the sofa and took the basket of eggs. The rest of us went about hiding various colors of plastic eggs and finally, it was time for the egg hunt to begin.

After half an hour all the eggs had been located except for those belonging to just-turned-nine grandson Clay. When Clay began to complain that he couldn't find his eggs, I asked what color we should look for. "Mine are blue," Clay said with a look of concern. Then he asked, "Did Poppy hide my eggs?"

My daughter affirmed that indeed, Poppy had hidden the blue eggs. Clay got a look of consternation on his face. I went to hug him and he placed his arms around me and then, he looked at me with the knowing look of a sage. The knowing and the understanding of a child mentally brought me to my knees.

Immediately, all the children and adults began a search for the eggs while Charlie sat on the sofa watching a baseball game. I went quietly to where he was sitting. He looked very relaxed and perfectly content. I asked, "Charlie, do you happen to remember where any of the blue eggs might be?"

Charlie smiled and shook his head and then returned to gaze at the television screen.

I asked again if Charlie had any recall as to where any of the eggs were and he smiled and asked, "Did I hide them?"

Eventually, all the eggs save two were recovered but it took nearly an hour, with everyone but Charlie invested in the search. I was fascinated with the hiding places Charlie had thought appropriate. It demonstrated total lack of awareness of the limitations of the mind of the child who would be trying to find the eggs. Charlie had hidden eggs inside of a suitcase which was housed inside a larger suitcase which was in the room of one of the granddaughters. He had hidden eggs inside packed boxes which had items yet to be sorted through and placed in their proper places from the recent family move. He had placed an egg inside a roll of toilet paper which was housed in a cabinet. I had to admit that the eggs were, indeed, hidden. They were hidden in the recesses of Charlie's atrophied brain and not even accessible to him.

After arriving home, I told Charlie I was really tired this year. He said, "I'll bet you are. You had to cook for a lot of people!" I reminded Charlie that our daughter and son-in-law had done the cooking and that we had just returned from brunch at their house.

"Were we there all day?" he asked.

"Yes, well, for most of the day," I replied.

"That's why we're tired then."

"Why is that, Charlie?"

"We were up all day," Charlie reasoned.

At this stage of the disease, I reminded Charlie to zip up his pants after using the toilet. I took his clothes at night when he removed them. On some mornings, I noticed him wearing the clothes I had placed in the hamper. At that time, Charlie might wear the same shirt or pants for a week or so. I reminded my husband to close his mouth when he chewed his food. I reminded him to use a napkin and to chew more slowly. Sometimes, I nudged him as he slept in the recliner lounger and I reminded him to breathe.

Chapter Fifty-Two

Anniversary

I just noticed that Charlie must be having difficulty putting on his socks. The heels of the socks are about at the ankle bone. It would drive me batty but Charlie didn't seem to notice. I reminded myself that I'd have to watch to see if he needs help with that now.

It was the day before our wedding anniversary and for the third year in a row, Charlie had forgotten. A flower deliveryman came to the door and Charlie answered it. I heard him ask the man who the flowers were for. Then Charlie asked, "Is it somebody's birthday?"

Charlie brought the flowering plant in to my office and set it on the desk. "I guess it's somebody's birthday, huh?" Charlie asked. I picked up the card which accompanied the plant and saw the sender was my sister. She had sent me an early anniversary plant, knowing that Charlie would probably forget the occasion. Her understanding touched me so much that I couldn't talk for a moment. Finally, I noticed Charlie just standing in front of the desk.

"It's from my sister, Charlie. She says it's just to remember how many wonderful years you and I have had together." Charlie smiled and returned to watch television.

In years past, we had gone out to celebrate our anniversary but this year, I just didn't feel in a celebration mood. I did not want to cook a dinner. I was feeling deprived and so very much wanted to be pampered. But, I recognized my feelings as the unrealistic feelings of a caregiver and decided to give myself a break. So, the next day on our anniversary, I ordered a pizza to be delivered.

Nothing Left to Burn - A Story of Alzheimer's Disease

As Charlie likes to eat early, we were devouring our pizza by six in the evening. I thought about making a pizza toast to us but then thought better about it. I was afraid my voice would reflect sarcasm and anger and I didn't want to hear it. While watching television, Charlie touched the remote control which is stationed in one of the cup holders just to his left. He'd been doing that a lot lately. Previously, I had asked Charlie about the touching. He's said, "It keeps moving so I touch it to see if it's in the right place." It didn't make a lot of sense to me but it suggested there may be a visual distortion of some kind.

By six forty-five, we had finished our anniversary pizza and Charlie was asleep on the recliner sectional. He started to grasp at objects in the air. That behavior had also been going on for some time. Sometimes, Charlie had his eyes open and at other times, his eyes were closed. If his eyes were open, I would ask what he was reaching for but Charlie was never able to explain his actions. "Just had to set it right," he would sometimes say.

And so, early in the evening on our anniversary night, Charlie was in a deep sleep. He repeatedly picked at his left arm with the fingers on his right hand. Lately, he had been digging into his skin at all times of the day. I noticed he had pulled off a scab and the skin was bleeding. I went to the medicine cabinet and got a couple of band aids. I carefully placed one on the bleeding scab and another on Charlie's left hand where he had also been digging. He did not awaken.

I thought back to our twenty-six years of marriage with mixed feelings. And then, I gently chastised myself for even including the past years in the memory bank. Charlie and I had experienced some wonderful years together and those were the years I needed to recall. Tonight, well, the calendar said it was our wedding anniversary but in reality, it was just another day with a man who increasingly bore no resemblance to the man I had married.

Chapter Fifty-Three

The Beautiful Climb

Sometimes, I try to distract the musings of my mind by doing a mental role reversal exercise. I imagine what it might be like if I was the one with the compromised mind and Charlie was my caregiver. I imagine myself as a rather difficult patient. I would be frightened of what I was missing in the recesses of my own mind and I might make things emotionally difficult for Charlie.

Charlie, on the other hand, would be a patient and tender caregiver. The house would be messy; the yard would be a tangle of vines; the clothes would pile up in the laundry room and the meals would be a bit haphazard. But, Charlie would be an attentive caregiver while my mind whittled away to a semblance of its former self. He would be accepting of me, no matter the symptoms and he would continue to love me.

At times, I might want Charlie to simply go away and leave me in peace – or whatever you might call such a withering state of existence. He would tend to *hover* over me and even in a compromised mental state, it would annoy me.

If I take the scenario far enough, I finally conclude that it is probably for the best that Charlie is the patient and I am the caregiver. He is suited well to his role, as he is oblivious and he cares little of what others may think. I am also somewhat suited to the caregiver role as I am naturally organized and structured. These are attributes which are helpful to a patient in mental disarray.

Nothing Left to Burn - A Story of Alzheimer's Disease

I have to remember the good times now. I have to remember the agony and the ecstasy of the times that Charlie and I shared uniquely as a couple. That is what we were. What we are now has little to do with sexual love and the excitement of feeling special, more special than every other couple on the face of the earth. It has to do with marriage and commitment and it has to do with the constancy of love.

When I think about challenge and staying the course, my mind jumps to the Cinque Terra region in Italy. It is August of 2006 and Charlie and I were vacationing in a charming village named Monterossa. Charlie planned the trip very carefully. He said we would have the opportunity to climb to five different villages by going up and down mountain trails. On the trails, one could see spectacular views of the villages by the Mediterranean Sea as well as various sculpted terraces. Charlie and I were both approaching our seventies and the staff at the restaurant where we dined our first night warned us that younger people than we had failed the hike. For years, I had been walking at least five miles a day and I felt confident that I could make the seven mile hike to the end of the fifth village. But, I had my doubts about Charlie. He had always been the kind of guy who would park in the closest parking spot to his destination.

The following morning, we ate breakfast, packed water and snacks in our small backpacks and we both donned hats against the intense August sun. We got about halfway up the first mountain which, according to the literature, was the steepest in the climb. Charlie asked to rest and then he said he didn't think he could make it to the top. We drank water and I asked if we could maybe walk a bit farther so that we could get a good view of the village below.

Little by little, I eased Charlie up the mountain with teasers and distractions which lessened his propensity to dwell on physical discomfort. When we reached the top, there was a stunning view of Monterossa and Charlie was immediately energized. We could see the next village of Vernazza down the mountain to our left and it was enough to entice Charlie to go on. I reminded Charlie that we could simply walk down that side of the mountain, stop for a tea and take the train back to Monterossa. Of course the steep decline down the mountain required a different set of muscles. I lead the way and tried to pace Charlie, stopping to admire vineyards and small farm houses along the way.

When we got to the village, we could see it was similar and yet distinctly different than Monterossa. We were encouraged to take a peek at the village. By doing so, we found ourselves back on the mountain trail, almost by accident. Charlie looked in the brochure describing the trail. "This one isn't so steep," he said. "I think maybe I can do it."

"It's just one step at a time, Charlie," I replied as I took off climbing up and away from the village. I was careful to stop briefly about every ten minutes to show Charlie something of interest. It seemed to rest him and give him motivation to continue. We reached the peak of the second mountain and looked down on yet another charming village named Corniglia. There was a mountain bridge approaching the village and the strait pathway resulted in the taming of sore muscles as we walked into the town.

We were now more than halfway to the fifth city and Charlie's face reflected increased determination to make it all the way. I had gotten a bit winded on the steep upward climbs but my muscles were cooperating just fine. We walked around the village and again stopped for refreshment before locating the path upwards and out of the city.

The path was again very steep. It was a series of ridges with a pathway which teased hikers to the very top. Again, there was a bridge across into the next village called Manarola. We did a very brief exploration, wanting to get to our final destination before dark.

Leaving the village of Manarola, there was a series of steps, hundreds of steps leading to the final village of Riomaggiore. That was nearly a killer for me but at that point, nothing was going to stop us from having hiked the villages of the Cinque Terre! Charlie sat on the steps and I told him we just needed to go a few more steps and then, a few more. I got him into a regular pace where we would climb a set of twelve steps and then rest and look at the sea view. In no time whatsoever, we made our way to the final village and found the train depot. At the depot, there was a simply marvelous mural which depicted how ordinary people had chipped away the rocks and the terraces, making routes through the mountains from one village to the next.

We took the train back to Monterossa and could barely rise from our seats on the train to walk back to our motel. We picked up a couple slices of pizza and retired early.

The next morning, we took our time in a hot shower and then strolled over for breakfast. Charlie chatted with the wait staff about our trek the day before and they were most impressed. Apparently, they told a younger couple at another table that we had just made the trip. The couple came to our table and asked to talk with us. After listening to our story, they decided that if a couple of *elderly* folks could make the trek, they were fully capable of doing so as well. Charlie and I met them the following morning at breakfast and they sheepishly confided to us that the first mountain hike had broken them and that they had taken the train back to Monterossa.

As I think of that trip now, I equate it to my current journey with Charlie. My life experience has equipped me to go into an endurance mode. Even though it's a new experience for Charlie, I only need to encourage him toward a set of stairs so that he gets part-way to his goal. By going partway, and then partway again and again, we will reach the end of our journey – together. And I know that eventually, I will leave my Charlie. It will be the end of the journey for one of us.

Chapter Fifty-Four

The Climb Gets Steeper

I now have to sit Charlie down on the bed to strip him of his dirty slacks so that I can wash them. When I ask him politely to please change his clothing, he always answers that he will do it "tomorrow." Although he still showers daily, he is not at all concerned about his clothing and that really bothers me. He was always a rather fastidious dresser before and this is just one more ongoing reminder of how quickly he is leaving me.

The childlike behaviors are also escalating. I had purchased a new set of towels some time back when Charlie was still helping to do the laundry. One day after he had discontinued *helping* me with that chore (at my request), I was folding the towels and I noticed that one of the bath towels and one of the small towels had bleach damage on them. Charlie didn't tell me about his *bleach accident* and I thought it was childish not to do so. I then examined the rest of the towels and was momentarily confused when I saw that one bath towel and one hand towel had a black **X** on the label. I had a suspicion as to what was occurring but I decided to test my theory.

I put the bleached bath towel on Charlie's towel rack and the bleached hand towel on his towel ring by the sink. After Charlie showered the following morning, I went in to check the towels. Sure enough, Charlie had removed the bleach-damaged towels from their places and then replaced the damaged towels with the undamaged towels marked with an **X**! I thought the gesture was very childish but I would never confront Charlie with his behaviors. Perhaps, it was simply time to replace the damaged towels and simply let it go.

***

I received a gift certificate for my birthday recently. It was to an Italian restaurant I really liked. Memorial Day week had been a rough one as Charlie's group had been cancelled for Memorial Day itself as well as for the next group on Wednesday. By Thursday, Charlie and I had been together for six days without a break. I had tried to interest him in puzzles and in crossword exercises and short walks around the neighborhood but he had no interest. I had taken him for an agonizing trip to run errands with me. A trip that should have taken me ninety minutes ended up to be a three hour and fifteen minute excursion. When we got home, I was exhausted and Charlie immediately said, "You forgot to get the soap I need."

I wanted to scream. Instead, I decided to use my restaurant gift certificate to take Charlie for an Italian dinner. We went early to avoid a crowd and were instantly seated in a booth which was some-what removed from the general crowd.

I reviewed the menu with Charlie and we decided on our order. When the waitress came less than a minute later, Charlie had forgotten what he wanted. I reminded him of what he had said looked good and he again approved the choice. He tried to order but could not find the entry on the menu in order to place the order. I ordered for us both.

Trying to provide some stimulation, I tried to engage Charlie in conversation. He gave me a blank look and then gazed at the tele-vision screen in the bar area. Our order came twenty minutes later and after multiple attempts to engage Charlie in conversation, I gave up and looked out the window at the brewing storm. It soon started to rain and then, the winds began to blow in a storm from the gulf. The weather seemed almost prophetic. Charlie watched television. I remembered the times when we first began to date and how I was so attracted to his mind.

Charlie's meal immediately caught his interest and he eagerly dug into his pasta dish. He spilled sauce on his pants and his shirt. There was Alfredo sauce on his lips running down to his chin. He did not seem aware. At one point, Charlie took out his lower partial dental plate and rubbed it with his napkin. He left it sitting on the table until I suggested he put the partial back in his mouth. I couldn't eat all of what I had ordered and I asked the waitress for a box for my left overs. I smiled at Charlie as my heart bled and ached. At the beginning of the disease process, Charlie had made me promise him that if he was in a position to embarrass himself in public, he did not want me to expose him to the public. Soon, I would be unable to take him to a restaurant.

On the way home, I asked Charlie if he needed more muffins. Before we had left for the restaurant, I had noticed he was down to his last one for the morning. He smiled and said he'd like to stop at the market across the street. They had homemade muffins, and Charlie always thought it a treat to get them even though we both knew it was a somewhat expensive market. As it was still raining, I pulled up to the front canopy of the market. As Charlie struggled to get out, he asked if there was anything I would like. I requested one, and only one chocolate muffin. "Only one chocolate, Charlie," I emphasized. I drove around the parking lot until I spotted Charlie at the door. I then pulled up to the canopy and Charlie struggled to get into the car with the grocery bag in his hand.

The bag looked to be filled to the top so I asked Charlie what else he had gotten other than his much-craved blueberry muffins. He grinned and said he had gotten a whole plastic container of chocolate chip muffins for me! I looked surprised and said I really had only wanted a single chocolate muffin and Charlie looked at me, shook his head and said, "Well, you should have told me then. I'm not a mind-reader, you know!" I was so relieved that Charlie would have his regular group meeting the following day.

***

Nothing Left to Burn - A Story of Alzheimer's Disease

I took Charlie for his regular six month dental cleaning. Afterwards, the dentist called me in to talk about the x-rays they had taken. Charlie had decay in almost all his remaining lower and upper teeth! I was shocked and I asked Charlie if he was still brushing with the electric toothbrush and using the floss and the mouth rinse. He just grinned and everyone in the room knew he had not been taking care of his teeth. Every night, I had put out the tooth care supplies on Charlie's sink and every morning, he had been putting everything back in the drawer – without using a thing!

The dentist recommended that Charlie's teeth be pulled so he could be fitted with full plates. I asked about the length of the procedures and I also mentioned that Charlie had experienced some choking incidents lately and I worried about the procedure being too stressful. The dentist asked Charlie if any of the teeth hurt him and Charlie said he was having no problems at all. We finally decided to do a watchful waiting approach. When Charlie started to experience discomfort, we would then decide on a course of action that Charlie might tolerate.

***

One morning, I asked Charlie to turn the sprinkler on the flower garden in the front.

"Where do you want it?" he asked.

"I want you to put the sprinkler so it will water the front garden, Charlie." I used my hand to demonstrate that Charlie should place the sprinkler parallel to the house in order to water the flowers and not the grass.

I went to put in a load of laundry and then went to the front door to check on Charlie. He had placed the sprinkler at a ninety degree angle to the house and was watering the grass. I opened the door and stepped outside.

"Charlie?"

"Yeah?"

"You need to turn the sprinkler the other way so it will water the flowers. The grass doesn't need to be watered. Just water the flowers, Charlie."

"Okay."

I watched as Charlie turned the sprinkler one hundred and eighty degrees and then went to turn on the water. It was again watering the grass.

"Charlie?"

"Yeah."

"We need to water the flowers, not the grass."

"What?" Charlie's hearing had grown steadily worse over the past year.

I yelled out, "Charlie, turn the sprinkler so it waters the flowers!" A neighbor across the street looked our way and probably thought I was verbally abusing my husband. Charlie again turned the sprinkler back to its original position which would water the grass.

I walked to the end of the front garden area shouting "NO!" as Charlie headed to the side to turn on the sprinkler. Charlie didn't hear me and turned on the sprinkler. I got soaked as I walked to the side of the house and asked Charlie to turn off the water. He complied and I went to the sprinkler head and turned it parallel to the front of the house. Then I went back to where Charlie was and I turned on the water. The flowers got gently watered as Charlie looked at me and said, "Why didn't you say you wanted it that way!"

***

I still tried to get Charlie to do simple tasks, just to keep his brain functioning. We were sitting out in the front garden when I noticed some of the flowers were beginning to droop. It was a warm summer day and we hadn't had rain for a couple of afternoons. The flowers in the pots always dried out quickly in summer and they required almost daily watering. I told Charlie I was going to water the plants.

"That's my job," Charlie said with a hurt look on his face.

"Okay," I said, "but please remember to water them with the nozzle set on shower. They're very delicate, Charlie, and we don't want to knock off the blooms using the heavy spray."

Charlie gave me a look that asked *'Do you think I'm dumb or something?'* He then reminded me that he had been watering flowers for years.

I sat back in my chair to enjoy the flower garden when the telephone rang. I had my cell phone outside with me but this was our land line so I quickly scurried inside the house. It was a friend calling and I talked with her for about ten minutes. I hung up the phone, opened the front door and looked for Charlie. He was watering the large tree out front so I went out to sit down again to enjoy the early evening. I glanced to my left and there I saw dozens of flowers petals on the ground. Charlie had used the jet setting on the hose attachment rather than the gentle rain shower intended for plants.

I took a deep breath. I let go of my disappointment and asked Charlie if he'd like a cold glass of tea while we sat a while longer. He finished his watering while I got two glasses of iced tea. We both sat outside while a dozen neighbors walked by with their dogs on leashes. I thanked Charlie for watering the plants and he had a look of deep satisfaction on his face. I knew the blooms would grow back.

***

Charlie was now having a great deal of difficulty rising from the new sectional we had bought not that long ago. Even with my bad right knee it was much easier for me to rise from the seat but Charlie had increasing difficulty as the months passed. Oftentimes, I would rise from my lounge chair and assist him in standing.

Oftentimes, Charlie would fall asleep right after he ate dinner. Lately, I noticed that he clenched his fists as he slept. I remembered my three babies sometimes sleeping with fists clenched in the first months of their lives. Charlie was becoming very childlike and maybe, he was reverting to a womb-like condition in his mind. If so, it might be a comforting feeling for him.

Charlie's chest would rise and then his stomach. More of his body now seemed to be involved in the breathing process. He seemed to struggle to breathe at times. Many was the night I would sit looking at my husband breathe, wondering if God would mercifully take him to the promised land before he became totally helpless. But, Charlie continued to wake up the next morning.

Still an avid consumer of television shows, Charlie processed less and less of what he was seeing and hearing. He would sit with a fixed gaze which would sometimes turn into a smile that would last for ten to fifteen minutes. I reasoned that his facial muscles were not getting messages to return to a more normal expression. He had increased incidences of *potty mouth* as he attempted unsuccessful to reply to something on the TV screen. Charlie had always had a marvelous sense of humor. Now, his humor was not generally something we would want expressed in polite company.

I would generally join Charlie in the evening as he watched television. But, since he always watched the same repeat shows, it was boring for me. Charlie could no longer hold a conversation about one of the shows. If I would ask about a given character, he would say "I forgot about him/her." If I asked about something that had just happened in the show, Charlie would say, "I didn't see that part."

By now, I had totally lost the companionship of the other adult in the house. Sometimes, feeling alienated, I would sit in the recliner adjacent to the one in which Charlie sat. At other times, I craved the feeling of closeness to another human being. I would sit in the recliner next to Charlie and take his hand and hold it as he watched television. He no longer grasped my hand in return.

***

One beautiful summer morning, I went out to the back lanai to do some reading. I had started a load of laundry and I still had another load to put in after the first one finished. I told Charlie I was out in the back and that I'd come in when it was time to put in the next load of laundry. "I do the laundry, right, Charlie?" I asked as a reminder to Charlie not to touch any machine in the laundry room.

Charlie nodded and continued to read his book. It was the same book he had finished the week before. It was the same book he had finished seven times now. I was happy that Charlie would sit and read. It was a small part of the professor that remained. But Charlie never seemed to figure out that he had read that same book over and over during a period of two months.

I knew I had forty minutes outside to read and relax. I read a chapter and then put down my book and closed my eyes and listened to the birds chirping and planning their own day. After forty-five minutes in which I read another four chapters, I went in to put the washed clothes in the dryer and put in another load of dirty clothes into the washing machine. I entered the laundry room and saw suds coming out of the washing machine. There were no clothes on the floor.

I stopped the machine and went into the den where Charlie was reading.

"Charlie, there's a sign on the washing machine that says only Karen uses the machines."

"Yeah, I know but I thought you were sleeping. I wanted to help you out."

There was nothing I could say except, "Thank you, Charlie, but you really need to do what the signs say."

I went to the laundry room and took all the wet clothes out of the washing machine and put them into the deep sink to soak out some of the suds. I scooped all the suds out of the washing machine into a bucket and then ran a cycle of only cold water. The cold water would rinse out the remaining suds. I rinsed the sudsy clothes in the deep sink and returned them to the washing machine and ran a regular cycle. Charlie had no idea what I was doing as he continued to read words most people would have memorized by several readings.

I went back into the den and asked Charlie what soap he had used. He said he used the one under the sink. I asked him to show me. He went with me to the laundry room and opened the cabinet underneath the sink, taking out the bottle of dish soap I sometimes used when cleaning up after painting or some such activity. The bottle of laundry detergent was next to the dishwashing detergent. I thanked Charlie for telling me what he had used and he went back to his den to read. I tried to find a hiding place for the dishwashing soap for the next time Charlie wanted to *help* me. I was running out of hiding places. And now, it was time to fix lunch.

***

Charlie just would not give up on trying to self-medicate. I would hide his medicines in one place, only to have him find them. He was a bit sneaky about taking the medications and I would generally discover his tricks when I went to check the bottle so that I could order a refill by mail. The pills never lasted the thirty days they were intended to last. I always told Charlie it was dangerous to take things I did not give to him but he would generally grin and walk away. It seemed as if there was some semblance of knowing what he had done. I thought of another hiding place only to discover it had been pilfered later as well. I found the secret was in moving the pills each and every evening after I placed them in Charlie's pill cup for the morning. I never quite figured out why he was so fascinated with the pills other than perhaps, to conclude that *more is better.*

***

This was a lonely time in the process of caregiving. I tried to anticipate Charlie's needs and I tried to anticipate how he could injure himself or damage something in the house. All the anticipation just wore me out. I went to bed tired and I got up feeling I had not slept at all. In truth, the new mattress I had purchased for myself the month before was allowing me to sleep for several hours. But I no longer felt rested upon arising in the morning. Upon opening my eyes, I would remember the day of the week. I tried to imagine

243

something I could do in the day that would bring me joy. As the months dragged on, I began to realize that even though I had felt moments of happiness when with others, it had been a really long time since I had felt a sense of real joy. I nearly buckled with the pain of that realization until welcome tears purged me of the need to think about my own needs for yet another day.

Chapter Fifty-Five

A New Day

Today when I awaken, I am just too afraid to bend for fear I might break. Again, it is the little things that threaten to shatter me. My usual coping skills are failing to keep me strong and motivated. I fear I might sink into a depression from which I will not emerge, not because I am too weak to do so but rather, because it would almost be a welcome hiatus to simply choose not to react to the real world. I lay awake in bed, listening for the shower to start. When it does not, I race out of my bed and run in to check Charlie. He is lying in bed and I touch him to see if he will respond. When he does, I say, "Charlie, you need to get up and shower. The bus will be here before you know it. I'll cut your muffin for you and peel the egg. Please hurry now."

I have not only awakened Charlie. I have awakened myself to the responsibility that has presented in the new day. And, I know with all certainty that this day will no doubt be the best of those yet to come.

Chapter Fifty-Six

A Vase of Flowers

At this stage of Charlie's disease, we could be together in the house for hours and he would not voluntarily initiate conversation. The only noise would be my own, when I went about doing the daily tasks. Charlie was content to sit in his office for hour after hour. I would periodically go in to try to interest him with conversation. He would always smile and provide a word or a short phrase which generally suggested his lack of comprehension. When with others, Charlie would listen diligently but would not volunteer to enter into the conversation unless someone directed a comment toward him.

I had lots of time to think now, too much time. Thoughts were sometimes intrusive, even when I was working on a task. I thought recently about how I miss the weekly vase of flowers. Charlie had always gone to get any groceries we required for the week and without fail, he would always hand me a bouquet of fresh flowers which I would cut and put into a vase. They would always last a week. But, it has been seven years since I have had a regular bouquet of fresh flowers in the vase. It should have been an early clue that something was wrong with Charlie but as with many future caregivers, we tend to overlook the small things for a while, deluding ourselves that everything is *normal.*

I think also about the wonderful meals Charlie fixed and how I probably took them for granted, much as Charlie now takes for granted the meals I fix for him. But, unlike me, Charlie loved to cook. My meals are nutritious but they are prepared more from duty and purpose rather than out of a sense of joy and fulfillment. I wish I had appreciated the meals more when they came on a regular basis. I recently told Charlie that I used to love the meals he cooked and he smiled and asked, "I used to cook?"

Charlie was always so very willing to run errands whenever I had even a small project. He would make several trips a day if necessary. Now, I grudgingly make my own trips for project supplies. Since I don't like that kind of errand, I notice that the number of my projects has decreased dramatically. My friends tell me that I have Charlie as a project and therefore, I just don't have time for the things I used to do. They praise me for my diligence with Charlie and his problems. This is in no way a statement of encouragement for me. Those who are caregivers will generally acknowledge that receiving praise for carrying out the duties that revolve around someone in need is not nearly as reinforcing as initiating a project you love and carrying it through to completion.

We used to go for rides and even though Charlie was never the best-focused driver on the road, he was adequate and he loved to drive. We would clean up the dinner dishes and take off for somewhere within a ten to fifteen mile radius. On weekends, we would take day trips to sites around our state. Except for perhaps a hurricane warning every few years, there was never a day we could not sightsee in Florida. It was a simple life but it was charmed. I had yielded my role as organizer and taskmaster of my family and I was content to be a passenger throughout our golden years of life.

I took Charlie out last night. We stopped at Panera and I ordered a bowl of soup. I read the menu to Charlie and he stood looking confused. "I'll have that too," he said.

After finishing our soup, I asked Charlie if he'd like to take a ride to Turtle Beach on Siesta Key. He smiled and said that would be a nice drive. I went over the bridge and turned left to go to Turtle Beach. Charlie started waving his hands and telling me I had gone the wrong way. I pulled over, stopped, placed his hands on his lap and again explained that we were going to Turtle Beach, not Siesta Key Beach. I reminded Charlie that Turtle Beach was one of his favorite fishing places. "Is it in Florida?" he asked. We went to the beach, got out of the car and walked to the water's edge. I had hopes of staying for a while as the ebb and flow of the tide came and went. It had always been relaxing for me. But then, Charlie urgently took my hand and said, "Time for ice cream!" He turned and started to walk back to the car.

I don't take Charlie shopping very often unless I have little or nothing scheduled for the rest of the day. When I do shop, I now ask Charlie to hang onto the shopping cart with me. It serves two purposes. It stabilizes my damaged right knee and it also keeps Charlie at my side. If not touching the cart, Charlie will wander when my back is turned, much as my preschool children used to do when something attracted their attention.

Charlie wants to go out frequently so I attempt to drive him short distances. I have apparently abused my right knee enough in my seventy-plus decades of life that it now needs a replacement. I have already had an arthroscopic procedure, cortisone shots and gel injections. And yet the well-worn body joint continues to protest with the slightest action. I fear the knee replacement surgery because of Charlie's needs and the length of the recovery time for the surgery. Also, my body tends to reject anything foreign and replacement parts are either made of plastic or steel, both substances which are not a part of my original body makeup. And then, there is the issue of the anesthetic. My parents both died of reactions under anesthesia and I have had several adverse reactions during prior procedures. I cannot take commonly prescribed painkillers and that could be an issue. I could go on and on and try to rationalize how I should not consider taking care of myself. In the end, I will do what needs to be done to keep my body functioning.

People tell me Charlie's *soul* is still the same and that I must now be content with memories as those memories are Charlie's "true soul". That is probably consolation to some. But, for me, I want the real thing. I can live with his having prostate cancer. I can live with the Barrett's Esophagus and I can live with my own arthritis. But I really want Charlie's brain back. I so very much *need* for Charlie to have his brain back. I want my vase of fresh flowers and I want them only from my husband. I am a stupid and stubborn child wanting what she cannot have.

Chapter Fifty-Seven

And the Days Dwindle Down

The days turn into weeks and then, into months without much change except a downward spiral that seems cruel and insidious. Friends now comment that Charlie seems "trapped" in his own mind but I know that there is precious little mind in which Charlie might hide. Charlie struggles to arise from his chair and when he finally completes the task, he stares about the room as if waiting for clues to tell him how to move.

There are tactile rituals now that remind me of when my children were in their infancies and they randomly reached for and touched objects simply for the stimulation. There is a cup holder near Charlie's lounge chair and I watch as his left hand moves in circles around the plastic rim of the cup holder. His three fingers circle several times and then return to a resting position on his groin. His right hand reaches for invisible objects. Content that he has accomplished his goal after about ten seconds of grabbing, that hand also joins the other.

Many are the moments now that Charlie stares at me as if to remind himself just who I am. Sometimes, he smiles and shakes his head in recognition and satisfaction that he still remembers. At other times, he stares until I speak.

"Is there something you need, Charlie?" I ask.

It now takes seconds for him to respond as if a thought has reverberated in his brain and when he speaks, I wonder if it is the echo. "No," he replies and that is about all I get.

Sometimes, Charlie will ask about dinner. Generally, it is

within minutes of his finishing a meal. Sometimes, he remembers the grandchildren and he asks if they are coming over. At other times, Charlie repeats part of a sentence I just uttered. In brain damaged individuals, this behavior is called echolalia. As a scientist-practitioner, I silently speculate about what neural pathways are now blocked and about how I might reach Charlie's remaining brain cells to make the most of what remains.

When Charlie falls asleep in his lounge chair, he now clenches his fists, much like a young infant who is exploring neural pathways. Charlie's clenching is involuntary and it tells me he is slowly working toward the final phase of being unable to control his own body. His hands tremble while performing simple tasks. I must now assist him in rising from a chair unless it is early in the day and Charlie has a chair that is a bit higher, with lots of hand support. The food I now prepare is cut into small pieces to prevent choking. I dread the time that Charlie is not able to eat and has to have a feeding tube. My man so loves to eat!

Mostly, Charlie just sits and stares at the television set when home but he will occasionally pick up a book and read. I am grateful that the scenes on the television screen do not bother him as they do many persons with Alzheimer's disease. I visualize in my own mind that the time is fast-approaching when Charlie might just sit and stare at a blank screen, not realizing the set can be turned on.

I have an important event coming up and in many ways, it terrifies me. I have exhausted treatments for my right knee. I have inherited the family arthritis but the biggest problem is that I have no cartilage in the knee and the upper and lower leg bones rub together, causing ongoing pain. It is difficult to drive and I can no longer complete many of the household tasks I used to do routinely. I had to make a decision about whether I would join the ranks of the elderly who are compromised in basic mobility or whether I would undergo a total knee replacement. Basically, it is a quality-of-life decision and despite the growing depression experienced in caregiving and the tremendous sense of obligation to Charlie, I have chosen to undergo the procedure.

Nothing Left to Burn - A Story of Alzheimer's Disease

My decision necessitated a lot of planning and preparation. I was able to get Charlie approved to go to the day care group five days a week instead of the three days he now attends. The grandchildren have been coming regularly during the summer to do chores which require ladders and kneeling. I know I must have a reasonable semblance of order in the house before going into surgery. If I can control my surroundings if only for a while, I will go into the surgical procedure with the essential positive attitude required to fight during the long recovery period. I had a month to plan and organize before the surgery and every day, I reminded Charlie of the upcoming upheaval in his routine. I thought that daily reminders might instill some sense of what was yet to come. I would routinely engage in perception checks to try to understand what, if anything, Charlie processed.

"Charlie, do you know about my going to the hospital?" I would ask.

"You told me you would go." I was pleased.

"What will I have done at the hospital, Charlie?" I ask.

"They will put a scope in your knee and straighten out the ligaments," he responds. "Then, you'll come back home and make my dinner," he adds.

Even though that is nowhere close to the invasive surgery and the extensive rehabilitation I will have, I am content that he has some notion that I will not be at home. That might help to lessen the anxiety and make it a bit easier for the caregivers who will keep Charlie safe during my absence.

"Charlie, do you remember who will be helping you out when I am in the hospital?"

Charlie thinks for quite some time and then, he says the children and the grandchildren will help him.

"And will you let them help you with decisions?" I ask.

"If they need help, I'll be sure to tell them what to do," Charlie answers. I know I have some work to do before Charlie is ready to cooperate with other caregivers.

All of my papers are now in order. I dread going into surgery because of my previously horrible reactions to anesthesia and the fact that I cannot tolerate most pain relievers. As mentioned before, both of my parents died under anesthesia. But, I understand that every month and every year I delay the surgery, is simply going to make it harder as I age. And so, Charlie and I make daily preparations. Charlie is unaware of the preparations. He is a passive observer to what I must do.

Everything which would be necessary to carry on should I not tolerate surgery is now in place. I tell my son about the advance directive I have made so that Charlie's needs will best be served. He looks at me with his *really, Mom* facial expression. But, he also understands that this is a necessary preparation.

I have tried to remain upbeat as I prepare for the surgery. I have attended a class with men and women intending to undergo knee or hip surgery. There is a man seated in back of me who says he has a wife with dementia and he has fears about his wife's ability to cope with what he must have done. I turn to him and we talk for a moment. We have the same concerns about our loved ones but we also have the same resolve to try to get ourselves more physically functional so that we might be more available as caregivers. Somehow, we both feel a bit relieved that someone has validated our own unique conclusions. We no longer feel quite so selfish.

Charlie is due for his annual Medicare physical exam. I have already taken him in for his blood and urine testing. Charlie is not concerned about the examination. On the drive to the doctor's office, he comments, "I'll bet he tells me I'm ready to drive again!" I love Charlie's eternal optimism but I ache at his unmet needs for efficacy.

When the doctor comes in the room, Charlie and I are both seated. Charlie has had an EKG that day and we await the results of the other testing performed the previous week. Charlie's PSA is now up to 18, with a recommended result which should not exceed 4. The doctor comments that he smells urine and Charlie looks blank. I tell the doctor that Charlie has worn full protection underwear for quite some time now and that despite the protection, we have to attend to bladder and bowel incontinence. The doctor shakes his head and notes this on the computer. All physician notes are now entered in the computer. It seems impersonal but it is necessary in order that physicians continue to see those on Medicare.

Charlie's urine results have come back with abnormal concentrations of several chemicals as well as bacteria and blood traces. The doctor tells me those abnormalities are common with Charlie's problems and that the incontinence causes infections and I must be on the lookout for signs of discomfort as Charlie probably won't tell me directly. Several flags occur on the metabolic screening. The doctor and I talk about various medications and finally decide to leave things as they are. He asks me if Charlie takes his prescribed medication regularly and I respond I give him the pills. The doctor asks Charlie if he swallows the pills and Charlie says, "I really couldn't say if I do." Our doctor turns to me and smiles.

Charlie's lipids are way out of whack but the doctor and I no longer have that as a primary concern. His EKG revealed some sluggish lower heart chamber activity and I remark that Charlie sometimes has irregular breathing. The doctor nods and he knows I already understand that Charlie's system is beginning to shut down.

As the doctor and I talk, Charlie begins to tap the examination table and he plays with the paper protector. I reach over and place my hands on Charlie's hands and say softly, "Still your hands, Charlie." The doctor comments on how lucky Charlie is to have me as a caregiver. He does not remark that I am fortunate to have Charlie as my husband. He asks if I need him to prescribe something for Charlie's anxiety and I say we'd rather handle the problems with behavioral management for now.

Our physician verifies that Charlie's advance directive is in order and he comments that we also have a DNR (Do Not Resuscitate) prepared and signed. During my own physical a month earlier, I had mentioned Charlie's breathing difficulties. I asked what to do should I find Charlie unresponsive and our doctor instructed me about calling 911 and then presenting the DNR document.

Charlie seems oblivious to the current discussion. He is anxious to leave. The doctor finishes his checklist and we briefly discuss my upcoming surgery. As he leaves the room, our normally direct, businesslike physician briefly pats me on the shoulder. It nearly brings me to tears.

I go to the office to get copies of Charlie's blood tests to present to the VA clinic when we check in next week. I ask Charlie to please go to the waiting room and sit down. He goes outside the office but, instead of sitting down, he stands by the reception desk until one of the receptionists asks if there is something he needs. I open the door and ask Charlie to sit down while I make an appointment for next year's physical. The receptionist shakes her head and smiles at me. I'm not sure I want all this sympathy. I don't want Charlie's *condition* to be so blatantly obvious. I make the appointment, step into the waiting room and help Charlie up from the chair. Others in the waiting room smile at me and I'm instantly angry that they all pity us. But, I immediately silently acknowledge that I probably would have done the same thing if I were the spectator in the lives of others.

Chapter Fifty-Eight

Caregiver Transitions

It was now the week of my scheduled knee replacement surgery and there was much to be done. On Monday, I met my son for lunch so that we could discuss the finer points of his involvement in the procedure and the recovery process. The conversation turned to steps I had taken for estate planning and asset protection and an image immediately sprang to mind.

Over the weekend, Charlie was running errands with me. We stopped at the mall to get something from one of the stores. Then, we decided to get a sandwich so we wouldn't have to bother with an elaborate dinner. After eating, I excused myself to go to the bathroom. When I went back into the food court, Charlie was standing, talking with a man and Charlie handed the man something. I hurried as quickly as I could to Charlie's location, saw that Charlie had handed the man his bank card. I immediately took the card from the man, thanking him for being willing to help Charlie. I led Charlie away by his elbow and asked what he had been doing. He said he wanted to get money from the ATM (automatic teller machine) and he had forgotten our access code. I had no idea that Charlie still had his bank card as I was sure I had put it away months earlier, thinking he might misuse the card. Apparently, he had found the card, put it back in his wallet and when looking through his wallet, it triggered some memory of the intended use of the card. I shuddered to think how the card could have been misused in my absence!

So, over lunch that day, my son and I discussed how to best protect our bank accounts if I should become disabled during surgery. We decided to arrange for transfer of certain checking accounts directly to my son in the event of my death or disability. Being an attorney, my son would then have immediate access to funds necessary to carry on estate dealings as well as help Charlie get situated in another living arrangement. Both my son and daughter already had durable Powers of Attorney for me and for Charlie in the event of my incapacity so acting in our behalf would, hopefully, be a smooth transition.

As I talked over issues with my son on that particular day, it became apparent that he was taking my concerns seriously. Finally, it had registered that I was older and vulnerable to what I was about to experience. There was one question after another as my son assured me he would confer frequently with his sister in the weeks to come. When my son dropped me at home, my eyes welled with tears as he hugged me and I entered the house. It was another milestone in our lives; my son and daughter saw me now as the Old Guard. That meant that I would one day be replaced in my duties as head of our family. Perhaps my family would not see it that way, but that was my take on it.

The following day, Charlie had his annual check-up at the local Veterans Clinic. It took no time at all. Despite all the recent publicity about the Veterans Administration facilities letting down their veterans, our local clinic seemed to be attentive and efficient. Afterwards, I dropped Charlie at home with one of the grandchildren while I went to the bank and made revisions to account access instructions. That took some time as the bank's legal offices needed to review the Power of Attorney I had for Charlie in order to approve my requests regarding the checking accounts. Even though the process was frustrating, I felt assured that the bank was checking thoroughly so that there would be no delays should our children be placed in a position of decision-making for Charlie and me.

Due to my numerous complications in past surgeries, my

orthopedic surgeon elected to schedule me as his first surgery on Friday morning. He would operate at 7:30 a.m. meaning I needed to be at the hospital at 5:30 a.m. Everything was arranged for Charlie. I would get up early and my son would pick me up. Charlie would be picked up to go to the Senior Center and he would attend five days a week for two weeks.

I remember awakening in the hospital, feeling a great deal of pressure in my right leg. The nurse informed me I was to press the button beside me for pain medication. I told her the knee did not hurt much at all but that there was substantial discomfort on the back of the thigh. As the pain block wore off, the pressure on my leg increased. Again the nurse asked me to push the button which would dispense morphine to me. I was allergic to nearly all common pain medications but for some reason, I could tolerate morphine. I pushed the button with no real result. I texted my son and he asked if he should come back to the hospital. I told him that I would just like to rest and try to fight the discomfort. I asked about the procedure and he said the knee placement had gone well but that the doctor had told him, "It was a wreck in there."

Soon the surgeon who assisted my surgeon of record came in. He asked me to move my toes and he pressed on various parts of my leg and asked about sensation. Apparently, his concerns about movement and circulation were assuaged and I asked why the back of my leg was so sore and tight. He explained that when the quad muscle had been cut, I had begun to hemorrhage and that he'd had to apply a tourniquet. He said I'd have substantial bruising for a while. Later, with the assistance of a walker and a nurse, I sat on the side of the bed and stood up, using the walker for support. That seemed to relieve some of the pressure on my leg. But, as soon as I lay down again, the pressure returned.

My son and daughter both texted me that Charlie was back from group. My daughter and son were both at our house and it was decided Charlie would go to my daughter's home as previously planned and that he would spend most of the weekend there. I later learned that he wanted to go home at night and he didn't want any-one staying with him. Fortunately, my family understood that was a potentially disastrous plan. Finally, my son-in-law took Charlie home to sleep in his own bed and my son-in-law simply spent the night in the guest room. He did the same on Saturday night. Charlie was not being quite as cooperative as he'd promised.

I ate little the first night and was given medication to help me sleep. The following day, the block was worn off and the dis-comfort in the back of my leg grew in intensity as the day wore on. I told my nurse that the pain did not seem to be coming from the knee but from the sciatic nerve. It took a while but eventually, my healthcare team was able to figure out that the tourniquet had proba-bly produced a sciatic spasm which just didn't want to quit. I was given a muscle relaxant and it finally calmed. I was able to get out of bed and walk about a bit. I was unsteady, but at least, I was up and running! Well, moving at least.

In the meantime, Charlie was watching television with the grandchildren and getting waited on royally. He was told I was doing okay and that apparently closed the subject for him. Our grandson snuggled up close to Charlie on the sectional at my daugh-ter's house. He explained the play-by-play of the Tampa Bay Rays baseball game as Charlie couldn't quite decipher what was happen-ing.

On Sunday, the healthcare team asked if I wanted in-home care upon discharge or whether I wanted to go to a rehabilitation facility. I strongly wanted to request the latter but I requested the former, knowing Charlie was getting more and more anxious with my absence. He would still be going to the Senior Center daily and I would have in-home nursing and physical therapy.

My son came to the hospital early afternoon. We had to wait for a walker and a commode to be delivered. I was instructed to use them at home for at least the first week or so. I was given prescrip-tions for an antibiotic, a muscle relaxant and a painkiller. After dropping me at home and assuring I was comfortably (and safely) in bed, my son took the prescriptions for the antibiotic and muscle relaxant to the pharmacy to get them filled. I had asked him not to bother with the painkiller as it was one which had made me very ill after a previous surgery. I decided to see how I tolerated the discomfort using only Aleve.

My son stayed at the house until Charlie was dropped off from group. Charlie came into the bedroom and smiled at me. He leaned down and patted the leg with the new knee and my pain level shot up to the ceiling! I explained to Charlie that I needed quiet and he left the room. I could hear the recliner mechanism and I knew Charlie was safely cushioned and already watching television.

As soon as one of the older granddaughters arrived to fix dinner for Charlie and spend the night, my son left. I could hear him reminding Charlie "not to bother Karen." It was a good television night and Charlie never once came into the room. My granddaughter made dinner, cleaned up and then came in to attend to my needs. All I wanted to do was rest. The sciatic nerve still tended to act up between doses of the muscle relaxant. My granddaughter attended to my needs and we all went to bed for the night. Charlie went to group the following day and my children both came over to check on my progress. The in-home care came to do an intake and to check on my knee wound. He approved six in-home physical therapy sessions.

I was up and using the walker when Charlie was dropped off. The walker seemed to confuse him but he appeared relieved to see me at home. He sat on his recliner and immediately turned on the television. When the oldest granddaughter arrived to spend the night, I told Charlie I was going back into the bedroom. He looked at me sweetly and said, "I'm sorry you broke your leg."

With the oldest granddaughter there, I had no qualms that things would go as planned in our home. She was to start her senior high school year in just two weeks and she was a no-nonsense girl! She slept in a room right across the hall from me and every time I arose to use the bathroom or just walk off the leg discomfort, she was right out the door, ready to help!

In two weeks, while Charlie continued to go to group, I progressed from the walker to a cane to walking without assistance. My physical therapist was tough but compassionate. He looked like the man on the bottle of Mr. Clean, with a shaved head and muscles that never seemed to stop. He thought my most difficult recovery would be from the sciatic nerve and the hamstring which seemed to have atrophied a bit. We worked on that until I finally said softly, "Uncle."

In the meantime, Charlie seemed content to go to group five days a week. We sat and talked at night and it became apparent he had no clue as to the nature of my surgery. I wore shorts one day while I was doing the set of exercises and when Charlie saw the deep purple on my thigh and lower leg, he commented, "Boy that was a bad fall you took! It's just lucky I was there to help you out!"

One night, Charlie remembered an incident in group. He told me another Navy man had confronted him. The man thought he had worn his own Navy hat to group and that Charlie had mistakenly taken his hat. Charlie told me, "He pointed his finger at me and everything!" I asked what Charlie had done and he said he didn't have to do anything because one of the helpers at group settled the incident. "I think there might be something wrong with him," Charlie said. "He might have Alzheimer's or something," he added. As a retired psychologist, I knew Charlie was seeing something in someone else that he just couldn't acknowledge in himself.

I suggested Charlie use his U.S.S. Randolph hat instead of the usual Navy he wore to group, explaining it would solve the problem of the hats. He thought the idea was *brilliant* so I suggested he get up at that moment and exchange the hats. He said he would remember in the morning. If there was one thing I *always* remembered, it was that Charlie *never* remembered. The incident repeated itself in group the following week and again, staff successfully intervened. I immediately switched the hats and from that point on, Charlie wore the hat with the logo of one of the ships on which he had served during his years in the Navy. When Charlie related the second incident to me, it struck me that he seemed a bit intimidated by the man. So much of my Charlie had slipped away.

Nothing Left to Burn - A Story of Alzheimer's Disease

My physical therapist came late one day and Charlie was just being dropped off. I introduced Charlie to the man who was assisting me in getting proficient with an artificial knee. Charlie smiled and raced past the man saying, "Okay, I gotta go pee." I simply smiled saying, "We aren't into formalities around here these days."

I would sit at night icing and applying heat to my swollen, metal appendage which would set off alarms in the airports. I thought that fact to be a potential annoyance but my grandson thought it was one of the best things that had happened to the family in quite some time! My daughter and son and the grandchildren continued to come and visit while they dropped off supplies and that brought a welcome hiatus to my days of recovery. I had been watching more television as of late and thought much of it to be boring and violent and just plain silly. Charlie sat mesmerized. He particularly liked to watch Texas Walker Ranger and the Andy Griffith show. Fortunately, those shows were on in the late afternoon when Charlie arrived home from group. Sun-downing had been a growing concern in the progression of his disease. While I sat icing my knee, I watched television with Charlie. It seemed as if all the Ranger shows were the same. Indeed, some of the shows were the exact ones Charlie had watched a day or two ago. He never remembered from one day to the next – or from one minute to the next. While I iced the thigh area and made up new scripts to Ranger in my head, Charlie would swat imaginary flies, play with the cup holder and ask what was happening in the show. That was now commonplace. Even though Charlie sat and listened to the television, he did not seem to understand the scripts or the plots.

By the third week after my surgery, I was assigned to outpatient physical therapy. My son would take me. Charlie went back to his three days a week at the Senior Center. When he returned home on Monday, he immediately sat in front of the television set and asked, "Can you take me for a haircut?' I explained that I could not yet drive but Charlie was confused. He thought since I no longer used a cane, I could certainly get back to driving him where he needed to go. He didn't want to go to the usual barber and then take the bus home as it was mid-August and hot. I suggested we call Scat Plus to pick him up and deliver him to the mall where he could get a haircut, return his library book and get a treat before coming home. I reminded Charlie that the mall had a Subway and he could get a lunch that would be relatively healthy. The ride was arranged. I charged Charlie's phone that night and turned it on for him the next morning. I reminded him that he only had to press one button to reach me.

Charlie still loved the mall but some of the stores were new. He used to locate areas by the old stores. But lately, he began to get confused. I noticed that problem just before my surgery when I had last let him off at our usual drop-off and pick-up place. So, the special needs bus then began to drop Charlie off right at the entrance to the food court. He didn't walk around much anymore. Rather, he sat on a cushioned bench and ate snacks and watched people. I would give him bus money and money for food before he left the house. At times, I hesitated to allow even that limited freedom but Charlie would get very angry if he thought I was treating him in a condescending way. So, the mall continued to be a limited *independent* trip for my husband. I knew even that privilege would soon need to be discontinued.

On the day of the planned haircut, I knew Charlie could see the barber shop as he entered the mall by the food court. As it turned out, if Charlie reported to me correctly, he stayed in that particular wing for three hours, getting the haircut and getting something to eat. He was no longer wandering around which in some measure, was a relief for me. The mall was becoming an unknown for Charlie. But, the old mall was still Charlie's favorite place to go, even though it was now becoming a limited and foreign place to him.

When Charlie was dropped off at home that day, he brought with him a large Subway sandwich. I asked if that had been his lunch and he said he'd brought it home for us for dinner. For several months before my surgery, my leg was so uncomfortable that once every couple of weeks, I would stop and get a Subway for us for dinner, supplementing it with a salad or fruit. Charlie loved anything that came from somewhere other than our kitchen. For him, food from a restaurant was *eating out.* Charlie must have had some trace memory of my Subway sandwiches. There was a big sign over the store where Charlie usually sat and the sign probably triggered a pleasurable memory. I thanked Charlie for *getting dinner for us.* I got out some paper plates and divided the sandwich in half, serving it with fruit which Charlie left on the plate. Other than the sliced turkey, there was nothing in the sandwich which represented our *usual* Subway meal. Charlie had apparently forgotten everything we normally put on the sandwich but we both ate it anyway. When he was finished, Charlie commented, "You know, I won't go there again. They just don't know how to make it right!"

Chapter Fifty-Nine

Timing is Everything

My son began to ask how much longer I could hold out before we all started to look for nursing homes for Charlie. My children were rightfully concerned. During my three day hospital stay, my blood pressure had returned to normal. Within a week of being home, it had again risen and we all knew the cause of the stress.

The inane conversations tended to increase my stress. Most people wouldn't think twice about answering such innocent questions but for me, the ongoing absurdity took energy I simply did not have.

"Is this Sunday or Monday," Charlie asked

"It's Thursday. Tomorrow you go to group, Charlie. Tomorrow is Friday and this is Thursday."

"Well, that's not right."

"It is right, Charlie. This is Thursday."

"Well, you're wrong. If this was Thursday, then tomorrow would be Friday. I only go to group on Monday and Wednesday. So, if I go to group tomorrow, this has to be Sunday."

Charlie, this is Thursday and you go to group tomorrow. You go to group on Mondays, Wednesdays and Fridays. Tomorrow is Friday and you go to group."

"See, you were wrong. I go to group on Monday, Wednesday and Friday and you said it was Monday."

"Let it go, Charlie. Please, just let it go."

***

265

Nothing Left to Burn - A Story of Alzheimer's Disease

During my recovery, I liked to sit out in the front. It is relaxing and even in the hot Florida summers, I always remained comfortable. For me, my Tuscan garden was an escape. But then, the glass front door would open. Charlie would get a chair cushion from the pile on the chair and he'd place the cushion on the chair adjacent to me. He would then sit and stare at me, hoping I would make voice and eye contact.

"It's beautiful out here, isn't it, Charlie?'

"What is beautiful?"

"I love the flowers and the bushes and the sound of the water fountain. And, of course, the songs of the birds are beautiful. It's all just so peaceful and relaxing."

"Birds aren't relaxing."

"Watching the birds can be relaxing, Charlie."

"Do they think so?"

"Does who think so?"

"You don't even know what you're saying."

A neighbor came to bring over a piece of our mail that inadvertently got placed in her mail box. We talked for several minutes about some of the changes in our lives and she volunteered to help me run errands while I'm recuperating.

When the neighbor left, Charlie asked, "Do we know that lady? She just came over and talked with us. I think that's weird."

I breathed deeply and answered, "Charlie, that's our next door neighbor Jean. You know we oftentimes talk with her son and her two granddaughters." We have lived next to Jean for seventeen years now.

Charlie looked vacant. Then, he looked at me and glared. I silently speculated he was angry that he was losing people that I still knew. I asked him, "You seem a little upset, Charlie. Can you tell me what you're thinking?"

Charlie frowned at me and said, "I'm not thinking anything."

And, I am horrified because I know Charlie is telling me the truth.

***

My physical therapist was a bit concerned that I was overdoing it with my rehabilitation efforts and I was under orders to take it easy during the long Labor Day weekend. I told Charlie we had lots of leftovers in the refrigerator. I stressed that he would be helping me a lot if he would simply heat up something in the microwave for our dinner.

Charlie went into the kitchen and looked in the refrigerator for an extensive period of time. He then got into the freezer and pulled out an ice cream bar and came into the family room. As he sat eating the treat, I commented to Charlie that he needed something nutritious. I smiled and said it was okay once in a while to start with dessert but that he also needed to have a healthy dinner. I again reminded my husband that I was to minimize the time on my feet and that he was to heat up dinner for us.

Back to the kitchen went my husband and this time, he pulled a frozen dinner from the freezer. He opened the carton and said, "These directions are stupid." I asked Charlie to bring me the box so that I might read the directions. He brought me the tray which contained the frozen dinner. I again asked for the box. He returned to the kitchen and brought me the box and he had put the dinner back in the box. I read the simple directions and then asked Charlie to take his dinner back to the counter and I would give him the directions.

Charlie returned to the kitchen with the frozen dinner, leaving the box with me. I told Charlie to leave the wrapper on the tray of food and to get a fork and poke several holes in the top.

"I already took the top off."

"Okay, Charlie, put the top back on and poke a couple of holes in the covering."

"That's hard. The covering is all loose."

"Hold the plastic wrap while you poke a hole in it, Charlie. Use a fork, not a knife, please."

"Okay, I did it. What now?"

"Leave the cover on top of the food. Put the tray in the microwave and close the door, Charlie."

"Should I leave the top on?" He only remembered the second sentence.

"Leave the top on."

"Okay. What button should I push?"

"Push the number 3, Charlie. Don't touch anything else. Just let the microwave do the work."

"Does it know what to do?"

"It does."

I had just reclined the chair I was on. I was *so* tired. But, when I heard the first of three beeps, I immediately cautioned Charlie. "Charlie, open the door but don't take out your dinner."

"I want to. I'm hungry."

"Charlie, please don't do that! Just get the two hot pads and take the dish at the sides. Set the dinner in the other bowl on the counter and let it cool for a moment."

"Okay. Oh wait. I gotta go pee."

I give thanks to the powers that be that by the time Charlie was finished in the bathroom, the dinner would be cool enough so that it won't scald his tongue. Otherwise, he would have risked burning his mouth just to get the food in as quickly as possible.

Charlie returned from the bathroom and I asked if he had washed his hands. He turned around and went back into the bathroom. My leg wound is still not completely healed and is subject to infections. I am constantly asking Charlie to wash his hands.

After again returning from the bathroom, Charlie brought in his dinner. He sat down and noisily began to eat. I asked him to please use his manners as I was very tired, not to mention, very irritable.

Halfway through his dinner, Charlie commented, "This is good. Just think, I made this all myself!" Charlie was perfectly content to sit there eating while I sat with nothing. If he had truly known how selfish his needs now were, he would have been so ashamed. But, my Charlie was not now a knowing being.

Chapter Sixty

Crying Over Spilled Milk

I was still struggling to heal myself. I needed to get back to driving so that I could free up my children to carry on with their own lives. They were wonderful about running errands and helping out but I knew I needed to push myself in order to again be independent and attend to Charlie's needs. But, it seemed like every time, I sat down to ice my leg and rest awhile, Charlie would get creative around the house.

After folding clothes I had just put through the washing machine and the dryer, I would ask Charlie to put away his clothes. The next day I would find the clean clothes in the dirty clothes hamper and would have to wash them again. After fixing dinner, my leg would be sore from standing on the solid kitchen surface. When we had finished eating, I would ask Charlie to wash two plates and put them in the dishwasher or to hand wash a skillet and put it away. I kept trying to find simple tasks he could still do just to keep the motor memory going a bit longer. But, if I didn't watch Charlie like a hawk, he would put the dirty plates back in the cupboard and put the skillet in the refrigerator or the stove. Thus, I usually ended up having to do the task over, resulting in just as much motion for my tired body.

And, then came the evening that I actually cried over spilled milk. Charlie went into the kitchen looking for a snack. I suggested he forgo the cookies, the blueberry muffins and the ice cream bars and have a glass of chocolate milk. He took the half-full carton out of the refrigerator, opened the top of the carton and then realized he needed a glass. He left the open carton of milk on the counter and opened the cupboard door, reaching in to get a glass. He did not close the cupboard door but while trying to place the glass on the counter, Charlie knocked over the carton of chocolate milk. I was only aware of the incident when Charlie exclaimed, "Uh, oh!"

I immediately asked about Charlie's apparent concern and he told me he had knocked over the milk. "It's all over the floor" he said with no particular concern in his voice. Not wanting to leave my icing procedure for spilled milk, I instructed Charlie to get paper towels and soak up the milk from the floor and to then use the wet sponge mop to clean up the residue. He only heard the first part about the paper towels. As you already know, Charlie loves paper towels and he always attends to a sentence containing those particular two words.

Fifteen minutes later, Charlie came back into the family room where I was attending to my nightly knee-icing. He held a glass of milk and a paper towel. I actually praised him for cleaning up a mess he had made. Charlie sat down and instructed me to turn to a program that wasn't "stupid." That meant a program that was a rerun from a long time ago. I turned on a channel I knew he liked and he sat back. I asked again if the milk was all cleaned up and Charlie said he had done a good job. I continued to read while the ice took down the swelling from the day's activities.

Shortly before we were to retire for the evening, I went to the kitchen to get a glass of water to take into the bedroom. I turned on the overhead kitchen lights and met with a scene of disaster! There was chocolate milk all over every single white cabinet in the kitchen. The stove, refrigerator and dishwasher were streaked with chocolate milk. I was stunned to see that the two by two inch backsplash tiles had chocolate milk all over them and to make matters worse, the chocolate milk was in the white grouting as well.

I called Charlie into the kitchen and explained that the milk had taken quite the journey in our kitchen and that his cleaning chores were not yet complete. I asked him to get a bucket from the garage while I got a sponge from the laundry room. I had visions of giving the kitchen a thorough cleaning but I knew that given the condition of my still healing incision, the sciatic nerve which was burning through my thigh and buttocks and the tight hamstring, I would have to hope that Charlie could at least do a superficial cleaning. I sprayed the affected areas down with Clorox spray cleaner and then, went to shower. I hoped the hot water and steam would relax my muscles and also help to reduce the stress I was feeling.

When I got out of the shower, Charlie met me and told me he was going to bed. "That cleaning really wore me out," he said. I truly felt sorry that I had asked him to clean up the mess with his limited abilities, but I was grateful that he had done the job. I would not know until morning the kind of job he had done.

The following morning, I stayed in bed to exercise while Charlie ate his breakfast and waited for his ride to group. It was when I dressed and went to the kitchen that my eyes began to form tears over the spilled milk. As Charlie's ride pulled out of the driveway, I scanned the appliances which were all glazed in a white residue. There was chocolate milk on all the cabinets from about one-third of the way down and the baseboards were covered with dark spots as well. The countertops had the same glaze as did the backsplash which also held various sizes of chocolate spots. I felt defeated and I thought of calling one of my children to come and help me. Even though I no longer took any pride in cooking, I did still get satisfaction from a clean kitchen with sparkling stainless steel appliances.

I went to retrieve the Clorox spray and began to tackle the backsplash with a small brush and a wet sponge. An hour and a half later, the backsplash was free of milk and I was exhausted. I sprayed down the countertops and also the stove top. Then, I got the stepstool from the garage and sat on it while I sprayed the top portion of the cabinets and then wiped them down. I was not able to get to the very bottom of the cabinets and I could not reach the baseboards.

Nothing Left to Burn - A Story of Alzheimer's Disease

My son called, saying he was in Sarasota and wanted to stop by for something. When I arrived, I explained the situation and he immediately began to clean the appliances, the bottom of the cabinets, the baseboards and the floor. "You really ought to take pictures of some of this stuff, Mom," he said.

"I really don't want to remember it, sweetheart."

"No, that's not what I mean, Mom. In case Charlie tries to fight you on getting needed help for him, you might need some evidence of all the things he's done," my son said. He was almost embarrassed to have said such a thing and yet, we both knew how spot on he was.

While Charlie was still gone, I remembered recent discussions in which I had asked him about attending group during the five week days. He had appeared confused but not opposed to such an arrangement. I called the Veterans Administration Social Worker I had previously asked when needing additional groups for Charlie during my time in the hospital. I explained that Charlie was requiring a lot more care and that I needed to begin to take care of myself. I felt myself tremble as I asked for additional groups for Charlie. The social worker asked, "Permanently?"

"That's right," I responded. "It needs to be a permanent thing for Charlie." I had just taken a step I had never ever wanted to take. But once the social worker asked a few more questions and said, "I'll see what I can do," I felt relieved. She said she understood my needs and Charlie's needs.

The feeling of having a community of caregivers was never stronger than at the moment a social worker I had never met said she would call the Senior Friendship Center and get back to me. I was asking someone else to share more of the burdens I felt in my caregiver role and I was not ashamed.

The VA social worker called later that afternoon and said everything was approved. She had already called the director at the senior center and the director had assured the social worker that she would call for additional rides for Charlie. When Charlie got home

272

not long after that, he said someone had come to tell him they were delighted that he would be in the group more days. I told him he would be home the following day but that after that, he would go to group Monday through Friday. He said, "Okay, I gotta go pee."

That evening as I lay in bed, I thought about how wonderful it was to have a community of caregivers. It mattered not that I hadn't met all of them. They were skilled, just as I had been in my profession, and I needed to place trust in them just as my patients had placed trust in my own abilities. I now had a local social worker, our family physician, the VA physician, the VA social worker, the director of the senior center and the staff at the Senior Friendship Center in my caregiving group. And then, there was my family, my precious family who had recently seen their once stoic and stalwart mother/grandmother with vulnerable lines on her face, stress darkness under her eyes and an artificial knee that would set off alarms in airports!

Chapter Sixty-One

The Pleasant Toddler

Even though Charlie was becoming cognitively like a toddler, his moods continued to be mostly positive. In my work as a Clinical Psychologist, I had seen so many men and women become angry and belligerent as their disease progressed. I was truly grateful that Charlie had maintained an *even keel* as it pertained to his emotional status. But still, I knew that his failure to express strong emotions was yet another part of the Alzheimer's process.

Once in a great while, Charlie would have a mild look of disappointment on his face. Those would be times when he perceived me to be more mentally astute than himself. I think one of the reasons he wanted to go to group was that he was still having some success with some of the cognitive exercises such as trivia games.

I estimated that Charlie's mentality was now fairly consistent with what we call the preoperational stage of functioning. This is approximately the age of a toddler, from two years until about five years. At this stage, a child is not keenly aware of the consequences of his or her actions and there is no abstract thought processing. Toddlers are somewhat full of themselves and it is definitely the "*me first*" stage of development.

I noticed that Charlie seemed consistent in his lack of unawareness of my needs while I was in the rehabilitation stage of the knee surgery. On days when I had worked particularly ... was truly worn out in the late afternoon, Charlie would arrive home from group and immediately want to know what I was fixing for dinner. If I told him I really didn't feel like fixing a big dinner, he would go and look in the refrigerator and then, go to his lounge chair and sit. It seemed to be an extreme example of a self-focused attitude which I had to totally ignore so as not to become angry. Inevitably, I would go to the kitchen and fix something for both of us. Charlie would always be pleased to have food served to him. Afterwards, he might stare at the substantial scar on my knee and ask, "Are you going to the doctor so they can fix your leg?"

Weekends were almost grueling for me now. Charlie still had three chores to do. I would tell him in the morning that it was time to dust the furniture and I would watch while he ran the dust cloth around objects, skipping some things altogether in a hit-and-miss fashion. He would then sit down at his desk and would not rise until I asked him to vacuum the three area rugs. Again, they would get a superficial cleaning and then, Charlie would sit in his office chair, seemingly exhausted. I would wait until the next day to ask him to push the dust mop around the floors. Because of his nearly total lack of exercise, Charlie would sometimes look very pasty after engaging in exercises with minimum motion. And then, he would almost always be resistant to doing anything that required physical effort. If it was to be an enjoyable experience, such as an activity involving food, Charlie could somehow find the energy to get into a car to go somewhere. Preschoolers can be just like that.

One morning, I decided to trim some of the plants in the front garden. Charlie watched me from the front office window and after I had been outside for over an hour, he came out and asked if he could help. I smiled at his willingness to assist me and said I would be very appreciative if he'd simply throw the trimmings into the yard waste container for me. He did so for almost half an hour, puffing along the way. He kept watching me take sips of the water I had taken outside. I suggested he go get a glass of water for himself and then return to finish cleaning up the front garden. After half an hour, he failed to come out so I went inside to assure myself nothing had happened to him. Charlie was sitting in the recliner chair watching television.

"Charlie," I said, "I really miss not having you outside with me."

"Oh," Charlie replied, "what are you doing outside?"

"Charlie, we are both cleaning up the front garden. Remember, you were helping to put the clipping in the yard waste for me."

"I was?"

"You were."

"Okay."

"Does that mean you will come out to help me, Charlie?"

"No."

"Why not, Charlie? I could use a good helper."

"I don't want to." And, that would be the end of the conversation. I had a typical toddler in a grown man's body.

Sometimes, when he watched television, Charlie would pick his nose. He would study what he had excavated and oftentimes, roll the nasal find in his fingers and throw it on the floor. Sometimes, he appeared curious about his own anatomy. He would scratch at his crotch and then, being unable to get at an itch because of the thick protective underwear, he would stare at his crotch as if he wondered if everything was still there. Apparently satisfied, he would revert to watching rerun of Walker Texas Ranger. Sometimes, when walking to the kitchen, Charlie would stop and look at the floor. He might retrieve a small piece of something (usually a carpet fiber) and then, put the piece in his mouth. If he didn't like the taste or the texture, he would either throw it back down on the floor or take it to the trash can in the kitchen.

Lately, Charlie had taken to spitting whenever he was out-

276

side. I wasn't sure if this was in any way practical due to a build-up of saliva or if it was a delayed imitation of having just watched a baseball game on television. On occasion, he would just go outside and disappear. He did not wander off. Rather, he would wait until I came outside to search for him. For me, it seemed as though Charlie was becoming totally right-brained. This is the impulsive, emotional part of the brain and that is exactly the side which seems to be used by the toddler as s/he begins to explore the world prior to brain maturation.

I think the behavior which most disturbed me during this phase of Charlie's illness was that of partial nudity. Lately, I had stressed being dressed properly as I remembered that nudity is oftentimes a component of dementia. I wanted Charlie to have rules and regulations for as long as possible so that I could feel reasonably comfortable with him in social situations.

Charlie would go into the bedroom to change from the clothes he wore to group. He would get down to his protective underwear and then, seemingly forget to dress in casual clothing. Sometimes, I would find him simply standing in the bedroom and I would then suggest he put on some shorts and a tee shirt. If he gave me a blank look, I would then get clothing for him and help him to dress. At times, Charlie would come out into the family room or the kitchen in his protective underwear.

"Charlie?'

"Yeah?"

"Where are the rest of your clothes?"

"Where are they?"

"Charlie, you clothes are in the closet. Please put on a tee shirt and some shorts."

"No."

"Why won't you put on clothes, Charlie? See, I have clothes on. We always wear clothes in case somebody comes to the house."

"Who's coming?"

"I don't know, Charlie. It's just polite to wear clothes when you're around someone else."

"I'm the only one here."

"I'm here too, Charlie."

"Yeah, but you don't care."

"Charlie, I do care. I like to see you dressed."

"Where did you hide my clothes?"

And so, I would take Charlie by his hand and take him to the closet where I would hand him a tee shirt and a pair of shorts.

"Can you put the shirt on me?"

"Yes, Charlie, I can help you with the shirt." I always put the shirt over Charlie's head and helped him put his hands in the armholes. "Okay, now you pull the shirt down, Charlie." I always wanted him to try to take part in a task so that the common activity would not be totally lost to him. I feared it would not be long before Charlie began to run around the house naked. And then, It would be time for yet another care decision. No one at group had complained about Charlie, so I guess he was keeping his clothes on there. Thank you for small blessings.

Chapter Sixty-Two

Our Days

"Uh, oh!"

This is often the way we start our days now. I had just dressed and I immediately followed Charlie's voice to the bathroom. He was standing by the sink in his protective underwear. He had a tube of toothpaste and he was holding it while the toothpaste oozed out of the tube. The toothbrush was covered with paste and the paste was now making a pile on the inside of the sink. Charlie was breathing rapidly and he had a look of anxiety and helplessness on his face.

I went over and immediately released Charlie's hand from the tube of toothpaste and his anxiety immediately disappeared. Not only was Charlie having problems initiating actions, he was now having trouble ceasing an action.

"What happened?" Charlie asked.

"I think your hand forgot to work for a moment, Charlie." I responded as I grabbed a tissue and began to wipe up the pile of toothpaste. I reminded myself to purchase toothpaste today.

"Nuh-uh," Charlie said in total earnestness. "There was something wrong with this barrel, not my hand."

I immediately surmised that the tube was now being called the barrel but I was not about to prolong our moment of "uh-oh" that day.

Nothing Left to Burn - A Story of Alzheimer's Disease

"Charlie, your breakfast is waiting. You need to dress and be ready for your driver. Come on, let's get those teeth brushed. Charlie brushed for about thirty seconds and left the toothbrush smothered with paste on the edge of the sink. I encouraged him to dress quickly and then sit down to breakfast.

In twenty minutes, Charlie came out of the bedroom, went to the kitchen table and then, he picked up his breakfast plate and took it into the den. He began to eat as he looked at the computer monitor. I had long ago quit trying to force him to eat at the table.

Charlie's ride to the Senior Center could come at any time within the period of an hour. It came early on that particular day. Fortunately, Charlie had eaten his breakfast so I helped him to stand and looked him over. I re-buttoned his shirt and sent him outside where the driver Freddie helped him into the van. I smiled in gratitude of the driver's careful handling of my husband.

Our "uh-oh" days could be anything but generally, they started in the morning when I was at my worst. I'd never been a morning person and since my knee surgery, I'd had the great urge to sleep in a bit. Restless nights will do that to a person. I now had a brace for my knee to try to force the knee down and extend the hamstring. It had not made my moods more pleasant so "uh-ohs" were particularly annoying these days.

On one day, an "uh-oh" might be a bladder accident. On another day, it might be failure to get clothing on properly. On another day, it might be that the shower wouldn't turn off. On those days, Charlie tried to turn the spray off rather than the faucet.

On other days, uh-oh moments might be outside and believe me, I couldn't run very fast at that time. Charlie might be stuck in a chair. He might have leaned over to pick up sticks and fallen or he might simply have had an event of visual distortion which bothered him. Above all, he understood that an "Uh-oh" from him would immediately bring help.

One day, I went into Charlie's den to get a phone number. There must have been hundreds of tiny ants, all attempting to get to the blueberry muffin crumbs Charlie left in the morning. I grabbed the can of ant spray and thoroughly blasted the offending critters and then proceeded to search the area for their place of entrance. I sprayed inside and outside of the window. I then proceeded to spray around the outside of all the windows in the house. I swept the floor and then vacuumed everything. When Charlie got home from group that day, I again explained how ants will try to find food everywhere and how I'd had to interrupt my day to take care of the muffin crumbs.

Charlie's reaction, you ask? He said, "I bet they really liked those muffins! I sure do!"

These days, Charlie would accept no substitutes. If we ran out of blueberry muffins for his morning breakfast, he would become anxious. If I tried to substitute toast with blueberry jelly, it would simply not fly. Charlie would steadfastly refuse the substitute and go without. Or, he might look in the pantry and get a blueberry snack bar and have that. There was simply no flexibility in routine and procedure anymore.

Every day was now a challenge for me. Charlie would lock up the house as soon as he returned from group. The window blinds would be drawn. I would unlock the doors and put up the blinds so as not to feel claustrophobic. Charlie would lay out his clothes and all his toiletries for the next day and I would put them away so that I could use part of the bathroom for my own needs. I would leave the clean clothes out as a reminder that Charlie needed to change clothing. Sometimes, he would change into old, worn clothes and simply put out the clothing worn on that day. I would inspect the clothes and most of the time, I would toss them into the laundry hamper and put out a new set of clothing.

On beautiful autumn days, I would open the windows and

Charlie would immediately close them. He "reorganized" things in drawers and cabinets so I would have to play "hide and seek" with my cookware and utensils.

One day while Charlie was in day care, I got a call from the Alzheimer's Association. They wanted their usual yearly donation. This year, I had already contributed to the Association via a walk-athon. One of my granddaughters did the walk. I was frustrated and probably talked a bit firmly when I explained that my husband had Alzheimer's and that I would really like to be taken off their calling list now. A very polite and understanding woman gave me her blessings and said we would no longer be bothered by calls from them. Sometimes, the smallest gesture can bring a caregiver back to life. That was one of those moments.

Chapter Sixty-Three

Living with Uncertainty

By this time, my days were both predictable and very unstable. Charlie attended his group at the adult day care center. They took care of him for six hours, five days a week now and I was able to get most routine chores accomplished. But there were still another eighteen hours in the day and for that time, Charlie and I were pretty much on our own. The weekends became very long now and I had to constantly check my own moods and behaviors lest I become disrespectful to a man who simply could no longer process the environment.

One day Charlie came home from group and I asked if anything new had happened. He initially said "No," but then a moment later he volunteered, "A new person came." Then, he added, "It was two new people." I asked if he had greeted them and he said he had. I reinforced his positive action and I was about to ask about another topic when Charlie said, "I gave them my card."

"What card, Charlie? What card did you give the new people?"

"My business card," my husband responded. Well, Charlie had not had a business for a very, very long time so I needed to follow up on this new enterprise. I felt I had lived and resolved this issue many months ago, but apparently not.

And so, I asked, "Do you have one of the cards you could show me?" I asked.

Charlie hunted through his wallet and he pulled out everything. It was packed! Finally, he handed me a card that he had used some twenty years ago. It had our home address and our home telephone number on it. My heart skipped a beat and I then clarified what had occurred.

"So you gave people you didn't know a card with our home address and phone number on it?" I asked.

"Yeah, they really liked it," Charlie said.

I thought for a moment and then, I responded, "Charlie, I think it's about time we clean out that wallet of yours. You can hardly get it in your pocket. It has way too many things in it."

Charlie looked at the wallet for a couple of minutes and then, he began to pull out cards. I was appalled when he pulled out a major credit card I had taken from him some time ago! I took the card and remarked to Charlie that it was dangerous to carry things he did not need. He insisted he needed the credit card and would not relinquish it. I had no idea how Charlie had hunted down the card but I was determined to take it and place it in a safe hiding place. Lately, Charlie had begun to rummage through drawers and cabinets, trying to find his medications bottles and I surmised he had run across his credit card during one of those searches. We ended up getting rid of ten cards that night. But, Charlie would not relinquish the credit card.

When Charlie went to bed that night, I took out the credit card from his wallet. I then searched the other cards and found a concealed weapons permit that I had removed months earlier. I had a vivid flash of someone accosting my husband, finding the card while searching for money and assaulting him while trying to find a handgun. I confiscated that card as well.

The following morning, Charlie's ride came and we said our good-byes to one another. He got out to the car and sat in the seat. I closed the door but, only a moment later, Charlie was back in the house. "I need my credit card," he pleaded. "Did I lose it?" he asked.

I went to him, hugged him and pointed him out the door

again. I said, "Charlie, last night we went through and cleaned out the cards in your wallet. We decided I would keep the card so you wouldn't risk losing it. You know it's such a hassle to replace a credit card."

Charlie stared and then he said, "Oh," and he got into the car. For days, I wondered if this would be a repeat issue each morning. But, Charlie never asked about the card again.

One day, my son came over to install a new printer in my office. When Charlie came home, he saw the old printer on the table and he asked what it was. I explained that our son had installed a new printer for us and that he would also soon remove Charlie's nonfunctioning printer as we had a new, working printer now.

That day, while Charlie was in group, I had begun to clean out several file drawers. I was determined to clear out some clutter. Charlie had always been a packrat and he had documents lying around that were absolutely useless. I ran across his birth certificate and was confused as I thought documents like that were already in our bank safety deposit box. I asked Charlie for the combination to his small desk safe so that I could put the gift certificate in for safe keeping until the time I could take it to the bank. It was his personal safe and I'd never had the combination. It goes without saying that Charlie no longer had the combination on ready-recall.

I tried several combinations but none of them worked. I wasn't concerned as I knew all our important documents were in the bank safe. But, in looking for the combination, Charlie had moved his computer mouse to the top of the computer. Pretty soon I heard, "Okay, who's been messing with my computer?"

I went to Charlie's den and he was pacing and anxious. He accused our son of taking the computer mouse. "See, here's the cord! He just unplugged it and took it away! Now, my computer is worthless," Charlie said in a panicky voice.

I quickly assessed the situation and then sat Charlie down in his desk chair. I showed him the mouse which he had placed on top of the computer and told him he had moved it while looking for something. I felt it best not to introduce the small safe combination issue. Charlie took the mouse from the top of the computer and placed it on the mouse pad.

"But look," he said, 'it's unplugged. I wish you wouldn't mess with my computer!"

I explained to Charlie that the cord to which he referred was the charging cord for his cell phone. He had not recognized it. I told him his computer mouse was plugged in and that he only had to point it at the computer. He placed his hand on the mouse and shouted, "No see, it doesn't work anymore. People have to stay away from my computer!"

I patted Charlie on the back, walked into the living room and turned on the television. "Charlie, I put on your favorite show, sweetheart. Come on in now while I start dinner for us."

Charlie obediently went in to watch television. While he was distracted, I went to the den, turned the computer mouse to the correct position and it worked fine. Later, Charlie went in to shut off the computer. He yelled out, "Comcast finally fixed my computer!"

"I didn't know it was broken, Charlie."

"Yeah," he answered, "it went out about a month ago."

At this stage of the disease, paranoia could have created far too much tension. There is absolutely no reasoning with someone who cannot process what you say. It was far better to distract and simply fix the problem, knowing there would be no constructive memory of the incident.

Lately, I had been waking up feeling very tired mentally. I remembered that I'd had some terrifying nightmares. Even though I couldn't remember much of the content, I reasoned that my sleeping mind must have been processing some of the stress of the day. During the daytime, there is precious little time to try to process the stress brought on by the caregiving role. You certainly cannot do it at the moment you are "taking care of business" and trying to prevent a catastrophe with your loved one. It makes sense that the unconscious mind would need to rid itself of some of the uncomfortable memory and feeling storage it accumulated. And so, the nightmares surfaced. Most of the dreams seemed to incorporate themes of being trapped and being without adequate resources to help Charlie. And so, I did the next logical thing: I began to attend a support group.

Chapter Sixty-Four

The Reluctant Witness

Charlie was missing the target on almost everything these days. He asked what a zip code was and then he asked what our zip code was. He thought he knew our address but he got the numbers all wrong. I got weary from answering questions I had answered two minutes before and then, before and before. I was getting so emotionally tired just taking care of Charlie.

I always carried a spare pair of Charlie's underwear in my car when we went out and another pair in my purse for when we left the car. We were oftentimes late running errands as Charlie would race to the bathroom at the last moment and spend half an hour in there. He got up earlier and earlier as the months progressed. His group attendance was the foremost thing for him and everything else went by the wayside. He expected my care and he got it daily while I grew weary.

I was concerned about what Charlie did in the bathroom for so long so I would get up and go to the nearly-closed bathroom door to try to discover Charlie's bathroom rituals. I worried about his safety and wondered if he might soon be needing some assistance with his grooming routines. Sometimes, he closed the bathroom door and at other times, he left the door ajar. He began to get up even earlier and I just couldn't bear to get up that early after a touch-and-go night of sleep. But, one morning, I awakened early and caught him as he came out of the shower. He spent considerable time trying to dry himself by dabbing at his body parts with the towel. He then struggled to get on his protective underwear. He had left the bathroom door ajar and his image was reflected in the mirrors so I didn't even have to open the door further to gain the knowledge I sought.

My husband sat on the toilet and put his legs into the openings of the underwear. I was pleased Charlie was sitting down as I was continually aware that he could easily fall and that would create even greater problems. Charlie would have to try several times to hit each of the two holes. Then, he would rise and go to the sink where over a dozen toiletries would have been put out the night before. He picked up his hairbrush and looked at it for a solid two minutes before putting it down. Then, he got his partial denture out of the container where it soaked overnight. He placed it directly in his mouth without rinsing it first. I grimaced. He picked up the electric toothbrush and pushed a button, turning it on. He placed it in his mouth and then, closed his lips on the handle of the brush. I nearly went in to help but I felt I needed to see the rest of the routine.

Charlie picked up the hairbrush again, looked at it and put it down. He picked up the tweezers and pushed at them several time, seemingly fascinated by the device. After nearly five minutes, he put down the tweezers and again went to the toothbrush. He turned it on and put it in his mouth. It appeared that the rotating brush touched Charlie's tongue, startling him. He jerked the brush out of his mouth and put it back on the stand, with the brush still rotating. He looked at the container of denture cleaner and picked it up. After a minute and a half, he dumped the liquid in the sink and put the container into the cabinet below the sink. He looked at the contents of the cabinet for a while and then stood up and looked into the mirror.

For several minutes, Charlie looked at all the items around the sink. He picked up a comb and put it back into the drawer. He began to pick at his skin. He picked at it until the skin bled and then, he wiped the blood on his underwear. He looked at the buzzing toothbrush and picked it up. He pushed the on button and the buzzing continued. He studied the toothbrush for quite some time and then pushed the other button. The toothbrush went silent. Charlie put it in the sink drawer and looked at the contents of the drawer. He pulled out some antibiotic ointment and squeezed out a large amount which he put on the skin sore he had just irritated.

Charlie seemed to study the open drawer. He took out several items and seemed to look at the print on tubes and packages. He then took out the electric toothbrush and put it in the sink. Charlie then picked up the brush, looked into the mirror, and finally, he ran the brush through his hair, smiling as he completed the task. Daggers were searing through my heart and I wanted to go in and brush his teeth and comb his hair and trim his beard and anything else that would help to make him the Charlie I knew. But, I knew I'd learn nothing if I took that kind of action. And so, I continued to watch. By now, forty-five minutes had elapsed since Charlie had exited the shower and put on his protective underwear.

Looking toward the shower, Charlie took a step and opened the door. It looked as if he was about to step inside and then, he appeared to notice the wet tiles. He closed the door and picked up the brush from the counter and again brushed his hair. He picked up the toothbrush, pushed the on button and then, he pushed the off button and put the toothbrush back in the holder. He started to pick at his skin again and then, he looked at the shower and opened and closed the door.

I was about to go in and ask Charlie if I could do anything to help when he suddenly shoved everything into the sink drawer. I high-tailed it out of the bedroom but left the door ajar. When Charlie came out of the bathroom, I asked, "Need any help, Charlie?"

Charlie didn't answer so I stuck my head in the room and asked again.

"No, I have to dress, that's all. I'll be out in a minute." And then, twenty minutes later, Charlie came out of the room. He had put on his pants, his shirt and his socks. His shoes were by the front door. As he shuffled all the time, I asked that he take off his shoes in the house so that he wouldn't mark up all the wood floors.

Charlie's hard-boiled egg, blueberry muffin and glass of chocolate milk were all out for him. I told Charlie I was going to hop into the shower and that I'd be out in ten minutes. When I came to the kitchen area ten minutes later, Charlie was in the den with his breakfast. I just couldn't figure out why he avoided the kitchen table. I had asked him a couple of weeks earlier and his answer at that time was, "Because we do that at group."

I thought I would approach the subject while it might still be fresh in Charlie's mind.

"Charlie, do you think maybe I should help you to get ready in the morning?"

"That's dumb! Would you want me to tell you what to do?"

"I guess not, Charlie but it seems to be taking a long time now. I just thought maybe you needed some help."

"No way."

"Charlie, when you put the toothbrush in your mouth, you need to put the bristles on your teeth and clean your teeth really well."

"I know that. I always put them in the box every night. That cleans them."

"But, Charlie, I mean the teeth in your mouth. You need to brush those teeth."

"I do," Charlie answered in an angry tone of voice.

I had to stop as I didn't want Charlie to go off to group in anything but a good mood. I told him we would go for a haircut on Saturday and he smiled and then saw his ride pull up into the drive-way. I walked him out the garage and then waved and closed the door. I went into my bedroom, pulled back the covers I had just made up and sobbed for fifteen minutes. What I had seen that morning was something no one should ever have to witness in a person they love.

Chapter Sixty-Five

Halloween Every Day

It was Halloween and Charlie's group was going to have a celebration. Each member was asked to wear a costume. Charlie had two potential costumes to wear; both were saved from previous parties. I explained to Charlie what was expected in group for the party and he immediately said he wanted to wear his kilt. Now, Charlie is not even close to being of Scottish heritage but I am. When traveling to Scotland many years previous, Charlie fell in love with the Scot traditions and the Scot people. He immediately declared himself a Scot.

The evening before the group party, I carefully laid out Charlie's kilt, shirt, cap, belt and a pair of short to wear underneath the kilt. The following morning, I went to the kitchen where Charlie was waiting for breakfast. He had the kilt on backwards and the shirt was tied in the front. There was no belt and Charlie was wearing his Navy hat.

"It looks like you've adapted the costume a bit, Charlie," I observed with a semi-grin on my face.

"What?'

"Where are your cap and belt, Charlie?"

"They don't fit." I picked up Charlie's kilt and while he smiled, I observed he had on only the protective underwear…no shorts.

"Mind if I alter things just a bit, Charlie?' I asked. I drew a blank stare.

I went into the bedroom and picked up the cap and the belt, along with the pair of shorts. Going to the kitchen, I saw Charlie had taken his muffin, hard-boiled egg and chocolate milk into his den. I followed him in and requested he stand for me.

I tucked in the shirt and turned the kilt to its proper placement. I put on the belt and put the large pin on the front of the kilt so that the kilt would not open. Then, I placed the bright red cap on Charlie's head and told him to go look in the mirror. I've never seen such a large grin!

"How did you make them fit?' Charlie asked.

"Oh, they just needed a little tweaking, Charlie."

"Did you do that on the computer?'

I thought for a moment and then responded, "No, Charlie, that tweeting. It's something that......" There was no sense explaining. Instead, I instructed Charlie to finish his breakfast and then, put on the shorts. Charlie finished breakfast and went into the bathroom. Then he came to the bedroom door and looked around, first for the front door and then, for me. He went to the front door and opened it.

"Where are you going, Scottie?" I asked as the front door slammed. I followed Charlie out as he explained he was going to wait outside for his ride. He looked around and asked, "Where is the Scottie? Maybe I can pet him."

I was facing Charlie's backside and took the opportunity to lift his kilt. Paper underwear was all I saw. "Okay, back into the house now, Charlie. You need to put on those shorts."

We went back into the house and into the bedroom. I asked Charlie to sit on the edge of the bed while I put his legs into the leg holes of the shorts. I asked him to stand and then, I pulled up the shorts and zipped and fastened them. As Charlie headed back out the door, I pondered whether Charlie would be successful in lifting the kilt, taking down the shorts and then taking down the underwear. I hoped I had not caused unnecessary stress for him.

Charlie's driver came right on time and he immediately

commented on Charlie's costume. He asked Charlie to wait a moment while he retrieved his phone and took a picture. Charlie complied and Freddie then helped Charlie into the car and buckled him in. I had a brief visual flash of doing those same movements with my young children.

As Charlie's car pulled away, I began to think about the beginnings of Halloween. The custom purportedly originated over two thousand years ago. Supposedly, it is the day when the living and the dead can intermingle. I thought at that moment that I would love to be able to receive counsel from some of my deceased friends and relatives. I then shuddered when I briefly thought about how Charlie sometimes seemed suspended between the living and the dead.

***

I am unable to get to sleep, visions of my life with Charlie shooting around like a rat in a maze with no entrance or exit. One of the flashbacks was vivid and persistent. It had been a game changer for us both.

Charlie and I were in a private practice together in Iowa. We were black and white, fire and ice and night and day in our personalities but had somehow complemented one another to form a thriving business. I wanted nothing to complicate our business relationship but apparently, Charlie wanted a different arrangement. He asked our office manager if she thought I'd go out to dinner with him. At the time, the office manager had immediately replied that I would never think of dating anyone who smoked as I was highly allergic to cigarette substances. The following morning, Charlie came into the office and announced to everyone within shouting distance that he had quit his thirty year cigarette habit. I was pleased but Charlie's decision in no way altered my feelings about him being a somewhat strange individual.

After a month, I was somewhat shocked that Charlie had actually quit his habit. He seemed to be waiting out a period of time. And then, just before closing one day, he came to my office and asked me to dinner. "I'll never pick up another cigarette," he announced with a bearded smile and bright blue eyes that just seemed to advertise mischief. I told Charlie I was flattered but that I didn't think we should complicate a working relationship.

"It won't complicate anything," he said. "It will actually be a resolution. And then, he left my office to allow me to contemplate.

I finished my case notes and prepared to leave the office. Charlie was still next door in his own office so I tapped on the door casing and said, "Charlie, you're really a sweet man but I just don't think I can accept your offer."

He tilted his head, smiles and replied, "Okay, but you know I'll ask again." I waved and left the office for the day.

A week to ten days later, Charlie made the same dinner offer. I think I felt sorrier for him than anything else. And so, I said, "Okay, maybe Friday night." Charlie lit up like a roman candle just off the launching pad.

"I'll pick you up, "he said. I thought I heard a trembling in his voice.

"No, I'd prefer to meet you there, Charlie." And so we made arrangements to meet at a fairly established restaurant.

That Friday, I was nervous and already regretting my decision to meet Charlie. He left the office early, after his last appointment but I had a couples counseling and stayed an hour later. I dropped by my house, cleaned up a little and then went to the restaurant and met Charlie. He looked as if he'd been waiting some time and might be unsure that I would even show up.

Charlie came to my car and opened the driver's side door for me. My initial reaction was that he was either highly anxious or that he was simply an old-fashioned gentleman. By the end of the evening, both attributes would prove to be true.

Charlie ordered a drink and then, two more. I sat drinking an unsweetened iced tea. We ordered our dinners and then Charlie began to ask me questions about books I had read and what I thought about various philosophers. I found myself mesmerized with his vast store of knowledge and I got totally into the discussions. This was something I had apparently missed for a long, long time and the conversation caught me up for three hours. We refused dessert but both agreed to coffee. Charlie was still verbally filling me with his intellectual prowess and at one point, I remembered looking down and seeing Charlie's hand covering mine. I wondered when that had happened. It both shocked and confused me.

I would find out in the months to come that Charlie was both a simple and a complex man. His needs were not at all lavish. He preferred a simple life, much as I had always lived. But his mind was just filled with bits and pieces of multifaceted knowledge. I had studied philosophy in undergraduate school and Charlie and I would spend hours debating the merits of the various scholarly, historical figures. Charlie allowed me to know and understand him at a deeper level and the more I discovered, the more I liked.

He was a professor at a large university program and a very outspoken faculty member. He was the state IPA (Iowa Psychological Association) President and also the President of the State Licensing Board for Psychology. He specialized in forensic psychology, doing consultations for several law firms locally and nationally. His mind never left me bored and it became a strong basis for a personal relationship and eventually, our marriage. Even after our move to Florida, Charlie sought to teach young graduate level minds and prepare them for a career in psychology. Having served in the military, he encouraged students to consider a military internship and residency and he became a liaison from the university to the military services. What bound me to Charlie was his creative mind. With his verbal fluency, he could talk his way out of anything, anytime. And now, that troubled mind threatened to be my undoing.

***

"Uh-oh."

"What is it, Charlie?" I was in getting Charlie's breakfast ready on a Saturday morning. I had just taken out the laundry basket to do our laundry for the week.

"There's no bucket in here," Charlie responded. I couldn't quite get that one so I headed toward the bedroom. Charlie was standing in the closet looking at the space which had previously been occupied by the net laundry basket I had recently removed.

"Charlie, I took the basket to the laundry room. What do you need to put in there?" I asked.

Charlie handed me the kilt from his Scottish costume which had been worn the day before and he said, "There's no place to put it."

"Charlie, that's a wool kilt. We don't wash it; we take it to the dry cleaners."

"But, it's dirty isn't it? You tell me to put dirty clothes in the laundry basket. So, I wore it and now, it should go in the basket but it isn't here. There's no place to put my kilt." I asked Charlie to go to the kitchen and eat his breakfast while I inspected the kilt and then, hung up the kilt on a hanger.

By the time I returned to the kitchen, Charlie was already in the den eating his breakfast. He was playing a game of solitaire on the computer while he periodically dropped crumbs on the floor. Fortunately, I had picked up another can of ant spray the day before.

I went to the laundry room to sort out the loads of clothes to be washed. There was nothing of Charlie's in the laundry basket! He had apparently hung up all his dirty clothes and now, my task was to try to remember what he had worn to group that week. I sorted through his closet and pulled out a pair of khaki pants, some socks stuffed into shoes and three shirts. I slipped them into the laundry room while Charlie was eating. When he finished, I went to his closet and got out a clean pair of pants and a clean shirt. I literally pulled up my husband and stripped him down to his underwear and redressed him. He looked surprised but he went along with my strange act. Afterwards, he just said, "You coulda just told me those weren't the right clothes."

Nope, I couldn't have done that at that particular moment. As I said before, you have to pick and choose your battles. Sometimes, surprise is the most functional action.

Chapter Sixty-Six

Peaks and Valleys

It was a time of ups and down, with down days prevailing. Once in a while, a spark of intelligence would flare and then, just as quickly, it would wane and Charlie would become the increasingly more severe Alzheimer's patient.

One night, we were watching a British show on the PBS channel. Charlie looked over at me and said, "I'll be shutting down soon."

I was startled and it took me a moment to respond. "I'm not sure what that means, Charlie," I struggled to say.

"Me neither," he replied.

I thought maybe Charlie meant he would soon go to bed. But whatever the meaning, Charlie stayed up to watch the show, going into the bedroom at his usual time. However, after that night, he began to go to bed earlier and earlier. I asked if he could sleep that early in the evening and he said he always fell asleep. But, when I would arise from my own bed around midnight, Charlie's bedroom light would frequently be on, with the television set glowing. Generally, I left well enough alone. I was actually content to believe Charlie was safe in the bedroom rather than wandering the rooms of the house or attempting to get out of the house altogether.

***

One day, I was sitting out in the front garden reading. I oftentimes did that in the late afternoon so that I could greet Charlie as he arrived from his day at group. I watched the car pull up and Freddie emerge from the driver's seat. He went to the passenger door, opened it and disengaged Charlie's seat belt. Then, Freddie helped Charlie out of the car. I went to the car to greet Charlie and Freddie said, "He's a good guy." I smiled at the driver and thanked my lucky stars that Charlie was surrounded by people who still recognized his human worth.

As Charlie and I headed through the gate to the garden area, I pointed to where Charlie might seat himself. Unless Charlie had to race to the house to go to the bathroom, we would often sit for a while so that he could tell me about his day. When I asked what had happened that day, Charlie replied, "Oh, not a whole heck of a lot." That was his usual response and I would generally have to try to trigger some memory by asking if there had been visitors or entertainment or I'd ask how Charlie might have done on the trivia games.

Charlie handed me a booklet and I read the title (*Caring for a Person with Alzheimer's Disease*). The booklet had been compiled by the National Alzheimer's Association. I asked Charlie if he had been given the booklet in group that day. He explained that he had just seen a stack of the booklets at the Senior Center and that he thought I might want one.

"Why did you think I might want the booklet, Charlie?"

Charlie thought for a moment and then responded, "I think you told me once I had Alzheimer's."

It was really the first time that Charlie had openly acknowledged his diagnosis and it really touched me. "So why did you want to give me the booklet then, Charlie'" I asked.

"I thought you would want to know how to take care of me," he smiled. Then, he sat and stared at the flower garden while my eyes became glossy with tears. It was just such a precious moment. My mind flashed back to the day that one of my preschool children had brought me a rough, handmade booklet colored with various flowers. I had asked why the booklet was being presented to me and my young son answered, "I thought you would want to remember how to take care of the flowers you have, Mommy." The booklet was precious. It had words like "water me" and "give me sun" written under the pictures. It was a moment that brought me to tears and I was grateful when Charlie abruptly got up and said, "I gotta go pee."

***

It was a busy day and I had a lot to do. But not long after Charlie got to the Senior Center, I got a phone call from the director of the day care program. She told me Charlie was acting out and being rude. For a moment, it startled me. Charlie had always gotten very favorable feedback from the staff. I flashed back to the past few days and realized that Charlie had appeared agitated the last few days. Our weekend had been very rough. The director told me Charlie had asked his driver to let him stay in the cab while others were picked up for the group. He had apparently wanted a longer ride that day. The group leaders had firmly told Charlie that he must get out of the cab and attend group. The director explained how it was an issue of liability and also, an issue of boundaries. She said Charlie had recently been wandering a bit and was not responding well to redirection. I assured the director that I would address these issues with Charlie and I volunteered that I also had been experiencing a few problems lately with Charlie's behaviors.

I ran a couple of errands and then, my cell phone rang again. It was the nurse from Charlie's group. She informed me that Charlie was being rude and sullen and that he was definitely "off" that day. She said they had just staffed Charlie and wondered if he might be having a physical problem that caused mental changes and behavioral abnormalities. She suggested that sometimes, conditions such as diabetes and UTI's (urinary tract infections) can cause those with dementia to act out. She suggested blood tests be run to rule out any physical problems.

I called the doctor's office and suggested that Charlie be seen as soon as possible as the Senior Center staff was concerned. They were very responsive and said we could see the Physician's Assistant if I could pick up Charlie early from his group. I emailed the Senior Center director that I would be picking up Charlie shortly. When I arrived, I went directly to Charlie's group room and the director and the nurse were standing together in discussion. I immediately went to them and told them I was taking Charlie to the doctor's office and that I was so sorry they'd had to cope with his foul moods.

Charlie saw me and came to where I stood. I asked him to get his jacket and hat. He was confused so I immediately stated, "Charlie, we almost forgot your lab work today. Come on now, I'll help with your jacket out in the hall so we don't disturb the others."

I got Charlie out of the group room and helped him on with his jacket. Then, I steered him out the door and into the car. He continued to look concerned. I decided it was useless to tell Charlie about the phone calls as his mentality would not absorb the information and I did not want to bring in others unnecessarily.

Charlie, do you remember that even though we've both had our physicals, the doctor likes to run labs on us in-between the visits just to make sure we're doing okay?"

"I guess."

"So, that's what we're doing today."

"Good. I'm glad you came. Group wasn't good today."

"Charlie, you love group. What happened to disappoint you?"

"I don't know but I wanted to ride with Freddie and they wouldn't let me."

"Charlie, they can't let you do that. It's against the rules."

"I like to ride.'

"Well, you're riding now. So, isn't it an unexpected treat to take a ride with me?"

"Yeah, I guess."

"So, Charlie, how did you let the leaders know you were angry at them?" I asked in as casual a voice as I could arrange at the moment.

"I wasn't mean."

"I didn't say that, Charlie. I asked how you let the people at group know that you were angry or disappointed about not going for a ride with Freddie."

"I didn't."

"You didn't?"

"No, I'm always nice."

"Okay, Charlie. If you remember otherwise, please do tell me so we can talk about it."

We pulled into the physician's parking lot, walked to the front door and took the elevator to the second floor. We checked in and sat down to wait. Charlie sat agitated and he said he needed to use the bathroom. I stalled him, thinking they would want a urine sample. Charlie sat wringing his hands. Then, the nurse opened the door and called Charlie's name. She asked him how he was and he said everything was just fine. The nurse handed Charlie a sample container and asked him to use the bathroom. Charlie was relieved and the nurse and I were able to talk a bit as to why I had requested that Charlie be seen. Charlie came out of the restroom and handed the sample to the nurse.

"Charlie, did you wash your hands?" I asked.

"No," he said.

"Please go back in and wash your hands, Charlie," I requested. The nurse told me where to go when Charlie finished. We went to the small examination room and the nurse asked a few more questions and then asked us to wait for the PA. Charlie and I spent the moments speculating on the PA whom we'd never met.

When she entered, Charlie immediately greeted the PA. She asked a few questions and quickly got the idea that Charlie was simply not tracking simple conversation. She continued to review Charlie's last blood tests and said that she did not suspect diabetes. After another moment, the nurse knocked and then brought in the results of the urine labs. Sure enough; Charlie had a urinary tract infection!

We got the prescription for the antibiotic and thanked the PA for her time. She had consulted with Charlie's regular physician to make sure the new prescription would not be in conflict with his regularly prescribed medications. She gave us greetings from the doctor and we left.

I decided to take Charlie to Panera for a nice bowl of soup while we waited for the prescription to be filled. The last thing on my mind that night was preparing dinner. We had a pleasant light dinner in our usual silence, with me bringing up topics of conversation and Charlie nodding or shaking his head while he raced through his meal. Then, we picked up the prescription and went home. I gave Charlie his medication and then emailed the director of the group program and thanked her for the heads-up call from the staff.

Before Charlie left for group the following morning, I gave him his medications and we talked about how he might have been a bit gruff with the staff because he hadn't been feeling well. He was very concerned that the driver Freddie might get into trouble and I assured him that would not happen. I again reminded him that apologies were always appreciated if others had been "gruff." Charlie's ride then pulled up and he greeted Freddie with a grin. I hoped he would remember our conversation.

That morning, I got an email from the program director informing me that Charlie had come into her office to apologize for bad behavior because he was sick with a UTI. I was so very pleased that Charlie had followed through with our conversation as I knew how difficult it must have been for him to keep the conversation in his mind all the way to the Senior Center. I was also touched that Charlie had been worried about Freddie. It was the first act of empathic concern that I had seen in some time. I went to work out at the gym thinking that this was indeed, a good day. Lately, there had been way too many more challenging peaks than relaxing valleys in our daily journey together.

Chapter Sixty-Seven

The Purge

"Uh, Oh!"

It was Christmas day and I was hoping it would be a day free of "uh-ohs." I had just put in the apple-cranberry pie to take to my daughter's house for Christmas dinner later that day. After having spent the morning standing in the kitchen baking, I needed to rest a bit. Charlie had been watching television programs the entire time and I was grateful that he'd stayed out of my way. I had already washed dishes once so that I could use the containers for the next project. I only had four or five dishes to wash now so I put the sink stopper in and ran about six inches of water in the sink, also squirting in some dish washing soap.

I called Charlie into the kitchen and asked if he could wash the few dishes, rinse them and place them in the other side of the double sink. He smiled as if he wanted to help and he began to run some water to rinse the dish he had just cleaned. I went into the bedroom to pull out some fresh clothes to wear to the Christmas celebration. After about three minutes, I had my selections made and I headed back to the kitchen. The water was still running.

Charlie was standing in front of the sink. His shirt was wet and water was up to the top of the sink and running onto the floor. I ran to the sink, pushed Charlie aside and turned off the water.

I tried to be civil as I asked, "Charlie did you think to let the water run in the other part of the sink where there was no stopper?"

Charlie looked at me as if I were speaking a foreign language. "We wash on one side and we rinse on the other side of the sink, Charlie," I said as I grabbed some towels and started to mop up the area.

For a moment, Charlie appeared confused. Then, he said, "If you run the water in the other sink, there's no place to put the dishes."

I looked at Charlie and then at the towel I had placed on the counter for the dishes to be placed after the rinsing. There was no use trying to explain. Charlie had forgotten how to wash dishes. This time, I grabbed my cell phone and took a picture of the overflowing sink.

On the way to my daughter's house, I explained about how holidays were special times in which we showed love and respect to others. I talked about using napkins, going to the bathroom to take out teeth and cutting food properly so as not to choke on food. Charlie said he knew all that.

As soon as we got to the driveway of my daughter's house, the children came out to help unload the car. Then my son showed up with several dishes of his own which would all be contributed to the family Christmas dinner. The table was beautifully set and the house looked warm, festive and inviting. We all sat down to dinner and I couldn't help but admire the way my daughter had organized things perfectly. After fifty-five years of hosting Christmas, I was gratified that my daughter and her family had learned how to put together a wonderful family celebration.

On occasion, I glanced at Charlie and he seemed to be holding his own at the head of the table. I would sometimes give him a clue to wipe his face with his napkin but he was otherwise doing well. He simply ate, ate and ate some more while everyone else talked.

When everyone was satiated beyond comfort, the grandchildren started in. The third granddaughter had braces and she noticed the butterfly napkin holders all had small magnets on them. She put the magnet to her teeth and sure enough, she soon had a butterfly on her braces. The four other grandchildren looked for places the magnet might stick and they became very creative. Suddenly, Charlie began to attempt to stick the butterfly on his teeth and he became frustrated when it wouldn't work. We other four adults were amused but we tried to spare Charlie's feelings. Finally, the youngest granddaughter explained, "Poppy, it won't stick to your teeth because you don't have braces. But see if it might stick to your spoon or your knife." Bless her kind little heart!

We moved to the living room to open gifts. We would have dessert later, after our stomachs were less extended. My daughter made up a dessert plate for her brother to take with him and the grandchildren got gifts from under the tree for him to take as well. He had other friends to visit. After getting a couple dozen hugs from nieces and his nephew, my son headed to the door. Charlie began to get agitated and he tried to rise from his seat on the comfy sectional.

"He has to take us home!" Charlie yelled. "He's leaving without us!" he added. I went to Charlie and reminded him that I had driven us here and I would take us home. He again looked confused but sat down and seemed to be able to relax. Charlie used the bathroom several times during the gift exchange and he seemed to be getting tired. I checked my watch to assure myself we would leave before the sun downing rituals commenced.

Following the gift exchange, there was dessert to be had! And, there were mountains of things from which to choose. Charlie chose them all! During the dessert conversation, the children commented on how grateful they were for their Christmas gifts and how surprised they were by some of the things they were sure would not be gifted this year. Our grandson said, "Well yeah, when I opened up that new bat, I was like Wow-Wee...I was so surprised!" Charlie immediately took off on that saying. "Wow-wee, pooh-pooh, pee-pee" before I motioned that we did not do potty-mouth phrases when in the company of others. It was a clue that we should soon vacate the premises.

It was a wonderful family celebration and I had been happy to yield the hostess job to those better qualified. Charlie had remained basically intact but I was grateful I left when I did as he began to decompensate on the way home.

"I gotta go pee."

"Charlie, you just went to the bathroom before we left."

"Then I want to go back and get some dessert."

"You had a plateful, Charlie, and our daughter made up a bag of goodies for you to take home."

"I want them now."

"Charlie, we've both had enough for tonight. We'll get sick if we eat more."

"I never get sick from eating. I could eat all day."

"Charlie, that's not healthy."

"You shouldn't tell me what to do. You're the one that had to go to the hospital."

It wasn't the time to hold a conversation. I remained silent.

"You were mean to me."

I remained silent.

"You didn't let me have enough to eat."

I remained silent. After about two minutes, I pointed out a beautiful display of Christmas lights as we passed by a church. Charlie said "Wow!" He rubber-necked at the display and forgot about the food. We had done Christmas with the family and it was a loving holiday to be sure. I wondered as I went to bed just how many more Christmases Charlie would have with us.

***

For some time now, something had been troubling me. I searched through a mental repertoire of things that could be bothering the caregiver of an Alzheimer's patient. Naturally, everyone who cared about me would routinely inject into our conversations the notions that I had to "take care" of myself. I was doing that. I had gotten the surgery on my knee; I was eating nutritious meals; I

307

was back at the gym; I was staying in touch with friends and family and I was attending a support group. I realized that even before my surgery a month ago, something was nagging at me and it was affecting my moods. I would get angry over small things and I would try to overcorrect Charlie even when I fully understood he could not accomplish more that his best. I began to get feelings of disgust about my own emotions and yet, there was something with which I was not coming to terms.

Being unable to get in touch with my emotional center, I began to problem-solve. In the past, action sometimes encouraged mental realizations what were hidden in the recesses of my mind. Beginning in September, I had talked at length with Charlie about how at some point in the near future, one or the other of us was going to need a caregiver. By including myself, I was able to get Charlie to listen to me. He did not feel threatened. He never used his office anymore and it was simply collecting more and more *junk*. I explained to Charlie that the office could make a potentially lovely caregiver room and that would allow us to stay in our home. I said we needed to make the transition before we actually needed the room. Charlie thought about it for a while and then asked, "What about my books?"

"You have so many books Charlie. I think we should begin to share them with others."

Charlie looked concerned so I continued, "But I think you should keep the books that are important to you. How about if you begin to go through the shelves, one by one? The books you want to keep, you can leave on the shelves. The books that can be donated, you can put on the floor. I'll box them up and donate them to the library."

Charlie studied my face, looked away and then, studied me again. "Okay," he replied. I smiled. I silently congratulated myself for that one.

Charlie turned back to the shelves and then said, "I want them all!"

My shoulders slumped and I knew I had not gotten the concept through to my husband. I realized I had given him too many steps in the process. I took Charlie by the hand and we went into the office. "We'll just do one shelf today," I said as I pointed to the top shelf on the right cabinet. I took out a book and handed it to Charlie.

"You haven't used this book for at least five years, Charlie. I think it's time for someone else to enjoy it."

"Well, that's just dumb. I need that book to teach."

My heart ached and I nearly sank to my knees. But we had begun something that I would not stop. "Charlie, we both retired years ago. I turned my books over to a colleague and now, it's time for you to do the same. Just think of the young students who would be overjoyed to have your books."

Since Charlie had always been an advocate for the students, I thought that statement might impact him. He placed the book on the floor and I was overjoyed. One-by-one, we did the same with all eighteen books on the shelf. When we were finished, about half the books remained on the shelf. There were still too many but I would scan those books carefully to try to ascertain which topics were still important for Charlie.

For several days after that, we took a shelf at a time and reduced the amount of books in the bookcase. I then talked with my son about putting in a closet so that the former office could be considered a legal fourth bedroom. He immediately thought that to be a good idea and began to assemble the supplies to build the closet while Charlie was in day care. While my son worked on the closet, I planned out the room. It would be simple. There would be a sofa bed so that the room could be used by anyone as a place of respite. When time came, the caregiver would have a room with a sofa bed, a dresser, a chair and a television set. The room adjoined Charlie's bedroom which was on the other side of the house from my bedroom. It seemed to be an ideal set up for us.

While Charlie was in day care, I would cull through the books remaining on the shelves and pull out a few for donation.

Nothing Left to Burn - A Story of Alzheimer's Disease

Then, I boxed up a shelf at a time. They would be stored in the closet my son was making. Even though Charlie could no longer read a book, he could always look in the closet and assure himself that the books he loved were still in the house.

The next step was to rearrange Charlie's master bedroom so that his desk, computer and personal memoirs could be moved it. We wanted to do this after the drywall was up and prior to the sanding. In November, my son moved in the desk and computer while I busied myself taking all the memorabilia off the office walls and trying to find places for them in the bedroom. While Charlie was at the Senior Center, we made the transition in one single day. I had bought a new bedspread for Charlie's bed. My son and I had rearranged the room so that it actually looked larger, even with the desk and memorabilia. Charlie's personal mementos from forty years of teaching and serving on various psychology committees and boards hung on two walls, seemingly smiling at Charlie as he lay in his bed. The Navy plaques gave the room some pizzazz and the family pictures now reassured Charlie of ongoing love.

When Charlie got home that afternoon, I took him immediately to the bedroom. He gasped and said, "This is everything I would ever want! And, the room is even bigger now!" I could not have prayed for a better response. I feared the change would be unsettling. But, it seemed that the transition had been made at the time there was a small opening in Charlie's flexibility. Instead of upsetting him, having everything Charlie needed and valued in one room seemed to be just what he needed. He no longer needed to search the house for his belongings. He took me in his arms for the first time in months and he had tears in his eyes as he said, "Thank you."

It was a short-lived moment but one I would treasure as Charlie then asked, "Could you turn on Walker Texas Ranger for me?" He went into the family room and sat on his lounge chair. I turned on the television set to the channel he wanted and the room was forgotten. I still had work to do but a mountain had been conquered that day.

In the days to come, the dry walling project was finished and the trim boards were applied. The closet door was hung and it was now my turn to decorate. My granddaughter came over during the early part of the Christmas break and primed and painted the walls for me. I shopped for and found the perfect sofa bed. I took a chair from my bedroom and placed it in the new room. I took an area shag rug from another bedroom and it beautifully complemented the sofa and chair. My son brought over two side tables and I experimented with odds and ends of lamps, eventually purchasing a matching pair. I placed a teak sofa table on one wall on which to place a new television I would purchase. One day while I was at the gym, my son decided to surprise me. When I came home after my workout, he was just finishing the connections on a brand new television set! "Merry Christmas, Mom," he said as he approached me with a hug. He then hung some curtains for me and the room was complete.

That evening as Charlie watched his shows, I slowly developed a headache from the volume that Charlie now demanded on the television set. When I asked him to turn it down, he obliged but it was obvious he could not hear his favorite shows.

"Charlie, why don't you turn up the set to where it's right for you? I'll go in the other room and watch a different show." Charlie hardly gave a shrug as he turned up the volume again.

I went into the new room, closed the glass French doors and turned on the television set to a nature channel. The sound was mellow and the picture crisp. I laid down on the sofa and took off my shoes. I could stretch out and my back and I felt immediately relieved. I grabbed the throw from the adjacent chair and placed it on my legs and torso. I could feel the tension in my back and legs recede and I closed my eyes and listened to the show. After several minutes, I opened my eyes and looked around the room. It was beautiful. It was a retreat. I decided to claim it as mine until the unknown caregiver would take possession. By then, it would be a bit worn and very comfy. I had not felt that sense of peace for some time now. And yet, something was still nagging in the deeper recesses of my mind.

***

Nothing Left to Burn - A Story of Alzheimer's Disease

Even with my temporary retreat, I could feel the tension as an ongoing companion. Unless I figured the source of my own anguish, I understood it would not be long before the bell would toll for me. All my life, I had relied on my body to bring me news from my brain, whether good or bad. I welcomed the information, even if it was negative. I knew that knowledge gained would then release the unbearable tension I had been feeling. I even tried to force it at night with a bit of deep relaxation. But, the knowledge was stubborn. It would come in its own time.

I was not at all prepared when it did come. It was a few days after Christmas. I had taken Charlie for another silent ride. I tried to initiate a dialogue but it was a monologue as usual. I missed companionship with my husband. Charlie was sweet and generally compliant but we were no longer equal companions. He smiled at me when I talked and it seemed to be a smile of appreciation. We stopped at a frozen yogurt shop and I helped Charlie to pick out two flavors he liked. We went to the counter and had the yogurt cups weighed as it was a shop where you paid by the ounce. While I was paying, I asked Charlie to go and pick out a booth for us. While getting change for me, I noticed the cashier staring at Charlie. He was standing by a booth. "You can sit down, Charlie," I said.

"Does he have Alzheimer's?" the cashier asked. She then looked sheepish and added, "I didn't mean to…well, my grandpa has it and you have to tell him to do everything."

I smiled and said, "Thanks for your concern," and I went to join Charlie. I watched as Charlie literally devoured his treat. I thought about how when I told him to go get into the car, he would stand by the door of the passenger side and I would have to tell him to get into the car. When at our destination, he would remain with his seat belt buckled until I told him to get out of the car. He did not voluntarily initiate anything anymore except for eating. There are some with Alzheimer's who lose that ability as well. Hopefully, Charlie would not be one of them; eating was his most favored hobby now.

On the way home, I began to get tense again and I could feel the anger rising in me. I thought the bell was about to toll but it remained silent. I got a headache trying to figure out what I was missing and finally gave up and went to bed early. It would be a night of epiphany for me.

***

I had been exhausting myself both physically and mentally over the holidays. Just being around others brought me both joy and fatigue. I fell into a sound sleep that night. At first, it seemed like a routine dream. I was taking Charlie to see our family internist for his yearly Medicare exam. I had brought all the right papers and I had prepared Charlie for the appointment. He sat in the waiting room with me, tapping his hands on his knees. We were called into the examination room and the nurse directed Charlie to sit on the examination table. She took his blood pressure and Charlie said it tickled. The nurse asked me questions and recorded my answers. She left, assuring us that our doctor would be in shortly. Nothing seemed amiss. It was simply a dream about a common occurrence.

The dream continued as the doctor came in and greeted both of us. He sat down at the computer and reviewed laboratory tests. He asked Charlie what was happening and Charlie responded, "Oh, not a whole heck of a lot." Charlie always says that. He is not able to formulate any kind of answer regarding current activities.

The doctor asked me a lot of questions and then he examined Charlie from head to toe. "I smell urine," he commented. I raised my eyebrows and he smiled. He sat in his chair and told me I looked a bit pale and drawn but added, "That is to be expected."

I wanted out of that dream right then. I knew I was going to ask a question that would result in me being granted the knowledge I had been avoiding. I felt my heart racing and I tried to get out of the dream. In the past, I'd been able to do that. But the dream played on and I asked the question.

"How is Charlie doing health wise, Doctor?" I asked.

And it happened. It was a simple remark, one the doctor

probably answered hundreds of times a year. But it penetrated my emotional wall and the dam burst forth. The bell began to toll and I knew the sound was a wake-up call for me.

"He's actually doing so much better physically than I'd expect," the doctor said. "He could even outlive you."

Everything went fuzzy in my dream as I took Charlie's hand for support. I don't know how we got out of the doctor's office. Again, I willed myself out of the dream and this time, I was successful. I awoke from the dream and I was drenched. My sweat glands had released every ounce of fluid they contained. There were tears streaming down my cheeks but when I reached up to my eyes to wipe them, there were no more tears. My ducts had given to the fullest. I felt the sweat on my body and on the sheets and the pillowcase. But, there was something else – far beyond anything I had ever experienced. My bladder had released its contents and I had soiled my own sheets. I had violated the sanctuary of my own bedroom, the one place all the problems disappeared for a short time while I slept. And yet, I was calm and totally at peace for the first time since I'd first experienced Charlie's illness.

I immediately hopped out of bed and my legs nearly buckled. I realized that the release was total and I had to move slowly. I stripped the bed and took the bedding to the laundry room and ran water to soak the sheets. I then hurried back to bed and lay down and covered myself with the quilt which had not been a victim to my purge. I hoped I was still relaxed enough so that my mind would clarify the knowledge I had just been given in the sleeping stage.

And then it came. And then, I smiled. The doctor had given me the information I needed to produce the growth I would now experience. I had known for seven years that I was a caregiver. Everyone told me that, my doctor, my family, my friends and yes, strangers as well. But, the doctor's pronouncement was so strong and so specific that I could no longer deny that I had inadvertently placed myself in that role – and *only* that role. Previously, I had been a daughter, a wife, a psychologist, a parent a grandparent, a crafter, an outdoors woman and reader and traveler. But now, this was my life; taking care of Charlie's body was my life and my only life. And furthermore, it could go on long after I left this earth, leaving me with a singular role of my own doing. I was doing my time while having committed no crime. It seemed to me to be an extremely confining role and that was not acceptable to me. Furthermore, I had not even questioned the solo role I had assumed for myself. I had been resistant to the information mainly because I had unwittingly placed myself in the role.

I came to the realization that because I had taken my wedding vows literally and seriously, I had assumed that the life prior to the onset of Charlie's Alzheimer's was the *better* and that this period of my life as a caregiver was the *worse.* And what's more, I had apparently vowed to do the role well, so well that the caregiver role was *my* role my *sole* role. I loved my adult children and my grandchildren and my friends but during and after interacting with them, I was still *the caregiver.* I had not lost all the other roles, but I had laid them aside in favor of doing a top-notch job in my latest role.

While cuddled up in the quilt, I vowed that when a negative thought entered my head, I would attempt to replace it with a positive image. If I could not accomplish that while in the house, I would go outside and listen for the warbling of a bird. I would sniff the aroma of a newly-bloomed flower. I would listen for the laughter of a child. I would keep my eyes, ears and senses open to the world available to me. I would not allow a television pundit or someone else's expectations to interpret my world and determine my moods. I would not allow myself to think of my husband Charlie solely as an Alzheimer's patient. I had experienced wonderful years with my husband and now, his body had chosen to continue after his healthy brain had nearly vacated the space it had occupied for decades of meaningful life. Charlie was now a man I no longer knew who needed care and I was available and willing to assist him. Others would help him as well, particularly as the weeks, months and years progress. If you were to ask me, I would say my caregiving role with Charlie was worth it. After the onset of the disease, he was still a dear man who now spent his days outside the normal roles in life. His days were his to live and I would continue to be there every step of the way.

But, after my epiphany, my purge, I would once again think of myself as a multidimensional person, a woman, a mother, a grand-mother, a retired professional woman and a woman who probably had some years left to add yet another role to my life. Some might my call my experience of purging a "kick in the pants" and others Divine Intervention. Some may say I came to my senses before it was too late and others may tell me it was a totally selfish conclusion. We all have our own interpretations of the parts of the elephant in the room.

Charlie has told me he has Nothing Left to Burn in his brain, but I have lots of neurons firing. I need to more fully use those neurons. I have adult children to love, grandchildren to cheer and friends to support. I have books to read and crafts to attempt. I have sunsets and sunrises to appreciate. And yes, I have caregiving to do. And I will become Charlie's advocate.

There is an old song which has recently made an appearance on my favorite radio station. It's a song which appeared in the 1970's by the unlikely group called Queen. I say unlikely because I've always been more of a classical music fan, with occasional lapses into popular tunes. The song is called *We Are the Champions*. The third stanza has a few lines that I might want used in my eulogy should anyone care to offer one upon my death (and hopefully, not before). It goes like this:

> *But, it's been no bed of roses*
>
> *No pleasure cruise*
>
> *I consider it a challenge before*
>
> *The whole human race*
>
> *And I ain't gonna lose*

We are the champions, my friend,
And we'll keep on fighting
To the end.............

I had been missing that feeling, particularly for the past two years. It was a feeling that I'd always keep on fighting, right to the end. I had gotten sucked into the quagmire of my husband's disease. Alzheimer's caregivers will oftentimes tell you that they sometimes seem to merge with the disease and it becomes a part of them, limiting where they go and what they do and how it thwarts their development during their "golden years." But now, in that single, shocking moment of purging, I had been granted another chance, another chance to fight for myself. And this time, I knew I would not yield.

Epilogue

There are a myriad of books on the progression of Alzheimer's disease and just as many books on the experiences of caregivers. My story goes on but my intention was never to demonstrate the horrible, terminal stages of the disease. Rather I chose to acquaint the reader with the subtle decompensation of the brain which constitutes the loss of those we know and love. Alzheimer's is a different way of leaving life and one for which none of us is prepared.

Along with the knowledge of what happens to our loved ones, we must also learn about ourselves as caregivers. We need to learn our own limits physically, mentally and emotionally. We need to constantly assess ourselves to assure that aside from the caregiver role, we have maintained our other identities. We need to feel okay about continuing to live when someone we love is dying a slow and painful or hideous death. We need to affirm our own humanness along with our commitment to our loved one's welfare.

We're oftentimes told by friends "If you don't take care of yourself, you can't take care of _____ (your loved one)." But, it's not as simple as that. We must guard against becoming immersed in the loved one's disease and losing ourselves. Caregiving is such a subtle yet urgent role that we get sucked in without knowing that much of our diverse, lifelong identities are falling away. We must disallow the ongoing desperation of the loved one's fight and find growth for ourselves. We must consciously choose life for ourselves, with all the disappointments, pain and suffering. For if we let the unconscious feelings choose for us, we have given up the fight we

318

intended for ourselves. If, however, we choose to go on fighting, we truly are the champions of our own lives. Pain and anger and disappointment should not be feared. Nor should those feelings become our means of existence. If we dare to feel deep pain and we get through it with even greater knowledge about ourselves, then think of the depth of the joy we will now be capable of experiencing. And no one would be happier for us than those who struggle toward certain death in the hands of a caregiver.

THE END

CONSIDERATIONS FOR CAREGIVERS

***Not all people who live with Alzheimer's or progressive dementia patients can or should be caregivers. Every single case is different. Some of us lack the education or skill sets to be able to care for certain illnesses while others may not have a personality compatible to the demands of caregiver. Some of us may not have a home facility that would keep the Alzheimer's patient safe. There is not a single thing wrong with acknowledging that you have passed on the caregiver role to others and will now assume the role of advocate, as a caring overseer. You are still giving care. In the later stages of Alzheimer's, it is nearly impossible to be the sole caregiver, even if your own personal motivation is to do so. *Care* is the definitive concept in caregiving, and there are many ways to give care.

***When you need help as a caregiver, I suggest you go to a group for Alzheimer's or at the least, a group which has knowledge about progressive dementia. Mixed grief and support groups sometimes create more frustration than relief for the Alzheimer's caregiver because other terminal illnesses are generally of much shorter duration and the course is more predictable. In many physical illnesses, the body is destroyed while leaving the brain basically intact to interact with and give input to the caregiver. The Alzheimer's caregiver must oftentimes make educated guesses and/or outright hunches about how to help loved ones. And in many instances, the Alzheimer's caregiver has little to no part in the actual death process of their loved one.

***It's not a particularly positive thing to vow to be the "best" caregiver (because your loved one deserves it). I tried that initially and it put tremendous and unnecessary pressure on me because I already had the knowledge I would lose a loved one in a hideous and tragic manner. I adapted the slogan "Pretty good" when interact-

320

ing with Charlie in the initial stages. When transitioning to the middle stages where brain degeneration is far more apparent, "Good enough" became my criteria. When progressing to the end stages, I adapted the single word "Passable" as I attended to his needs. There were many times when friends would ask about Charlie. I would tell them the latest news while assuming they would assess my caregiving as less than the man deserved. When I would then be complimented, it would always surprise me and cause me to reassess just how hard I was being on myself. Perhaps we all wonder if we're doing enough when in truth, we only need to simply doing our best. I long ago ceased allowing "performance ratings" as they relate to caregiving and caregiving role.

        ***While working in long-term nursing facilities during my practice, I would oftentimes be called to the bedside of patients who were dying. Sometimes, family would be there; sometimes not. Remarks would be made as to the effect that the patient "died a peaceful death" or that a family member was pleased that they were there to help ease the loved one into the transition from life to death. There were many beautiful moments which tended to put staff or families at ease. And, indeed, I felt privileged that the family included me in their good-bye. But, we Alzheimer's caregivers (with isolated exceptions) must not set ourselves up to experience a "beautiful death" for our loved ones. We must take the bits and pieces of death which occur over a period of years and reframe them as the memories we will carry in our hearts. To carry memories of degradation and the ravaging of the mind and the body is counterproductive to healing. Endurance is one of the most difficult of disciplines. If we endure and carry the love and surprises offered by our loved one early on, we will have fought the fight well and productively in the end.

        ***One of the most difficult decisions for the caregiver is to try to determine just how much knowledge the loved one needs. There is a paper-thin line between giving information which might allow greater cooperation and giving information which will depress and anger the loved one. When Charlie first asked me his diagnosis, it was early in the Alzheimer's process. He later denied he had the disorder. Even later, he brought me a booklet which told me how to care for him. But now, if Charlie asks why he can't remember things, I will give a simple answer such as "Most of us forget things, Charlie. It's Saturday, not Monday." And then to disallow discouragement at not remembering things, I follow with, "You're right! It is Saturday and we have a lunch date with Frank and Alice today.

***As a follow-up to the above, I *did* routinely give relevant information to family and friends as they would be the ones to support me when I began to crumble. I learned that most people would only ask what they could tolerate knowing and I would adjust my responses to that realization. I would always try to end my conversation with something positive, such as "Charlie is so gentle and sweet. You just can't help but love him." That doesn't mean I didn't cry when alone, or scream or ask God why Charlie and I had to endure this. It simply means that I still had boundaries which were essential to the continuation of ongoing social support. My sister would allow me to vent unconditionally by email and on many days, it was a lifesaver for me. Her simple words would pull me back into the now and I could then lessen the effect of then.

***Simple things seemed to soothe Charlie as the disease progressed. I might hold Charlie's hands when he was anxious. I might read a children's fairy tale and he would smile. I might take him for a ride to one of the Keys. When we would go over a bridge, he would stare at the water and I could ask about his years in the Navy. They were not yet lost to him. Even though my husband did not retain current information, he remained capable of recalling his early years. I oftentimes played music and we would both sit on the sofa and close our eyes and listen. I think it reminded Charlie of when we went to concerts together. When having a bad day, I would try to prepare something familiar for Charlie for dinner. It would soothe the frustration of not knowing the world at large.

***Going out seemed to keep Charlie less disoriented. We

would go to familiar places and do the same things again and again. We'd go out and have yogurt. We'd drive out to a lake and sit. We might go to the lanai and look at the stars while drinking a chamomile tea. Even after fifteen minutes outside, Charlie would often appear exhausted. But, when we returned to the house, he appeared better settled in the house. If Charlie was agitated or frustrated, a simple change of location or environment would then allow him to readjust to more familiar surroundings.

***

Acknowledgments

My family is one anyone would be proud to call their own. My two adult children and the grandchildren have never wavered in their support of my husband and me. They anticipate our needs and make arrangements so that I need not further humble myself by asking for help. I am always included in the hectic lives of the grandchildren and their activity and love is a source of inspiration during the times I question my own abilities, both as a senior citizen and as an Alzheimer's caretaker. My lifelong friend and sister always attends patiently to emails in which my frustration and sense of hopelessness has, at times, tested even her patience.

My undying gratitude goes to the Senior Friendship Center in Sarasota, Florida. Without their talented staff, my life would be drastically different than the life I live today. In particular, I wish to thank Debbie and Paula for their ongoing understanding and support. Every day, they make decisions which alter the lives of those under their care. The group leaders and nurses are wonderful, always knowing what to do and never judging.

To my marvelous friends.......Never a day goes by when I fail to hear from one of you. Oftentimes, your messages arrive just at the time I want to curl up and forgo the rest of the day. And then, your concern for my well-being lifts me up and gives me the courage to continue to stay the course. Without fail, I receive love and hugs from you all, whether you live a mile away or thousands of miles from my house. Margaret, Carolyn and Jim, Elaine and Lee, Bonnie, Char and Daryl, Virginia, Jan, Ina and Bill, Marge and Al, Faye,

Bonny, Ellen and Marty, Debra and Steve, Lois, Susan and Garret, I feel blessed to know you all.

To my support group.....You are a fantastic group of courageous caregivers. Your trials and errors have helped countless people maintain a sense of dignity and sanity through a long and difficult process.

To the Veterans Administration in Sarasota.....Your support of a Veteran was never more appreciated than the day you approved my husband for services.

To our family physician Dr. David Reichel....Your care, support and understanding of both our needs is a valued and trusted bond.

To Mary and Gary (publishers).....Your belief in this literary project was heartwarming. Your encouragement and talent helped to bring a reluctant author to the point of absolute belief in the project.

Other Books by Dr. Pirnot

GENERAL
As I Am
Just a Common Lady
The Learners of Owamboland
Keeper of the Lullabies
Eating Through the Earth
A Christmas of Grace

CHILDREN'S PICTURE BOOKS
The Blue Penguin
A Colorful Day
Rainbows are the Best
Sam's Perfect Plan
The Door in the Floor
Night Traveler
Just Hanging Out
The Colors of Myself
Please Be My Hands

MID-GRADE READERS

Ordinary Kids Series:
Peter, the Pole and the Knob
The Above All Others Principle
Potsie and the Apparition of Brave Wolf
Morgan and Clive
The Days and Nights of Crighton Immanuel

Skymasters Series:
Galaxy Girl
Under the Universe

Through a Black Hole
The Multiverse

Silky and Sly:
The Ghost of Gasparilla
The Victorian House

To contact Dr. Pirnot **go to:**
www.drpirnotbooks.com

CPSIA information can be obtained at www.ICGtesting.com
Printed in the USA
BVOW08s0146280415

397975BV00008B/101/P